KIERSTEN SCHIFFER

the playlist diaries

Book 1 ▶▶ Fast Forward My Heart

SWEET LIGHT
PRESS

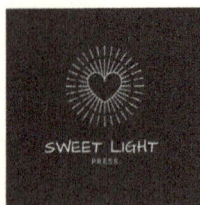

Published by Sweet Light Press

Copyright © 2022 by Kiersten Schiffer

All rights reserved.

ISBN: 979-8-9857701-0-0

e-book ISBN: 979-8-9857701-1-7

Cover Design and Formatting by Damonza

To all my crazy, passionate, hopeful classmates from the '80s. Teenagers who grew up sitting at the front table of Pizza King, cruising the square until midnight, getting drunk at the All-Nighters, and driving for miles and miles around the back roads of southern Indiana.

You know who you are. This story is for *you*.

Damn, we had it good, didn't we?

CHAPTER ONE

"EMOTIONAL RESCUE"

Indiana- August 1981

SOMETIMES A DECISION is just a decision.

And sometimes a decision changes your life.

What happened that night at Amaro's back-to-school party falls into that second category. Which is probably why I remember it so clearly, even now. But I'm getting ahead of myself. Because, as everyone knows, a single decision never stands alone. Something always comes first. Each of our choices tied to the one before, like the squares of one of those never-ending scarves magicians pull out of their sleeves. And the choice that came right before my Decision That Changed Everything was so simple it was laughable: I decided to go down in the basement to get a beer.

My best friend, Stacie, warned me not to go.

"Be careful. Jimmy's probably down there waiting for you," she said as I left her upstairs flirting with a guy on the basketball team.

"I'll keep an eye out," I assured her. It wasn't like me to ignore her suggestion, since she usually knew better than me about everything. But I needed the sweet escape of the beer so badly the risk seemed worth it.

Before we'd left Stacie's house tonight, I'd told her what Jimmy had said in band class earlier that week. About how he'd claimed I was a lot hotter this year and that every time I bent over to set up my drum the sight of my ass gave him a raging boner. Which wasn't all that extraordinary, considering Jimmy claimed to have a raging boner about one thing or another at least five times a day. (I think the last one was from Miss McMurray, our chemistry teacher, lighting a Bunsen burner. So that kind of gives you an idea of just how sensitive Jimmy's dick was.)

The real reason I had to look out for Jimmy was because he'd told me yesterday he wanted to find me tonight and "get with me", whatever that caveman sentence meant. I assumed he was just teasing since there was no way the most popular boy in school could like me, a mere sophomore with "microscopic titties" (the way he'd described them last year), odd colored hair, and a penchant for telling crude jokes. I was sure my underclassman invisibility would be enough to keep me safe as I fought through the press of kids downstairs, making my way toward my target: the keg floating in a pig trough smack dab in the middle of Amaro's rec room.

I was only a few steps from victory when I felt a hand

close around my wrist. Suddenly I was pulled roughly through the crowd. I struggled to stay on my feet as I bashed against a maze of sweaty bodies gyrating to the blasting music, unable to see where I was going or who was dragging me there.

Elbows and knees and damp skin slammed into me until my mystery guide and I burst through the throng into blessed fresh air with an almost audible pop. I stumbled a few feet forward before I finally figured out where I was: In a dark hallway with Jimmy Huskerson grinning drunkenly down at me.

"I've been looking everywhere for you!" Jimmy slurred, pressing me up against the wood panelling with the length of his hard body. "I *reallllly* need to talk to you, Red," he said, using the nickname the boys had given me when I'd started high school last year. A nickname that wasn't very accurate because my hair was actually strawberry blonde, not red. A detail that had sent the guys into hysterics the first time I'd corrected them. A mistake I hadn't made since.

"Well, it looks like you found me, Jimmy," I said with fake cheer. I had to kind of grunt each word since the weight of his body prevented my lungs from fully inflating. "Right in front of you. Completely here on my own volition." I was pretty sure he was too drunk to understand my sarcasm, or what the word *volition* meant.

My heart hammered wildly as I tried to wrestle out of his vice-like grip. But Jimmy was pretty much a Stretch Armstrong doll come to life, so fighting him was useless. I tried to relax and act like I was cool with

3

whatever the hell was happening to me, even though I'd never even held hands with a boy before, much less felt such a, um… *rigid* part of their anatomy pushing into my crotch. My friend, Scott, always teased me about how inexperienced I was with boys. He claimed it was because I was saving myself for my long-time love, John Travolta. It always pissed me off when he said that. Probably because it was so true.

Gazing up at Jimmy, I couldn't help but notice how handsome he was. Green eyes, blonde hair, the star of the basketball team. I should've been thrilled to be kidnapped by him. But I also noticed how many bruises peppered his arm. They were from the fist fights he bragged about incessantly. Fights he claimed he always won without even breaking a sweat. Jimmy may have been hot, but he was also one of the biggest bullies in our school. I didn't want to find myself on the receiving end of his wrath.

He reached down with one hand and started rubbing my ass in big circles, like he was trying to make a genie to fly out of my back pocket and grant him three wishes. I tried not to laugh at his clumsy efforts.

"So, what do you want to talk about, anyway?" I asked, as if we were both there to discuss the weather. I tried to hide how scared I really was. Knowing Jimmy, it would probably only turn him on more.

"I want to talk about these smokin' hot jeans you're wearing tonight," he said with another vigorous rub of my right ass cheek. I fought back an eye roll. Jimmy's vocabulary had stopped expanding in sixth grade. *Hot, smokin', bangin', bitchin'.* Those were pretty much the only adjectives he knew.

"You like these?" I glanced down at the Calvin Klein jeans I was proud to say were exactly like the ones Brooke Shields wore in her risqué TV commercials. Brooke was my idol. I would do anything to look like her. "I got them at Ayres in the mall. I think they'd still have your size if you get up there quick. They *would* look good on you," I teased, desperate to keep the conversation light.

Jimmy laughed at my lame joke, then glanced down the hallway at where almost every kid in our high school was screaming about how they wished they had Jessie's girl. The crazy scene distracted him for a split second. I knew this was the part in the movies when the poor hostage fought and punched and kicked her captor in the nuts, then made her brave escape. But since I was as far from brave as a girl could get, I just stood there frozen, waiting for what Jimmy would do to me next.

He leaned back a little and cupped one of my boobs. "These are awfully nice."

I made a face. "I thought you told me I needed to see the doctor for the bug bites on my chest. Wasn't that how you described them last year?"

He gave me a lewd grin. "Well, you've obviously matured over the summer."

I laughed really hard at that. Not only because it wasn't true (believe me, I'd know if my boobs had grown even an eighth of an inch), but because I thought it might be a good diversion tactic, a way to shift Jimmy's weight off me a little. But he didn't budge. God, he was heavy.

Jimmy's face clouded over as he noticed me struggling underneath him. I relaxed against the wall again, reminding myself to be careful. I'd seen firsthand what

happened when Jimmy got pissed. I knew all too well what he and his posse of bullies did to people who got on their bad side. And with what they knew about my mom (well, with what *everyone* knew about my mom really), I could only imagine what I'd have to endure if they set their sights on me. I'd already lived through enough of their lesbian jokes to last a lifetime. I didn't want to have to face that humiliation all over again.

At the entrance of the hallway, a group of girls glanced down at Jimmy and me tangled up together. They whispered furiously to each other, glared at me, then went back to whispering. I knew every one of those girls would've traded places with me in a heartbeat. I wanted to call out and beg one of them to switch places with me, to save me from my so-called good fortune with Jimmy. But despite them all being so close, I was too scared to open my mouth and ask for help.

Jimmy leaned in, lips hovering precariously close to mine. *Please God, no. Please don't let my first kiss be like this.* I twisted my head away, and he planted little, wet kisses along my neck. It felt like a million spiders crawling all along my skin. It was all I could do not to scream. How the hell was I ever going to get away from him?

"Just relax. I promise you'll like this," he whispered in between kisses. The urge to punch him right on his square jaw and knock his slimy lips off my skin, swelled inside me like a gathering tsunami.

I squeezed my eyes shut tightly and prayed for a way to escape. It wasn't the first time Jimmy had touched me like that. He'd started coming on to me in band

class when school started a few weeks ago, telling me in graphic detail at the things he'd do to me if he ever got me alone. When he'd grabbed my ass the first time, I'd instinctually slapped his hand away. It had been a mistake. He'd gawked in disbelief at his reddening hand, then accused me of being a lesbian just like my mom. Which wasn't true, despite how the kids at school loved to say it was. That's why I had to stand there and not flinch or struggle. Why I had to let him grope me and even pretend I liked it. Because letting Jimmy touch me like that was the only way I could prove to everyone I liked boys, not girls.

He gave my boob a hard squeeze. Then did it again. And again. *Does he really think girls like this?*

"Awwooooga!" I honked like an antique car in time with his next squeeze. (The guy just wouldn't quit.) He burst out laughing, exactly the way I'd hoped he would. It was how I usually defended myself against him in band class. I'd tell him and his goons crude jokes, act silly, do impressions of the teachers; anything I could think of to crack them up. It had mostly worked so far. But that had been in the safety of the school walls. And when Jimmy wasn't as drunk as this.

"I've always wanted to fuck a redhead," he said, grinding his hips hard into mine. My stomach twisted hearing the sharp-edged word. *Fuck.* There was no way I could pretend I didn't understand what he wanted from me now.

I struggled to distract him. "Oh, I'm sure doing it with a redhead is just like doing it with any other girl," I said. Then I lowered my voice conspiratorially. "Except for the part where afterward, we steal your soul."

Jimmy's head jerked back. "What?"

I blinked at him innocently. "Your soul? Are you partial to it?"

His face clouded over in confusion.

"It's a joke, Jimmy."

He let out a sigh of relief, as if he'd actually believed I could steal his soul. *God, what a dummy. Good looks really do cover a multitude of sins, don't they?*

"That's what I like about you." He pointed a finger at my face. "You're *soooo* damn funny." The whites of his eyes were bloodshot, one of them almost all the way closed, which made him look like a pirate whose patch had been lost at sea. "You seem like a girl who likes to have a good time." He wagged his eyebrows lecherously.

"Funny because I feel more like a girl who likes to not get her ass kicked by your girlfriend."

Had he forgotten about Tina, his notoriously unstable girlfriend? She was a card-carrying member of The Pack, a group of girls so mean they'd rack you up on a locker just for looking at one of their boyfriends. (Imagine a pack of wolves in heat, but with Farrah Fawcett haircuts and you've got the general idea.) And if a wrong glance earned you a mild concussion, I didn't want to think about what they'd do to a girl whose micro-boob was now resting in one of their boyfriend's hands.

"Don't worry," Jimmy said. "Tina's not here."

"Yeah, so what?" I tipped my head at the crowd through the doorway. "You really think all those people are going to keep your little secret?"

His face hardened, reminding me again I had to be careful. "Don't worry about Tina. I can handle her," he snapped. Then he wagged his eyebrows again. "In fact, maybe I could handle you both at the same time. You'd probably like that, wouldn't you? It seems like something someone like you would get into."

Someone like you. The insinuation was clear. Again, I fought back the impulse to knee him right in the balls.

"That's not something I would get into, Jimmy," I said through gritted teeth. Just then, I noticed Stacie pushing through the mass of bodies in the basement, coming right at us. She was easy to spot in the crowd because she was taller than even most of the boys in our school. She held her red plastic cup up high in one willowy arm, blonde hair curling with sweat along her round cheeks, a look of sheer loathing on her face. I knew what she was thinking. She called going to parties like this "rubbing elbows with the unwashed masses."

Seeing I was in trouble, Stacie bounded down the hallway and straight to my side. Unlike me, she wasn't afraid of anything.

"Tina's here." She stared down at Jimmy. I loved how she towered over him. And how clearly uncomfortable that made him.

Jimmy pretended to be unfazed but took his hand off my boob awfully quick. "Yeah... so what? She's doesn't tell me what to do." He scanned the room nervously.

"She was looking for you," Stacie went on. "She's probably on her way down here right now."

Hearing that, Jimmy stood up, releasing me from the wall. It felt so nice to take a full breath again. I glanced at Stacie and she cocked one eyebrow. For a second, I wondered if she was just making up that Tina was there, but then I saw Tina's mousy brown head at the top of the stairs. Jimmy must have seen it too, because he took off down the hallway away from me.

But before the crowd engulfed him, he turned back to me.

"Don't worry, Red. I'll get rid of her. Then I'll come back and find you."

He disappeared, not waiting to ask what I thought of his plan, which was no big surprise. He was Jimmy Huskerson after all. Any sane girl in a fifty-mile radius would've been honored to have her boob honked by him.

Stacie flipped off Jimmy's back as he walked away. I collapsed against the wall, trying not to think of what would've happened if Stacie hadn't shown up.

"What am I going to do?" I was safe for now, but how was I going to hide from Jimmy for the rest of the night?

"There's only one thing you can do," Stacie said, pulling me toward the staircase. "You've got to get the hell out of here."

❧

When Stacie and I burst out onto the back deck of the house, it felt like breaking through the surface of a pool after being held under water for too long. A myriad of smells punched me in the gut as I gasped in the summer air. Newly shorn grass, spiced with sweet clover. Wet dank mud, swirled with cow manure. Tangy smoke so faint it seemed to have traveled some great distance, then dissolved right at our feet. The smells of a farm. The smells of a life that used to be mine, back before my mom decided she wanted to take an art class at Indiana University to "do something for herself for once" then met Karen and ended up doing way more for herself than my dad and I ever expected she could. One seemingly simple decision that changed all our lives forever.

I wanted to stand on that deck staring out at the shadowed pastures and just suck it all in and let myself be taken back to my old life for just a little while longer. But then a guy brushed by my shoulder and headed down the stairs. Stacie and I looked at each other and shouted, "Scott!" in unison. She and I were obviously thinking the same thing about how I was going to get away from Jimmy.

We caught up with Scott as he headed toward the driveway.

"Hey, wait a minute!" I called out.

Scott whirled around, a thick shock of brown hair falling over one eyebrow. Seeing us, he broke into an enormous smile. "Hey, ladies, what can I do for you?"

"Are you leaving? Can I go with you?" I begged, looking up at him. Scott was a senior, just like Jimmy. He even wore a letter jacket like Jimmy, although Scott had earned his varsity letters for tennis, not basketball, which meant his didn't count for much around here.

He looked surprised but reached out for my hand. "Shit yeah, Red. I'd love that."

"Ugh, Scott, not like that!"

He let go of my hand, looking disappointed. "Well, like what then?"

Scott was my best friend next to Stacie, so I wasn't really worried about pissing him off. We were both used to this dance. We'd go along as normal friends, then he'd ask me out on a date. I'd say, "That's incestuous Scott. You're like my brother!" and he'd act offended, and I'd have to force myself to say something nice to him. Then we'd be friends until he tried to ask me out again. Repetitive, but in a sweet, kind of reassuring way.

"She needs to get out of here," Stacie said. A door slammed behind us. When I looked back at the house, Jimmy was leaning on the deck railing above, pointing at me and mouthing the word *later* so exaggeratedly it looked like his lips were made of Silly Putty.

"That's why she has to get out of here." Stacie nodded at the deck. "Do you have your car?"

"No, my cousin's coming to get me."

"Which one?" I asked. "Frank? J.B.? Butch?" People in Cold Springs had so many cousins they couldn't keep track of them all. Which, for some reason, they seemed to think was a good thing.

"No, my cousin Will."

Stacie and I must have looked confused because he went on. "He's in college. Maybe you don't know him?" Scott seemed surprised by that possibility.

As if cued by a hidden movie director, a white car roared up the dirt road, churning up a cloud of dust worthy of the General Lee on the Dukes of Hazzard show. It skidded to a stop beside us. Music blared from the speakers. Loud, familiar, but something I still couldn't quite name.

"That's him now," Scott said, reaching for the door handle that was somehow perfectly aligned with where he stood on the grass.

"C'mon, you guys can go with us," Scott said, climbing into the back seat.

I took a step to leave, relieved to finally have a way out, but Stacie hesitated. "Actually, you go. I'm going to stay here."

"Really? You're going to stay here? By yourself?" I suddenly wasn't so sure about my plan anymore. Stacie and I always did everything together.

"Michelle's here. I won't be alone. And I uh, kinda wanted to see if…" she trailed off.

"See if you could run into Mark?" Mark was Stacie's latest crush, the reason we were even at the party for the basketball players in the first place. It seemed there were some of the unwashed masses that Stacie had developed a bit of a tolerance for.

"Well, maybe. He asked if I'd come tonight."

"Hey you!" A voice barked from inside the waiting car. "You going with us or not?"

When I turned, the driver was leaning over the guy in the passenger seat. His face was in shadows, but the outline of him looked really cute. Dark hair, waving and dipping almost too perfectly, kind of like John Travolta's.

"I'm coming. Just give me a minute already!" I yelled back.

When I turned to Stacie, she raised her eyebrows, nodding at the car. "Shit. He looks hot." I swear to God, the two of us possessed the exact same brain.

I grilled Stacie to see if she really wanted to stay without me. But before I could make completely sure she was okay, Scott's cousin barked again. "Get in the car already!" He sounded really annoyed now.

I rolled my eyes and gave Stacie a hug, whispering in her ear, "Why do all the cute ones have to be assholes?"

Stacie pushed me toward the back seat. I laughed as I climbed in the car, replaying my funny asshole comment over in my head. I was so relieved to get away from Jimmy I wasn't thinking of much else. I couldn't believe I'd been praying for a way to escape and then *poof!*, out of nowhere, my prayers had been answered.

At the time I didn't know the magnitude of that moment. I had no idea that open car door was about to reveal way more to me than just a red leather back seat and a cooler full of free beer. Choosing to leave the party was so simple, so thoughtless, I figured I'd forget about it right away. But to this day I still remember that night. Boy, do I ever remember. Because getting in that car at Amaro's back-to-school party… that was the decision that changed my life.

CHAPTER TWO

"(I CAN'T GET NO) SATISFACTION"

HE IGNORED ME for a long time. Scott's cousin with the cute, shadowy outline. But it didn't really matter because the further he drove me away from the party, and the further I got away from Jimmy, the better I felt. Corn stalks swished by the car windows, their tight rows opening every so often to reveal wide pastures blanketed in creamy moonlight. The sight of the familiar fields made me feel like I could take a full breath again. I had no idea what was going to happen with Jimmy on Monday after he found out I'd ditched him, but I didn't want to think about that right then. I just wanted to let myself sink into the rumble and flow of the driving car and pretend for a little while longer that the world outside its two doors didn't exist anymore.

The jagged notes of music blasted so loudly I couldn't make out any of the animated conversation Scott's cousin was having up front. His passenger was Rob

Grinfeld, who I'd known forever. He was the starting center on the basketball team, a gentle giant who didn't talk that much. Which, from the way Scott's cousin had been blabbering on to him nonstop ever since we got in the car, seemed like a perfect arrangement for the two of them. I doubted the poor kid could've gotten a word in edgewise even if he'd wanted to.

I'm not sure *talking* was the right word to describe what the dark-haired boy was doing up there in the driver's seat. It was more like a theatrical performance of some sort; all sweeping arms and pointing fingers and head tosses so wild and vehement, he would've made even the most dramatic Shakespearean actor feel like he needed to up his game.

The whole demonstration was so strange and yet so captivating I couldn't take my eyes off him. I was dying to know what could make anyone that passionate about anything, but with the stereo so loud, all I could decipher of his soliloquy was a random word here and there. Quick phrases that sporadically broke through the thick batting of music packed around us. Random blasts of "I said" or "I went" or "I told". *I* this and *I* that. That's what I remember the most about the night I first met Will. Everything he said started with *I*.

When he finally turned the music down, it felt like the air around us had been sucked out of the car along with notes.

"So, who's your little friend, Scott?" Will asked, peering at me in the rearview mirror.

I cringed at the way he'd sing-songed the word *little*.

I hated that word, and the fact he'd said it in such an annoying big-brother way.

"Oh, this is the lovely Red," Scott said, like I was a prize heifer he was presenting at the 4-H fair. "Red, this is my cousin, Will." Scott lowered his voice, "he's Coach's son." Coach was my gym teacher and the coach of our winning basketball team. I wasn't sure why Scott needed to whisper his name in front of his own son.

Will narrowed his eyes in the mirror, examining me closer. "Red, huh? Because of the hair?"

God, not this again.

"No. Because I'm a Commie," I deadpanned. *See Mr. Big Shot? I can be annoying too.*

Will let out a sharp laugh. "A little girl with a smart mouth. I like that," he said to Rob like I wasn't even there. I noticed he'd used that word again. *Little.* It was funny how quickly he'd picked up that it bothered me.

"So, you're Mitch's brother then?" I called to the front of the car. Mitch, a sophomore like me, was Coach Calder's younger son.

Will huffed loudly. "Mitch's brother? *Mitch's brother?* Since when have I ever been Mitch's brother in this town?"

Scott was trying hard to hold back a laugh.

"It's more like Mitch is *my* brother," Will corrected indignantly.

"Oh sorry," I said, but secretly smiled to myself, pleased I'd bothered him, just like he'd bothered me.

"So, you've never heard of me then?" he asked, seeming flustered now. "Will Calder? Of the '79 team that went to States?"

Now I knew why he was surprised I didn't know him. Our team making it to the Indiana State Basketball Championship back in 1979 was the biggest event to hit Cold Springs since the limestone from our quarries had been used to build the Lincoln Memorial. The match-up in the finals paralleled a classic sports underdog movie: little Cold Springs taking on the giant Crispus Attucks High School from Indianapolis to fight for the trophy.

The David and Goliath aspect of the game had caught the attention of *Sports Illustrated* and they'd run a four-page article on the big event the week before the championship. But back then I was only in seventh grade, and my mom had just moved out to live with Karen and my dad's skin cancer (which had been in remission) had come back but inside his brain this time. I'd needed to be home every night to help him feed the cows because he was too weak to lift the hay bales anymore. Or drive the tractor alone. Or push the wheelbarrow out to the manure spreader. That's why the basketball team wasn't really my priority. All I knew was there was a lot of crazy hype and build-up, which ended with us somehow losing by one measly point in the end.

"No, I've never heard of you," I said, even though I could already tell it would upset him. "But then again, that was an awfully long time ago."

Will made an *offff* sound like I'd just punched him in the stomach. Everyone started laughing, but Scott seemed to think it was especially hilarious. He was heeing and hawing and clutching his stomach like he was watching a skit from *Saturday Night Live* play out right in front of him.

"Hey, it had to happen someday, old man," Scott called up to Will. "Legends can't last forever!"

"Fuck you," Will said to Scott. But even though he was laughing, I noticed how the car sped up, how he started taking the corners really sharply after that.

A few minutes later, Will motioned to Rob to get something from the floorboard. Then Will handed a glistening bottle of beer back to me. "Here. A peace offering," he said.

I snatched it up quickly, eager to add to my fading buzz. "Thanks. But why a peace offering?"

"You know why," he said, like he and I were playing some kind of game and he'd just conceded me a point. My heart sped up, thrilling at the sudden familiarity I felt with this mysterious boy.

He waited until I tipped the bottle to my lips before adding, "Although I doubt a *little* girl like you is old enough to drink it."

I laughed, choking on my beer. He winked at me in the mirror, so I raised my bottle high in a mock toast. *Touché asshole. Touché.*

A while later- after we made it over a stretch of potholes so rough Scott and I had to clutch onto each other to keep from being bounced off the seat- Will called back to me.

"So, tell me something about yourself, Red."

I froze in my seat. My answer shouldn't have been that hard. Here was a cute college boy asking me about myself. I should've told him some interesting tidbit like the fact that I didn't have a curfew and that my mom was very lenient when it came to me dating older boys. (She didn't have much of a leg to stand on as far as age gaps in relationships went, since Karen had only been in her early twenties when they first met.)

But saying that would've meant bringing up my mom, which was off limits. I had to be careful to censor myself after what had happened. I couldn't just come right out and say the first thing that popped into my head like I used to. I had to run through my responses first, check all the paths the answer might take, so I could make sure it wouldn't accidentally lead back to my strange family along the way.

I was sorting through my various choices (*no I can't say I used to live on a farm because then he would ask where the farm was, and why I didn't live there anymore, and then he'd know what had happened and...*) But while I was trying to come up with something Scott piped up for me.

"Red's a cheerleader," he said proudly, as if my being a cheerleader had something to do with him. I wouldn't have led with that one fact, but it did provide a lot of information in a few words. The basketball team was royalty in Cold Springs, so being a cheerleader put me at the edge of their court, both literally and figuratively.

Will surveyed me, his disembodied eyes floating in the rectangular mirror in the middle of the car windshield. I couldn't make out their exact color but I could tell that they were a light shade, (blue? green maybe?) dark lashed, and (dammit all to hell) strikingly beautiful. I held my breath, waiting for what he'd say next.

"You're a cheerleader, huh?" he finally said. "I can see that."

My cheeks burned at what felt like a compliment. I half expected him to make some kind of joke about me liking to be around girls all the time. (How many times had I heard that one?) Then I would've known he already knew the truth about me like everyone else did. But when he didn't, I realized the flip side of not knowing anything about this college boy was there was a chance he knew nothing about me either.

"Well, I'm only on the J.V. Squad," I said softly, moving toward the open window to get more air on my burning face.

"Only? *Only?!*" Will seemed outraged for some reason. "Never say the word *only* before you talk about yourself."

"Why not?" I asked, surprised by his sudden vehemence.

"Because the world is only too happy to cut you down and try to turn you into something small. It's your job to keep yourself big."

I made a face. Was this guy serious? He sounded like Casey Kasem at the end of the Top 40 Countdown: *Keep your feet on the ground and keep reaching for the stars.* Real life people weren't supposed to talk like that.

I huffed. "Uh, if I remember correctly, you're the one who keeps calling me little."

"I only did that to see how you'd react."

"And how did I react?"

"You got pissed off," he said smugly, still talking only to the windshield.

"Wow, genius. How'd you figure that out?" I rolled my eyes.

"Never mind that. The real question is, why did it make you so mad when I called you little?"

"I have a feeling you're about to tell me, right?"

"Yeah, I am," he volleyed back. "It's because, deep down inside, you know you're not."

I sat there, stunned. I looked at Scott, confused, but he just made an exasperated face like he'd heard it a million times before. What was going on? Weren't we supposed to just be driving around drinking beer? Why was Will talking about all kinds of big, philosophical things, like my feelings about myself deep down inside?

"I'll give you an example, Red," Will barreled on. "Take me. I'm never going to say I'm *only* a basketball player. I'm going to say," he raised his voice louder, "I was the best damn basketball player to ever come out of Cold Springs High. You see the difference? That's how you keep yourself big."

Scott leaned close and whispered, "He gets like this sometimes. Just ignore him."

But I was intrigued now. Ignoring Will was the last thing I wanted to do.

"So you're saying I should brag then? That's what you do?"

"It's not bragging if it's true."

I laughed. "Wow, Scott. I didn't know your cousin was a motivational speaker." I leaned up and poked my head next to Will's. "How much you charge per hour for this bullshit, anyway?"

"Hey, laugh all you want, but I know what I'm talking about. Ask Rob here. He knows."

Rob raised a hand like he was taking an oath in court. "Yes, I can attest that I have completed the Will Calder course on confidence, and it does work. I wouldn't be the starting center on the basketball team right now if it wasn't for him."

I glanced back and forth between them, trying to figure out if they were teasing me, but they both seemed strangely sincere. I didn't know Will at all, but I knew Rob. Not only was he one of the nicest boys at our school, he was one of the smartest too. In fact, with his perfectly combed hair and dark-rimmed glasses, I'd always kind of thought of him as a brainy, Clark Kent/ Superman kind of guy. If he actually believed Will knew what he was talking about, then maybe it was true.

I sat back in my seat, dazed by the entire interaction. I'd never met a boy that talked to me the way Will just had.

"Sorry," Scott whispered again, "like I said, he goes off on tangents like that sometimes. We're all just used to it by now."

Will stopped the car at a stop sign. He was smiling as he glanced to the right before he made the turn, and the moonlight lit his lovely profile in a thin line of white, making him look almost otherworldly.

"So, Red," Will went on as he accelerated down another dark, gravel road. My entire body tensed, waiting for what was coming next. "What kind of music do you like?"

His voice was light, but I sensed another trap. And

from the way Scott and Rob were glancing at each other with tight smiles I had a feeling my instincts were right. I tried to think back to what music Will was playing when I got in the car, but I'd been so preoccupied I couldn't remember. And unfortunately, the stereo was quiet now. I decided to just throw an air ball and blurt out the music Stacie and I were singing into our hairbrushes as we got ready tonight.

"I don't know, like Air Supply and..."

Gravel spun loud under the wheels as the car screeched violently to a halt. Scott and I slammed into the seat in front of us. I looked out the windshield, half expecting a dog to be standing in the headlights or maybe even a cow, but the road was empty. When I looked over at Scott, he made a grim you've-done-it-now face, and my heart sunk.

"Do you want to walk back to town?!" Will shouted, pointing out the window in what I assumed was the direction of Cold Springs.

The only sound in the car was the low rumble of the idling engine. I looked at Scott again, but he just shrugged resignedly, like the outburst was normal. Will was still staring straight ahead so I couldn't see his expression. What the hell was going on? He wouldn't really make me walk back to town, would he?

"Are you serious?!" I yelled back.

"I am if you think Air Supply is good music!"

I had to agree with him that Air Supply was kind of cheesy and the jumpsuits they wore were pretty hideous, but their ballads were still awfully catchy. I didn't think liking them warranted being thrown out of the car in the middle of the night.

"I think I'll take a piss since we're stopped," Rob mumbled, throwing his door open and getting out.

"Me too," Scott said. He climbed over me, leaving the door open to the humid night air and me alone in the car with Will.

Once they were gone, Will put the car in park and turned around in his seat to face me squarely for the first time. I knew I shouldn't stare at him so openly, but I couldn't help myself. Back in the driveway, I'd taken one quick look at his shadow and decided he was cute, pinning the label to him as thoughtlessly as someone calling the sky blue, or snow cold. But now, seeing him clearly in the overhead light of the car, I realized Will was way more than just cute.

Along with the black hair, he had a straight nose and light blue eyes, just like I'd imagined. An artist like my mom would've probably described his features as having good composition (if his face were a painting and not made of actual flesh and bone like it was.) All the angles and curves of his face came together in such lovely, symmetrical ratios. I'd never seen anyone as handsome as him in real life, much less staring back at me only two feet away. A sick feeling suddenly rolled through my stomach. I reached up to smooth my hair and froze at the mess I found there. Why the hell hadn't I used that hairbrush at Stacie's house instead of just singing into it all afternoon?

"There is only *ONE* band that's worth listening to," Will proclaimed like he was a preacher and the driver's seat his pulpit. "The greatest band that ever was... ever is... and ever will be..." He pushed in a cassette tape and turned the volume up really loud. A fuzzy guitar rhythm filled the air, followed by a seductive voice snaking men-acingly through the car.

"And that band is..." Will stabbed a finger at me, cuing me to fill in the answer. Thank God, I finally knew who it was.

"The Rolling Stones!" I cried, surprised I could even get any words out at all.

"Right! And the song is?"

I let out a breath, knowing I had a chance to redeem myself from my horrible Air Supply answer. "*Satisfaction*," I said, feeling the meaning of the word as it slipped through my lips.

"Right again!" He was so excited he reminded me of my Government teacher, Mr. Glinden, when some-one finally got an answer right in class. "Although the proper working title is 'I Can't Get No Satisfaction'. Mick got a lot of flak for using the double negative, but the song wouldn't be what it is today if he'd given in to the pressure and changed it."

He was thoughtful then, eyes looking past me as if he were a million miles away. He was talking like he was a close personal friend of Mick Jagger's; like he'd sat at a table and discussed the naming of this iconic hit over a cigarette and a bottle of tequila back in 1965. What was with this guy anyway?

There was almost this palpable glow coming off him now. I leaned up in the seat, wondering what the edges of that light would feel like if it touched me. I wanted to sit there and talk to him for the rest of the night. The only problem was, I didn't know anything about The Rolling Stones.

I fished out the one bit of trivia I knew from the back of my mind.

"I heard one of The Rolling Stones died of a drug overdose in a swimming pool," I said to his beautiful lit up face. "Guess he didn't wait an hour to swim after he snorted that coke, huh?" I laughed weakly, instantly regretting opening my mouth. *Oh my God, what a stupid thing to say.*

But to my relief, Will brightened even more.

"That's right! Brian Jones. Actually, he'd just been fired from the band. Couldn't handle the rock 'n' roll lifestyle." His eyes danced with life. "The death certificate said, 'death by misadventure.' What do you think of that? Death by misadventure. I love it!"

I wanted to mention that even if the words on the death certificate sounded cool, the whole thing still involved dying, which pretty much cancelled everything else out. But instead, I agreed with him.

"Sounds like a good way to go!" I said cheerfully, feeling like I'd been possessed by someone way stupider than I truly was. *Good lord, what's happening to me?*

"Well, you know what, Red?" Will said seriously. "Brian lost his dreams. And after that, he lost his mind."

"Uh huh," I agreed dumbly. *What the hell is he talking about?*

Scott climbed back in the car and Rob settled in the front, slamming the door hard behind him.

"Is he droning on again?" Scott asked in a low voice. Then louder, for Will's benefit he said, "Will's the family philosopher. Right, Will?" Will seemed to exhaust Scott for some reason.

"You could call me that," Will said, either not picking up on Scott's sarcasm or else choosing to ignore it. "All I know is... it's only rock 'n' roll," he took a long swig of beer then looked directly in my eyes, "but I like it."

While I was trying to remember how to breathe again, he went on. "You know what, Red?" He waved a finger at me again. "I like you. You're an okay girl."

Then, as abruptly as he'd stopped, he turned away, dropped the car roughly into gear and gunned it down the road. I sat there, dazed and reeling, trying to figure out what had just happened. Why it felt like my entire bloodstream had become carbonated with liquid happiness. This strange boy had just called me an "okay girl", which wasn't really that great of a compliment when you got right down to it. So why the hell had it felt so damn good?

CHAPTER THREE

"START ME UP"

AFTER THAT, WILL started talking in some kind of gibberish. Turning around in his seat as he gunned the car down the road, pointing at Scott and me, going on about men coming on radios and white shirts and how Scott couldn't smoke the same cigarettes as he did. It was as if he were in a weird trance, like how those evangelical people chant and speaking in tongues when they're supposedly possessed by the holy spirit.

"What? You can't have cigarettes?" I hissed under my breath to Scott. "But you don't smoke, do you?"

"No dummy, I don't smoke," Scott sighed heavily. "You don't get it... he's quoting the song. Those are the words from 'Satisfaction'."

"Ohhhhh," I said, relieved. I sat back in my seat and listened to Will again. Were those really the words in "Satisfaction"? I'd never really understood what Mick had been singing about other than the chorus. He always seemed to mumble a lot. And groan and grunt a bunch too.

As it turned out, Will knew exactly what Mick was saying. Every single word, in fact. He turned up the volume and sang loudly, almost like he was trying to drown Mick out. It shocked me how uninhibited he was. He wasn't even that good of a singer, but he didn't seem to care. He sang and gestured wildly, imitating Mick's well-known persona like we weren't even in the car with him. He was totally lost in the music. I couldn't figure out if he was drunk. Or brilliant. Or maybe both. I'd never seen a boy act that free before.

Will kept driving, furiously clicking cassettes in and out of the stereo in what seemed like some curated order that I didn't understand.

When a rare snatch of silence came in between songs, I saw my opening. "So where do you go to college?" I called up to him.

He turned down the music. "I go to ISU. Following in the great Larry Bird's footsteps."

I made a face to myself. Who would choose to go to Indiana *State* in yucky Terre Haute when they could go to super cool Indiana University in Bloomington? I already knew with 100% certainty that IU was where I was going when I finally escaped from our boring little town.

"So why would you come back to Cold Springs when you're in college?" I asked. "It must be way more fun up there. I can't wait to get out of this hellhole. Once I graduate, I'm never, ever, ever coming back."

Will turned to Rob and shook his head like I'd said

something terribly childish. My face went red seeing his expression. Why did I have to say 'never, ever, ever' like that?

"I see you have the old, grass-is-always-greener mentality then," Will called back to me. "I know that one only too well. But let me just tell you from experience. If you think college is going to save you, you're wrong. What you're going to find out when you do finally get out of here, is that you're still the same old you. Only now you're just you in a different place."

I was so confused trying to sort out his tangle of words, I couldn't even think of a quick comeback. He abruptly turned up the music, obviously done talking to me. I felt so stupid, so rebuffed by his sudden dismissal. I rode along, staring out the window, desperately trying to find a way to talk to him again. The songs were clearly my doorway to him, but since I didn't recognize the ones he was playing now, I couldn't find any way through.

Luckily, a few miles later, a series of twangy guitar chords filled the car, followed by an easy drum rhythm that even I could've played. I wanted to pump my fist in the air. Finally, a song I knew. This one was on the radio all the time now.

"*Start Me Up!*" I shouted, even though Will hadn't even asked. Maybe I could still win a few more points from him. Maybe I could fish another compliment out of him like before.

Will braked hard, slamming the car into park on the deserted road. Then he whirled around in his seat to face Scott and me.

"This is the part of the night," he shouted, "when

we DANCE!" Then he swung his door open and disappeared out into the night.

The rest of us followed him out into the dusty ribbons of headlights that seemed to stretch for miles down the empty road in front of us. Will and Scott pranced around the thin strip of dirt like it was a stage, while Rob leaned sedately on the hood of the Monte Carlo, bobbing his head in time with the music. As the music swelled, Will slipped into a full-on Mick Jagger imitation; flapping his arms like a rooster, craning his neck, and sticking his lips out really big as he sang. He looked so stupid, and yet he didn't seem to care what anyone thought about him. *Will doesn't care what anyone thinks about him*, I thought to myself. The concept was so foreign I had to repeat it a few times before I could even make sense of it.

He looked like he was having so much fun. For an instant I wondered how it would feel to be like him, what it would feel like to not care what anyone thought about me either. I slowly tried it out, first joining in with an invisible tambourine, then adding a few hand claps here and there where the song dictated. Eventually, I got so carried away I ended up finishing the last two verses as a full-on backup singer, shouting the dirty parts at the top of my lungs and everything.

When the music finally faded away, we were all laughing, gasping for air, hitting each other on the back like we'd just performed in front of a crowd of 60,000 screaming fans instead of just a field full of cornstalks. I fell against the driver's side door, breathing hard, clutching the side-view mirror just to keep myself from floating away. Clutching my heart to keep it from floating away too.

Scott leaned up against the car, chest heaving. "See, aren't you glad you didn't stay at that stupid party, Red? Stacie doesn't know what she's missing."

I hopped up on the hood of the white car. The warmth of the idling engine flooded pleasantly through the seat of my jeans.

"Yeah, a bunch of drunk boys who don't know how to sing." I pretended to be annoyed, but, everything inside me felt buoyant. Like I'd just been transported to another planet that had a lot less gravity on it than the one I was on before.

Will walked from further down the road straight toward me. He was bathed squarely in the headlights now, wearing a light blue polo shirt and faded Levi's, his body trim and athletic just like I knew it would be. His skin still held a summer tan, the brown of his arms fading to cream where his short sleeves landed, and his blue eyes danced above a broad smile. He was close now. Standing in front of the car, only a few feet away from me.

"Yeah, what does that party have that we don't?" Will asked. "You've got Scott and Rob and me. What more could a girl need?" He spread his arms out to the side, palms up. "How about me? I mean, I'm not bad looking, am I? There could be worse guys to hang out with, right?" A knowing smile spread slowly across his face.

He was clearly teasing me again. Someone that looked like him didn't need to ask a question like that.

It felt like he'd just read my mind and knew how much he thrilled me and now was trying to make me reveal myself, which I sure as hell wasn't going to do.

"Well," I stalled, trying to look cool by leaning back on my arms the way I'd seen Brooke Shields pose in her Calvin Klein ad. (Of course, the effort was in vain since Brooke had a lot bigger boobs than I did and in that ad she'd only had on a sheer shirt with her jeans, not a boring, striped button down like me.)

Heart pounding, I tried to think of a clever come-back. I remembered a phrase my dad always used to describe Cher when he and my mom watched *The Sonny and Cher Show* when I was little.

I shrugged, doing my best to feign indifference. "Well, I guess I wouldn't kick you out of bed for eating crackers if that's what you're asking."

All three boys erupted in laughter as soon as I finish my deadpan delivery. Their reaction surprised me. The joke wasn't really all that funny. Still, they laughed and laughed, clutching their stomachs like I deserved to be called over to Carson's couch after finishing my stand-up set on *The Tonight Show*.

Scott high-fived me and Will did the same to Rob saying, "You hear that, Rob? She wouldn't kick me out of bed for eating crackers. So, I've got *that* going for me!"

I rolled my eyes fighting to keep a straight face. After all, Karen had taught me the golden rule of comedy: Never laugh at your own joke.

"We've got a hot one here, boys," Will said, gestur-ing at me.

"A red hot one!" Rob added, the sound of his voice surprising me. I felt a strange satisfaction that he'd spent his few precious words talking about me.

"A little girl with a smart mouth. I like it," Will said, staring at me hard. I stared back, trying not to flinch even though it felt like the hood of the car had just disintegrated underneath me and I was free falling through the air.

Will stood so close in front of me he was practically touching my knees. "Hey, I never said I was great," he said, leaning so close I could smell the beer on his breath, "*just bloody good.*"

I had no idea what he was talking about, but his smile was so beautiful at that moment I couldn't look away. Sometimes in books they described someone's smile as infectious, but Will's was way more than that. Something lit inside my chest as I stared at him; a whooshing of heat that overtook me in one startling split second, like when you turn on the burner of a gas stove and it bursts into flames all at once.

Suddenly I imagined Will reaching out, putting his hands on my knees, and spreading my legs apart, then grabbing my hips and sliding them down the car hood until they met his. Then I saw him lean in and kiss me passionately, one hand tangled in my hair, the other one sliding up underneath my shirt.

I looked away quickly, face flaming. Where the hell had that come from? I'd never even kissed a boy before and now I was imagining myself spread eagle on the hood of a car with one? Did I think I was in the middle of a Metallica video or something? Maybe all those televangelists were right after all. Maybe that new MTV station was actually corrupting my young, impressionable mind, just like they'd said it would.

Will was still way too close. "Mick said that."

"Huh?"

"I never said I was great, just bloody good," Will repeated. "Mick said that. In a *Rolling Stone* interview. 1969. The Stones were getting bashed by the punk-assed Beatles. So, Mick says *I never said I was great... just bloody good.*" He stared out into the night, smiling like he was recounting something he'd lived through himself. "I love it!"

"That's really cool," I mumbled, counting the stones on the road under his feet until he finally walked away.

When Will was far enough away, Scott leaned over. "Yeah, just so you know, pretty much everything Will says, Mick said first." I noticed how he whispered it, like he was letting me in on some deep dark family secret.

Scott and Rob walked down the road to check out something rustling in the weeds, leaving me alone with Will again. He had his back to me now, staring down the path of the headlights out into the night.

A chorus of peepers galumphed from an unseen pond in the distance, accompanying some unfamiliar song that had clicked on stereo behind me. I watched Will's silhouette, half of me hoping, the other half terrified he might turn around and talk to me again. I kept repeating *"he's an asshole, he's an asshole..."* over and over in my head in a vain attempt to calm my heart, which was still hammering like jackrabbit feet against my chest from the memory of his smile.

I decided to recreate another of Brooke's modeling poses I remembered from *Seventeen* magazine, so I'd look good in case he came back. *Turn sideways, glance coyly over one shoulder.* But before I could get in position, Will whirled around and startled me and I ended up sliding down the hood, arms flailing as I tried to get a grip on the slick paint.

He was fighting to keep a straight face as he came closer. I pulled myself upright and acted like I'd done the whole thing on purpose just to make him laugh. Now not only was my heart about to explode, but I was having trouble breathing too.

"What else do you know about the Stones then?" he asked when he got to me.

"Um, I don't know..." Without air and the proper blood supply, my brain felt like it was soaked in wet cement. It took what felt like a herculean effort to pull even the tiniest bit of information to the surface. "Uh, they have a new album." *God. That was stupid. Everyone in the entire world knows that.*

"Yeah... what's it called?"

I swallowed hard. The cement was slipping down into my throat now. "*Tattoo You*," I croaked.

His face brightened. "Right!"

I slumped over in relief, then pretended I was checking to see if I tied my shoelace to cover it up.

"Do you have it?" he pressed.

Shit.

"Uh... no."

He narrowed his eyes at me, clearly disappointed. So that was it then. I'd blown it. There would be no hands on my knees, no spreading apart of my legs. No pulling my hips hard into his. No hands in my hair and passionate kisses. No tongues in my...

"You can't always get what you want," he said, interrupting my fantasy.

I grabbed the car hood underneath me. *What the hell?! Had he just read my mind?*

"Huh?" I said.

"The song. 'You Can't Always Get What You Want'. Do you know it?"

"Oh, you're talking about the song! Oh, thank God..."

He scrunched up his face. "Yeah. What else would I've been talking about?"

"Oh, nothing, nothing. I just thought you were saying that I couldn't actually get what I wanted. Never mind!" I rambled on incoherently. "The song. Yes! I know the song. Of course I do!" For some godforsaken reason I started to sing. "You can't always get what you want... you can't always get..."

His face had the expression of someone witnessing a seven-car pile-up who can't tear themselves away. I stopped myself abruptly. Took a deep breath and cleared my throat. "Yes. I know the song." Then I bit my lips between my front teeth to stop myself from saying anything else stupid.

He was laughing outright now, and even though I knew it was because he thought I was so weird, I didn't really mind. I just loved watching the way he tipped his head up to the sky. The way his Adam's apple moved up and down and his eyes squinted into two crescents as he laughed. God, he was so hot.

"Do you want to learn more about the Stones, Red?" The question felt like a red carpet laid at my feet. I leapt onto it way too eagerly.

"Yes! Of course I do." *Shit. Dial it back. And quick.* "I mean... I guess that'd be cool."

The smug smile was back. "Good." He leaned toward me, pointed a finger at my chest. "Get 'You Can't Always Get What You Want.' Listen to it. Learn it. Then we'll talk about it next time." It was clearly an order, not a suggestion.

I was so stunned by his forcefulness that by the time I sorted out what he'd just said, he was already walking away. I opened my mouth to call out to him, to ask what he meant by next time, but my voice was drowned out by him barking at Scott and Rob to get in the car because it was time to go.

I slipped off the hood and struggled around the car, my head whirling so violently I had to clutch the rearview mirror, then the door handle and finally Scott's outstretched hand just to make my way into the back seat.

Will barely talked to me the rest of the night, but I didn't even care. I was too busy staring mutely into the blackness roaring by outside the window, tumbling his words around and around until they became lovely little polished stones in my mind. Each of them holding one simple promise: There was going to be a next time.

CHAPTER FOUR

THE DEN

"HERE, IT'S THIS one," Karen said, pulling a cassette out of the rack at the record store. She scanned the back of the case. "Yeah, there it is... down at the bottom... 'You Can't Always Get What You Want'."

When Karen had woken me up this morning and asked if I wanted to go with her to Bloomington to meet my mom for lunch, at first I'd said no. My head was pounding, not only from the beer I'd drunk but from staying up half the night thinking about Will; about his smile, the way he'd laughed at me, the way he'd told me I was an okay girl.

But Karen had kept begging. "C'mon," she'd whined, pulling the pillow out from under my head while I'd groaned and tried my best to ignore her. "We're going to the Trojan Horse... I know how you love your gyros."

I growled at her to stop, but she'd only tried to entice

me further. "Oh, don't be so bitchy... it'll be fun. We can go a little early and shop on Kirkwood."

Karen and I always killed time waiting for my mom at The White Rabbit, this freaky little novelty shop that sold funny posters and fake dog poop and refrigerator magnets with obscenities on them. Usually I'd jump at the chance to go with her, but just thinking about riding in the car with her, with the crazy way she always drove -speeding and swerving and cussing at all the assholes that seemed to only show up when she was behind the wheel- made me feel like heaving.

But just as I started to scream at her to get the hell out of my room, I remembered what store was right next to The White Rabbit.

I popped my head out from under my covers. "Could we go to The Den too?"

The Den was a record store, a place I knew I could find the song Will had told me to listen to and learn so we could talk about next time. *Next time*. There were no two lovelier words in the English language to me right then.

Now Karen had found the cassette, but she wouldn't hand it over. "Wow... there're a lot of good ones on here." She flipped it over and started reciting the entire set list maddeningly slow, "'Brown Sugar', 'Satisfaction', 'Honky Tonk Women', 'Street Fighting Man'..."

"Can I have it please?!" I snapped. It took every ounce of restraint I had to not rip it out of her hand and race back to the car as fast as possible so I could slip it into the stereo and start deciphering the secret message Will was obviously trying to send me.

She finally handed it over. "Yeah, you should definitely get that one. It's like a greatest hits tape."

She walked off to browse the Queen section, and I finally got the chance to look at the cassette. On the front were the silhouettes of five heads, each one descending in size, stacked inside each other like a set of hairy Russian nesting dolls. At first it looked like it was five profiles of the same person, but when I looked closer, I realized only the biggest head had Mick's fat lips. The smaller ones must've belonged to the other band members, whoever the hell they were. I imagined the whole band gathered inside some big wig record producer's office, having the mockup of this album cover slapped down in front of them, and realizing they'd all been downsized into mere shrunken heads living inside Mick's skull. I wondered how that had gone over.

Karen slipped into a little room in the back with a doorway shrouded by strands of beads where they kept the guitar sheet music. I already knew from experience that room was super boring, so I flipped through some albums trying to look like I fit in.

Karen played guitar and sang lead vocals in a band, so we came here a lot. I always felt like I was too young to be inside, like Karen had somehow snuck me in when the bouncer had stepped out to go to the bathroom. The store had all kinds of pipes and weird contraptions made of glass on the countertops and it smelled funny, like a mix of tobacco and incense and musty straw. I could almost imagine any minute the police busting through the door and yelling "Everyone, down on the floor! This is a raid!"

I knew I was being stupid. The Den was a legit store. An iconic spot just on the edge of the Indiana University campus that also sold sweatshirts, tiny vials of Tylenol, and packs of gum and candy bars for the college students that lived across the street. But still, there were a lot of weird things in there too. Things that seemed just on the border of criminality like displays of hangover cure pills, flavored tobaccos, and those silver clips with strips of leather and feathers hanging from them.

When I was younger and Karen first brought me here, I'd asked her what those feathered metal things were. "They're called roach clips," she'd said, "but not for the kind of roaches that have legs if you know what I mean." I hadn't known what she meant, so I'd said, "but if a roach doesn't have legs doesn't that just make it a worm?" She'd laughed so hard, but it wasn't the kind of laugh that made me proud of myself. And I'd been even more embarrassed when she'd repeated what I'd said to her friends in the band later, and they'd laughed just as hard too.

"Shit, she's so adorable!" they'd said while I was standing right there. God, I felt so stupid. I had no idea what was so funny until a year later, when I was hanging out watching the band practice in our living room.

"Here's your roach with no legs," Karen's friend Chip said, showing me the tiniest twisted cigarette clamped in the feathered instrument's teeth; the kind of cigarette that smelled different from my mom's. Chip was gay too, just like the other two girls in the band. He was the drummer, Crystal played the keyboard, and Lola played the bass guitar. I'd known all of them almost as long as I'd known Karen. They were almost as funny, and almost as talented as Karen. Almost, but not quite. That probably should have been their band name. Almost, But Not Quite. It was a lot better than the cheesy one they had now: The Professor and Mary Annes, which in my opinion was way too cute for the kind of music they played.

As I waited near the counter for Karen, I saw a basket filled with all kinds of metal pins. They had sayings on them like "Why Be Normal?" and "Support Apathy" and "Make Love Not War". Peering into their candy colors, one button made me do a double take. I pulled it out and looked at it closer. The words "If It Feels Good Do It" were printed in bold black letters on top of a yellow background. I read them over and over, struck by how simple the slogan was. *If it feels good do it. If it feels good do it.* Six teeny tiny words that suddenly made so much sense to me.

I thought of dancing on the road with Will last night. Of how much fun he looked like he was having; of how it had seemed like something that would feel so good, so I'd done it, just like the pin said. And look how that had turned out: with me walking around now, feeling like I was living inside one of the romantic movies I loved so much. Maybe this pin was on to something.

Karen came up beside me. "You getting that too?" she asked. For some reason, I didn't want her to know I liked the pin as much as I did.

"Yeah, maybe. Stacie might want it."

The girl behind the counter pointed over my head to

Karen. "Hey, didn't you play at The Brass Lantern last Friday night?"

The cashier girl looked like a student, but not like all the preppy ones with their khakis and striped belts and collars of their polos flipped up. This girl had really short spiky hair, a bunch of leather wrist bands and was wearing way too much black eyeliner.

"Yeah, I did an acoustic set there Friday," Karen said. She was trying to act all casual, but I knew how much she liked to be recognized. The only thing she liked better was when someone sang one of her songs back to her.

"Oh… yeah… I love your stuff!" the girl squealed, clapping her hands together. "Especially that one. 'The Battle in Me'. That one gets me right here." She hit her chest so hard I was afraid she'd just accidentally plunged one of the spikes from her wrist cuffs right into her heart.

"The battle in me," the girl started singing. *Oh God. Here we go.* "Am I real or am I make believe?" She closed her eyes and started dancing all crazy, which was a little strange since it was a slow song. She went on, "If you call my name, who will come…." She trailed off like she couldn't remember what came next.

Karen filled in quickly, singing, "The best or worst of me? Will you think less of me? The battle in me." She sounded a million times better than Goth Girl. Karen could sing a Kit Kat commercial and make it sound like it should be nominated for a Grammy, that's how good her voice was.

"Yeah! That's it!" Goth Girl said, like Karen was the

one that needed reminding. "It's just so... so... poignant you know."

Karen stared up in the air, clearly enthralled by the girl's review. "Poignant. Yeah. I like that," she mumbled, fingers twitching in her pocket like she wanted to pull out a gum wrapper and scribble the word down so she could repeat it into a mirror when she got home.

"Well, thanks." Karen tried to sound all humble, but I already knew she was going to tell this story to my mom later. And probably inflate it to where the girl was asking for her to autograph her chest with a Sharpie so she could have it tattooed there later.

I wanted to mention to the girl that I'd helped Karen write that song. That she'd taken it from a poem I'd written and, for some reason, had shared with her in a rare moment of weakness. I mean, Karen had added a bunch of lines to it and written the music, but still. I considered it a collaboration of sorts. I'd felt so alone when I'd written those words. And yet it was cool to think that maybe there were other people out there, like weird Goth Girl, that understood those same feelings too. That my poem was actually *poignant* somehow. Maybe I was the one who should've been writing that word down on a gum wrapper instead of Karen.

"It's so cool I got to meet you," Goth Girl said, cheeks flushing. The dreamy look she gave Karen made my stomach twist in a weird way. I glanced at Karen's face, trying to see what Goth Girl saw. Although the word pretty was way to girly to use about Karen, I guess if you wanted to get technical about it, that's what she was. She was one of those kinds of people that made old ladies mad. *If only she'd wear makeup and not cut her hair so short, my with those green eyes and high cheekbones, she'd be beautiful!* Yeah. Forget that. Karen thought painting your face to fulfill archaic male desires was demeaning to women and she'd never stoop to such blatant degradation. *Blah, blah, blah.*

"Can I buy this, please?" I asked, stepping in front of Karen to break Goth Girl's stare.

"Oh, right... yeah." She grabbed the cassette away from me, seeming flustered.

"I'll meet you outside," Karen said, pulling her sunglasses down like she needed to disguise herself from all her fans waiting outside.

I put the button on the counter. "Is she a friend of yours?" Goth Girl asked breathlessly once Karen was gone.

"Who? Her?" I tipped my head to the door. For some reason, the question startled me. Was Karen my friend? I'd always thought of her more like my second mom. Someone who did my laundry and cooked dinner for me (if you call frozen pizza or mac and cheese dinner.) Who drove me to practices and forged my mom's name on permission slips when she was too busy to do it herself.

But then again, we did hang out a lot. We liked the same movies (always funny ones like *The Jerk* and *Meatballs* and *The Blues Brothers*). And she always seemed to enjoy it when I went with her to band practice, the grocery, and all her other errands. And she had looked awfully disappointed when I said I wasn't coming with her this morning.

I blinked back at Goth Girl, still not finding an

answer. Trying to file Karen away in one neat category always made my head hurt. My feelings about her were way too complicated for one simple word.

"Yeah, I guess she's my friend," I said, just to shut her up.

She looked out the window at where Karen was waiting for me. "God, you're *so* lucky."

The odd feeling in my stomach came back again. I wanted to reach over the counter and twist the dog collar on Goth Girl's neck so hard she turned purple. She didn't even know Karen. She didn't have the right to tell me whether or not I was lucky to know her.

I waved the pin in her face just to get her to stop ogling Karen. "Again, can I check out now, please?"

Breaking from her trance she glanced at the pin. "Oh, this is a good one!" She pointed to her leather vest where she had the same button pinned. "That's the way I live my life. If something feels good, I do it!"

"Well, good for you," I muttered, still not sure why I was so mad at her.

"It only makes sense." She tapped the keys of the register without even looking at it. *Beep. Beep. Chaaa-goom. Beep. Beep. Beep. Chaaa-goom.* "I mean, we all just ultimately want to feel good, right? Isn't that why we do everything? So why not just bypass all the so-called rights and wrongs and find what feels good first? Then just follow that off into happiness?"

"Uh, yeah, I guess that makes sense."

"Simple isn't it?" She smiled big at me as I handed her the money, feeling dazed because the way she'd explained it really did make it sound simple. God, why

hadn't I thought of it before? Simple instead of complicated. Easy instead of hard. Maybe everything I'd ever
thought had just been backwards. Maybe this stupid
little metal pin really was the answer to everything I'd
been looking for all along. Ironic that I'd found it on a
counter next to a rack of Trojan rubbers and a box of
spicy beef jerky.

Goth Girl dropped the cassette in a little paper bag,
hesitating a moment to wave the pin at me before she
dropped it in too.

"It really is the secret to life. You should try it
sometime."

I took the bag and gave her a tight smile, thinking
back over how good last night had felt again.

"Oh, don't worry," I called over my shoulder as I
walked away, "I think I already have."

CHAPTER FIVE

I DON'T CARE

As I LEFT the store, I stopped to look through the plate-glass window at Karen outside, leaning on a lamppost in her sunglasses, waiting for me. I thought of the cashier saying how lucky I was to know her.

I'd certainly felt that way when Karen and her friends had first started coming over to our house back when I was only eleven. My mom met Karen and her group of friends in the art class she was taking at Indiana University that fall. "The Girls" was how my mom referred to them.

"The girls are coming over after class."

"The girls and I are going to the movies this weekend."

"The girls are going to come keep us company while your dad's away this weekend. Won't that be fun?"

The girls were all in their twenties, way younger than my mom, who had a husband and kid in sixth grade, and clearly shouldn't have been hanging out with people half her age. Looking back now, the whole situation prob-ably should have seemed strange to me, but since I'd had no reason to ever doubt my mom's judgement before, I didn't stop to question it. I just liked when the girls came over. They were so cool and fun with their flannel shirts and baggy overalls; their hiking boots with red laces and clunky soles that matched the tread of the tractors that were parked in our barn up the hill.

I made a point of gluing myself to their sides every minute they were at our house. I loved how they laughed so much and danced around the living room to Heart music and chugged Bartles and James fruit coolers. How they talked about big important stuff like the ERA amendment and how Reagan's trickle-down theory would never work and how Christian conservative Anita Bryant could take her anti-gay movement and stick it up her orange-scented ass.

The girls were so much more interesting than my dad, who I barely even knew. He'd been a pilot in the Air Force, which meant he was deployed in one war or another for most of my childhood. Now he was like some really strict stranger that had shown up at dinner one night a few years ago and never left. All he ever talked about was which cow was about to calve or how Roger Staubach was the best quarterback ever. He was nowhere near as fun as my mom's new friends.

My favorite of all the girls was Karen. She was super funny and super sarcastic. She could play the guitar and sing and draw and paint better than anyone I'd ever met in real life; maybe even a few on TV too. Every-one clamored for her attention, even me, but my mom was the one who got it the most. She and Karen were always disappearing to look at the artwork my mom had done before she'd had to drop out of college when my dad got stationed in Texas just before he went to Vietnam. I remember feeling proud that Karen liked my mom so much. I guess in all my eleven-year-old wisdom I reasoned that if she liked her, then by another kind of trickle-down theory that meant she liked me too. Of course, at the time, I had no idea just how much (and in what way) my mom and Karen liked each other.

I remembered the day I'd found out the truth. My mom and Karen were off somewhere like always and the other girls were watching me, even though I was way past the age of needing babysitting. We were all eating popcorn in the kitchen of our farmhouse, and I was telling them how I'd written a funny poem comparing the taste of bacon to true love, which they thought was hilarious. I'd wanted to read it to them to make them all laugh, so I'd run into the living room to find my notebook.

That's when I saw them together; my mom lying flat out on the couch with Karen lying on top of her. I stood there in the doorway, just staring at them. All I could think about was when my mom took us to the National Gallery of Art when I was little and we'd seen a Picasso painting. It was a weird thing to think about at a time like that, but it must have popped into my head because, just like the Picasso, I couldn't make sense of what I was seeing. My mom's arms and Karen's arms all intertwined, their legs scissored together, Karen's head bending down, their lips pressing together. It didn't make sense at all.

Just like all the random shapes and mismatched eyeballs and floating ears of the Picasso hadn't made sense to me at first either.

At the museum, my mom had told me you had to let your eyes blur a little so you could take in the whole of the painting and not just each of its parts. And that's exactly what I did that day in the living room. Then all of a sudden, *whoosh*, I saw what was framed right there in front of me. And the next second, the reality of my mom and Karen slapped me so hard across the face it felt like the skin of my cheek had just been torn right off my bone.

One girl saw me frozen in the doorway and grabbed my arm. "Don't go in there," she hissed as she pulled me back into the kitchen. The shame of what I'd just seen flooded hot through my body as I stumbled backwards, trying to arrange my face into the smile that had been there only seconds before.

I pretended it didn't bother me. Tried to disguise how badly I was reeling by telling the girls a knock-knock joke about an impatient cow and a long story about how in class that day Steve Hamish had scared me by jumping out from the coat closet with his eyelids turned inside out.

Later, after some low murmurings between the girls and my mom -after they'd all hurried out the door and Karen had stopped to say she was sorry to me but didn't explain why- my mom sat me down at the kitchen table. She talked about gross things like love and feelings and how they sometimes came up when you didn't expect them and in ways you could never have planned. She said a whole lot more, but I tuned her out after a while. I just kept scribbling on my notebook saying, "I don't care", "I don't care", over and over and praying she would stop talking.

After she finally released me, I ran off to my bedroom and tried to do just that; I tried to learn how to not care about anything or anyone anymore, so I'd never have to feel that stupid ever again.

But even though I liked to think I'd hardened myself against life, it was obvious my attempts hadn't fully taken. Because now, as the door of the shop jingled, as Karen smiled when she saw me walking toward her, dammit if my heart didn't lift a little. I still had no idea if Karen was my mom or my friend or a little bit of both. All I knew was that at that moment, as much as I hated to admit it, I really did feel lucky to know her. It was the most messed up part of me, the part I still couldn't quite understand: How could I actually love the person who ruined my life?

CHAPTER SIX

A DIFFERENT WORLD

"Man, that cashier's got good taste in music, huh?" Karen said when I got to her.

"Yeah, right… just because she liked yours." I opened up my cassette as we crossed the street to the park, where we were supposed to meet my mom. We found a bench right along the sidewalk and I unfurled the cardboard liner from the case. "I mean, you could have mentioned I helped you write that song," I mumbled.

Karen looked surprised. Like she'd forgotten I'd even been involved at all. "Oh yeah. Right. I guess I could have."

"No shit, Sherlock."

"Hey, how about this? I'll give you a writing credit when I cut my first demo tape, okay? Your name will be printed right in the notes, just like those guys' were." She pointed to the paper in my hand. Printed in italics after every song on the list were the words 'Jagger/Richards.'

"I'm not holding my breath," I grumbled as I scanned down all twenty-one songs. "Wow, so they *wrote* all these too?"

It was hard for me to imagine Mick Jagger sitting at a desk with a pen and piece of paper, writing something. I wondered if he'd had to jump up every once in a while and squeal or grunt or kick his foot out in the air like he was karate chopping something while he was doing it.

I'd been writing since I was a little kid. Not just poems that sometimes got turned into songs, but stories and essays and movie scenes (with a girl who suspiciously resembled me inserted into all the lead romantic roles). It was weird to think that Mick Jagger and I might have something in common. Maybe I could somehow work that into a conversation with Will the next time I saw him. *Oh, by the way, did I mention I'm a writer like Mick? Yeah, I wrote a song too. It's going to get recorded someday. My name's going to be printed on the liner notes and everything.* Then I remembered I couldn't say any of that because then he might ask me who my song was going to get recorded by, and I could never tell him the truth about Karen.

"Yeah, those guys are one of the most prolific song writing duos in rock history," Karen said. "They call them The Glimmer Twins. Mick Jagger and Keith Richards."

I memorized the unfamiliar names in case they might come up as one of Will's quiz questions. That was, if I ever got to be in his car again. *Keith Richards. The Glimmer Twins.* Got it. I wanted to ask Karen to tell me everything she knew about The Rolling Stones, but I was afraid she'd want to know why I was so interested in them all of a sudden. She was already suspicious when I asked her about the song in The Den.

"That's an old song. Why do you want to hear that one?" she'd asked when I brought up "You Can't Always Get What You Want".

"Ummm… just some kids were talking about it last night." Actually, just one kid. Who wasn't even really a kid if you wanted to get technical about it.

Karen had looked at me kind of funny then. I was never really that good at lying. I always got really self-conscious thinking about what my face looked like and then my mouth would start twitching all weird. It was a dead giveaway. Especially to her, since she knew me so well. That's why I'd had to look away when I was talking about the song. Thank God, she'd let it go.

Karen and I sat on the bench and people-watched while we waited for my mom, making jokes under our breath about the students walking by. We never ran out of material to work with when we came to Bloomington. It always amazed me that we were only 30 miles north of Cold Springs and yet it felt like we were in a completely different world.

There were so many different kinds of people here. Preppies, nerds, farmers, jocks. Whites, Blacks, Asians, almost every ethnicity you could think of. Three stoners playing hacky sack, and another guy who looked like he was homeless, sleeping on a park bench. And nobody even cared. Everybody was just walking around doing their own thing like it was all totally normal, which was so completely unlike Cold Springs. Down there, the only difference between people was whether they worshiped at the Baptist, Methodist, or the Presbyterian Church. The only variance in skin color came from how long they stayed in the tanning bed at Sunshine Tan and Nail Salon down on Peterson Street.

There were gay people in Bloomington too. Although Karen usually had to point them out to me since even up here (other than in the gay bars where Karen's band played) they still mostly had to hide. It made me wonder if there might be some gay people hiding out in Cold Springs too. It was crazy to imagine, but if what my mom and Karen said was true, then homosexuals weren't as much of an anomaly as the churches down there claimed they were. Gay people were, in fact, everywhere. God, if I said that aloud down in Cold Springs they'd probably burn me at the stake.

I finally saw my mom walking up the side street from Atwater where her office was. She was wearing a long printed skirt and a blue gauze blouse with colorful embroidery around the collar. It was the kind of outfit that would get you called a "gosh-darn hippie" if you wore it on the streets in Cold Springs, but in Bloomington, my mom fit right in. She was walking with a girl who looked like she was only a few years older than me. They were both smiling and laughing about something that was obviously totally hilarious. I'd never seen the girl in my life, but I instantly hated her.

When they got to us, my mom introduced us to the girl. She said I was her daughter, but she didn't even qualify who Karen was to her, probably because we were in Bloomington and people didn't need any qualifiers up here.

"Oh, my gosh!" the girl gushed, looking at me. "You're *soooo* lucky to have Ruby for a mom!"

I plastered on a fake smile. "Uh, yeah, I guess."

More like, I would be lucky to have her as a mom if she didn't have to spend all her time listening to all your problems, bitch.

Lately, I'd been getting sick of my mom's clients. I thought my mom had to be all confidential about who she counseled, but her clients didn't seem to worry about keeping their therapy with her a secret. Wherever we went, there was always one of them that would find her; tracking her down at the mall or hugging her on the street or interrupting us when we were eating dinner out. They were always raving and gushing, just like this girl who had taken it upon herself to tell me how lucky I was. What was it with people telling me that today anyway?

After a few more minutes of gushing, which I pretended to listen to, the girl finally tore herself away, and my mom sat down on the bench between Karen and me. Exactly as I expected, Karen told her the entire story of the girl in The Den recognizing her. But I had to give her credit, she ended up telling it without all that much embellishment.

I wished Karen would just shut up for a minute. I mean, it wasn't like I was really going to tell my mom anything about last night. About meeting Will and about the weird way I'd felt ever since. I'd never just come right out and ask her if it was normal to feel so nervous and excited and happy and worried all at the same time when you thought about a person. It wouldn't have been like me to talk to her about stuff like that. But still, I would've liked to have had the chance to try if I wanted to.

Karen finally took a breath and asked where we should go to eat. My mom made a face. "I hate to tell you guys this, but I can't go out to lunch. Barb had an emergency and I have to take her 2:00 client."

Karen didn't even try to hide her disappointment, but I did. I was pretty good at it by now since I'd already had so much practice.

"I'm sorry," my mom said, turning to me. The breeze picked up a piece of her short, frosted-blonde hair, making it stick straight up off her head. It somehow consoled me she had no idea how stupid she looked. "Did you get a new tape?" she asked, pointing to my hand.

"Yeah. The Stones." I felt like being mean to her, but it was hard to be mean to my mom because she was always so cheerful and nice. So, I settled for what I usually did: Just kept my mouth shut and thought about all the things she didn't know about me now. About how she used to know everything about me and now she knew nothing. It was stupid, I knew. But it was all I had left. My thoughts were the only things I had to take away from her. The only way I could punish her for all the things she took from me.

"What else did you get?" she asked, pointing at my bag.

"Oh, this," I said, pouring the button out into my hand. I couldn't wait until she read my new motto. Surely that would shock her a little.

But I was the one who was shocked when she started laughing.

"Oh, my gosh!" she said, "I used to have that same pin when I was a teenager!"

"What? You did?" That wasn't at all the reaction I was expecting.

"Yeah. Well, maybe not when I was a teenager," she admitted begrudgingly. "Maybe more like when I was in my twenties. When I was in art school."

I should have known. My mom was always telling stories of the civil rights marches she went to when she lived in South Carolina and how she was there for Martin Luther King Jr.'s big speech down in D.C. My mom didn't just look like a hippie. She honestly was one.

"Yeah, I loved that pin," she mused, running her fingers over the shiny words. "I'll have to find mine. Heck, it's probably an antique by now, huh?!" She playfully bumped my shoulder with hers.

Karen leaned over and read the motto again. "I don't know," she said. "I don't think that's a good rule of thumb for a fifteen-year-old to be going by."

And there it was. The reaction I'd hoped for, but not from the person I'd wanted it from.

"Oh, I don't know," my mom said. "I think it *is* good advice. Tapping into the way you feel is a good way to make decisions, in my opinion. That's what I was just telling my last client." She tipped her chin toward where the gushy girl had disappeared.

I took the pin away from her, imagining what it would feel like to poke her last client all over with the sharp part on the back. "Yeah, well, I might just give this to Stacie."

I couldn't believe my mom actually liked the pin.

That she was pretty much telling me to do whatever the hell felt good to me. Moms weren't supposed to say things like that. They were supposed to tell you to follow rules and be home by ten o'clock and to change your jeans because they were too tight to wear out in public. But of course, my mom wouldn't say any of those things. She probably had one of those "Why Be Normal?" pins I saw back at The Den too, because she was about as far from normal as any mom could get.

&

I watched my mom as she left to go back to her office. There was something about the slant of the sun, the way the trees were mottling on her back as she walked away that made me think of being back on the farm with her. It was when I was about six years old, and we'd been up all night with a mother cow laboring to have a calf. Things weren't going well and we'd had to call the vet. He'd wrapped some ropes around the tiny protruding hooves and together we'd finally pulled the calf out of the birth canal, but right afterward the huge cow had collapsed and started hemorrhaging all over the straw and there was nothing the vet could do to save her. It was a terrible scene, my mom holding the momma cow's head in her lap, rocking and crying, wailing "No, No..." over and over again while the calf stood over his dead mom crying just as loudly.

We'd stayed up all night with the baby calf, feeding him from a bottle and letting him curl in our laps for warmth. But when we'd had to leave him the next morning to do our chores he'd cried so loudly again, bleating over and over like a heartbroken foghorn. To me, it sounded like with each bawl he was saying, "Mommy! Mommy! Where are you?! Mommy?" I wanted to run back to my bed and put my pillow over my head so I didn't have to hear how sad he was anymore.

I remembered how all that day I couldn't stop thinking about the poor calf with the dead mom. I stayed so close to my mom's side that she almost tripped over me a couple times. She'd even accidentally hit me in the head with her elbow when she was scattering feed to the chickens, that's how close I'd stayed next to her. But my mom didn't complain. She just held my hand and kept me close. I was sure she knew something was wrong, but she didn't ask me. She just waited until I was ready to talk.

It wasn't until we were pulling weeds out of the garden as the summer sun dropped low around us that I finally said what I'd been thinking all day.

"Mommy, when you die, I want to die the very next day," I'd told her in a shaky voice.

She'd stopped and sat back on her heels, a clump of weeds hanging mid-air in her hand. "Oh, honey, why do you say that?"

"Because," I said, trying to sound matter of fact, even though the words were all lumping up in my throat, "I never want to live in a world without you in it."

She'd dropped the weeds and reached over the ruffle of lettuce leaves to hug me. "I know why you're thinking about this... and it's okay," she'd said into my hair. Then she'd held me out at arm's length and looked into my eyes. "But you don't have to worry about me, sweetie. I'm not going anywhere."

But now, sitting on the bench across from The Den, watching her walk back to her office and disappear once again, all I could think about was how I wished she hadn't lied.

CHAPTER SEVEN

"YOU CAN'T ALWAYS GET WHAT YOU WANT"

THE NEXT FRIDAY night Stacie, Scott, and I were sitting at the front table in Pizza King, the local hangout uptown, watching cars cruise around the town square.

Stacie was trying to find us a ride out to the drive-in because she'd heard Mark and his friends were there. It turned out that after I'd left the party with Will the weekend before, Stacie and Mark had snuck off and made out in one of the tractor barns. Unlike me, Stacie had kissed a few boys before, but they'd mostly just been awkward pecks with boys in our grade, a few gropes when she'd played 20 Seconds In Heaven in some kid's dark closet. But she'd said with Mark it had been totally different. I'd made her describe just how different and she'd given me every little detail, even the part where he'd put his tongue in her mouth which Stacie claimed made her get all tickly in parts way farther south than just her mouth. It sounded kind of gross to me, but it must've felt good to her because she seemed awfully desperate to do it all over again this weekend.

"Why don't you have your car again?" Stacie asked Scott. She looked beautiful as always, wearing a tank top with one of her stepdad's dress shirts over it with a man's floral tie as the belt for her jeans. Stacie never wore boring old polos or sweatshirts like the rest of us. In fact, Stacie didn't really do anything like the rest of us. That's because she wasn't a native like pretty much everyone in our school. She'd moved to Cold Springs from Indianapolis in sixth grade, so she was way more cosmopolitan than that. I wasn't a native either since I'd moved here from Virginia in second grade, but that didn't mean I was anywhere near as cool as she was.

"I told you," Scott said dejectedly. "My dad figured out I'd been adding water to his gin so he took my car away for a week."

Stacie huffed, still scanning the packed restaurant for someone to hit up for a ride. "You know, we only let you hang around us because you have a car," she teased Scott. "What good are you to us now?" She tipped her head at me. "Right? Tell him." I knew she wanted me to pick up the baton and pile on Scott like usual, but I was too busy staring out the plate glass windows, searching for any signs of Will's shiny white car.

"Yeah, you're a total dweeb, Scott," I mumbled halfheartedly, then went back to my single-minded sur-veillance of the street.

Things had kind of spiraled out of control for me the

past week. Whenever my mind had a second to wander, I found myself in full on Walter-Middy-style fantasies about Will. Like tonight; I already envisioned Will pulling up along the curb, dashing into the restaurant, desperately searching for me. Sweeping me in his arms to kiss me passionately while every girl in the restaurant watched, each of them turning green with envy by how lucky I was to be with such a handsome boy. James Thurber had nothing on me.

That was not at all what happened.

A couple minutes later, the dazzling white of the Monte Carlo slid into the frame of the window, just like I'd prayed it would. Will parked in the lot across the street and headed directly toward the restaurant as I floundered in my seat, trying to look cool. My heart felt like it was about to pound its way out of my body by way of my throat. I thought I was doing a good job of disguising my panic until Stacie made a face at me from the end of the table.

"Are you okay? You look like you're about to barf."

I jerked my head, motioning to the street where Will was now standing beside of a car full of kids, talking and gesturing in his big outrageous way while a line of traffic formed behind them.

"Ohhhhh," Stacie said. I had forced her to listen to me describe every tiny detail of last weekend over and over again those past few days. Each of my stories about Will proceeded with the same adamant disclaimer. "I know I'm being completely stupid, but…"

A second later, Scott noticed his cousin outside. "Hey, I know. I'll get Will to give us a ride to the drive-in."

"Yeah. That might work," I said casually, as if I hadn't been secretly praying for that exact scenario to happen all night.

Will finally untangled himself from the car and jogged the rest of the way to the door. He was more dressed up than he had been the other night, wearing a button-down striped Oxford and dark jeans, like he'd just come from having a fancy dinner out somewhere.

He didn't come over to us at first. He was too busy high-fiving and back slapping and waving to people calling out from the back booths to talk to us. My God you would've thought the guy was running for mayor with the way he worked the crowd. He was as big a force outside the car as he was in it. But after a while of seeing his impact on people, watching them gather around him to lap up any bit of him they could get, I couldn't help but feel even more hopeless about my crush. Not only hopeless, but mindlessly unoriginal too. I clearly wasn't the first person to worship Will Calder. And I clearly wouldn't be the last either.

He finally sauntered over. My skin flushed hot with him standing so close to me. I busied myself talking to a couple of guys sitting at the other end of the table so my red face wouldn't give me away.

I kept my head turned, but listened intently as Scott asked Will for a ride to the drive-in.

"Sure, I can give you a ride," he said, then hesitated. I thought I could feel him staring at me, but I told myself it was only wishful thinking. Will probably didn't even remember who I was.

"Hey, Red," he called. I froze in my seat. "What are you doing? Pretending to ignore me?"

I turned and faked being startled. "Oh sorry. I didn't see you there." Stacie rolled her eyes.

"Yeah, right," he said, giving me a smug smile. I hated how he always seemed to know what I was thinking. I looked away quickly. It was too jarring to see his brightness, his beauty, set against the grey backdrop of the restaurant. It felt like the part in *Wizard of Oz* when everything suddenly transformed from black and white into a million shades of color.

"I'm just going to go find Rob," Will said, heading toward the jukebox in the back. "I'll meet you guys at the car."

As I scrambled onto my limp noodle legs, I heard Will barking Rob's name. He sounded exactly like his dad, Coach Calder, yelling at us in gym class.

As we left, Stacie hung back. "Shit. He really *is* as hot as you said."

"*Shhhhhh*," I hissed, like she'd yelled it to the entire restaurant instead of just whispering in my ear.

As we shuffled single file out the door, I felt someone come up so close behind me I could feel the phantom brush of their chest against my back. I was too scared to turn around to find out if it was Will, but from the heat burning along my skin, it seemed like my body had already decided it was.

"Are you going to make me laugh again like you did last week, Red?" Will's voice was low, close to my ear.

Desperate for a quick comeback, I said, "Yeah, but probably not on purpose."

He chuckled behind me, and I smiled to myself. It looked like my prediction had already come true.

∽

When we got to the drive-in, we didn't actually drive in like you're supposed to. Instead, we turned down an overgrown dirt path that ran just behind the theater. You couldn't hear the movie from back there, but you could see it through the trees, which was enough for us because nobody really went to the drive-in to watch the movie anyway.

Cars were parked along the road in the woods and a bunch of kids were gathered around a fire burning in an old oil drum. As Will pulled the Monte Carlo over to let us out, I saw *Animal House* playing on the wooden screen through the shutter of the birch trees, John Belushi's face looming huge over the parked cars, his cheeks packed fat with mashed potatoes.

We piled out into the night. Stacie headed directly to the fire in search of Mark. Scott hooked his arm through mine, pulling me to follow her. My heart sunk when Rob hopped up on the hood of the car to watch the movie and Will stayed behind with him, leaning against the driver's side door with his beer. *Dammit. I'd waited all this time to see Will and now I'm not going to be anywhere near him? Just my stupid luck.*

But just as we were leaving, Will called out to Scott.

"Red's going to stay here with me," he ordered, voice as steely as a Tombstone sheriff's.

Scott whirled around, looking deflated. "What? Why? She's my friend Will."

Will threw his hands up. "Can't she be my friend too?"

My stomach did a massive somersault. *Goddamn. Fuck. Hell. Did he really just say that?*

"Fine," Scott said, releasing me with a huff. "But don't keep her captive all night."

"I'm not keeping anyone captive." He arched one perfect eyebrow at me. "You're coming to me on your own free will. Right, Red?"

I gave a cool shrug, trying to hide my soaring heart. "I mean, I guess I could spare a few moments of my precious time."

I walked toward him, barely feeling my legs under me. "But only if there's free beer involved," I said, trying to look bored.

Will gave me a sly smile, like he could see right through my act. He reached in a red cooler by his feet, pulled out a dripping bottle of Budweiser and handed it to me.

"Of course, my dear. Anything for you."

✎

Will and I leaned on the side of the car, watching the movie, drinking our beers. My heart was pounding from being so close to him, but I kept reminding myself the only reason he wanted to talk to me was because of the homework he'd given me.

"So, you listened to the song then?" he said, right on cue.

I stood ramrod straight, clicked my heels together, and gave him a stiff salute. "Sir, yes, sir!"

He laughed, head tipping back, eyes crinkling into sweet, blue crescents. A flood of warmth surged in my chest. I decided that if I could do nothing but make him look that way for the rest of my life, it would be enough for me.

"I like that," he said. "You can salute every time you see me if you want. I don't mind."

"Yeah, I bet you don't."

He handed me his beer. "Here, hold this a sec." He went to the passenger window and leaned in so far that his waist teetered on the edge of the door frame. His shirt rode up and exposed a patch of skin just above the top of his jeans. I stared at it, imagining what it would feel like to reach out and touch it. To run my hand along his narrow waist and then up the smooth expanse of his back. When he turned back, I looked away quickly hoping he couldn't read my mind again.

A few seconds after he rejoined me, the first notes of "You Can't Always Get What You Want" wafted out of the car window.

When I'd gotten home from The Den last weekend, I'd locked myself in my room and blasted the song so loud Karen had to pound on my door and tell me to turn it down.

It had surprised me when the music had started and there weren't any electric guitars screeching through the speakers. Instead, the sound of a choir had filled my room, women's voices operatically singing the words Will had slowly spoken to me beside his car the night before.

Eventually Mick's familiar voice had replaced the

choir, singing simply to the strum of an acoustic guitar, a single horn calling mournfully in the distance. The sound of it made my chest ache. It reminded me too much of when the military honor guard had played "Taps" at my dad's funeral earlier that year; three of the players standing beside us, one lone horn echoing from some place far off in the distance.

"So, what did you think of the song?" he asked.

"I really liked it. I mean, it's no Air Supply but..."

He smiled big but didn't say any more. We both stared out in the same direction, listening as a drum cadence and funky guitar rhythm braided into the song. Will nodded his head in time to the music, but I couldn't move at all. I felt like a block of stone next to him. It was hard to pay attention when all I could think about was what I was going to say to him when the song ended.

I took a deep breath and tried to focus on the song. It had soothed me when I'd listened to it in my bedroom. I prayed it would do the same now. I stared at the actors on the movie screen, their lips moving mutely, and let the layer of rhythms wrap around me until slowly I started to relax. Eventually, I became so lost in the music that when the song built to its crescendo, I couldn't be quiet for one second longer.

"I love this part!" I shouted to Will when Mick started on the last triumphant verse.

"Me too!" Will shouted back.

Mick and the choir's voices swelled louder, and I felt like I was being lifted higher and higher in the air with each line of the song. The canopy of trees above us captured the music, amplified it, then shot it back down, even more intense than it was before. I looked up into the trees, half expecting the branches to be lined with angels perched above, swaying in time with the music. That's how beautiful the song was.

The feeling was almost otherworldly, like something spiritual was happening right there on the overgrown road behind the drive-in movie theater. The song had been moving even in the confines of my tiny bedroom. But mixed with the trees and the night and Will standing next to me, it suddenly became so much more.

When the last notes faded away, I felt filled up. Achy even, but in a good way. Like my chest was being pushed from the inside out by the residue of what the music had left behind.

"Wow, that was cool, huh?" I said, unable to contain myself. I wondered if Will had felt the same way I just had.

Will nodded, seemingly as out of breath as I was. "Yeah, really cool." He smiled over at me. "What do you think of them adding a gospel choir?"

"Genius! Totally genius! Just the way it's so unexpected. You know? Like who would expect The Rolling Stones to be singing with a choir?"

"I always say the exact same thing," he said. "Fucking Lennon and The Beatles claim the Stones were just copying 'Hey Jude'. But that masterpiece," he motioned to the stereo, "is a million times better than The Beatles' five-lined little ditty."

I nodded furiously. "Yeah, much, much better." I noticed it was the second time he'd bashed The Beatles. I made a mental note to myself. *The Beatles are the enemy. Never bring them up.*

I'd only had one beer, yet I suddenly felt drunk. Like everything inside me wanted to spill out, completely unchecked and uncensored for all the world to hear.

"It really is a masterpiece, like you said. It's just so, so, big, you know? It makes me... it makes me..." I stopped. I needed to be careful or else Will was going to think I was crazy. "Oh, never mind."

"What were you going to say?" he prodded. "The song makes you what?"

The light from the movie flickered across his face, making his eyes flash from light blue to dark blue. There was no doubt in my mind that I was going to answer him. I'd only known Will for barely a week and yet I could already tell he was someone I'd never be able to say no to.

"It's just the song makes me feel something, you know," I started slowly. "Like really *feel* something inside me. I just think it's amazing how some random notes, put in a certain order and played in a certain way, can change the way your body feels, you know? And then you put them in a different order, and they make you feel a completely different way. It's really cool. Like some sort of magic or something." I looked away so I could finish. It was so much easier to talk to him when I didn't have to look at his face.

"It's like I knew exactly what Mick and Keith were thinking when they wrote it. Almost like I was there with them, even though it was a long time ago and nowhere near here. It's crazy really… like some kind of musical communion across time and space, you know?"

Oh, my God. What had I just said? Had I just told Will I believed in time travel or something?!

"But that's just what I think. It's probably stupid, I know." My voice trailed off limply.

I looked down at the ground, my face flushing hot. I didn't dare look over at Will. It felt like the entire world had just screeched to a halt. No wind blew. No leaves moved. No lights flickered. Why had I just told him all that?

"Actually, I don't think it's stupid at all," Will finally said. "In fact, I think I know exactly what you mean."

When I finally let myself glance over at him, he was staring at me, his eyes scanning my face like it was the first time he'd ever seen me. For once in my life, I felt like I'd said just the right thing.

"Wow… so… yeah," Will said, looking down at the ground, shaking his head a little. He seemed almost speechless, which surprised me. "So, what do you think it all means, Red?"

"Oh… well, um." This was it. The moment I'd known was coming, but suddenly I couldn't find any words. I'd studied every word of the song so I could be ready and yet all the notes I had scribbled just disappeared out of my head so quickly I could almost feel a rush of air blowing out of my ears.

"Well, um," I tried again, swallowing hard. "I think it means that you might not always get everything you want, but in the end, you'll get what you really need."

Oh. My. God. That was the worst answer ever. I'd basically just repeated the title of the song back to him.

"That's all you think it means?" Will snapped, clearly unimpressed.

Everything felt like it was falling apart. This was not going at all like how I'd hoped it would when I'd fantasized about talking to Will again.

"Are you going to answer the question?" he pressed.

"Yeah... I... I..." My brain was one big fog. I clutched around desperately, but only came up with a handful of mist. How did a person form a sentence, anyway? I used to know. Now I wasn't so sure.

"So let me ask you a different question then, Red," Will said, obviously sensing my distress. *Please Lord*, I prayed, *let this have a Yes or No answer.*

"Have you ever wanted something you couldn't have?"

I wanted to shout "Yes. You!" but thank God, I had the presence of mind to hold myself back. Instead, I mumbled, "Uh, I don't know," like a moron. The question felt way too personal. Like he'd bypassed a whole lot of polite pleasantries and jumped straight into asking about my deepest, darkest secrets.

"I'm sure there's something," he leaned over and elbowed me playfully. "C'mon, try. Tell me something you want right now that we could work on for you."

Had he just used the word *we*? I scanned my mind, desperate for something to say.

"Well, there is something but it's a long shot." It wasn't like me to open up and yet I felt this strange need to please him.

"What is it?"

"You know how they always pick two seniors to write a column in the newspaper about school?" He nodded. "Well, the other day in Creative Writing Mrs. Anderson was complaining about how they couldn't find any seniors who wanted to do it this year. And Stacie and I were talking about how much fun it would be if we could write it..."

He furrowed his brows. "You consider that *fun*? Writing a column? Sounds more like homework to me."

"Well, I think it would be fun. I love to write. I've been doing it forever."

"Okay, so you think writing is fun." He made a face like I'd just said I liked to volunteer for Chinese water torture experiments in my spare time. "So, did you ask her if you guys could do it?"

"No. I mean, they've only ever had seniors write it before. I don't think they'd ever let a couple of sophomores do it."

"You don't think? *You don't think?*" he erupted. He stood up tall and wagged a finger at me. "You see, right there's your problem."

My heart galloped in my chest. Uh oh. I'd said the wrong thing again. "What?"

"You've already assumed you can't do it before you even tried!"

"But it's never happened before," I tried to reason with him. "Why would they just suddenly change all the rules for me?"

He huffed loudly, then leaned down in my face. "Because you asked," he said really slowly, like I wasn't understanding something simple. "Get it, Red? You've got to put yourself out there. Go for what you want. No one's going to come hand it to you. No one's ever going to just read your mind and say, 'Oh, I think maybe this little red-haired girl huddled all quiet in the back row wants to do this. Let's save her the trouble and give it to her before she even makes the effort to ask for it herself.'"

"Little red-haired girl? You make me sound like some kind of *Peanuts* character!"

"What I'm saying is you have to believe in yourself. You gotta at least give them the chance to say no to you before you say no to yourself first!" He was breathing fast now, eyes dancing like he was rallying an entire troop for battle, not just plain old me, slumped there beside him already waving my white flag.

"You sound like one of those inspirational posters they have in the guidance room," I joked, hoping to make him laugh again so maybe he'd let the whole thing go. "You know, the ones with the soaring eagles and the vast canyon sunrises or the widdle bitty kitty with his paws clutching on for dear life telling you to 'Hang In There'."

But he didn't laugh. In fact, he looked more serious than I'd ever seen him.

"Stop joking around, Red. This shit's important."

I made a face. Why was he so worked up about this? Why did he even care what I did in the first place?

He barrelled on. "I'm telling you, I know what I'm talking about. You just gotta trust me." He smiled down at me. I swear to God it felt like there was some kind of palpable energy radiating off of him and onto me. "And here's the best part about asking for what you want." He leaned closer again. "They just might say, yes."

I blinked at him, letting myself imagine just for a moment what it would feel like if what he was saying was true. What if Mrs. Anderson did say yes to me? Man, that would be amazing. It would feel so good to be given an honor like having my own column with Stacie. Suddenly, I thought of my *If It Feels Good Do It* pin. So, was this what that phrase meant? I was supposed to do what felt good, like asking to write the column? Was Will agreeing with that motto just like my mom had?

"You're going to do it," Will proclaimed loudly. "You're going to go to Mrs. Anderson and ask her if you can write the column and then report back to me next weekend."

Next weekend?

Even though the thought of seeing him again thrilled me, I still couldn't give in that easily. "But what about what Mick just said. You can't always get what you want. Remember that?" I argued.

"But what if this column turns out to be the some-thing you *need* part of the song?"

I pretended to weigh over all he'd said, like I was still trying to decide, when I already knew I was going to do exactly what he'd told me to.

"Ok... maybe I will."

He let out a harsh puff of air, then said in his cocky way, "Oh, you obviously don't know me very well, Red. I don't accept maybes."

"Fine, I'll do it," I said firmly, not wanting to think

about the nerve I was going to have to muster up to go through with it.

"Good," he said, looking pleased. It thrilled me how happy he seemed with me.

With that decided, we both went back to drinking our beers and watching the movie. I thought of what we must've looked like there, standing next to each other, leaning on the car. If someone didn't know any better, they might've thought we were a couple out on a date, watching a drive-in movie through the romantic tendrils of tree limbs. I finally relaxed even more. But looking back, I probably shouldn't have.

"What about you? Have you ever wanted something you couldn't have?" I asked, leaning over a little so that my shoulder brushed his. I figured we were close friends by then, so I could do funny little things like that with him.

If it had been a few months later, I would've noticed how his grip tightened around his beer bottle. How his mouth curved down just a tiny bit and his body went rigid the second I finished the sentence. But I hadn't learned any of that yet, so it completely shocked me when he turned and stood right in front of me, shaking his head like he couldn't believe I'd had the nerve to ask him what I just did.

"Oh, you don't get how this works." He narrowed his eyes at me. "*I* ask the questions, and *you* answer them. Not the other way around."

My head jerked back like he just slapped me. Then, like an involuntary reflex, the rage shot out of me so fast I didn't have time to snatch it back.

"Fine! But you don't have to be such a fucking ass-hole about it!" I yelled in his face, shocked at the words that had come out of my own mouth.

His eyes went so wide I wasn't sure what he was about to do next. It turned out to be the last thing I expected. He burst out laughing.

He laughed and laughed, stumbling to the front of the car to call out to Rob, "Did you hear that, Rob? This girl just called me a fucking asshole!"

"Seems like she knows you pretty well then," Rob called back, not even looking away from the movie. That cracked Will up even more, so that by the time he made it back to me his cheeks were wet with tears.

I must have looked confused because he explained, "Nobody's ever had the nerve to say that to my face before."

"Well, it's obviously long overdue," I muttered, relieved, but still a little confused by his reaction.

He shook his head. "Man, you're too much, you know that?" He smiled down at me. "I don't think I've ever met a girl like you before. You're.... I don't know. Just different."

My body turned to ice. *Different.* The word I'd been running from for four years now. Was it just an offhand comment or did Will already know the real reason I was so different from everyone else?

"So, what if I am an asshole?" Will was still grinning broadly. "Does that bother you?"

"Pffff," I waved a hand. "No way. I'm used to being with assholes. I'm around guys all day long." I slipped into a bad New York accent. "All of them raging jerks,

I tell ya. Little fuckers that run home to their muthas if you so much as look at 'em cross-eyed."

I literally had no idea what I was saying. All I knew was I would blabber nonsense forever if it meant I could watch him laugh for a little while longer.

When he finally caught his breath, he tipped his head to the side a little and gave me an odd look.

"You're pretty weird, you know that?"

"I thought you said I was an okay girl."

"You are an okay girl. But you're a *weird* okay girl."

"Well, I'll take that as a compliment coming from the Grand Poobah of weirdness himself."

He bowed a little, like he was accepting the honor with great pride.

"Weird is good," he said. "At least to me it is."

My face burned from what seemed like another compliment. I was glad it was too dark for him to see it. Being with Will made me feel off balance. Like everything was a test and half the time I was getting the answers right and the other half I was getting them wrong and there was no way to ever know which one was which ahead of time.

We stood there staring at each other for a second too long. He broke away first, blinking a few times like he was trying to clear his head.

"Are you going to answer the question then?" I said, feeling a newfound power coursing through my blood. "Is there something you wanted that you couldn't have?"

"Yes," he said. I waited for him to add more, but he just stood there, staring out into the night, not looking at me.

"Well? What was it?"

"Oh, I think you need to wait a little longer until I tell you *all* my secrets."

I huffed, embarrassed that he'd duped me into revealing all I had to him, when he clearly wasn't going to reciprocate.

He stood up, shifted back and forth on his feet like he suddenly needed to be somewhere else. I sensed a door closing. I knew I had to slip through it quickly to avoid the humiliation of having it slammed shut in my face.

"I better go find Scott and Stacie," I said before he could dismiss me like I knew he was about to do. I dropped my empty beer bottle into the cooler and turned to go.

"Yeah. You better go," Will agreed. He looked like he wanted to say something else, but he didn't, so I just waved and walked away.

I hadn't made it too far when he called out to me.

"Hey, Red!"

"Yeah?" I turned back to him.

"Tops."

I made a face. *What did that mean?*

"It's a song," he said, "get it – "

"I know, I know," I interrupted, pretending to be annoyed, even though my heart was soaring higher than the drive-in movie screen. "Get it, learn it, then we'll talk about it next week, right?"

He nodded, giving me a smile so sexy it would churn my stomach for the next seven days straight.

I walked away, but just as I was almost out of earshot Will called out, "See you next week, weirdo okay girl!"

And that was the first of many lessons I'd eventually learn about Will:

He always got the last word.

CHAPTER EIGHT

ACCOMPLICE

THE NEXT MONDAY I'd just made it to the top of the three stairs to the drum section when Jimmy leapt out of his chair to block my path.

"Hey, Jimmy, what's up?" I asked, my heart quickening in my chest.

As it turned out, I hadn't had to worry about dealing with Jimmy after the party. When we'd gone back to school, Jimmy acted like nothing had happened between us. All he did was ask, "Where'd you go the other night?" absentmindedly.

"I was there. Didn't you see me?" I lied, hoping maybe he'd been so drunk he wouldn't remember I had ditched him. He'd gotten a confused look and dropped it, which only confirmed what I suspected. Jimmy was so wasted he had no idea what he was saying when he claimed he wanted to be with me. It was the only explanation that made sense.

"I need you to do me a favor," he said now, puffing out his broad chest. There was a big red mark on his cheek like he'd been slapped. I wondered if Tina had found out about our little incident in the hallway after all.

"What kind of favor?" I asked, dreading what he was going to say next. His buddy Steve was standing behind him, giggling like a maniac.

"I need you to go distract Tommy," he whispered in my ear.

"What do you mean, distract him?" I glanced over at where Tommy Terwilliger was sitting still as a statue in his chair, looking like he was trying to will himself into the concrete wall behind him. I knew that feeling all too well.

Tommy was the senior boys' number one target to bully in band class. I used to be target number two, but since I'd started letting Jimmy touch me I seemed to have fallen further down their list. I felt sorry for Tommy because, unlike me, he was completely defenseless. He had way too many strikes against him. Not only was he clearly poor (I'd heard he lived in the trailer park next to the railroad tracks), but he also probably weighed less than 100 pounds, wore Coke-bottle glasses and spoke in an unfortunately high voice which made him sound like a girl. I had no idea if he actually was gay, but the boys had decided he was. They called him fag and buttfucker and cocksucker every chance they got. The poor guy might as well have had a bullseye printed right on the back of his dirty terry-cloth shirt, that's how many strikes he had against him.

"I need you to keep Tommy's attention so he doesn't see me," Jimmy hissed. His breath smelled like the menthol Skoal he kept in the back pocket of his jeans under a ring of faded denim.

I looked at Tommy again, then back at Jimmy, wishing I could think of a quick one-liner to get me out of this, but nothing popped into my head. The boys had played countless pranks on Tommy over the past year. I had no idea what they were going to do to him next, and I wasn't about to ask. All I knew was, if I didn't go along with them, all my work at getting on their good sides would be destroyed. And then, my name would be at the top of their hit list again.

"How am I going to distract him?" I whispered back.

"I don't know, Red," Jimmy snapped. "Rub your ass up against his leg. Make him cream his jeans or something."

Steve giggled at Jimmy's crude suggestion, and I suddenly wished I hadn't eaten so much vanilla pudding at lunch.

"Just go," Jimmy pushed me toward Tommy.

I did what he said because as much as I hated to admit it, I kind of enjoyed when the seniors treated me like one of the guys. It made me feel kind of special when they laughed at my impressions or pulled me into their upperclassman powwows to tell them a crude joke. It was wrong I knew. But I got some kind of sick satisfaction out of knowing the senior boys liked me.

I grabbed a piece of music off a stand as I made my way over to Tommy.

"Um, Tommy... can you help me with this?" I asked,

opening up the folded piece of paper and holding it in front of his face. Jimmy shuffled around behind my back, close to where Tommy had set up his drum.

Tommy looked up at me, startled. I hardly ever talked to him, except maybe to ask him to hand me a mallet or move the marimba out of the way. He was like a drowning victim to me. If I got too close, I knew he would only pull me under with him. That's why most of the time I pretended I didn't notice him struggling to stay afloat right there next to me.

He stared at me as if he couldn't understand why I was asking for his help. His thick glasses were smudged with fingerprints and his hair fell across his pimpled forehead in greasy strings. I tried to be as disgusted with him as the boys always were. I mean, wasn't he just asking to be bullied, showing up to school looking the way he did every day? Couldn't he at least shower or change his clothes once in a while? Shouldn't he at least try to be more normal? Then the boys wouldn't have such a good reason for picking on him all the time the way they did.

"Uh... help you with what?" Tommy stammered in his squeaky voice.

"I can't remember where we're supposed to switch to the brushes on this piece," I asked. "Can you show me?" Tommy was a terrible drummer on top of everything else, even worse than me, so it was crazy I would even ask for his help.

Tommy squinted at the page. A look of panic crossed his face. *Oh God. He doesn't know the answer. This kid can't catch a break.* I decided to let him off the hook.

"Is it right here?" I asked, pointing to the right spot in the lines of music.

Tommy nodded furiously at me. "Yeah... yeah, that's it." He seemed suspicious, jumpy. If he'd been a soldier he probably would've been diagnosed with shell shock and been given a psychiatric discharge to get him out of the war. Every day last year I'd prayed that he'd just quit band and save himself from Jimmy and his goons. Save me from having to watch the cruelty anymore. But to my surprise, he'd survived last year and had signed up to do it all over again. I couldn't figure out why he kept coming back until I realized that maybe every class was like this for Tommy. That for him, being bullied wasn't a once in a while occasion, it was just a way of life.

Jimmy walked behind me and slapped me hard on the ass. "All good, Red."

I still wasn't sure what kind of plan I'd taken part in until our conductor Mr. Weinreight commanded us to our instruments a few minutes later and on our first strike of "The Power of Gold" Tommy's entire drum stand collapsed with a deafening crash.

The snare rolled on its side all the way across the floor of the drum section. Then, to the delight of Jimmy and Steve, it somehow built up enough steam to bounce down the three steps of our raised tier until it finally came to a clamoring stop by the classroom door.

Mr. Weinreight slammed his baton onto his music stand. The entire band came to a warbling halt as Tommy scurried after his escaped instrument.

"Do we have a problem with setting up our drum, Mr. Terwilliger?" Mr. Weinreight sneered with contempt. He ran his hand menacingly down his conducting baton like he wished he could hit more than just the music stand with it. Mr. Weinreight always seemed to be just one clarinet squawk away from erupting into a psychotic rage. He scared the shit out of all of us. There was even a rumor that he was a former Nazi hiding out in southern Indiana to escape being prosecuted for his horrific war crimes. That's how evil we thought he was.

The entire band class turned to where Tommy crouched by the door, cradling the runaway drum in his hands. Ripples of laughter floated down the stadium classroom, the loudest coming from the top where Steve and Jimmy were falling all over themselves with the hilarity of their prank.

"No... uh... no," Tommy said, scampering awkwardly up the stairs, his drum clutched under one arm. When he passed by me, I turned away so I didn't have to look into his foggy, over-magnified eyes.

After class, Jimmy found me. "Nice job, Red."

He laced his fingers in mine and pulled me close. Luckily, the bass drum was blocking Tina's view of us from the saxophone section.

"That was pretty funny," I said, adding the world's fakest laugh.

"Yeah, we got that fucking fag good, huh?" he said. He watched, waiting for my reaction.

"Yeah, we got him good," I said, swallowing hard. I could tell Jimmy wanted me to call him that horrible name, but I just couldn't do it. I hoped my omission wouldn't be the trigger that set Jimmy off again.

Relief swept over me as Jimmy broke into a huge smile. "You're one of us now," he said with a wink.

My stomach sunk as I watched him walk away. *Was that true? Was I one of them now?*

After Jimmy left, I saw a flash out of the corner of my eye as Tommy slipped past me and out the door. I struggled with myself, part of me thinking I should follow him out into the hall and apologize when the boys weren't looking. Explain to him that I didn't want to be Jimmy's accomplice, but I had no other choice.

But the other, weaker part of me kept me anchored where I was. I told myself there was nothing wrong with the choice I'd made. That any rational person in my situation would've done the same thing. After all, I just probably saved myself from a year's worth of teasing and ridicule. Maybe a stronger person would have been able to stand up to Jimmy. But I wasn't a stronger person, was I? I was just me. Trying to survive with a handicap just as bad as a high voice and Coke-bottle glasses and a trailer for a house.

Besides, it wasn't like I'd shot up the band room with an AK-47 or helped Jimmy rob a bank or anything. I knew better than to do anything terrible like that. I'd just helped with a silly little prank. A drum fell. Some people laughed. No one had really been hurt.

CHAPTER NINE

ASKING

"So, what was it you wanted to ask me about?" Mrs. Anderson said, looking up from her desk.

"It wasn't just me who wanted to ask you. It was Stacie too," I clarified, my heart slipping into the same staccato beat that came every time I thought about what I was about to do next.

Will's words rang in my head: *You're going to go to Mrs. Anderson and ask her to let you write the column, then report back to me next weekend.*

Normally, I would have never been so bold as to ask for something I wanted outright, but I really didn't want to disappoint Will. So here I was standing in front of Mrs. A, shaking in my shoes with nerves, silently begging Stacie to get here quickly and provide me some much needed back up.

"Could we just wait for a second until she gets back? She had to run and get something out of her locker."

"Of course." Mrs. Anderson smiled. "I've got all the time in the world, honey. No need to worry."

I knew I was making way more out of this than was necessary. Mrs. A was my favorite teacher in the entire school, there was no reason for me to be so nervous. Ever since I first walked into her classroom for Creative Writing last year, she'd done nothing but make me feel at ease. And yet I still felt like I was standing on the ledge of a twenty-story building looking down and swooning from the height. I wanted to change my mind. I wanted to dive back to safety like I always had before, but I couldn't because this time I wasn't on the ledge alone. This time, the ghostly image of Will was there with me, his hand planted firmly on my back, pushing me to jump.

"You can just hang out like always." She nodded to the desks behind me where almost every afternoon Stacie and I and a few other kids debated back and forth about all the world's problems and how we'd solve them if only anyone would listen to us.

Mrs. A was the only teacher in the school who did listen. She'd sit quietly at her desk grading essays, pretending not to be eavesdropping on us, until she finally couldn't hold back. Then she'd chime in with some other perspective we'd never considered before that would take the conversation in a totally different direction. It was like what I imagined college would be like someday. Lively debates and arguments where all ideas were welcomed, not just the ones that aligned with church teachings, which most people in Cold Springs took as literal gospel.

Mrs. A went back to grading her papers, stopping

every once in a while to push up her glasses. They were so huge and round they took up most of her face, which I secretly thought made her look like the owl from the Tootsie Pop commercial.

"Your 'Place I Call Home' essay was really fantastic," she said, not looking up.

"Really?" I tried not to let myself get too excited. Mrs. A was so nice she probably said that to all her students.

Normally, only juniors and seniors could take Advanced Creative Writing. But when Stacie and I told her we really wanted to take it, Mrs. A had gone to bat for us; charging up to the principal's office muttering about how 'this school needs to reexamine whether they're actually helping or hurting kids with all these asinine rules of theirs!'

Whatever she'd said to Principal Wallace had worked because the very next day Stacie and I were taking our seats in the back of Mrs. A's tiny basement classroom for the 45-minute class that would end up being the favorite part of our day.

"I was hoping it was okay I wrote about Pizza King, you know, instead of my actual home," I said.

"I thought it was brilliant," she said, her red pen jerking along the edge of the page she was grading. "So brilliant. In fact, I was thinking of having you read a bit in class tomorrow. I want to talk about how we can view our personal experiences in a different light. How we should think past traditional labels. How homes can be more than just the standard four walls."

"Oh, I don't think I could read it in front of the

class," I said, a lump rising in my throat at the thought of standing in front of all those older kids. They already called me a brown-noser for being in there in the first place. I didn't need to give them any more reasons to hate me.

"You could stay at your desk. You wouldn't have to get up in front of everyone," she said. I could tell she was purposely trying to keep her voice light. Like I was a baby fawn reaching for the grain in her outstretched hand and she was trying to move really slowly so she wouldn't spook me.

"It's a great example of what I asked everyone to do with using metaphors," she said, still not looking up. "The way you wove in the baseball references. How you called Pizza King... uh, how did you put it again?"

"The home plate in our game of teenage life," I quoted, trying to squelch my rising pride again.

"I think the class could learn a great deal from your example."

"Well, you could read it to them, couldn't you? I don't mind," I offered.

She looked up at me. "Yes. I guess I could do that. If that's what you want."

"Yeah. That's what I want," I said, relieved. "Just don't say who wrote it, okay?"

She shook her head at me. "You really should take credit for it."

"I just don't want people thinking about the word home and me in the same sentence. You get that, right?"

She sighed heavily, deflating a bit in her chair. "Yes, I know exactly why you don't want to talk about where you really live. Why you don't want to bring up your family."

Mrs. A was one of the few people that understood what I was going through. When we still lived in town, my mom and Mrs. A were good friends. They'd met in the Women's Club and bonded over their days as hippie protestors, their love of Carole King, and hatred of Ronald Reagan (a stance they had to whisper about since it wasn't acceptable to admit inside the Cold Spring town limits).

As a Girl Scout troop leader, my mom had enlisted Mrs. A to help us earn our poetry badge and in turn my mom painted the elaborate backdrops for the theater productions Mrs. A directed. When the scandal about Karen broke and an enraged group of citizens called for my mom to give up her Girl Scout troop and not be around children because of her 'lax moral standards', Mrs. A stood by her when her other friends distanced themselves from her, first figuratively and then literally, when they crossed the street whenever they saw her coming.

At first my mom wanted to fight back and do everything she could to keep her Girl Scout troop, but I begged her to please just resign quietly so she wouldn't embarrass me any more than she already had. She did what I'd asked, even though I knew I had hurt her. After that, I'd stopped asking her to come to my games, my band concerts, my teacher conferences. I thought if she wasn't around everyone would just forget about the whole scandal and I could go back to being normal like before.

Despite my shunning, she tried to stay involved, but

then she got busy with her job and Karen and it became a new norm that I was on my own when I was in Cold Springs. I became a pseudo-orphan, just like I wanted. The only problem was, I hadn't realized the price of going it alone was the loneliness that came along with it.

I picked at a dirty piece of Scotch tape stuck to the corner of the desk and prayed for Stacie to hurry. I was nervous enough about what I was about to do. I didn't need to relive all the details of when everything in my life had fallen apart all over again.

"I just worry about how closed off you've become," Mrs. A pressed on. "I remember when I first met you. What were you? Like in fifth grade?"

"Yeah, I guess."

"When Gary and I came over for dinner you weren't shy at all. You'd sing for us, show us your artwork, tell jokes. You loved taking center stage." She smiled fondly.

I rolled my eyes. "God, I was obnoxious back then."

"No you weren't! You were delightful!"

"That's not what my dad used to say. He always told me I was trying too hard to get attention and I needed to tone myself down or else people wouldn't like me. He said my 'act wouldn't fly' when I got older and wasn't so little and cute anymore."

She shook her head. "Well, I'm not sure that's the best thing to say to a child."

"He was right though. I'm glad he told me the truth. My mom never does. She just thinks everything I do is perfect which, lord knows, isn't true."

Even though I'd never been that close to my dad and hadn't fallen into the depths of grief like I probably should've when he died, I still sometimes wished he was around. At least then I might have a chance to get a second opinion from someone who really knew me. Have a way to get some honest feedback to help me figure out the hard truth of who I really was, apart from my mom's so obviously biased viewpoint.

Mrs. A gave a heavy sigh and stared out the tiny basement window that looked out on the walkway in front of school. All you could see from down here was a line of tennis shoes militantly marching by as kids shuffled toward the buses to go home.

She furrowed her brows. "Are you doing okay?" she asked, lowering her voice. "Are things getting any easier for you?"

Mrs. A knew all the horrible ways I'd been treated when the news of my mom's affair had broken. How kids would suddenly stop talking when I sat down at the lunch table, shove crude notes in my locker, scribble *carpet-muncher* and *lezbo* on my notebook when I went to the bathroom. How they whispered just loudly enough for me to hear about how my mom was going to hell for the sin she was committing by being gay.

"Well, people still make fun of me," I admitted softly, thinking back on all the cracks Jimmy had made in band class about me liking girls. "I just wish it would all stop. I just want it to go back to the way it used to be." I looked over my shoulder at the empty hallway. It felt strange to be talking about this inside the school walls; to let down my guard in the place where I was the most vulnerable to attack.

"Of course you do, honey. That's understandable."

It surprised me how good confiding in her felt. "I mean, just last week we had a substitute teacher... you know Mr. Willis with the pocket square and the matching argyle socks?"

"Yes, he was quite the Dapper Dan, wasn't he?"

I made a face. It sounded exactly like something my mom would say. In fact, it almost made it seem like I was talking to my mom, except for the fact that I would never reveal to my mom the things I was about to tell Mrs. A. It would hurt her too bad to know what I had to endure because of her.

"Yeah, I thought he looked pretty nice. And he was nice too, trying so hard to make things fun for us, to get us involved. But the second he stepped out of the room, Dan Bledsoe shouted, 'that guy is as queer as a two-dollar bill!' and everyone laughed so hard. And then they all turned and looked at me, just waiting to see my reaction. I know they all wanted me to get all upset about it. They wanted to see me blush and squirm and get embarrassed because they'd called him gay."

"Yeah, I can imagine. Kids can be so cruel."

"Believe me, I know that only too well." My voice cracked a little, "But I sure as hell wasn't going to let them win. I wasn't going to cave like they wanted me to or run off to the bathroom crying. So I just laughed right along with them like I'd never heard anything so funny in my life." I shook my head, looked down at where I was now scraping at nothing because the piece of tape was already ripped to shreds. "God, I'm such a traitor."

Mrs. A cocked her head to one side. "And you feel

bad about that? I mean, anyone could understand why you'd go along with them."

Her words made me think of how I'd gone along with helping Jimmy in band class. For a split second I considered telling her about what he'd asked me to do. But I stopped myself, knowing that what I'd done was way worse than just laughing at some substitute teacher.

"But I shouldn't have just gone along," I said. "Why couldn't I have been strong like Stacie always is? Why didn't I stand up to them? Tell them how stupid and prejudiced they are and if anyone's going to rot in hell it's going to be them."

Mrs. A didn't even wince at my language. "At your age it's awfully hard to stand up to your peers, honey. I know it is. Especially in a small town like this."

"I never want to give them the satisfaction of seeing me upset. That's what they want and they're never going to get that from me!"

It was only when Mrs. A sat back in her chair, eyes wide, that I realized how loud my voice had gotten. It shocked me how I'd let myself admit as much as I had. I had a sudden, overwhelming urge to jump up and run out the door and never come back.

"I just want you to know I'm here for you," Mrs. A said quickly, as if she sensed my urge to bolt, "You can talk to me anytime. You know that, right?"

"I know."

"I keep meaning to call your mom sometime. See if we could get together one of these days. I miss her."

"I'm sure she'd like that."

Mrs. A and her husband had come to a couple of

Karen's gigs and even had dinner at our house a few times too, but it had been a while ago. I could tell by the look on her face that I wasn't the only one feeling a bit like a traitor right then.

"Okay. I'm finally here!" Stacie said, breezing through the door, mercifully bursting the bubble of regret Mrs. A and I seemed to be sharing.

Stacie waved a sheet of notebook paper in the air. Last night we'd made a comprehensive list of all the reasons Mrs. A should pick us to write the column even though we were only sophomores, and it broke the rules our school had always followed before.

But it turned out we hadn't needed to write down any reason other than that we really wanted to write the column because as soon as I asked (which I'd insisted on saying the words myself so I could tell Will I'd done exactly what he'd told me to), Mrs. A leapt to her feet and exclaimed, "Oh my god! That's a great idea! Would you guys really do it?"

We both breathlessly nodded and Mrs. A started pacing around the room, muttering to herself, "Oh my goodness you two will be wonderful. I mean, I'll have to ask the principal but since no one else will do it, I'm sure he'll agree. He better agree or he'll get another earful from me, that's for sure. Oh, this is going to be wonderful!"

She clasped her hands together and came over to where Stacie and I stood side by side. "Oh my goodness, I would've never thought of this," she said, squeezing us together in a tight hug. "I'm so glad you asked!"

CHAPTER TEN

PINKY SWEAR

THE NEXT AFTERNOON, Stacie and I were hanging out in her bedroom trying to brainstorm ideas for the newspaper column. Ever since we moved off the farm, I spent more time at Stacie's house than my own. Stacie's stepdad had built the log cabin himself when they moved to town and I always felt like I was on the set of *Little House on the Prairie* whenever I was there. Everything smelled like wood smoke and freshly cut pine trees. The beds all had hand-stitched quilts and instead of a regular piece of wood, the banister to upstairs was made of a smooth branch which always made me feel like I was climbing up into a treehouse instead of just the second story of a house. It was a far cry from the tiny fixer-upper ranch that my mom bought when she left my dad because Karen had liked the 'vibe' of it, whatever the hell that meant.

"We've got to change things up," I told Stacie. "We

can't just do the boring old news stuff everyone else has done for years, reporting on the Business Club's field trip and who made the honor roll. Who the hell wants to read about that?"

Stacie rolled her eyes. "Well, considering what they have for news around this town, we could probably report on the janitor changing the trash bags and people would hang on our every word."

"Yeah, the bar is pretty low. But still, it's cool we get our own byline in a real newspaper though, don't you think? I bet we can put that on our college applications."

Cold Springs High was so small it didn't have the funds to print its own newspaper, so the school news column always ran in the Tuesday edition of the town paper, *The Cold Springs Gazette*. I knew Stacie didn't really consider the Gazette a real newspaper, but I was still excited to see my name in print, my headshot running alongside the *Warrior Report* headline every week, just like a real-life reporter.

"See? There are some perks to living in a small town!" I said cheerfully.

"Okay, I'll give you that one." Stacie tried her best to look disgruntled, but I could tell she was excited about her newly found fame too. "But it's the only good thing about living here."

"I know," I agreed with Stacie like always. Over the years, she and I had turned bashing Cold Springs into a varsity sport. Nothing got by us without some kind of snide remark: The FFA jackets made the boys look like spokespeople for corduroy fabric; the shorthand class handed out chastity belts along with their spiral notepads; the history class was so behind the times they still referred to Istanbul as Constantinople.

Even though I complained as much as Stacie, I secretly didn't think all of Cold Springs was that bad, although I never would've admitted that to her. When we'd moved to our new ramshackle house, we weren't in Cold Springs school district anymore, so my mom had tried to get me to go to school in Bloomington instead. She said it would be a fresh start for me. A chance to meet new people and have new opportunities. You would've thought I'd have jumped at the offer, since all I did was complain about Cold Springs, but the thought of changing schools terrified me. How could I leave my friends? Especially Stacie, who stuck up for me and didn't whisper behind my back like everyone else did. Plus, I'd worked so hard to make the cheerleading squad. I didn't want to give that up and risk never being a cheerleader again. Things were hard enough already. I couldn't believe my mom could actually be so thoughtless as to suggest making it even harder.

"I know what we could do!" Stacie lifted a finger in the air. "We could write a scathing expose on Jimmy and his henchmen and how they bully everyone in this school."

My body went rigid. I hadn't told Stacie about how I'd unwittingly become Jimmy's accomplice in band class the other day. I knew she'd be disappointed in me for going along with what he'd asked me to do. But Stacie didn't understand how things worked in there. Saying no to Jimmy wasn't as simple as she made it out to be.

"Oh, I don't know if that's a good idea." I tried to make

my voice light so she wouldn't suspect why I was trying to draw her off the expose idea. If Stacie went through with an article like that, wouldn't I now be exposed as a bully, too? Jimmy's words rang in my ears. *You're one of us now.* Please God. I hoped that wasn't true.

"But think of it," Stacie's eyes lit in excitement, "we've got you as an informant on the inside. You could collect the evidence until we have enough on them to make our case."

"What is this? *All the President's Men?*" I gave a weak laugh. "We just started writing the column, Stacie. We're no Woodward and Bernstein."

"Not yet, we're not."

I rolled my eyes. Sometimes Stacie's confidence was inspiring, but other times like this, it was awfully annoying. "We can't get Jimmy and the guys in trouble," I said, "They're on the basketball team."

"So?"

"So, you know everyone's saying this is the team that's finally going to get us back to States again. The town would come after us with torches and pitchforks if we did anything to jeopardize that." I held my breath, hoping she would see my obvious logic.

She let out a defeated sigh. "Yeah. I guess you're right." It wasn't like her to back down, but even Stacie knew that basketball was a force not to be reckoned with in Cold Springs.

I went back to shuffling our notes around, relieved that it seemed like she was going to drop it. "Besides, they're not that bad," I mumbled without thinking, "they're just playing around."

Out of the corner of my eye, I saw her sit up taller. *Uh oh. Why couldn't I have kept my big mouth shut?*

"They're not that bad?" she said incredulously. "What's with you all of the sudden? You're always complaining about them. Didn't I just have to rescue you from being forcibly groped by Jimmy the other night? Don't tell me you actually liked that?"

"Of course not." My heart raced faster thinking of Stacie's question. It wasn't the first time I'd agonized over how mixed-up Jimmy made me feel. Didn't I sometimes, deep down inside, actually like it when he paid attention to me? Even if his compliments were lurid and suggestive, they were still technically compliments; and dammit if they didn't sometimes still feel really good.

Stacie reached over and grabbed both of my arms and gave me a little shake. "Oh, my God! Don't tell me you're starting to relate to your captors? You know what they call this, don't you? It's a classic case of Stockholm Syndrome."

There was a little smile on her face, so I knew she was just teasing me, but I was still annoyed. "Stop it. It is not." I wriggled away from her grip.

We both laughed. "Remember Patty Hearst with the Symbionese Liberation Army?" Stacie bent her head to look right in my eyes. "If Jimmy tries to talk you into robbing a bank, promise you'll come to me first."

I rolled my eyes and pushed her away, not liking that she'd used the same bank robbing metaphor that had popped into my head the other day.

She giggled at her joke, then went back to scribbling ideas in her notebook. I was relieved we didn't have to talk about Jimmy anymore. Still, how could she have compared me to Patty Hearst? I remembered when the story had been all over the news: the rich girl kidnapped only to reemerge months later helping her captors rob a bank. My mom had to explain the term brainwashing to me. At the time, I'd wondered how such a thing could even happen. How could Patty have not seen what they were trying to do to her? Her captors' motives were so clear, anyone could see they were using her to get what they wanted. But now that I thought about it, maybe the stress of captivity had blurred Patty's judgement over time. Maybe she really believed she had to go along with the Army just to save herself. I certainly could understand that feeling. Giving up your morals just to save your own ass. Still, there was no way that was what was happening between me and Jimmy in band class. I knew what brainwashing was. I was way too smart to ever let that happen to me.

❧

A while later Stacie left me on the bed and went to sit at her vanity in the corner of the room. She studied herself hard in the mirror.

"Do you think my cheeks are too fat?" She poked at her skin, making hard indentions in her cheeks.

"No way," I said. "Remember the quiz we took in *Seventeen*? It said you had a round-shaped face, just like Valerie Bertinelli and she's *sooooo* pretty."

It had thrilled me when the quiz said I had an oval-shaped face just like Brooke Shields, even though that was the only body part of Brooke's I resembled in any way.

"Yeah, I guess you're right," she said, although she still seemed unconvinced. She picked up a container of blush and a tube of mascara, then set them back down dejectedly. All of Stacie's makeup vials were mostly unused because she and I didn't really know how to put it on right. We'd try it out sometimes on a Friday night, then chicken out and wash it off right before we left the house because we always felt so ridiculous; like our efforts to look more grown up only drew attention to the fact that we weren't.

"Why do you even ask that?" I prodded. It was strange for Stacie to ask about her looks since she always seemed so confident. Being so tall and willowy and blonde, all the boys at school flocked to her. What did she have to worry about anyway?

"Oh, Mark just called me chipmunk cheeks the other night."

I looked down at my notebook so she couldn't see me make a face. *Stupid Mark. Why did she even listen to him?* He was a notorious ladies' man at school, always dating two girls at once, causing drama all over the place. As the leading scorer on the basketball team last year, he was now poised to be the star of the team when the season started in a few months. He was cute enough and pretty tall (one of Stacie's biggest turn-ons). Still, it surprised me that she would even give someone as shallow as him the time of day.

"Mark wouldn't know the Taj Mahal if it fell out of the sky and landed on his head," I grumbled.

Stacie laughed and didn't disagree. It was a running joke we had. On the day we first met, back in sixth grade, our geography teacher, Mr. Belkins, had held up our new textbook and pointed to the white building on the front and asked the class if anyone could name it. I knew the answer but hated how everyone in class huffed really loud every time I got a question right, so I just sat there and waited for him to tell us since I knew no one else was going to get it. Then I'd heard a disgusted grunt from behind me. When I turned around, there was a girl I'd never seen before slouched too desks back, her long legs taking up half the aisle.

She'd raised her hand like it weighed a thousand pounds, then rolled her eyes when Mr. Belkins called on her. "It's the Taj Mahal," she'd said flatly, then scanned the room with an expression that clearly said, "What the hell am I doing here?" Which was the same feeling I'd had ever since I'd moved to Cold Springs. I caught her eye and made a face, like I was as disgusted as she was, and we'd become instant friends; forever bonded by the clear intellectual superiority we held over our classmates. (A quality I usually kept a lot quieter than Stacie did.)

"Mark is hot so I can overlook that he's a dummy," Stacie said. "Besides, I just want to make out with him, not marry him."

Stacie used that logic all the time. As a staunch feminist, she felt it was her right to be as free as the boys were when it came to dating around. Although I had reason to believe there was more to her detachment than just wanting to exercise her equal rights. When your dad leaves you when you're three years old and never contacts you again like Stacie's did, it kind of messes with your trust in men.

"You know who does know what the Taj Mahal is," I started lightly, "Rob."

"Oh God, I knew you were going to do this."

Mark hadn't been at the drive-in the other night like Stacie had hoped, so we'd all just hung out and drank beer and watched some guys reenacting the *Raiders of the Lost Ark* movie they'd seen up in Bloomington that afternoon; diving and rolling in the leaves, cracking fake whips, and wrestling invisible snakes.

Rob had eventually come over and hung out with Stacie and me. He'd surprised us by adding to the *Airplane* and *Monty Python* quotes we were bantering back and forth. Rob was pretty funny when he said more than two words. As the night wore on, I could tell by the sheepish way he kept glancing at Stacie that he liked her. On the ride back to Pizza King, he even switched seats and let Scott ride up front so he could sit in back with her.

"Yeah, so he's smart?" Stacie relented. "I already know that. We're in French class together, remember?"

Stacie came over to the bed and stretched out with her head on the pillow. I scooted up next to her and did the same, curling in a C shape toward her as I went on.

"Rob's like really smart. He's on track to be salutatorian. Did you know that?" I had to be careful not to come on too strong about Rob. Stacie never liked doing what other people told her to do. Although I was already stupidly fantasizing about her and Rob double dating with Will and me one day.

"Yeah, so? He's just going to community college and then come back here and run his dad's dairy farm. How can I relate to someone like that? I mean, can you imagine wanting to stay in this hellhole town forever?"

I usually went along with all of Stacie's Cold Springs bashing, but when she made fun of farmers it always hit a nerve.

"Running a dairy farm isn't an easy job," I informed her. "And that operation the Grinfields have up there, believe me, they are pulling down some big bucks. One day Rob will pretty much be running his own corporation." I wanted to add, "so quit being such a snob, Stacie!" but I didn't. Instead, I said, "Besides I thought you only cared about making out with boys, not marrying them. Why do you care about what he does when he graduates?"

She must have sensed she'd upset me because she backed down. "Fine. You're probably right," she conceded. "But the problem with Rob is he's just too nice."

I laughed. "Too nice?!"

"Yeah. I can tell already he likes me too much. He's always being all sweet, asking if I need help with my homework, volunteering to carry my books." When I rolled my eyes, she went on. "You know what I'm talking about. You're the same way! Plenty of guys chase you around and you won't give them the time of day either."

"Only because I question the sanity of any guy that would like me!"

"Stop it!" she shoved me hard on the shoulder. "You know what I'm talking about. Nobody wants it to be too easy. Nice just isn't a turn on sometimes."

"I guess," I admitted, rolling onto my back. We laid side by side on the bed staring up at the ceiling, not saying anything for a while.

What she'd said about Rob being too nice made me think of this past summer when we'd visited her grandma's house near Terre Haute. It was July and so blazing hot and humid all we could do was lie on the couch under her grandma's air conditioner, eat popsicles, and watch Wimbledon all day long.

We'd become totally obsessed with John McEnroe. Whenever he came on the screen we'd scream, "There he is, there he is!" tumbling over each other to get to the TV to turn up the volume and adjust the aluminum foil on the antenna so we could get a clearer view of him. Of the wild curls spilling over his red headband; the signature bad boy pout perpetually plastered across his face in all its Technicolor glory.

It was his tantrums that thrilled us the most. We loved how he argued with the umpires, arms flailing crazily. Yelling "Open your eyes!" or "Chalk flew up!" when they made what he considered a bad call. Or how, when he made a mistake, he'd throw his racket and storm around like a toddler who hadn't had his nap; pace the court like an escaped predator, his wiry body coiled so tightly you were pretty sure that any moment he might leap into the crowd and choke out anyone who dared to boo him. No one knew what the hell McEnroe was going to do next. That's what made him so exciting.

"Shit, he's so sexy when he gets like that," Stacie had muttered around slurps of her grape Flavor Pop during one of his outbursts.

"I know. So damn sexy," I agreed, even though it didn't feel right to be turned on by something so clearly wrong. That wrongness reminded me of how I now felt about Will. That forbidden lust that was so tantalizing. I was starting to realize that when it came to sexual attraction, desire and logic didn't always go hand in hand.

The clock on her bedside stand ticked loudly in the silence.

"But Rob's really tall," I said, more just to make her mad than anything.

"Ugh! Stop!"

"Alright, alright. I'm just saying he's much taller than Mark."

"Do you really want me to lecture you on who you should or should not like?" she raised an eyebrow like she knew I didn't want to go there.

"No. I would rather pretend that I'm a rational human being and have not completely gone off the deep end over a college boy who I can never have."

"That's what I thought," Stacie said. "Let's stop talking about boys. It's so pedestrian. We don't want to become the kind of girls whose only interest is what boy they're currently screwing."

"Screwing?! How did we get there? You know I haven't even kissed a guy yet!"

"You know what I mean. Figuratively speaking." She wagged her eyebrows. "Although with the way I'm going with Mark, things might not be so *figurative* in the near future."

My heart whirled at what she was insinuating. Was Stacie actually considering having sex? That seemed impossible. Had she forgotten we were only fifteen years old? The only thing we knew about sex was from the porn tape my mom had brought home from her Human

Sexuality class a few years ago. Stacie and I had snuck it out of my mom's office and watched it when we were alone one afternoon. And I use the term *watch* loosely because we'd ended up mostly covering our eyes every other second and screaming, "Do you think she likes that?!", "Why is his thing that weird color?!" and then a prolonged, "*GROOOOSSSSS!*" when the guy did what he did on the poor girl's face at the end.

When we'd clicked it off afterward, we'd both agreed that it would be a while before we ever wanted to be involved in something as disgusting as that. But Stacie had obviously changed her opinion about sex. And with the way I kept thinking of Will lately, I was pretty sure my opinion about sex was changing too. Although it was awfully scary to admit that. Even if it was only to myself.

"Yeah. Let's not talk about boys anymore," I said, not liking the way my stomach was rolling, thinking of all the changes ahead of us.

"Right, no boys. Hey, I've got an idea. Let's make a pinky swear right now," Stacie said, rolling over to me and hooking her little finger in mine. "Let's not be like all those other girls at school that are always fighting about guys. Let's never, ever, ever, let boys come between us."

I broke into a huge smile and squeezed her pinky tightly in mine.

"Of course we won't. We'll never, ever, ever, let boys come between us," I chanted emphatically. It was such a no-brainer I barely even thought about the words as I said them. That's how easy keeping our pact seemed to me at the time. Little did I know how hard it was about to get.

CHAPTER ELEVEN

SPORTS ILLUSTRATED

I TRIED TO talk myself out of it. I knew it was only going to make things worse. I knew it was only going to feed the obsession, make it more out of control than it already was, but I still couldn't stop myself.

I leaned over the desk of the school library. "Mrs. Walker, do you have…"

"Sweetie, can you just give me a minute?" Mrs. Walker interrupted me, turning to where Angie Davis was waiting on the other side of the desk holding a tower of books that almost reached her chin. It was going to take forever for Mrs. Walker to go through them all. Flip each book open, squish her silver date stamp into the ink, and then smash it on the little lined paper glued to the back page.

I knew it was a sign from the Universe that I should leave and not do what I was about to do. I could still stop the momentum of my hopeless crush on Will, but the anticipation that trilled so deliciously in my chest anchored me in place. *What can it hurt?* A soft voice crooned inside my head. *You want to see it. And it's right there. There's absolutely nothing wrong with that.*

A few minutes later, Mrs. Walker finally whirled around to me. She was wearing black cat's-eye glasses connected to her neck by a fat silver chain and a really old-fashioned brown plaid suit. "Okay dear, what can I do for you?"

I leaned in closely. "Um, I was wondering if you had a copy of the *Sports Illustrated* from March of '79? You know, the one with the team?" I whispered, my face warming like I was asking her to hand over a *Playboy* magazine. "It's for a report I'm doing... for English."

Mrs. Walker's eyes went wide, as if she'd just seen something terribly shocking like a periodical filed between two dictionaries; a book returned with a page dog-eared.

"Well, yes, we have it," she said primly. Did librarians actually get together in groups to practice that tone? "But why would you need it? Don't you have your own copy?"

I wanted to burst out laughing. It was the same reaction I'd gotten from a few of my classmates when I'd asked around about the magazine earlier. "Actually no, I don't have my own copy." I glanced around like I didn't want anyone to hear. "You see, I was abducted by aliens in late February of '79 and they didn't return me home until after the issue went out of print."

She shook her head in disdain. Joking about something as serious as the 1979 Cold Springs basketball team was obviously not at all funny to her.

"Well, we have it in our archives," she sighed.

Archives? Our library didn't even have a copy of The Thurber Carnival book I was looking for last week, but now we have archives?

"But you can't take it out of the room," she snapped.

"That's fine. I can just take some notes here."

"Alright, I guess I could go get it for you," she said warily, looking me up and down like she was determining if I was worthy of what I was about to receive. I made my best attempt at looking upright and responsible, like what I imagined a knight might look like right before King Arthur placed Excalibur into his outstretched hands. It must've worked because she dug a set of keys out of her drawer and headed off down a shadowed hallway.

All I heard was the clicking of multiple locks and deadbolts. By the time she came back, I was half expecting her to be dragging a wooden treasure chest wrapped in chains behind her. Instead, there was only a grey cardboard box in her hands.

"This is an acid-free box," she said, setting it gingerly in front of me as if a copy of the original Constitution was nestled inside. "You see, magazines are printed on very cheap paper. They disintegrate very quickly."

I nodded eagerly, trying to look enthralled. *Just give me the damn magazine, lady.*

"That's why we keep it out of sunlight and don't handle it very often." She shot me a sinister look, clearly wishing I'd rethink my selfish request to touch it.

"Am I going to have to wear little white gloves or something?" I said, laughing.

She opened a few drawers. "I used to have some here somewhere."

When she didn't find the gloves, she looked pointedly at my hands.

"Just washed them," I said cheerfully, holding them up to her for inspection. "No Cheetos for lunch or anything."

Again, she wasn't amused. She carefully lifted the lid off the box. To my surprise, a beam of light did not instantly shoot out of its confines and up into the heavens. Instead, there was only a magazine inside. On the front was a picture of Larry Bird in his Indiana State uniform charging to the basket with the title "Bird Takes Flight" in bold red letters next to him. Pretty ironic that another Indiana team would dominate the cover of the issue that featured our school. If anyone from the outside world ever wondered about how we Hoosiers felt about basketball, they only had to look at that one magazine for proof of the power it wielded in our state.

I held my palms out flat and let Mrs. Walker place the magazine on them, then considered bowing to her as I turned to walk away.

"Now be careful with it," she warned.

"Oh, I'll be careful," I called back, walking with exaggerated deliberateness. But after a few steps, not being able to help myself, I pretended to trip just to give her a minor heart attack.

"Oh, dear!" she gasped behind me as the magazine danced above my hands.

"Whoops, just a little bump in the carpet here," I said, regaining my footing while she fanned herself furiously. I tried to duck behind a set of shelves for some privacy, but Mrs. Walker caught me before I could turn the corner.

"Why don't you stay where I can see you, young lady," she said sternly. I guess my little comedy show backfired on me. *No good joke goes unpunished in this place.*

I grudgingly settled into a table in full sight of Mrs. Walker and the few other kids scattered at tables around the library and flipped to the beginning of the article.

The left side of the page was filled with the silhouette of a boy shooting a basketball into a hoop tacked to the side of a barn with the sun setting orange and red on the cornfields behind him. The words "Back Home Again In Indiana" were emblazoned on the bottom half of the page and below that in smaller print, "A Story of Hoosier Hysteria and the Little Team that Could".

My heart sped up just thinking about what I was about to read. I knew immediately the boy in the sunset wasn't Will. He was too tall. The boy in the picture would've probably played center for the team, whereas with Will's body type, he would've played either forward or guard.

Most people thought cheerleaders didn't know anything about basketball, but that wasn't true. You couldn't spend as many hours in the gym as we did and not know at least some of the intricacies of the game. In fact, our cheerleading coach made it a requirement for us to learn all the rules so we knew exactly which cheers to lead, at which time. She even asked Coach Calder to drop into our practices sometimes and try to stump us with basketball regulation questions. Every few weeks he'd wander into the hallway during our practice and start throwing questions as quick as he chucked balls at his players' heads when they missed a free throw shot.

"What do you do when defense coverage is too tight and you can't get the ball in-bounded?" he shouted one afternoon.

"You hit the ball off the defender's body, so it goes out on him. Then the clock gets re-set," I answered back as fast as I could.

"Good! Good!" he'd walked closer, aiming his next question only at me. "And how many seconds do you get back to try again?"

"Five."

"And when does the clock start running?" he asked, his face only inches from mine.

"When someone on the court touches the ball."

"Nice job," he said, high fiving me. "I've said it before and I'll say it again. We've got the best damn cheerleaders in the Tri-County region!"

That's when it hit me, how much Will was just like his father with the quizzing and the pointing and the high-fiving and the sudden unexpected praise. I'd been proud of answering Coach Calder's questions right that day. The same way I'd been proud when Will liked my answers in the car and behind the drive-in. Now all I had to figure out was how I could keep getting my answers right for both of them.

When I started reading the article, it was shocking to me that it didn't begin with any facts and figures about the impending game. Instead, the first paragraph described in vivid detail a scene of a school bus carrying our basketball team as it pulled into a parking lot at night with a police escort flanking its sides. The author wrote about the shine of the lights on the wet pavement, the cut of the state trooper's hair, the smell of decaying cornstalks mixed with the diesel fuel of the bus. He continued, unfolding the story of our town with such beautiful details that I could hardly believe it was the place where I lived.

He wrote of farmers in overalls leaning over wooden counters, sipping coffee, and discussing the previous night's game; of grandmas sewing quilt squares while quoting free throw stats; of caravans of cars snaking over county roads every weekend night with boys' names and jersey numbers painted in shoe polish on their windows; of church halls packed with townspeople laying out banquets of lavish food for the team the night before each game.

Even though there were pictures to go along with the writer's descriptions, I didn't need to look at them. His words were enough to bring the images to life. His words and the fact that I'd seen each of the scenes a million times in real life. (Although I was starting to wonder if I really had ever seen them before.) The way he'd written the article made it feel like a piece from *National Geographic*, as if our town was a remote village in the Andes that the author had stumbled across. Now he was trying to describe it to the rest of the world to convince them a place like where we lived actually existed. I couldn't believe it, but for the first time ever, I almost felt proud to live in Cold Springs.

I found Will's name only a few paragraphs later.

Although at first glance the Warriors don't appear to be much of a physical threat to their opposition, their secret weapon is senior captain Will Calder, who has somehow cobbled the rag-tag group of farmers' sons into a cohesive scoring machine. This year he has led the group to an undefeated season with the one-two combination of an unrelenting work ethic and the sheer force of his will.

Junior starter Caleb Carter echoed that sentiment when asked about his team leader. "Yeah, we all say we've been willed into the finals," he laughed. "Get it? Willed, because that's his name. Will's pretty much the one who's responsible for getting us to where we are today."

Although there is no denying the role of his leadership in the Warriors' success, there is an elephant in the room (or more aptly, on the court) when it comes to star Will Calder. The senior captain and four-year starter just happens to be the coach's son. On some teams that might be considered a problem, with favoritism and unfair playing time being common complaints from the scrutinizing crowds that pack these Indiana gyms every weekend. However, that doesn't seem to be the case in Cold Springs.

"Oh no, Will definitely doesn't get special treatment," senior center Joe Buckley said. "In fact,

it's probably just the opposite. He works harder and practices longer than any of us. Coach is probably hardest on him. I wouldn't want to be his son!"

Although he laughed while saying it, Joe seemed concerned his comment would get back to the coach with the most wins in all of southern Indiana. The man whose thick grey hair and frequent court side temper tantrums remind many of another famous coach in residency at nearby Indiana University: the infamous Bobby Knight.

"Make sure you write I was joking when you print that," Joe told me nervously when the interview was over. "I don't want to run even more laps than I already do."

Joe doesn't have any reason to worry. Coach Calder's tough-love relationship with his middle son is no secret in this town. Down six points in the third quarter of the regional semi-finals to a physically stronger Bakerville team, Coach Calder had no problem benching his son after he was called for a flagrant foul, a decision with which the hometown crowd was clearly dissatisfied.

"He needed some time to think that over," Coach Calder explained. "Will's greatest downfall is his temper. Don't get me wrong. He's one hell of a ballplayer, but he can get too emotional on the floor. Most of the time, it lifts the team up. But sometimes it can bring them down too."

Whatever detriment Coach believed happened during that regional game was forgiven when Will (finally released from the bench in the fourth quarter) scored 16 straight points in three minutes to lift the team past Bakerville High and into the regional finals. The younger Calder's inspired performance that night was of no surprise to anyone in this town. Most of the residents revere the charismatic senior with the movie-star good looks as a savior who walks amongst them. When he enters a room, he's instantly surrounded by hometown fans. They pepper him with questions about how he broke the full-court press against Central or suggest new defense tactics or simply ask him what pie he wants for this week's pregame meal.

"Will is what holds everything together on our team," gas station owner Willie Reed proclaimed while pointing to the tousled-haired youth talking to reporters after a pep rally. "Players like him with a heart like his, they don't come around all that often. I don't know what we're going to do when he graduates."

All the attention seems overwhelming, even from a bystander's perspective. Yet, this poised young man seems to take it in stride. When asked about his philosophy on the game, Will sounded more like a seasoned army colonel than a 17-year-old basketball player.

When I turned the page to read more, I nearly fell out of my chair. The entire right page of the magazine was taken up with a picture of Will. He was standing on railroad tracks in his red senior letter jacket, staring directly into the camera. One hand was held out to his side, palm up, with a basketball suspended in mid-air above it like he was a magician caught in the middle of a levitation act.

I couldn't breathe. Or blink. Or think. I could only stare at him. He was so damn beautiful. His cheekbones picked up the angled light and the shiny black waves of his hair sliced sharply against the cloudless sky. His eyes, though narrowed in a fierce expression, dominated the image their color so vividly blue they almost didn't seem real. The magazine clearly knew what they were doing by giving him a full page spread. I imagined that picture of him was probably still pinned up on the wall of girls' bedrooms all over the state.

My heart began racing. It was almost like he was standing right in front of me. Without thinking I traced his face with my finger wishing I could feel his skin not just the glossy sheen of the paper. I had to force myself to look away and keep reading.

"I see every game as a war," Will said, with no hint of the teenaged jocularity of his teammates. "Every ball possession is one battle in that war. With focus and determination, I can lead my troops to win each of those battles until we end up winning the entire war. That's what we're going to do in the end. We're going to win the war."

I gazed at his picture again but this time I noticed how his features looked just the slightest bit different compared to the boy I met on the dusty road a few weeks ago. In the picture his face was a little rounder than it was now, younger, and more innocent. And his narrowed eyes, meant to appear so sinister, looked like those of a boy pretending to be more battle-ready than he really was. Yet, the Will I met on the road clearly didn't have to pretend anymore. His battle was over. And he wore the scars to prove it.

I couldn't help but feel sorry for the boy in the picture. The one who thought he could beat the odds simply by wanting something bad enough. I felt sorry for him because I knew something he didn't: Only a week after he stood on those railroad tracks in front of that photographer, all his dreams were going to be shattered.

❧

"I knew it!" Scott's voice boomed through the library behind me a few minutes later. I jumped like a gun just exploded in my ear accidentally crumpling the magazine in my hands. A loud gasp came from the circulation desk. When I turned around Mrs. Walker was halfway out of her chair looking like she might hurdle the desk to get to me in time to rescue the priceless artifact.

"It's okay. It's okay. I didn't hurt it!" I reassured her before she got a leg over the counter.

"I knew it!" Scott said again as he flopped into the chair next to me. I closed the magazine although I knew it was useless since he'd obviously already seen what I was reading.

"You've got your panties all wet for Will, don't you?"

"*I do not have my panties all wet for Will!*" I shouted. Every head in the library swiveled in my direction all at once.

I lowered my voice to a whisper. "I do not have my panties wet for Will," I repeated.

Scott laughed at me, tipping back in his chair, and clutching his stomach like he'd never heard anything so hilarious. It took everything I had not to give his chair a hard push so he would fall all the way over on his head.

"Now, now. Don't feel bad, Red," he said as the chair careened back down on the carpet. "It happens to a lot of girls. You're not the first and God knows you won't be the last."

"Stop it, Scott. I'm just reading a magazine."

"Oh, right. Looked more like drooling than reading to me."

"I'm writing a report!"

"On what? How fast your panties get wet when you look at Will?"

I grabbed Scott's wrist with both hands. Squeezed it tightly then twisted the skin in opposite directions. "Stop it! I mean it."

"Ouch, ouch! Okay. I'll stop," he whined trying to wrench his arm away.

I let go and we stared at each other for a few seconds. My face felt hot and sweaty like it was throbbing in time to my heartbeat. It was no use trying to pretend to Scott.

"I'm sorry," Scott finally said, "I was just teasing you."

"Don't make fun of me," I said through gritted teeth. "I hate when people make fun of me."

"I just can't believe that you of all people. Miss I-Don't-Give-A-Fuck-About-Anyone might actually have the hots for someone."

"Stop. I give a fuck about people."

"Yeah, right. Who? John Travolta? Richard Gere? Those are the only guys you seem to care about."

"They are not!"

"Is that who you're saving yourself for?" Scott sing-singed annoyingly. "One of your movie-star crushes?"

"I'm not saving myself for Richard Gere!" I said. "I mean, John Travolta maybe."

"I knew it!"

"Well, I have to keep myself available, you know. Just in case he lands his Cessna in one of these cornfields and asks to whisk me off to Cannes."

"Whisk you off to where?" Scott asked.

"Never mind," I said, internally adding Scott's name to the list of those who probably knew nothing about the Taj Mahal.

Scott plowed on. "You get asked out all the time by guys, Red and you always have an excuse why you can't go."

"You're just mad I won't go out with you!"

"Yes, I'm mad about that, but we've already gone through that. You have some strange idea about us being related or something. Which, for the record, I think is bullshit."

"It would be incestuous, Scott. You're like my brother," I said. "Besides, I hang out with guys all day long. You know that. I probably spend more time with guys than girls."

"True. You like to flirt, but that's about it." He leaned in closer like he was sharing some kind of secret. "You can't always live in your fantasy world, Red. There's a real world out here waiting for you. Believe it or not, it's not half bad."

"Don't worry about me. I'm fine." There was no way I was going to explain why I liked my fantasy world so much better. How it was the only place where I had complete control of everything that happened to me.

"All I'm saying is you shouldn't get fixated on Will. It's a total waste, just like you're wasting your time waiting for John Travolta." He shook his head. "I knew I should've said something after the other night."

"What? What about the other night?"

"It's just I could tell you were all googly over him."

"*I wasn't ALL GOOGLY over him!*" I shouted. The kids around the room turned to gawk again.

"I wasn't all googly over him," I said softer this time.

"You were like…" Scott pretended to be me, making enormous eyes and lolling his tongue out of his head.

"STOP it, Scott!!" I grabbed his wrist again.

"Ouch! Don't do it again!"

"I did not look like that!" *Oh God. Had I looked like that?* My face burned just thinking about it.

"Like I said before, don't feel bad," Scott consoled me. "He has that effect on girls."

I huffed trying my best to look indignant.

"Listen. There's something else you should know." Scott looked down at the magazine. I still had my finger wedged in the pages holding the spot where Will waited patiently for me to return.

"Open that back up," he said.

I did what he said, but this time I didn't look directly at Will because I knew it would only make my face turn redder and then Scott would laugh at me again.

But Scott wasn't laughing now. "Now turn the next page," he ordered seriously.

An ominous feeling settled over me as I did what he asked. From the look on Scott's face, I knew I was about to see something upsetting. At the top of the next page, there was a smaller picture nestled in the columns of words. On first glance, I could tell it was a girl and a boy. On second glance, I made out that it was a cheerleader and a basketball player. On third glance, it finally registered that the basketball player was Will and the cheerleader next to him was way more than just his friend.

In the picture, the two of them were sitting in folding chairs on the sideline of the court. Will was facing forward and the girl was turned sideways leaning close to him, both of them smiling big. The girl's brown hair feathered away from her face and she was wearing a lot of makeup; blue eye shadow and really pink blush and maybe even some lipstick. Our coach would never let us get away with wearing makeup like that to a game. Not that I'd ever want to. But I guessed that's what girls did back in the seventies. Underneath the picture was the caption: "*A lot of courting goes on next to the courts in Indiana.*"

I could feel Scott staring at me. "Yeah, so?" I snapped

even though I barely had enough air in my lungs to form the words.

"I just thought you should know. Will has a girlfriend."

It felt like a fist had just hit me square in the stomach, but I didn't want to let Scott know how upset I was.

"I don't care, Scott!" I wheezed. "It's not like I think I'm going to date him or something!"

"Well good. Because those two," he pointed at the offending image, "have been together forever."

"Well, good for them!"

"Her name's Penny."

"Yeah, so?! She's named after a coin. Good for her!" *Okay. Calm down now. You're totally losing your cool.*

Scott gave me a funny look. I took a deep breath and tried again.

"So, like, how long have they been together?" I asked.

"A long time. Like since they were your age, Red."

"Jesus Christ. Since they were sophomores? All the way until now?"

"Yup."

"So, they're the same age then?"

"Yeah. Both graduated in '79."

I stared hard at Scott wishing he'd read my mind so I didn't have to ask what I really wanted to next. I knew when Will graduated which meant I kind of knew how old he was, but I still wasn't completely sure. I could've been off by a year or so. I really needed Scott to tell me exactly how old Will was. Then I'd know once and for all just how far off limits he really was.

"Which makes him?" I prodded Scott.

Scott finally understood what I was asking. "Oh, you want to know how old Will is?"

I shrugged like it was his idea not mine.

He took a deep breath. "He just turned twenty," he informed me. He looked up in the air calculating. "That makes him five years older than you, Red." He said it so morosely it sounded like he'd just broken the news to me that Old Yeller had rabies and we were going to have to take him behind the barn and shoot him.

"Yeah, so? Who cares?" I said, my voice rising higher. "It's not like I want to *date him* or something!"

"Of course, you don't. You already said that," Scott said way too agreeably. Which only made me want to twist his wrist again.

We stared at each other as the silence pinged between us.

"But just so you know," Scott said, "Will loves to play around with girls' heads. Tease them and lead them on, but it means nothing. It's all just fun and games to him."

"Like I care?"

He watched me, a slow grin spreading across his face.

"What? What are you smiling at?"

"I just think it's sweet," he poked at my chest. "The Tin Man actually has a heart in there somewhere."

I rolled my eyes. I wanted to yell at him again, but the Shakespeare quote '*the lady doth protest too much*' rang in my head. Besides, I teased Scott brutally too and Karen always said that if you wanted to be in the business of dishing out jokes you had to learn to take them. (Although I still wasn't very good at that part.)

"Alright, I'll leave you two lovebirds alone now," Scott said, pointing at the magazine. He slapped his hands on his thighs like he was about to stand up.

A terrible thought came to me. "You won't say anything to him, will you?" I asked. I'd never be able to look Will in the eye again if Scott told him about my silly infatuation.

"Of course not," Scott said sweetly. I relaxed a bit. Scott and I liked to give each other a hard time, but we really were good friends when it came right down to it. In fact, I hated thinking about what I was going to do without him when he graduated this year.

"I only want what's best for you," he said giving me a playful push on the shoulder. "You know that, right?"

"Yeah. I know. Same here," I said, giving him a push back. That was about as mushy as I could get.

"That's why I thought you should know about Penny. I wasn't trying to be mean," he said looking more sincere than I'd seen him in a long time. "I just wanted to make it clear. Will's taken, Red. You can crush on him all you want, but you can never have him."

CHAPTER TWELVE

FIGMENT OF MY IMAGINATION

"I THINK YOU need more speed!" my friend Holly called from the end of the gymnastic mat set up on the gym floor. It was after school on Friday and our cheer captain had called an extra practice so we could make sure we were at top form when basketball season started in November. It was still a whole two months away, but since our school's domination in basketball was such a big deal, everything related to the team (even us cheerleaders) had to be perfect.

I walked down to where Holly was standing. As always, she looked adorable in her tiny white socks with pink pom-poms on the back and her long brown hair swept up in a high ponytail.

"More speed, huh? Anything else?" I asked.

"I think you need to reach up and back a little more," she said demonstrating the angle with her arms. "You're close. You've almost got it."

Holly and I had been working on our full layouts with our coach up at IU for months. It was a hard trick, requiring more twists and rotations than we'd ever done before. Holly had perfected hers at our lesson last week. Now I was desperate to land mine too.

In a normal world, I should've hated Holly with her sheet of silky hair, perfect white smile, and perpetually tanned skin that made her look like she just stepped out of a Coppertone suntan lotion ad. It certainly would've made things a lot easier if I could have. But in a nasty twist of fate, it turned out Holly was even nicer than she was beautiful and even smarter than she was nice. Her mere existence didn't seem fair to me. I thought everyone had one Achille's heel that made them human and not gods. They were pretty, but mean. Smart, but ugly. Athletic, but dumb. But not Holly. She had the perfect combination of everything. It was like someone had dropped her all the way into the river of Styx, then fished her out with a net so that every inch of her body came out soaking wet without a mortal heel to her name.

I lined up to try again. "You can do it!" Holly called, clapping wildly. The rest of the squad waited behind her, watching, probably half hoping I'd land on my ass again like I had the time before just so they could get another good laugh at my expense.

I took a deep breath and focused. Our coach had drilled into us that gymnastics required not only strength of the body but of the mind too. I let the room around me fade away until all I could see was the thin mat in front of me. My thoughts were already seconds in the future, visualizing each aspect of the trick just like my coach had taught me, feeling it deep in my bones before I ever made a move.

I ran hard down the mat, then hurtled and punched and tightened and twisted, my body taking all the data from my past falls and recalculating it just slightly so that when I whipped my legs back to the ground, it was my feet and not my ass that landed on the mat this time. I straightened up slowly and stuck my arms triumphantly into the air.

All the girls exploded in applause.

I looked down at myself standing solid on the ground, my mind now lagging seconds behind. "I did it!" I cried in disbelief.

Holly led the group hug, beaming at me. She looked as genuinely happy as when she'd first landed the trick herself.

"I knew you could do it!" she told me as the rest of the girls fell away.

Everyone went back to what they were doing, but for some reason, I still heard clapping behind me. I whirled around and almost collapsed when I saw Will standing by the boys' locker room, clapping for me.

I blinked at him. *How much time had I spent upside down today? Had all the blood rushed to my head and made me hallucinate or something? Why would Will be standing in the gym in the middle of the afternoon, clapping for me?* It just didn't make sense.

I was just about to shake my head really hard, like people in cartoons do when they can't believe what they're seeing, when Will called out. "Nice job, Red!"

I looked over at Holly and she was staring at him

and it looked like she'd heard him too. So that meant he really was standing there. He was real, not just a figment of my imagination.

"C'mere, Red," he shouted, doing one of his crazy hand waves. Yes. It was definitely him, standing by the door to the parking lot, wearing shorts and a faded red Cold Springs jersey with the number 22 printed on the front with a basketball planted on the floor between his feet.

I jogged slowly over to him, trying to smooth down all the hair that had fallen out of my ponytail without looking like I was trying to smooth down all the hair that had fallen out of my ponytail. I didn't even want to think about what the rest of me looked like. It couldn't have been good since I had on my Girl Scout camp t-shirt with the hole in the armpit and the crumpled gym shorts I'd found at the bottom of my locker after school. Then I reminded myself that I was being stupid for even worrying about what I looked like since, as Scott had so kindly reminded me, nothing was ever going to happen between me and Will anyway.

"What are you doing here?" I asked when I reached him. "I thought you were a vampire. You only came out at night."

My heart lifted when he laughed. Watching his lips part, all I could think about was how many thousands of times the girl in the magazine article had kissed them.

"Real funny, Red."

Looking up at him, I realized how strange it was to be so close to him under real lights. I'd only ever seen him in headlights and movie reflections and the bulb in the overhead of the car. I noticed for the first time that although the skin on his face was completely smooth (so unlike the pimple-faced boys in school), the edge of his jaw wasn't. It was lined with the faintest shadow of stubble.

My God, I thought. Will is a *man*.

A *man* with a *beard*.

A *man* with a *beard* and a *girlfriend*.

A *man* with a *beard* and a *girlfriend* and is so obviously *way too old for me*. (Now I was sounding like one of those add-on songs I used to sing at Girl Scout camp about the green grass growing all around and around...)

The thrilling wrongness of it all flooded hot and tempting along my skin. Even though I knew I had to stop thinking all these lurid thoughts about Will, it still took everything I had not to reach up and run my hand along his jaw just to find out what tiny black whiskers felt like.

"I was just playing a pickup game outside," he answered the question I'd already forgotten I'd asked. "I came in to find my dad. Good thing I did, huh? I got to see that." He pointed to the gymnastic mat behind me.

He hooked the toe of his tennis shoe under the basketball and kicked it into his hand without even looking. "Man, you're really good!"

I shrugged, not wanting to brag, although I had a feeling Will might like it if I did.

He went on, "And you're clearly way stronger than you look." His eyes scanned down my body. *Oh lord. How long had it been since I shaved my legs?*

He pointed to my arm. "That's quite a bicep."

"Oh this? It's nothing." I flexed it, rotating my fist so the muscles rolled under my skin. I'd never admit it out loud, but I was proud of my muscles. I'd worked hard for them.

"A lot of throwing hay bales and practicing gymnastics will do this to a girl," I said.

"You're giving me a run for my money," he said, flexing the arm not holding the ball. His bicep was hard and carved and perfect in every way.

I tried not to stare, but I couldn't help myself. His arm was just too lovely. I stood there and gawked, trying to ingrain the vision of his beautiful muscles in my memory so I could have it for later that night, when I was alone in my bed. (I needed something new to think about since my memory of those tight white pants that John Travolta wore in *Saturday Night Fever* had faded a bit lately.)

I finally tore my eyes away. "Um. Yeah, so guess what? I asked Mrs. A about writing the newspaper column like you told me to."

His eyes lit up. "And?"

"She said we could do it."

"Alright!" He held his hand up high for me to slap. "That's awesome! See, I told you so."

"Why do I have a feeling you say that a lot?"

"Well, I *do* know a lot of things. You could learn a lot from me, you know."

I had to keep repeating, *he's only teasing me, he's only teasing me* over and over to keep my face from bursting into flames.

"Which reminds me," he said, "did you listen to the song?"

He tossed the basketball in the air, then caught it lightly in his palm as he waited for my answer. It reminded me of the picture from the magazine with the ball frozen mid-air next to him. Except now the picture was alive and real and standing right in front of me.

He kept tossing and catching, tossing and catching, over and over again. It was so natural to him. It seemed like he didn't even realize he was doing it. The measured throw, the perfect spin, the gentle catch, repeated with such precision that even when he took a step toward me, the ball still landed perfectly centered in the curve of his hand.

"Yeah, I listened to it," I said. "I really liked it."

It was another one of my lame answers. I knew I should've said more, but I was too distracted by a single bead of sweat slipping slowly down the middle of his neck, sliding leisurely past the hollow of his collarbones and into the valley of his chest where it disappeared into the V of his jersey. I stared at the spot, transfixed, imagining the rest of its trip downward.

When I looked up, Will was watching me, watching him. He had a little smile on his face that told me he knew exactly what I was thinking. Too late, I realized that my mouth was hanging open. I closed it quickly, but not before his smile spread even further.

"Hey, I gotta go." He nodded to the door outside. "The guys are waiting for me. I should be at Pizza King a little after nine. I'll find you and we can talk more about it."

Oh, my God. He was going to find me. Will Calder was going to make a point of coming to Pizza King a little after nine o'clock with the sole purpose of finding me.

Again, the fantasy unfolded in my mind: Will walking into Pizza King calling out to me in front of everyone, "Hey, Red, let's go!"; me running to his side as all the girls watched in envy and grabbing onto his arm as he escorted me to his waiting car where he would bow and open the door for me and then I'd climb in and we'd...

"Did you hear me, Red?" He waved a hand in front of my face.

"Yeah, of course I heard you. A little after nine," I said stammered, hoping he hadn't noticed my pink cheeks.

"I'll see you later then." He gave me a funny look, then clutched the ball under his arm and slipped back outside.

I stood there staring at the closed door, feeling dizzy and off balance, like the entire gym had turned into a swirling kaleidoscope of colors all around me. Had that really happened? Had Will really been here at my school on a Friday afternoon watching me practice gymnastics? Talking to me? Telling me he was going to meet me later? It seemed so odd, considering only a few weeks ago I'd never even laid eyes on him. And yet it was starting to seem like every time I turned around, he was there.

CHAPTER THIRTEEN

THE SOCIETY FOR UNREQUITED LOVE

As WE WERE putting away the mats after practice, I noticed Scott by the edge of the bleachers doing this weird head jerk thing trying to get my attention.

"What is it?" I snapped when I finally joined him. "Are you having a seizure or something?" I wasn't in a hurry to talk to him since I figured he'd seen me with Will and was just waiting there to make fun of me again.

But it wasn't me that was on Scott's mind. "So, did you get a chance to ask her?" He tipped his head at Holly, who was dutifully cleaning up some trash by the ball racks.

"I told you when I wrote you back. There's no point."

Scott and I passed notes back and forth every day. This week the topic of his writing had abruptly changed. Instead of his normal musings about what had happened on the *Simon and Simon* TV show the night before or the filmstrip he'd watched in history class, he'd started writing only about Holly.

He'd gone on and on about how fabulous she looked in the color blue, how sweet she was because she'd shared her White-Out with him in typing class, and the adorable way her eyes crinkled whenever she laughed. (Like I didn't know all of that already.) In today's note he'd even asked if I could maybe set him up with her, reasoning that since she and I were such close friends and he and I were such close friends, it only made sense that my two close friends became close "friends". (The quotation marks were his, not mine.)

"Couldn't you just try? For me?" he pleaded, pulling me further down the bleachers so no one could hear us.

It was hard not to feel sorry for him. I already knew how many times the girls in his grade had rejected him. Even though Scott was cute enough, in his own gawky way, there was an unwritten rule at Cold Springs High that girls couldn't date guys their own age because they were too immature. (After overhearing a couple sophomore guys have a lengthy discussion about whether Batman or Spider-Man would win in a wrestling match I tended to agree with that rule.)

"Like I said, it's not you. Holly doesn't date anyone." It was the same thing I'd written to him that afternoon.

I wasn't just telling him that because I was mad at him for making fun of me about Will. Holly really was totally oblivious when it came to boys. She had no idea that all the boys in school idolized her, dreamed about her, and would probably wrestle both Batman and Spider-Man just to get a date with her.

"Yeah, I know," Scott said, dejectedly. "I thought maybe you could at least help me try."

The way he said it made me think of Will telling me I had to at least try to get what I wanted instead of just assuming I could never have it. I had tested out his philosophy with Mrs. Anderson and it had worked for me. Maybe it could work for Scott too.

To test my reasoning I called Holly over, whispering under my breath to Scott as she got closer, "Okay, here's your chance. Follow my lead."

I felt Scott tense beside me as Holly stopped in front of us, her silky ponytail swishing over one shoulder. Goodness, she was beautiful.

"Scott's giving me a ride uptown after practice. You want to go with us? He can take you home along the way."

Scott chimed in loudly, "Yes! I have a car!"

I waited for him to say more, but he just sat there staring dumbly up at her. It wasn't quite what I had in mind when I told him to follow my lead, but at least he'd said something.

Holly nodded at where her older sister was heading into the girls' locker room. "Callie's taking me home. So, I don't need a ride."

"I have a car!" Scott blurted again for some unknown reason. When I looked over at him, his face had frozen into some kind of weird contortion I assumed was supposed to be a smile.

"Yes, Scott has a car," I nudged him hard with my elbow, hoping to unstick him and make him say something different. "A really nice car, don't you?"

"Yes. I have a really nice car," he parroted back. "And I know where you live too." Sweat was beginning to bead on Scott's forehead.

"Okay," Holly said, looking worried.

I plowed on. "I'm just starving and I thought maybe we could all stop up at Pizza King. Grab a stromboli before it's time to head home."

"Hmmm." She scrunched her face, considering my offer. I knew she'd probably never go for it, since her parents didn't like her riding around with anyone other than Callie. It was one of the reasons she never came out with us on the weekends. The other reason being the fact that she didn't drink. If you didn't drink or cruise around in other people's cars, then there wasn't much else to do on the weekends in Cold Springs.

"Probably not today," Holly said. "I'd need to ask my parents first. Maybe another time?"

"Another time would be good!" Scott piped up. I cringed at his over eagerness. Of course, Holly was probably clueless about his crush on her so there really wasn't any reason to be embarrassed for him.

"Oh sure. Sounds good," I said. "Just thought I'd ask."

"See you guys later!" Holly said, running toward the locker room.

"Another time then!" Scott called out to her. "Because I have a car and I know where you live!"

Once Holly was out of sight, I punched him hard on the shoulder.

"That didn't go so well, huh?" he said morosely.

"What the hell was that? I have a car and I know where you live? You sounded like a crazy stalker!"

"What can I say? I panicked."

"Thank God she left before you told her you hide in the bushes and watch her undress at night!"

"How do you know I do that?"

I whirled to him, eyes big.

"Just kidding!" he laughed. But I glared at him for a few more seconds just to make sure he was really joking.

"Well, at least I tried." I felt a new kinship with Scott after the exchange. Clearly we were both members of the same club now: The Society for Unrequited Love.

Still, it was hard to see him so dejected.

"Hey, you know what," I said, bumping his shoulder lightly. "I'm going to keep trying to help you with Holly. You never know what could happen, right? When she gets to know you better, she's going to love you."

"Are you sure?"

"Of course! What's not to love? Any girl would be lucky to have you."

Scott made a face at me. He wasn't used to me being so nice to him. Hopefully he hadn't pieced together that I was still entertaining the far-fetched notion that one day there might be a time when he could help me with my unrequited love too.

"Thanks, Red!" he said, hugging me tightly to his side.

I leaned into him, trying to think of ways to bring he and Holly together. Yet as I imagined the possible scenarios, some problems began to crop up.

"There's just one thing. In order to have a chance

with Holly you can't cuss so much around her. She wouldn't like that," I instructed.

"I can definitely do that. No cussing."

"And you probably shouldn't be so handsy at first. That might scare her off. You have to rein back all the hugging and touching."

He pulled his arm off my shoulder and sat up straight. "I thought you liked my hugs?"

"I do, but I'm used to you. Holly's not. You're kind of like an acquired taste. You're going to have to go a little slow."

"Okay, Okay. No touching then. At least not at the beginning. What else?"

"You'll need to stop drinking."

"Stop drinking?!" he yelled. "Like all together?"

"Well, at least around her."

He pondered that for a few seconds, seeming to struggle this time. "That's going to be hard, but I'll do it for her."

I thought back over all we'd covered so far. "So, no touching, no cussing, no drinking. Oh and no gross jokes, no burps, no writing disgusting limericks in her notes."

"Jesus Christ, Red. All that?"

I realized what all my new rules really meant. "Yeah, you're basically going to have to become a completely different person, Scott."

"Wow." He rubbed his hands together, thinking hard before he went on. "Well, if you really think it will give me a chance with her, then I'll do it."

Just then, Holly and her sister walked by in all their tanned-skinned, white-smiled glory. I almost fell off the bleacher when Holly looked back over her shoulder and called to Scott, "Another time, right?" If I thought it was possible for her, I would've almost called it flirtatious.

Scott nodded, mouth hanging open in shock as he watched her disappear out the gym door. He turned to me, eyes shining. "Oh my God. I think she might like me!"

A few seconds earlier I would've told him not to get his hopes up. Yet with that one backwards glance from Holly, all that had changed.

"Yeah," I mumbled, still trying to make sense of what I'd just seen. "I can't believe I'm actually going to say this, but I think you might be right."

CHAPTER FOURTEEN

"TOPS"

"No. Get up front," Will barked as I started to crawl into the back seat of the Monte Carlo.

I surveyed the bucket seats up front, not understanding what he wanted me to do. "Where am I supposed to sit? On Rob's lap?" I asked, pointing inside.

I'd been alone in Pizza King when the car had pulled up in front exactly at 9:00, just like Will had promised. Stacie was riding around with Mark and Scott was at a party for the tennis team. Yet no amount of nerves or nausea or harping inside my head about how delusional I was being, was going to keep me from getting inside that car.

Rob was standing on the street holding the passenger side door open for me while cars cruised slowly by beside us. Will was too busy rummaging through the cassettes piled in a plastic bin on the floorboard between the seats to even look up at me.

"Sit here, on the console," he said absently, patting the padded square of leather between the two seats. "You'll have to straddle the gearshift, but you're tiny, you'll fit." He studied the back of a cassette intensely then, apparently not finding what he wanted, tossed it roughly back into the pile.

Traffic was building on the street behind us, but Will didn't seem to notice.

I hated how he wouldn't look at me. I wanted so badly to get his attention. "I've barely just met you and you're already asking me to straddle something?" I huffed. "I mean, shouldn't you at least buy me dinner first?"

It was a joke I would've normally made to the guys in the drum section. It would've felt right at home between all their various dick and ball sack jokes, but I probably shouldn't have said it to Will. Not when the thought of straddling him wasn't at all funny to me.

Will looked up and stared right into my eyes exactly the way I'd wanted him to. Then he burst out laughing. Behind me, Rob laughed too. Of course, they did. Me and Will. Dinner. Straddling. Ha! The idea was just so absurd.

"Just get in the car already, Red," Will commanded. I could tell he was trying to sound annoyed, but he really wasn't.

I climbed in beside him, unprepared for the fact that this new seating arrangement meant my shoulder, hip, and leg were going to be pressed into Will's body for the rest of the night. As we roared off, the entire left side of me burned like someone was holding a blowtorch to my skin. While my right side, pushed equally as hard against Rob, felt nothing at all.

"You good there?" Will asked as we headed out of town.

"It's okay," I said coolly, when in truth I felt like I could've ridden all the way to the coast of California on that hard little seat as long as he was the one driving me.

"So, where's Stacie tonight?" Rob asked, handing me a damp bottle of Budweiser. Most of the boys around here drank cheap beer like Schlitz or Old Milwaukee, but I noticed Will always had the more expensive brands in his cooler.

"Stacie's with Mark tonight." I felt bad disappointing Rob.

"Oh, yeah? That's cool," Rob said, drinking his beer quickly. I glanced over at Will, and he raised an eyebrow like he was thinking the same thing as me about Rob having the hots for Stacie. I liked how Will and I could already communicate without using words.

For the next twenty minutes, Will and Rob talked back and forth, mostly about basketball and some kind of job they did on the weekends together that involved fixing up houses. I didn't really mind them ignoring me since it gave me time to get a good enough beer buzz to finally join the conversation.

"You guys work together then?" I asked when there was a lull.

"Yeah, I work for his grandpa's real estate company on the weekends," Rob said.

"Finnegan's Real Estate," Will said. "You ever heard of it?"

"Yeah, I have," I said, my heart tugging with an old memory.

The day the real estate agent had pounded the Finnegan sign at the end of our driveway had been one of the worst of my life. I hated that sign and what it meant for the future of our beloved farm. I even used to throw fistfuls of mud at the smiling face of the old man on the front who claimed he could *Turn All Your Home Dreams into Reality.* Couldn't see he was turning all my dreams into nightmares?

So, the old man I hated was Will's grandpa, huh? If this were another town I might have considered that quite a coincidence. But since Cold Springs was so small and the odds of bumping into someone's relative were pretty high, that meant the serendipity wasn't so shocking.

Rob went on. "Yeah, we fix up some of the foreclosure houses for resale. Run errands back and forth between the branches. Do all the shit no one else wants to do."

I turned to Will. "So that's why you're back here on the weekends?"

"Yeah. Gotta earn some of my own money. My parents are trying to teach me a good work ethic and all that other happy horseshit."

Even with his explanation something still nagged at me. "It's just, I don't remember seeing you around here before." I tried to sound casual. I cheered at the basketball games last year. Since his dad was the coach, wouldn't he have been at some of them? It seemed impossible that I could've missed noticing someone as handsome as him standing on the sidelines.

"I used to work at the branch in Terre Haute since it was closer to school," Will said. "But a few weeks ago I decided it might be nice to come home again so

I switched to working back in the Cold Springs office on weekends."

I swallowed hard. A few weeks ago? He and I had met a few weeks ago. Could his wanting to come home have had something to do with me?

He broke into my thoughts. "Basketball season's starting soon. And now that my dad and I are getting along better he said he'd let me help with the team this year. I want to try it."

"Oh right. Because of basketball. That makes sense." *Of course, it's about basketball. Why the hell would it be about anything else?*

When the highway eventually ran out, Will turned onto a road so narrow and dark I could only see a few feet of gravel in front of the car. He drove slower, the engine lowering to a dull purr beneath the throb of electric guitars pulsing through the speakers. Since I'd been in the car, five Stones songs had played in the exact order I'd memorized them. It made me think this might be my lucky night since I was pretty sure Will was playing the same *Hot Rocks* cassette I had at home.

"Man, you know all the words, huh?" Will said to me after a while.

I shrugged. "Well, not all of them."

I didn't mention I also had a notebook full of deep-level analysis and probable symbolic interpretations for every word that Mick and Keith had written on the cassette just in case Will happened to ask. Boy Scouts weren't the only ones who were taught to be prepared.

"You're going to fit right in on The Ride," Will said, flashing his cover-boy smile.

"The what?"

"The Ride. It's what I call this." He circled his finger around the car.

I must have looked confused because he went on. "It's what we did on the weekends in high school. Cruising around, drinking, singing, solving the great mysteries of life. You know, stuff like that."

I burst out laughing. *Solving the great mysteries of life?* He made it sound so dramatic.

"So, you actually named what you did on the weekends?" I asked incredulously. "Like you called it The Ride? With a capital T and a capital R?"

"Of course," he said matter-of-factly. "Everything I do is in capital letters."

I glanced over at Rob, hoping maybe he'd roll his eyes signaling to me this was all one big joke. But he was nodding along like Will was making perfect sense.

"Okay. The Ride. I got it." I lied.

"I've decided to bring it back again for a limited time engagement. One last world tour."

"A world tour, huh? You mean like what rock bands do?"

"Exactly!" Will shouted over the music. "I knew you'd understand."

"Well, I don't know about that."

"I've got me and Rob and Scott. Maybe others that I deem worthy." He glanced over my head at Rob. "I think she'd make a good Marianne, don't you?" he said like I wasn't even there.

I looked back and forth between their two nodding heads.

"I'd make a good who?" I asked, confused.

"You'd make a good Marianne Faithfull," Will said, like I should've known exactly what he meant. "She was a groupie for the Stones back in the sixties."

When I heard the word groupie, my entire body flushed so hot I could almost feel steam droplets clinging to the inside of my polo shirt. "I don't want to be your *groupie*!" I shouted.

This was bad. Like really embarrassingly bad. I remembered the smug smile Will had on his face as he'd watched me look at his bicep earlier that afternoon. The way he'd caught me leering at the drop of sweat on his chest. He obviously thought I was just following him around so I could lust after him. (Which was pretty much the truth, but I sure as hell didn't want him to know that.) I was clearly just one big joke to him. The little girl groupie chasing after his heels like a lovesick puppy.

"What's wrong?" Will elbowed me in the ribs.

"I don't want to be your groupie! That's what's wrong!"

"Why not?" He seemed almost offended. "Marianne was a big part of The Rolling Stones back in the early days."

"I don't care. I'm not anyone's groupie!" I hated how upset I was getting. I didn't want Will to know he was bothering me.

"Calm down, Red." His tone was so condescending it made my blood boil. I felt him staring at me, but I was too afraid to look back. What if he was laughing at me? What if he and Rob were winking at each other over my head? Both about to explode into hysterics about the silly girl who thought that two older boys actually wanted her with them tonight when the real reason I was there was to be the butt of their jokes?

Will tried to explain. "They also called Marianne their muse. Does that sound better to you? Do you like muse better than groupie?"

I shook my head, still mad, even though it seemed like he was trying to apologize.

He bumped his shoulder into mine. "Come on." His voice was low now. The sound of it made a weird tugging feeling inside my stomach. "I didn't mean anything bad by it."

"It doesn't even make sense," I complained. "If I'm Marianne, then are you saying you guys are The Rolling Stones or something?" I bumped his shoulder the same way he had mine, except a little harder. "Because news flash! You're not!"

When I turned back to the windshield, the road in front of us had veered so sharply to the left it looked like we were about to collide into a wall of cornstalks. Instead of braking like any normal person would have, Will sped up like he was about to drive straight off the road and into them. Then at the last second, he wrenched the steering wheel hard to the left. The Monte Carlo's back tires fish-tailed over the gravel so violently it felt like we were floating over the road instead of driving on top of it. When I was sure we were about to be swept away in a flash flood of dirt and rocks, he called out, "We may not be The Rolling Stones! But aren't we the next best thing?!"

I was falling off the console, clutching onto the padded ceiling to keep from landing right in Rob's lap. Luckily, the back tires caught traction and Will somehow expertly maneuvered the car around the corner and onto a long straightaway. Then he wove down the road, jerking the steering wheel back and forth so it felt like the car was surfing across an enormous gravel wave.

Will was laughing and Rob was laughing and I was laughing, even though I didn't want to because I wanted to stay mad at Will. I couldn't though, because the feeling of not knowing which way he was going to go or what he was going to do next, was so exciting that I wanted it to go on forever. I wanted him to just keep driving and acting crazy and making me mad then making me happy over and over again just for the sheer thrill of the friction of it all.

The headlights of an oncoming car sliced through the windshield as we got to the end of the road and Will finally crammed on the brake.

"So how about we forget that whole Marianne thing if it's going to make you so mad," he said as we all caught our breath.

"I wasn't mad."

"Right," Will said with a smug grin. "What if I said I had another name for you, then?"

"Oh boy." Rob kicked at the beer bottles that had rolled out from under the seat during the commotion. He seemed to be as afraid of what Will was going to say next as I was.

"Oh boy is right," I grumbled. "What am I going to be now? Your mascot?"

"No. Although I do kind of like the sound of that," Will teased. I punched him hard on the arm.

He didn't flinch. Instead, his hand swept dramatically across the windshield as he declared loudly, "You're going to be Red of The Ride!" He gazed straight ahead like the words were hanging in front of us in flashing marquee lights.

I couldn't figure out if he was teasing me again, if this was just the next stage of an elaborate joke he was playing on me.

He lifted his eyebrows and finally looked right at me. "So? What do you think? Do you like it?"

His eyes danced in anticipation like he couldn't wait for my answer. The sincerity in them made me think that none of this was a joke to him.

It felt like the possibility of seeing him again hinged on me admitting the truth in that moment. But damn, it was hard to say out loud. "Yes, Will I like it," I muttered, terrified by how willingly I'd exposed myself.

"Good!" he said, with way more enthusiasm than my simple response deserved. "Because if you like that you're going to fit in just fine around here."

⁓

An hour passed and Will still hadn't played "Tops", the song he'd assigned me last week.

"You play drums?" Will asked me during the drum solo in "Jumpin' Jack Flash".

"Yeah, just like Charlie Watts," I said, throwing in the nugget I'd learned from the liner notes on my cassette.

"Nice," he nodded, clearly impressed by my new knowledge.

"This is my favorite part of the song actually." I said it hoping to spur him to turn it up louder so he would have to put his hands between my legs to reach the dial.

Just as Will's hand hovered over my thighs, Rob interrupted him.

"Hey, dude, don't forget." He pointed to a driveway we were just about to pass.

"Oh yeah, sorry." Will slammed on the brakes and started up the gravel road next to a big white sign that read *Grinfield's Holstein Farm* in kelly green letters.

"Oh man, I haven't been here in a long time." I looked past Rob at the shadowy outlines of two barns at the top of the hill. "Not since haying time. What, three or four years ago?"

"Yeah. I'd say it's been at least three," Rob agreed.

Twice a year all the farmers in town pooled their collective resources during haying season and went farm to farm helping each other get their hay cut and baled before the rain came. It was always one of my favorite times of year, even though it was invariably boiling hot, and the work was back-breakingly hard. There was just something about doing the grueling work all together like one big extended family that seemed to make it so much more fun.

"I remember how you were always so little and the guys would give you a hard time," Rob said.

"Yeah. They didn't think girls were supposed to be out there. My dad didn't really have any other choice though. I was all he had." I regretted the words as soon as they were out of my mouth. Mentioning my dad might spur Rob to say something about him dying and then he might feel like he had to say the same stupid shit everyone always did about how sorry they were for me. Then I'd want to punch him right in the nose because I hated when people felt sorry for me. I really didn't want to punch Rob in the nose. He was way too nice for that.

I was relieved when Rob went on with no mention of my dad. "You'd always show them. You'd get in there and throw as many bales as they would and shut the guys right up."

"Yeah. What a bunch of assholes."

"Well, not all of them." Rob nudged my shoulder with his.

"No. I didn't mean you, Rob," I said. "You weren't like all the other guys."

It was funny that in the past few weekends we'd been together, I hadn't remembered those times putting up hay with Rob. I guess that was how much I'd bottled up my memories of that time.

"I remember right out there." Rob pointed at the pasture we were driving by. "All the guys were laughing at you for some stupid reason and you got so pissed. Your face got all red and you were stomping around, throwing things. I really thought you were going to punch someone!"

"You held me back and told those jerks they'd better shut the hell up or else you were going to put a pitchfork up their ass!" We all cracked up. It was hard to imagine quiet Rob ever saying something as harsh as that.

Will had stopped the car in front of a big white farmhouse and for once sat quietly and listened instead of talked. I silently pleaded for him to dig through his tapes again and forget everything he'd just heard. I didn't want him to know anything about my past. These past few weeks I'd held out hope that somehow, he was one of the few people in town that didn't know the truth about me. I liked how anonymous I could be when I was with him.

"I keep forgetting you're a farm girl, Red," Will interjected.

"Well, more like I *used* to be a farm girl."

"Used to be?"

His confusion lifted my heart. There still a chance he knew nothing about me.

Rob met my eyes. In them I could see him saying he wouldn't reveal anything I wanted to keep to myself.

"Yeah, we've moved since then," I snapped, frantically trying to steer Will away from the subject of my family life. "You said you're working with the team this year?"

"Yeah," Will said, glancing at me suspiciously almost like he knew he was being called off of something important. "Just when I can fit it in my schedule."

"That means you're going to be coaching Rob?" I had no idea where I was going with this. I just wanted to change the subject any way I could.

They smiled at each other like they had an inside joke.

"What? What's so funny?" I asked.

"It's just that Will's been coaching me for a while," Rob said. "I owe everything to him actually. He's totally changed my game."

Will shrugged, uncharacteristically humble all of

a sudden. I remembered Rob saying he had graduated from Will's school of confidence although I still had no idea what that meant.

"Ask him to tell you the story of what he did for me sometime. It's a good one," Rob said. I noticed how he looked at Will with such obvious admiration.

"He's already taught you all he knows? Did he tell you how to see every play as a battle then add them all up so you'll eventually win the war?" I quoted the phrase Will had used in the magazine article.

When Will's eyes went wide, I realized my slip.

"It looks like someone's been doing her homework!" he said, laughing at me.

My heart dropped. "No, I wasn't!"

"Yes you were! Only a few weeks ago you didn't even know I existed. Now you know the exact words I said in *Sports Illustrated*!"

I huffed. Crossed my arms in front of me. There was no way to defend myself.

"You went and found the article, didn't you?" Will asked with a knowing smirk.

I tried to ignore him but he kept elbowing me and laughing. "Huh? Huh? I'm right, aren't I?"

It was hard to keep a straight face. "I just wanted to find out if all that stuff you were saying was true, that's all."

"You were trying to find out more about me," he teased. I could feel my face burning.

Rob swung the car door open. "Hey, leave her alone," he yelled at Will. "or else I'm going to put a pitchfork up your ass!" We all laughed together. I wanted to hug Rob for saving me once again.

I was so flustered from defending myself it wasn't until Rob was outside the car that I realized what his leaving meant. Will and I were now alone.

෴

I slid over to the passenger seat so fast you would have thought a geyser of hot lava had just erupted out of the console.

"I guess it's just you and me now," Will said, trying not to laugh at my not-so-subtle attempt to get away from him.

"Um, you can take me back to Pizza King." My heart was pounding so loud I was sure he could hear it all the way across the car.

He made a face. "But we haven't talked about 'Tops' yet."

"I'm sure you probably have other things to do."

"Not really."

He watched as I scooted even closer to the passenger side door. "Relax. I'm not going to do anything to you," he said, looking amused. "As you might have read in that article you 'just so happened to stumble upon'," he air quoted, "I have a girlfriend."

"Right. I know. Penny. You two have been dating forever. Since you were sophomores like me." *Oh God. Why the hell couldn't I just shut up?!*

The smug smile was back. "I don't remember that part being in the article." He raised an eyebrow. This guy had me behind so many eight balls everywhere I looked was a wall of black.

Will maneuvered the car onto a thin thread of road that led us even further from town, even deeper into the night.

"What time do you have to be back?" he asked.

"Oh, I don't have a curfew," I said proudly. Maybe now he'd see I was way more grown up than he thought.

He furrowed his brow. "Why not? What are you like, twelve? And you have no curfew?"

I could tell he was trying to piss me off again, so I purposely stayed cool. "I'm fifteen, by the way." I wanted to say fifteen and a half, but I knew that sounded way too childish. "And my mom works late so she's asleep when I get home. She never knows what time I get in."

I told him about how I'd moved out of the school district and my house was kind of far away. As long as I could catch my own ride, my mom didn't really care what time I got home. She was just glad she didn't have to come get me herself. When he asked me where my house was, I told him.

"That's not too far away," he said. "But then again, I'm a guy that likes to drive." He did the veering thing with the car again for effect.

"They drive me to school during the week. So they said if I want to go out on the weekends I'm on my own for rides." I froze, realizing I'd slipped and said the word *they*. What if he asked who I meant by *they*? Lucky for me, Will just nodded, seeming to absorb it all.

Watching Will's expression, I didn't feel quite as proud of my lack of curfew. He was obviously figuring out that it meant my mom didn't give a shit about me. I hated the end of the night on the weekends when I'd start getting desperate about how to get home. I'd have to search around, begging people to give me a ride, even though it was always out of their way. It killed me to ask people for favors. It made me feel like such a sad little orphan. A lot of times I'd stay with Stacie, but she had a curfew and lately I'd been wanting to stay out later. I needed to drink more, party longer, so I could postpone facing the real world as long as possible.

"And your dad won't come to get you either?" Will asked.

For once I didn't panic at someone bringing up my dad. Hearing Will ask about him actually gave me hope. It meant he didn't know as much about me as everyone else in town did.

"Oh, my dad's dead," I said cheerfully. I'd found when I used that upbeat tone, that cutting directness, it made people uncomfortable. Then they'd usually drop the subject quickly.

"Oh, sorry. I didn't mean to…" Will trailed off. It was the first time I'd ever seen him flustered.

"It's no big deal." I waved a hand flippantly in the air. "We weren't that close." Images of my dad flashed through my mind: him correcting the way I held my fork, telling me to quiet down because I was too loud, saying all the kids at school were going to laugh at me if I didn't stop sucking my thumb before kindergarten. Basically, disapproving of everything I did.

"I don't think my dad really even liked me that much," I mumbled to my reflection in the window.

My body seized when I realized what I said out loud. Why did I keep revealing things to Will I normally kept to myself?

"Well, if it makes you feel any better, I don't think my dad likes me that much either," Will said quietly. When I glanced over at him, he was frowning at the windshield.

"Must just be a dad thing, huh? Being hard asses all the time."

"Yeah. I guess they think they have to be all tough to make up for how soft our moms are?" he said, face brightening. "Because my mom...she loves the shit out of me!"

I laughed at his strange choice of words. I started to say, "yeah, my mom loves the shit out of me too," but then I remembered talking about my mom was off limits.

I gave him a huge smile. "Guess what? I didn't even cry at my dad's funeral." I couldn't help but brag. It was one of my proudest achievements.

"You didn't?"

"No. It was a full military funeral too. My dad was a pilot in the Air Force so there were all kinds of gun salutes, a flyover, horns being played." I pointed to my beaming face. "And not one tear. Pretty good, right?"

He blinked over at me, like he couldn't tell if I was being serious or not. "Well, that's... that's... uh..."

"Cold?" I said, again feeling proud. People said that about me a lot. I considered it a compliment.

"No. I was going to say *strong*."

I made a face. He was clearly bullshitting me now. There was no way he really thought I was strong. Although thinking back to when I'd seen him in the gym earlier, it *was* the second time he'd used that word about me today.

"Well, crying is for pussies," I said, mostly just to make him laugh, which worked. God, he was so easy to crack up.

"You definitely aren't like other girls then," he said. "I thought girls cried at everything. Movies. Commercials. When you happened to be fifteen minutes late for dinner because you got stuck at work but she insists it's a sign that you don't care about her feelings anymore." He rolled his eyes.

"Wow. Pretty specific on that last example, bud."

He gave me a sheepish look, like he hadn't meant to let that slip. Maybe I wasn't the only person in the car spilling way more truth than they normally did tonight.

✍

A little later Will cleared his throat dramatically. "Time to listen to the song now," he said in his most professorial voice.

"Alright, I'm ready!"

He pointed to the overflowing basket of cassettes between us. "You gotta find it first."

"You don't think I can find it?"

"I'm not sure. I guess we're about to find out."

I grabbed the basket and began digging through the pile of tapes. "Tops" was on the Stone's newest album, *Tattoo You*. The bright red cover would make it easy to spot even in the dim light. But with Will staring at me as I searched, I was still nervous.

"Here it is!" I whipped the plastic case in the air,

wanting to slap a huge kiss on the tattooed face of the man/woman on the front. Some people said it was a painting of Mick, but I didn't think it looked like him at all.

Will remained stoic. "You got the right album, but can you find the right track?"

"Of course!" I struggled to open the case.

"You can't look at the song list." He commanded as I slid the cassette into my hand.

"How could I even see it? It's too dark."

"Well, let's see if you can cue it to the right spot."

"Can you just shut up and let me work here?" I huffed.

My hands shook as I tried to line the cassette up with the thin mouth of the player. It took me a few tries before the stereo finally swallowed it with a satisfying clatter of plastic. I closed my eyes and pressed the fast-forward button, letting my mind drift back to the thousands of times I'd cued up the song on the boom box in my bedroom. It was the eighth track on Side B. With an obscure placement like that, it was a song that most likely would never be released on the radio. Which made me wonder again why Will had chosen it for me.

The tape whirled beneath my finger as I prayed to release it at just the right spot. If I nailed this, Will would see how well I'd followed his direction. Then maybe, just maybe, he'd deem me worthy enough to give me another assignment for next week.

When I let go of the button, there was a second of silence. Will's foot slid off the accelerator and the car coasted as the two of us locked eyes waiting for what came next.

When the first notes of a piano plinked through the speakers, I shot both arms in the air in triumph.

Will beamed at me. "Perfect cue!"

A huge breath whooshed out of me. I couldn't believe I'd passed his test. I didn't know what that meant, but I had a strange feeling my victory was about way more than just cueing up a song.

Settling back in my seat, I let myself enjoy the song I'd grown to love over the past week. While "You Can't Always Get What You Want" was grandiose with its choir and soaring crescendo, "Tops" was surprisingly simple yet still beautiful in its own right.

Instead of screeching guitars, an easy piano rhythm pulled the listener gently into its melody. As Mick sang, he alternated between an exaggerated drawl and a seductive purr, adding his signature quivering falsetto at the end. It was that pleading quiver, that heartfelt begging, which made my stomach drop out from under me every time I listened to it.

Will and I sang the song together, but I couldn't bear to look at him. The first time I listened to it, I had a notebook close by so I could take down every word, sure I'd have a hard time understanding the song's message. But once the lyrics unfurled, all those fears had faded away. "Tops" was one of the rare Stones songs that left nothing to interpretation.

In it, Mick was trying to convince a girl that he would make her a star. He flatters her and begs her and promises her the world if she'll only listen to what he says. Mick will put this girl on a pedestal, he sings. Hand her success. Take her to the top, just as the title stated.

When I listened to the tape my bedroom, I'd soaked in every word, pretending Will was the one singing the lines to me; that I was the one he was begging to take to the top. Of course, I knew I was just being delusional again. No one in their right mind would ever see me as a star.

"So why do you think I picked that song for you?" Will asked when the song finally ended.

I remembered the line at the beginning of the verse that had frozen me with recognition the first time I'd heard it. "Was it because of the part where he's telling the girl she should leave her small town behind?"

"That's it. It reminded me of you. How you told me you wanted to get out of Cold Springs so bad. How you said that once you graduate you're never coming back here."

"I remind you of the girl in the song?"

"Yes, you do."

My stomach flipped like we'd just plummeted down a mountain even though we were still careening down the flat wedge of road. I was just getting up the courage to ask him who the Mick part in the song was when he beat me to the punch.

"Do you think I can show you the steps? Help you taste the sweet wine of success?" he asked, quoting the words of the song.

"Oh, you're Mick Jagger now?" I asked, trying to calm my flipping stomach.

"Like I said before, I'm the next best thing." He

glanced at the road every once in a while, but mostly he just looked at me.

He went on. "I'll make you a success, just like the song says."

What the hell is he talking about? "Right. And how are you going to do that?"

"I'll make you believe in yourself."

I thought of what Rob had said earlier about Will turning him into who he was now.

"Is that what you did for Rob?"

"Exactly," Will said. "That kid was so gangly and uncoordinated when I got my hands on him. He could barely dribble the ball halfway down the court without kicking it out of bounds, much less hit the basket with it."

He sat up straighter in his seat, invigorated by talk of his own prowess. "I took him under my wing. Worked with him after practice. Spent hours on drills with him after I'd graduated. Now he's been the starting center for the past two years."

"That's great, but I'm not really basketball player material."

"No worries," he said with a sweet smile. "I can turn you into whatever you want to be."

"So, I'm your next project? You're bored and you need a sad little loser to fix up in your spare time?"

"See. Right there," Will pointed at me, looking grim. "That's the first thing I'd work on."

"What?"

"The way you talk about yourself. You should never cut yourself down. The rest of the world is all too ready to do that for you. You don't need to give them a head start."

I shook my head. "Where do you get all this stuff? All these weird ideas of yours?"

"From the music," he said matter-of-factly.

"From the music?"

"Yeah, it's all in the music. Everything you need to know about life is all right there." He pointed at the stereo.

I wanted to shout at him, "It can't be that simple!" Then I realized it was the same thought I'd had when I'd first seen the *Feel Good* button at The Den. First the button and now Will. Could it really only be *me* that was making my life so complicated?

Will noticed my doubt. "Don't worry. I'll explain it to you as we go. The music will guide us."

I still couldn't understand what he was asking me to do.

"Guide us to where? There's no place to go!" I pointed out the windshield at the same dirt road we'd been circling around all night.

"What? You don't think songs can transport you? Take you to another place and time? Funny, because someone once told me they can. Like some kind of musical communion across time and space. I think that's the way she put it."

I blinked at him, completely stupefied that he was repeating the same words I'd said to him behind the drive-in. He'd actually memorized them, as if what I'd said that night had been something worth remembering.

"But I still don't understand. What do you want me to do?"

"Just say you'll join The Ride. Commit to coming with us every weekend," he said. He sounded so much like the Marine recruiter that spoke at our school assembly last spring I wanted to laugh out loud. "C'mon Red. We need you," he pleaded.

My stomach felt the same sick way it had when Mick begged the girl at the end of "Tops." I wanted to give in and tell Will I'd like nothing better than to follow him blindly down his self-proclaimed yellow brick road. Yet, there was still something I couldn't understand.

"But I don't get it. Why me?"

"I told you the other night. You're different. I saw that the first night I met you. You're not like other girls."

"Oh, right. That." *Different.* The word I'd been running from for all these years. For the first time ever it sounded like something to be proud of coming from Will's mouth. "What if I don't like being different?"

"Well then, that's another thing we'll need to work on," he said. He probably wished he'd brought a clipboard so he could keep track of everything he needed to fix about me. "I'm going to convince you. You've got a lot going for you. You're smart and pretty and you're fucking funny as hell."

I wanted to reach over and push a button on Will's shirt to rewind him so I could hear that sentence over and over again for the rest of my life. And yet I still couldn't believe it.

"Will, I'm not pre-"

"Stop it," he reprimanded sharply.

I let the compliments hang there the way he'd told me to, but it made me feel all itchy and uncomfortable.

I couldn't figure out why he insisted on thinking I was so special. He seemed so sure about it. He was almost as sure about me as he was about himself.

"Seriously, you could go far in high school if you listen to me," he went on, sounding as confident as a boy who would compare a basketball court to a battleground, his team to an army.

"You're crazy!"

He leaned toward me. "Yeah, I've got nasty habits. I take tea at 3:00," he said in a British accent.

"You're not helping your case," I said, laughing. *Does he really think he's the next best thing to Mick Jagger?*

His crystal blue eyes seared into mine. "Yeah, I might be crazy. Then again, what if I'm the sanest person you've ever met?"

I was so off balance. For the first time all night I couldn't think of a sarcastic comeback. "Can we just listen to the song again?" I asked breathlessly.

Will rewound the tape until "Tops" started over. This time as we sang together he barely took his eyes off of me.

My face burned from his attention. I was thankful it was dark in the car and he couldn't see how flushed my cheeks were.

"You think I can take you to the top?" he called over the last verse to me. The music was so loud he had to shout.

"What?" I yelled back to him. There was no rational response to his question.

"I'll take you to the top," he sang to me exactly the way I'd fantasized he would. "Do you believe me?"

I made a face, twirled my finger by my ear. "I said, you're crazy!"

Will grinned like I'd just given him the world's greatest compliment. "Join us on The Ride. I promise. We'll go places." He nodded knowingly.

I watched the moonlight glide rhythmically over his face, illuminating each of his perfect features in undulating waves. There was no smug look now. No taunting flash in his eyes. He seemed serious. As if he really believed all the outlandish claims he'd just made to me.

I reminded myself again that he had to be playing with me. Having fun with the little girl he wanted to drag around as his own personal groupie. But at that moment I didn't really care. I didn't want to think about whether Scott was right about Will just playing games with me. Or, whether it was wrong to be alone in a car with a boy so much older than me and had a girlfriend too. Or, even if I was being delusional by letting myself think about him as much as I did.

I just wanted to feel good right then, right that very second. I wanted to feel the rhythm of the car moving, listen to the sound of the music, and think about the things Will had just said to me. Feel how nice everything became when they got all mixed up together. I thought of my past weekends. Of never knowing where I was going or how I was going to get there. Of being that lost girl floating in the breeze with no direction, with no one in the entire world caring where she landed.

Will was saying he cared. He wanted me to be with him. If I joined him I would have someone out there who expected me to be somewhere at a certain time. Who would keep his promises. Who would always be there to pick me up when he said he would. That gave me an idea. Maybe there was another problem Will could help me solve.

When the song ended Will stopped the car in the middle of the road and looked at me hopefully. "What do you say, Red? Do you want to join The Ride?"

"On one condition," I said, trying to sound as stern as I could.

Will's eyes lit up. It was almost like he was happy I hadn't made it too easy for him. "Lay it on me."

"You always have to give me a ride home when the night's over." I held my breath, part of me not believing I had the nerve to bargain with him when he was already offering me so much.

His face broke into the same beautiful smile that had made my ears whoosh the first night I'd met him. "Of course. I'd be happy to give you a ride home. That's no big deal at all."

It may not be a big deal to you, I thought to myself, *but it is to me.*

He leaned over the console. "So? Does that mean you're with us?"

I pretended to struggle with my decision for a few seconds longer. Then, when I thought I'd made him wait long enough, I sighed heavily. "Yes, Will. I'm with you." I hoped he noticed how I'd turned the plural into the singular in that sentence.

I couldn't believe how genuinely happy he looked.

"Great!" He reached over and grabbed my hand off my lap. For a second, I thought he was going to raise it to his lips and kiss the back of it, just like a prince in a fairy tale. Instead, he flipped it over, pulled a cassette out of his bin, and slapped it in my palm.

"Here's your next song."

CHAPTER FIFTEEN

"BATTLEFIELD"

IT WAS 1:30 in the morning when Will finally took me home. Walking in the door, I was still flying high. Partially because of all the beer I'd drunk but mostly because the most handsome, most intriguing boy I'd ever met in my entire life had just asked me to spend every weekend with him.

My stomach dropped when I saw Karen sitting at the dining room table strumming her guitar.

"What rhymes with battlefield?" she asked as I tried to quietly slip by her to get to my room. She frowned down at a notepad filled with a bunch of scribbled sentences. I exhaled in relief seeing the pages because it meant she was writing music and when Karen wrote music she didn't notice anything around her. Not the time, or place, or in this case the drunk fifteen-year-old swaying back and forth right in front of her.

"I'm adding a new stanza to the song we wrote."

She strummed the shiny chestnut guitar on her lap. *We wrote.* At least now she was giving me a little credit for it. "I need something else to rhyme with battlefield."

I flopped down in the chair beside her, the wicker of the seat squeaking in protest underneath me. "God, can't you come up with anything on your own? Do I always have to be the creative genius around here?" I teased.

"Shhhh. Your mom's sleeping," she hissed, not even laughing at my joke. I hadn't known I'd been so loud. Yelling over the music all night in the Monte Carlo must have deafened me a bit. "She's got another 12-hour shift at the clinic tomorrow so we can't wake her up."

"Again?" I said in a lower voice.

"Yeah. Again."

Great. Another weekend of barely seeing my mom. With only her income to support us now, it seemed like all she did was work. She was gone so much I was starting to wonder if we would even recognize each other passing in the hallway. Pretty soon, we'd have to resort to having a code phrase to identify ourselves like the spies in the movies. She'd say, "The eagle has landed," and I'd say, "on a planet made of cheese," and then she'd know I was truly her daughter and I'd know once and for all I even had a mother.

Karen waved a hand in front of my face. "So, how about that rhyme? Battlefield, remember?"

"Um, let's see. How about *clattle-sealed*? Or *flattle-bield*?" I offered half-heartedly. My capacity for rhyming was not at an all-time high. My mind was too jammed up with the memory of sitting half the night with Will's incredibly hot body pressed up against mine.

Karen shook her head. "Real funny. Thanks for nothing."

She wrote something on the notepad, scribbled it out violently, then stared past me with a glazed look on her face which I'd seen many times. Karen was intense on a good day, but when she was making new music she became a super concentrated version of herself. Like a spoonful of Kool-Aid powder straight out of the packet.

She ran her fingers through her short hair. It spiked all crazy around her head like Jesus's crown of thorns. She tapped the table in frustration, seeming so distressed I started to feel sorry for her.

"Let me see that." I pulled her notebook across the butcher-block table. I could barely read her frenzied scratching.

"Here," I said, wrestling the pencil out of her hand. "How about you switch these words around in this sentence?" I circled a word, then drew an arrow to put it in a different spot, marked another word out and rewrote it further down on the page. "It will flow a little better. Then you'll have the word *love* on the end which is way easier to rhyme with than battlefield."

She pulled the notebook back and mumbled my reworked sentence softly to herself. "Yeah... I like that." She took a deep breath, visibly relaxing. "That's much better. Thanks." She took the pencil out of my hand and waved it at me. "You know something? You should be a writer one day."

She was teasing me since she already knew about my plans to go to journalism school at IU, move to New York City after graduation, land an internship on *The*

David Letterman Show, then eventually work my way up to write for *Saturday Night Live.*

I cringed, suddenly remembering that for some asinine reason, I'd blabbed those exact plans to Will tonight after he'd asked me to explain why I was so desperate to leave Cold Springs one day. Oh God. I'd only ever told Stacie and Karen about those stupid dreams of mine. Why in the hell had I blabbed them to Will when I barely even knew him? I was starting to wonder if Will laced his beer with some kind of truth serum or something. How else was he able to get so much information out of me?

I surveyed the room dreamily. The lines on the wood paneling waved back and forth making me feel kind of sick. I made a pillow out of my arms and rested my head on them like we used to do during indoor recess in elementary school. But when I closed my eyes, the waving feeling didn't go away. In fact, it only seemed to get worse.

"Had a few too many?" Karen asked. When I opened my eyes, she was looking straight at me. The glazed look was gone, and she was back in the dining room with me.

"Maybe just one too many," I admitted, dropping my head down again.

Karen punched me on the shoulder. "Hey wake up! Go get a glass of water. Take an aspirin. I need you!"

I groaned loudly, trying to act like she was a pain in my ass, secretly thrilled she needed me. It was weird to think I could be of value to anyone, other than just giving them a passing laugh.

As I slowly made my way into the kitchen, I thought of how nice it was that Karen wasn't lecturing me about drinking and staying out too late at night. It was the one good part of her being so young: unlike my mom, she still remembered what it was like to be my age.

I downed a few Tylenols, rummaged through the pantry for a snack, then came back to the table with a bowl of pretzels. I figured they'd be good for soaking up the extra beer in my stomach.

As I forced the food down, Karen started playing the song from the beginning, only the melody this time without any words. She tipped her head back and let her fingers fly over the strings, her pale green eyes narrowed in concentration.

The music was so light and soothing. It was surprisingly upbeat for a song about fighting battles and getting shrapnel to the heart and all those other horrible metaphors I'd written back when I was sure I'd never let myself care about anyone.

Now the guitar music lulled me back to the memories of the past few hours and I wondered if I'd already broken that promise to myself. As much as I hated to admit it, I already cared a lot about Will. How could I not when my body flooded itself with all kinds of delicious sensations whenever I was near him? Such excitement, such anticipation, such longing. All my obsessive thoughts were becoming harder and harder to control with every passing day. The more I tried to push them away, the bigger they seemed to get.

I wished I could ask my mom about the strange new emotions I was experiencing. She would know what was going on with me. She would probably tell me way more than I wanted to know since oversharing was her thing.

A classic example was when she gave me the birds and the bees talk when I was only eight. She couldn't just explain sex in general terms like everyone else's mom did. No, she had to make a big production out of it. She'd taken out her sketchbook and her Canon pencils and drawn beautiful, realistic pictures of a man and a woman to use as a reference; sketching and cross hatching and shading, creating such detail that the couple's anatomy took on an almost photographic quality. Then she'd droned on about what happened between a man and a woman during the act of sex, pointing and circling, drawing arrows up and down to show the correct placement and movement of each body part.

The only problem was I had been too young at the time to understand. When she finished, I sat there confused. "So, you and daddy only did that one time? To get me, right?"

She'd become flustered and said something about how men and women had sex not just for making babies, but because it felt good when they did it. That still hadn't cleared things up for me.

"It doesn't look like it feels good when the chickens do it," I'd said. "The rooster always grabs the back of the chicken's head and pulls her feathers out and she screeches like he's killing her or something."

That had cracked my mom up. She'd agreed with me about the scary chicken sex ritual, then explained humans took a lot more pleasure in each other's bodies than animals did.

Back then, I hadn't gotten the whole concept of "taking pleasure in each other's bodies." Now I understood it perfectly. I'd taken an overwhelming amount of pleasure in Will's body when I'd stared at him in the gym today. Was it normal to think of touching him as much as I did? Did that make me some kind of nymphomaniac or something? Did I need to be put on medication? Or given aversion therapy to snap myself out of this? I had no idea. How ironic that just when I finally understood what my mom was trying to tell me back then, she didn't have the time to sketch out those elaborate examples anymore.

I propped my chin on my fist and watched Karen play the melody over and over until I was so swept away that when a question bubbled into my tipsy mind I couldn't stop it from slipping out.

"It must have been hard for you and mom to get together, huh?"

At first, I thought Karen was so zoned out that she wasn't going to answer. Then she mumbled, "Yeah, I guess."

I should have just left it at that and yet another really important question kept nagging at m.

"Especially because of the difference in your age and all." I tried to sound casual although I didn't feel that way. My heart sped up as I waited. Karen's answer could change everything for me. At least in theory.

She shrugged, still staring down at her strings. "What about it?"

"Just… well… because you were so much younger than her and all."

"Yeah, so?"

"I was just wondering if it was a problem. I mean, do

you think age makes a difference in whether two people can be together?" I felt like Jack Klugman on the *Quincy M.E* show, trying to force a courtroom confession from an unwitting defendant. I just needed to hear the words out loud.

She answered so quickly it was clear she'd been posed the question a million times already. I guess when you're almost twenty years younger than the woman you're living with, you have your defense ready for interrogations like mine.

"No, I don't think age makes a difference at all," she said righteously. "What matters is how two people feel about each other. Sometimes that doesn't always follow the standards society says is right. That still doesn't mean there's anything wrong with it." She sounded like she was reading off a prepared statement.

"Of course. I agree with you totally." I kept my tone measured, fighting the urge to pump my fists in the air in victory. I rolled the words around in my head. *I don't think age makes a difference at all.* I filed the thrilling sentence away in the very unlikely chance I might need it for my own defense one day.

I was so bolstered by her unwitting support that I blurted out, "I'm sure it was the being a lesbian thing that was the hardest part."

This time Karen stopped playing and laid her hand flat against the strings to stop the reverberation. I could almost hear a needle scratch against an imaginary record in my head.

"Not that you had any choice in that part," I added quickly. "I know it's just who you are and all." I'd heard

Karen and her friends talk about it all the time. About how people treated them like they had a choice about being gay, when in fact they didn't. Still every time I heard them say that I was confused by one detail.

"Because you were born gay, right?" I asked her.

Karen and I both sat up taller in our seats and stared at each other. It wasn't typical for me to ask her a question like that outright. Karen and I talked all the time. We just didn't talk about serious stuff. We mostly just cracked jokes and made fun of TV commercials and reworked popular songs into crude ditties. We never talked about things that truly mattered.

"Yes, I was born gay."

"How did you know you were gay?" I couldn't believe how much I wanted to keep this conversation going.

She searched the air above my head, thinking. "Well, I didn't exactly know what it was at first. I just knew I was different. I didn't like the things my sisters did. Playing with dolls and wearing frilly dresses and doing my hair." She made a face as if the thoughts disgusted her.

"I know. I've seen the pictures," I said, laughing. Karen had a creased snapshot of her with her mom and two sisters lined up on Easter morning, all of them wearing matching pink dresses. Karen was on the end with her face screwed up so tightly it looked like she'd just been force fed a pile of dog shit right before they snapped the photograph.

"Yeah, I'm not a dress kind of girl," she said, motioning to her baggy cargo pants.

"So that's how you knew? You didn't like to dress up?" My mom told stories about me when I was little and how I never wanted to take off my green coveralls that matched my dad's. How I'd wear my cowboy boots with my shorts all summer long and refuse to brush my hair for weeks at a time. I sure as hell didn't enjoy dressing up either when I was a kid. In fact, I didn't like it all that much now, yet that didn't make me gay.

"When I got older, I had a terrible crush on my babysitter," Karen said. "She was my older sister's best friend. I knew it wasn't right, but I kept thinking about her in ways I wasn't supposed to."

I nodded. I knew all about thinking about people in ways I wasn't supposed to.

Karen went on. "It was a relief when I found out there is a name for what I am. That there are other people out there that feel the same way I do. It helped me to not feel like such a freak, you know? Even though my mom kept telling me I was."

She bowed her head over the strings again and plucked the top one with her thumb over and over. I felt bad for making her think about her family. I knew how much it hurt her. My mom and I were Karen's only family now because her real family had disowned her the day she moved in with us. Karen hadn't spoken to any of them in three years now. She'd chosen us over them. Technically, she'd chosen my mom over them, but I liked to think I was a tiny part of the deciding factor too.

Karen looked at where I was slumped on the table and smiled a devilish smile. "Why are you asking me about this? Do you think you're gay or something?"

I slapped both palms on the table. "No, I don't think I'm gay! God, Karen!"

She burst out laughing. It was the one subject she knew really got to me. She knew how sensitive I was about people thinking I was gay. I had to fight it all day long at school. I didn't want to have to do it at home too.

"I'm just kidding. Calm down," she said, trying to wrench her smile away.

"You know I don't think that's funny."

"Sorry. Sorry. Don't worry. No one thinks you're gay. My God, no red-blooded lesbian would ever lust over John Travolta as much as you do." She raised one unplucked eyebrow. "I mean, some red-blooded gay *guys* would for sure, but that's a different story."

We laughed together and I relaxed again. I wasn't sure why I'd brought up the subject in the first place. I had never, ever asked my mom or Karen about any of this stuff. But now that the proverbial floodgates were open, more questions began pouring through me.

"Do you think *all* gay people are born that way?"

Karen thought for a moment. "No, not everyone. I think there's a spectrum with varying degrees of tendencies. Some people are on one side. Some people on the other. Some people hang out in the middle somewhere. Like a dial on a radio or something."

I must have looked confused because she went on. "You know you can like both men and women, right? You don't have to choose."

"I know that," I huffed. "That's not really what I was asking though." I wished she would just read my mind so I wouldn't have to say it out loud.

She stared at me for a few seconds. Our brainwaves must have finally melded somewhere over the bowl of pretzels because she suddenly said, "Oh! You want to know if I think *your mom* was born gay?"

I shrugged and tried to pretend that question had just come to me instead of being trapped inside me for years now.

"I was just wondering," I started slowly. "Because she was married for a long time. And she had me. And she didn't seem to ever be that way before."

Karen watched me. It seemed like she wanted to be careful to pick just the right words. There was something tender in her eyes I was seeing for the first time. Something that made me wish I'd asked her these questions a long time ago.

"I think sometimes people just fall in love with other *people*, you know? Despite what form that person takes," she said. "You fall in love with what's inside a person. And, as I said before, sometimes that love doesn't follow the rules that other people believe are right. But that doesn't mean you have to listen to them."

I nodded. I understood feelings that didn't follow rules. I was pretty sure my feelings were card-carrying anarchists based on what had been going on inside my head lately. The way I kept thinking about Will was definitely not right at all.

"So as far as your mom goes, no, I don't think she was born gay. I don't think she set out to have a relationship with another woman. But I do think she was smart enough to understand what she was feeling when we met and not put boundaries on those feelings just because it didn't match what the rest of the world had deemed as acceptable."

I rolled my bottom lip between my teeth. Bit on it as I consider what she'd just told me.

"Do you get it?" she asked after a while.

"Yeah. I guess."

"Attraction all starts here," Karen said, pointing to her heart. "Not here." She tapped her head.

Something in her words struck home. "So it's something you *feel* more than you can explain with words?" Once again, I thought of my *Feel Good* pin.

"Yeah, I guess that's what I'm saying." She seemed kind of unsure, which wasn't normal for her. "You really should ask your mom all these questions. She's the professional. She'd love to be talking to you about all of this."

Karen was right. My mom would've loved to have known everything I was currently thinking. Which was why I couldn't give her the satisfaction of having a truthful conversation like this with her. She had to pay some kind of price for disrupting my life the way she had.

When I ignored Karen, she pressed further. "Why are you asking about all this relationship stuff anyway? Is there someone you're interested in?" Her eyes went wide. "Do you have a crush on a boy or something?!"

"No, of course not," I shot back. There was no way I'd ever admit the truth to Karen. She would have teased me mercilessly if she knew I cared about anyone, much less someone as off-limits as Will. "You were making me write that stupid song about love and all that shit. It just got me thinking."

She looked at me suspiciously. I'd probably gone too far, tipped my hand too much, asking about the age difference thing. I needed to reel myself in now.

"I'm more just curious about that stuff for the future," I went on. "Like a *looong* time from now."

"Right." She didn't seem too convinced. One of the drawbacks of us spending so much time together was that Karen always knew when I was lying.

"Plus, I thought it was pretty clear from what I wrote in that song, that love stuff creeps me out. I'm staying as far away from it as possible."

She looked down at her notepad. "Yeah, you do have some pretty rough imagery here. Battlefield. Mines. Shrapnel."

"See? To me, love is horrible bloody carnage!"

She laughed, her eyes squinting to thin slits. "As you so eloquently described it!"

I wanted her to keep laughing, so I milked it more. "Jesus Christ, why the hell would anyone do that to themselves?" I pointed at the lines on the page. "That's true masochism if you ask me!"

She nodded. "You're right. Love can be awfully painful sometimes." Her expression glazed over again like she'd slipped into another world.

Enough seconds ticked by that I thought the conversation had ended. I stood to leave, hoping I could get away before I incriminated myself any further. Just as I got to the door to the hallway Karen called out to me.

"You know what though?"

When I turned back, I was shocked by the seriousness in her eyes. "Most of the time love isn't horrible bloody carnage," she said with a wistful smile. "In fact, most of the time it's the best damn feeling in the world."

CHAPTER SIXTEEN

HEART TO HEART

THE NEXT NIGHT a knock came at my bedroom door.

My mom peeked her head inside. "Can I come in?"

"Oh. You're home already?" I sat up in my bed and slammed my journal closed. I'd been writing about my time in the car with Will. Mrs. Anderson taught us that if you free-write without editing or thinking too much about your words, sometimes a truth comes up and surprises you; helps you make sense about a subject you need to clarify. So far, seeing all my mixed-up feelings about Will written out in black and white had only made me even more confused.

Mom walked to the edge of my bed. "My last client cancelled, so I got to come home early." As she got closer, I kept my head down, sure she'd take one look at my face and instantly read my mind about all I'd just written.

She pointed at my journal and pen. "You're writing I see."

I started to say, "No shit, Sherlock!" but stopped myself at the last minute.

"Doing a writing assignment for class," I lied.

"I'm so glad you're still enjoying it," she said. "Remember when I went to my medium and she told me my daughter was going to be a wordsmith?"

"Yeah, I know," I rolled my eyes. "You've told me a hundred times."

She tipped her head at me, looking hurt. "I thought you loved that story?"

"Back when I was a little girl. Not anymore."

I used to beg her to tell the story of the medium's prophecy. Now I could tell she was only using it to soften me up, to convince me we were still close when, in fact, we were a million miles apart.

"It's true what she said, you know," Mom plowed on, undeterred. "The way you wrote so many stories when you were little was quite extraordinary. Let's see, what were some of them? I remember one called *Legends of Secret Horse City* and wasn't one *The White Stallion of Zanzibar*?"

"Yeah, and *Black Beauty Comes to America*. I was a little enmeshed in the equine adventure genre in elementary school."

She stared dreamily past me at the huge rainbow poster hanging above my bed. It matched my rainbow curtains, which matched my rainbow bedspread, which matched my rainbow pillowcases, which matched my rainbow rug. Karen and her friends helped me pick out the decor when we moved in, never once mentioning to naïve twelve-year-old me that rainbows might have another symbolism I didn't understand at the time. No wonder they'd kept laughing and elbowing each other as we'd shopped. It was just another example of how clueless I'd been when I was younger.

"You were always reading, always writing when we lived on the farm," Mom said. "I remember us walking through the fields and you saying, 'I'm writing a book in my head right now, Mommy. Everywhere I go. I don't feel like I'm living my life. I feel like I'm narrating it.' Narrating! Can you believe you used that word?"

"Again, I've heard that story a hundred times too."

"You were so advanced for your age."

"Yeah. I was a real savant back in the day," I said flatly.

Although it was normal for her to tell stories about me being a precocious child, this time they seemed stilted. Like she'd stood behind the door before she walked in and planned each of them in order, all part of her carefully crafted opening remarks.

"I was so proud of how creative you were. And I still am. You're such a brilliant girl!"

"Right. I'm so amazing. Woo hoo!" I did a half-assed fist pump. My mom was completely delusional when it came to me. She thought I was the smartest, kindest, most beautiful girl that had ever walked the earth. Which was so obviously untrue I couldn't trust one word that came out of her mouth anymore.

She pulled the chair out from my desk and swiveled it around to sit right next to my bed. In our farmhouse, my room was so big I could do three cartwheels across it. This shit-hole house was so small there was barely enough space in my room for a dresser, a desk, and a twin bed.

"So, how are you doing?" She patted my leg under the covers.

Her voice was light. Too light, in fact. Karen must have told her how I was grilling her last night.

"I'm fine."

"What's going on with you lately?"

"Um.... nothing I can think of."

She sighed, most likely mentally flipping to another chapter from her Adolescent Psychotherapy textbook. After a few seconds of deliberation, she came at me with a different approach.

"How's school going?"

I broke into a smile, delighting in her mistake. She'd slipped and asked a close-ended question, the ultimate no-no for therapists. Man, she was off her game tonight.

"Fine," I countered, shutting her down easily.

Again, she hesitated. She was probably using the time to recall her training on how to deal with difficult patients.

"Have you been having fun?" she asked. Ah ha! Now she was rallying. Trotting out one of her standard lines. Mom thought the key to life was learning how to make everything fun along the way. She was such an out-of-touch hippie.

"Fun?!" I asked incredulously.

"Yeah. Are you enjoying yourself at school? Learning new things? Expanding your horizons?" Mom never asked me about my actual letter grades. She thought grades were completely irrelevant, invented by the hierarchy to judge and divide people instead of bringing them together as equals, the way we were all supposed to be in her Kumbaya world.

"Oh yeah, it's a blast being a high school sophomore! I love getting up at 6:00, sitting at a desk all day, eating shitty lunches, then coming home to do homework half the night. My sides hurt from laughing so much!"

She shook her head. "I blame Karen for all this sarcasm. You never used to be like this."

"I was always like this. Karen just taught me how to express myself more."

She tried to hide her exasperation. "So, school isn't going well?" She slipped into her sickly smooth therapist voice, which made me want to reach up and shake her shoulders until all her practiced patience ran out and she became my plain old mom again.

"It's fine." I kept reminding myself to be careful and not let her weasel her way any closer. She had a magical way of making people pour their hearts out to her. Ever since I could remember, no matter where we were (at the feed store or the gas station or the grocery store), she would somehow end up in a deep meaningful conversation with whatever farmer or trucker or housewife she happened to bump into. After only ten minutes of talking to my mom, some poor grizzled guy in overalls would tell her how he and his wife fought over who did the dishes at night. Or how his 89-year-old mom had just been diagnosed with cancer. Or how he sensed there was something missing in his life. Something he knew he wanted but hadn't quite put his finger on yet.

Mom would listen. Ask some questions, then listen

some more. Not only listen but be genuinely interested in his response. I guess that's what drew people to her. The way she always made whoever she was with feel like they were the most important person in the world. She used to make me feel that way too before Karen became the most important person in her life and I became a meager second place.

"So school is fine, but it could be better?" she pushed.

"It's school, Mom! It's not meant to be good. In fact, the dictionary synonym for school is prison. There's not much anyone can do about that."

I hated myself for being so mean to her. But if I didn't keep a wall between us I might break down and tell her about everything worrying me. About Will and how I couldn't control all my looping thoughts about him. And how I had to go along with whatever Jimmy wanted so I wouldn't piss him off. And how vigilant I had to stay at school to keep people from making fun of me because of her and Karen.

"So, are you sure there's nothing you want to talk to me about, honey?" she asked.

"I can't think of anything." I said, gritting my teeth.

"Nothing you've been curious about?"

Oh, Karen had definitely told her about last night.

"Nope. Nothing at all."

"Oh. Okay." She picked at a string on my bed-spread. She was obviously trying to decide whether to throw Karen under the bus and confess everything she knew about my questions.

"I guess I'll leave you alone," she said, standing up. She must have gotten to the chapter in the textbook that said not to push the patient if they weren't ready to talk yet. "If you do ever have anything you want to chat about, I'm here. Remember that." She looked down on me with so much sadness in her eyes, I would've had to have been Charles Manson not to feel sorry for her.

"I will," I relented a bit. "I mean, you usually know what to say to make me feel better."

She smiled and I continued. "But if you ever pull the whole 'and how does that make you feel' shit on me, I'm out!"

She laughed. The gesture smoothed her cheeks, made her look a little less tired than usual. "It's a deal."

I could tell she didn't want to leave. The Stones sang softly from the boom box next to my bed, telling Ruby Tuesday how much they'd miss her when she was gone.

"Oh hey, I almost forgot!" Her eyebrows shot up. She reached into the pocket of her sweater and handed me a tiny metal pin. It matched my *If It Feels Good Do It* pin, except the words were in red and right in the middle was a cartoon of a floppy-eared dog scratching himself. The blissful expression on the dog's face cracked me up.

"That's awesome!" I sat up in my bed and took the pin from her.

"See, I told you I had one too."

"Cool!" I rubbed my hand over the shiny surface, flipped it around where rust mottled the metal on the back. "This thing is really old, huh?"

"I guess it's kind of an antique. Just like me!"

"Neat." I tried to hand the button back to her, but she pushed it away.

"Oh, you can keep it if you want. You said you were going to give the other one to Stacie."

I'd forgotten about my lie. "Oh, actually I decided to keep it." I pointed to where my pin sat at the edge of my desk. Since it was too embarrassing to wear in public, I carried it in my pocket every day. I didn't want anyone to see the motto and question me about the outlandish idea.

"So, I don't need yours." I handed the pin back to her again.

She begrudgingly took it back. "Alright. If you don't want it."

Seeing her face made me hate myself all over again. Why couldn't I just be nice to her? She was making such an effort to reach out to me.

"Do you think that motto works?" I asked, hoping she'd accept my olive branch.

"Oh yes. As I said before, you have feelings for a reason."

"You said they help you make choices, right?" I repeated what she'd told me the day in the park when I'd first shown her the pin.

"They do. I often say your emotions are your guidance system. They're there to help you gauge whether you're going toward or away from the things you truly want, deep down inside."

Deep down inside? You mean the place I'm too scared to even admit exists?

She went on. "The problem is, most people don't let themselves fully feel their emotions. You know, really feel them in their bodies." She scrunched up her face as if she were demonstrating the process. "And if you don't take the time to stop and identify how you feel, you have no data to help you make decisions."

I let her words roll around in my mind. In the past, I'd genuinely enjoyed our mother-daughter talks about deep philosophical stuff. She had cobbled together such interesting theories about life based on all the psychology, New Age, and ancient western religion books she read. Where the ideas originated from didn't matter. She absorbed whatever resonated with her. (That was the word she used: resonated. As if she were a bell or something.) Then she blended all those beliefs into her own kind of philosophy. One I assumed her clients must've resonated with too, based on how busy she'd been lately.

"You have to figure out what you're feeling first?" I asked.

"Yes, it's crucial," she said, more serious now. "Because so many times people plow ahead and make choices based on what other people think is right, not on what they themselves feel deep down inside. The sad truth is, the majority of people are very detached from their own emotions. I try to teach them ways to get in touch with them again."

I considered her concept. "Detached, huh?" I remembered Scott making fun of me in the library. Laughing about me being the Tin Man who didn't have a heart. I prided myself on tricking everyone into believing I didn't care about anyone or anything. But it was becoming more and more difficult to keep up that charade.

"I can show you what I mean if you want," she said, sitting back down beside me. "I do this simple process to help people get in touch with their feelings. Do you want to try?"

Normally, I would've gone on a tirade about her not treating me like one of her clients. (It was my standard defense tactic when she pushed me to talk about anything important.) Yet her invitation piqued my curiosity. Maybe her crazy process could help me figure out what I should do next.

"I guess it wouldn't hurt to try," I said, pretending to be disinterested.

"Great!" She clapped her hands together. Seeing my expression, she tamped her enthusiasm down a little. "I mean, this is all up to you. We'll just do a few basics."

I shrugged. "Whatever you want. Doesn't matter to me."

"Alright. Close your eyes and take a deep breath. Then tell me how you're feeling right now."

I did what she asked and right away, the feelings I'd had when I was writing in my journal about Will popped to the surface again.

"I feel nervous," I blurted out.

"Wow. That was awfully quick. Are you sure?"

"It wasn't hard to identify. I feel that way a lot lately."

"Well... um." Even with my eyes closed, I could tell I'd upset her. "I know you had anxiety problems when you were little, but I thought you were better now."

"Nope. Not better. Just better at hiding it."

She didn't speak for a few seconds. I could tell it was killing her not to pry deeper into the subject, but luckily, she stuck with her plan.

"Alright." She cleared her throat, starting over again. "Tell me how that feels."

"I told you already. It feels like being nervous!"

"I want you to dig a little deeper. Tell me how being nervous feels to you." Her therapist's voice was back. I had to admit, it was awfully soothing. "Take a deep breath and feel it in your body. Use descriptive words to make it more vivid. Don't just name it with the word *nervous*."

I waited a few seconds to respond, trying to do what she'd asked of me. "Ummm. There's this kind of sick feeling in my stomach..." I started slowly.

"Good. What else?"

I took another deep breath. It was difficult to come up with other words. I was always too busy fighting against my crazy thoughts to notice how they felt in a flesh-and-blood way.

"There's this kind of jittery feeling just under my skin. And I feel tense," I went on, noticing the feel of my fingernails digging into the soft part of my palms. "My muscles are all clenched up." I opened my mouth and moved my jaw back and forth. The relief was instantaneous. Why hadn't I thought to do that before?

"Really, really good," Mom said. "Sick, jittery, tense, clenched up. That's how nervousness feels to you?"

"Uh huh."

"Now I want you to just sink into that feeling. Don't try to force it away. Just notice it. Accept it. Don't be afraid of it."

I opened my eyes just so I could roll them at her.

"Why would I be afraid of a feeling? It's not like it's the boogeyman or something."

"Oh, you'd be surprised," she said with a knowing smile. "Feelings are pretty much the only thing people are afraid of."

I tipped my head at her, confused. I'd have to dissect the sentence later when I was alone again. There was something inside it that resonated with me (gag!), but I wasn't quite sure why.

"Now close your eyes again," Mom said. "Good. I want you to think of something that makes you feel good. Something easy and simple that you know will make you feel happy. For example, sometimes people think of petting puppies or walking in the forest or —"

"Oh God," I mumbled, "please don't say rainbows."

"I wasn't going to say rainbows," she huffed. But when I opened one eye to peek at her, she was staring at my rainbow poster, looking a little sheepish. "It has to be something you choose. Something that works for you. Maybe that funny samurai guy you and Karen like on that *Saturday Evening* show...."

"Mom! He's not just a funny samurai guy!" I erupted. "He's John Belushi!"

"Well honey, you know I'm bad at names."

"And it's not the *Saturday Evening* show, it's *Saturday Night Live*. Everyone knows that!"

"Well, *Saturday Night*, *Saturday Evening*, whatever it's called, it doesn't matter."

"Okay, now I have to change my answer. Now I'm not nervous. Now I'm angry. Good work, Mom!"

"Now, stop," she scolded in what was clearly not her

standard therapist's voice. I smiled to myself; proud I'd made her lose her cool.

"Can we please get back to your good-feeling thoughts?" she asked.

"Fine." I took a few deep breaths, then let my mind drift to the one image I knew for sure would send me soaring into my own little orbit of happiness.

It was of Will turning to me in the car, the waves of his black hair illuminated in the dashboard lights, his baby blue eyes boring into mine as he said, "You're smart, you're pretty and you're fucking funny as hell." I took a deep breath and let the snippet play over and over in my head. *"You're smart, you're pretty, and you're fucking funny as hell.... You're smart, you're pretty, and you're fucking funny as hell..."*

I chanted the words, focusing on the lovely image of his smiling face, until I felt like I was back in the car beside him and not still in my bed.

"Do you have your soothing thought?" Mom startled me back to reality.

"Uh, huh."

"Describe how you feel now."

"Um... I feel really light. As if my entire body is floating a bit. And my chest has this kind of achy feeling in it. But it's a good kind of achy feeling," I qualified, trying to think of a better way to describe it. "Like it's being stretched open a little, which actually feels quite pleasant." I decided not to mention the other pleasant sensation pulsing between my legs.

"That's perfect."

"And my throat." I pointed to my neck. "It feels

kind of bubbly. Like I just drank some Coke, or I want to giggle or something." And then I did just that.

"I want you to remember that feeling. Ingrain the sensations in your mind. When you find that good-feeling place, then that's when you want to make your decisions. From the place where you feel open and clear about what you honestly want before you take action."

"Okay," I mumbled.

"That's why that motto from your pin works. Because when you feel good first, *then* you do it, it means you're following the path that's right for you."

"I get what you're saying," I said, thinking back on how good I'd felt when I'd said yes to Will after he asked me to join The Ride. If what my mom was saying was true, I'd done the right thing in agreeing to Will's offer last night. It meant I was right to keep spending so much time with him.

"Let's practice some decision making," she said. "From this place you're in right now, what do you feel like doing next? What impulses are coming to you?"

"I just want to lie here and rest," I mumbled.

"Then that's what you should do!" she said, as if it could be that simple.

My eyes flew open. "I can't. I still have homework to do." My body tensed thinking of all the things I still had to finish. The change was so jarring it physically hurt. I couldn't believe how much more noticeable the tired, achy feelings in my body were compared against all the delicious sensations I'd just conjured for myself.

"How did you feel when you had the thought about resting?"

My head flopped dreamily to the side of my pillow as I relaxed again. "So relieved."

She smiled big, looking proud. I guess I must've been doing well at the lesson.

I blinked up at her as a new realization popped into my head. "Actually, I could finish my homework in the morning. I forgot I have Study Hall first period. Geez, why didn't I remember that earlier?"

"Because when you're all tight and nervous, it's difficult for you to hear your guidance. But when you relax and open yourself up, even if it's just for a few minutes, you allow all kinds of new information to flow to you."

I rolled my eyes. "You're getting all freaky and New Age on me again."

"It's not just New Age people who use this. Athletes utilize this technique all the time. They call it getting in the zone. They open up, stop thinking so much, and get grounded in their bodies. It calms their nervous system so they can tap into their instincts and follow their guidance on what to do next. And from that place, they're able to do incredible things."

I nodded, thinking of the dreamy state I slipped into before I did a gymnastics trick. A place where the world fell away and there was nothing left but just me, my body, and my single-minded goal. Maybe I could use the same technique on Will; make kissing him my single-minded goal. Now that was a trick I really wanted to land.

I smiled at her. "I enjoyed that exercise," I admitted. My arms still felt like they were floating up in the air instead of resting on the covers beside me.

"See how powerful that can be?" she said. "Getting back in touch with yourself is something you can work on every day. Just small simple steps. Taking the time to stop and ask yourself how you feel in a moment. Identifying which emotion you're feeling before you act. If you're scared, nervous, worried about what other people think about you, then your guidance is clouded. And that's when you get confused and make decisions that aren't right for you."

"Oh, I know all about being confused," I mumbled softly, not wanting to return to reality just yet.

"You do? Well, do you want to talk about —"

"Mom, can you go now?" I interrupted her.

She looked hurt but nodded like she understood. She gave me a kiss on the forehead and told me good night before she left. As she slipped away, I felt guilty for sending her away so abruptly, but there was only so much emotional honesty I could handle in one day. She'd said it herself: *small simple steps.* After all we'd been through over the past few years, she and I were going to need a whole hell of a lot of those small steps to ever get back to the place we used to be.

CHAPTER SEVENTEEN

RULES OF THE RIDE

THE NEXT MONTH whirled by in a tornado of Stones
music, cold beers, and deserted gravel roads.

Now that I was a part of The Ride, everything had
changed. Before I met Will, my life was one big, nebulous
cloud of uncertainty. What would I do on the weekend?
Could I find a party? If I found a party, how would I get
there? If I got there, would I even be welcome inside?
But with Will next to me, all those worries disappeared.

Now my weekends had structure, a schedule, times
to meet and places to go. Now my weekends had rules.
And although it didn't surprise me how many rules Will
enforced (he was a leader after all and leaders always
had expectations for their followers), what *did* surprise
me was how much I liked them.

First Rule of The Ride: Be at Pizza King by 9:30!

Will would pull in front of the restaurant, select the people he deemed "Ride-worthy", then grant them access to his privileged vehicle. Rob was almost always in attendance, but Scott and Stacie and a few of Will's high school friends rotated in and out based on their availability each night.

Will allowed variations in the group. Except for me. I had committed to The Ride and that meant he expected me to always be waiting for him. (An expectation I had no problem fulfilling.) In fact, I loved that he'd added that caveat to his rule; loved that I was the only person on The Ride who wasn't optional to him.

Second Rule of The Ride: Red always sits up front!

Most of the time, I perched on the console, Rob commandeered the passenger seat, and other members were relegated to the back. Scott hated that rule, especially on the nights when the numbers didn't fall in his favor and he got stuck in the back seat all alone. He'd whine for me to sit in the back with him, but Will never allowed me to leave the front seat.

"The system breaks down if everyone doesn't do their job!" Will would bark in his platoon-leader way.

The only time Scott ever got to sit up front was when Stacie came along and Rob gave up his seat to sit in the back with her. Stacie and Rob always had such a great time together. They'd laugh and talk about school and politics and movies. But no matter how hard I tried to get Stacie to see Rob as more than just a friend, she stubbornly refused to shift her romantic sights off stupid Mark.

It was no secret Will spent the first part of the night with his girlfriend, Penny, but she never joined us on The Ride. Her exclusion seemed strange to me, but I sure as hell wasn't going to complain about it. At first, I couldn't figure out why I was there when she wasn't; why Will had picked me out of all the girls who would've clamored to be by his side. Yet as time passed, his reasons became clearer.

Third Rule of The Ride: Do your job!

Thank God, my job was easy. I was Will's trusty assistant. He didn't call me a groupie anymore since he knew I hated that term. However, he did still call me Marianne from time to time, which wasn't as annoying. (I could get onboard with being a muse. That sounded kind of romantic to me.)

My primary duties consisted of handing Will beers whenever he called for them and finding whatever cassette he wanted to play next.

"I think it's time for some *Beggar's Banquet*," Will would say, sending me rummaging through the storage box until I found the right tape. I'd slap the cassette into his outstretched hand like a nurse handing a surgeon a scalpel. At first I didn't have all the track numbers memorized like he did, but each weekend I got better at anticipating which song he wanted.

We eventually turned my duties into a game. He'd name an album, and I'd guess what track he wanted.

When he asked for the *Get Your Ya Ya's Out* cassette I'd say, "You're thinking a little 'Honky Tonk Women'?" When he asked for *Some Girls* I'd guess, "You want to hear 'Beast of Burden'?" I quickly learned he played songs that matched his mood, and it didn't take long before I became as much of an expert on his emotions as I was the music.

Once I'd made my guess about what song he wanted, he always answered the same way: "How did you know, Red?" Either I was really good at the game, or he liked to let me think I was.

My other job on The Ride was to make Will laugh. If our story had been set in medieval times, I would've definitely been Will's court jester. It was an easy role for me because Will seemed to think everything that came out of my mouth was hilarious. He especially loved when I told funny stories about myself. The more outlandish or risqué the story, the harder he'd laugh.

I told him about the time I'd streaked across the lawn playing Truth or Dare at Stacie's house. How I pissed on a fire to put it out at Girl Scout camp. About the time I crashed into the crowd during a tumbling run at a gymnastic meet and ended up crushing some poor old man's glasses.

I'm not sure why I told Will all the embarrassing stuff I'd done. I probably should have painted myself in a more flattering light. Pretended to be a sophisticated woman with a worldliness that defied her mere fifteen years instead of the bumbling idiot I truly was. But that was the effect Will had on me. He kept laughing and I kept blabbing. It seemed to work for both of us. For a few hours a week he got to be happy, and I got to believe I was the most interesting girl in the world.

Fourth Rule of The Ride (the only one I didn't like):
You're on your own at parties!

I hated how Will ditched us once we got to a party. He'd always migrate to a group of older kids I didn't know. While I'd wander around aimlessly, pretending I was having the most fabulous time of my life when all I really wanted was to be back in the car next to him.

At the parties, Will flirted with a lot of girls, exactly the way Scott had warned me he would. Girls circled around him, laughing too hard at his jokes (which I knew was fake because Will wasn't that funny), touching his arm, fixing their hair when they thought he wasn't looking.

I'd stand across the fire and secretly eavesdrop on Will and his latest round of admirers. His conversations always progressed the same way: He'd quote a bunch of weird Stones lyrics (like asking some poor blonde if her mom was a "tent show queen" or if she thought she'd ever be someone's "beast of burden" or if she liked to get "whipped just around midnight".) Then the girl would get flustered by his gibberish and try to respond appropriately. *Is a beast of burden a donkey? Because I really love donkeys!* Invariable, whatever girl he toyed with ended up making a complete fool of herself.

At that point, Will would catch my eye across the fire and wink, bringing me in on his private joke. My skin would burn, not from the heat of the flames, but from knowing Will and I now had a secret language. A language forged of Rolling Stones song lyrics that only he and I understood.

At first, I worried that I'd be forced to see Will with another girl. That I'd have to feel the sick envy of watching him run his hand along a girl's cheek, bend to kiss her like I so badly wanted him to kiss me. But over time, I learned that wasn't a risk. Although Will flirted mercilessly, he never went any further. He always carefully extricated himself from any girl that leaned into him a few too many times; always gave a slick excuse for why he couldn't go out back so they could be alone like she wanted.

Of course, I held on to the futile hope that one day Will would see me as more than just a mascot he dragged around to make his fictional "last tour" seem more legit. But that dream became even more hopeless at a party one night when one of the prettiest girls I'd ever seen practically threw herself at his feet. He'd expertly slipped out of her grip, then quickly rounded up the members of The Ride, telling us it was time to leave.

When Scott questioned Will about the incident as we roared away, the answer he gave made his perception of me crystal clear.

"Man, Renee wanted you bad tonight, Will," Scott slurred from the backseat. "Why didn't you take her up on her offer? I would've hit that for sure."

I glared at Scott. Not only because he wasn't supposed to be drinking, but because he shouldn't have been talking about "hitting" on any girl now that he and Holly had been on two dates.

Will stared at Scott in the rearview mirror. "Wouldn't have been worth it. Penny has spies everywhere."

At first, I let the comment slip by with barely a second thought. But later I realized what the implications of that statement really meant for me. Will was so careful about not letting the girls at the party touch him for fear of Penny's wrath and yet he drove around with me pressed into his side every weekend for all the world to see. That meant to him I wasn't even in the same category as those other girls at the party. In fact, I was starting to wonder if Will even saw me as a girl at all. To him I was just funny Red, little sophomore Red, get-me-a-beer-Red. Too young, too childish, for his girlfriend to even consider me a threat.

CHAPTER EIGHTEEN

"GIMME SHELTER"

"Okay." Will took his hands off the steering wheel and rubbed them together like he was about to sit down to a delicious meal. "Time for the song!"

We'd dropped off Rob, so we were alone. It was the way things always went for us now. At the end of the night, once everyone else on The Ride had left, we'd spend our last hours talking about whatever song Will had assigned me the previous weekend.

He seemed to have a structured coursework prepared for me, but so far his choices had been so random I couldn't figure out his pattern. We'd fluctuated through a few Stones classics from the sixties, some obscure B sides from their more recent releases, a plaintive ballad, and some guitar-screeching rock songs.

Will curated playlists for me, scribbling song titles on the back of gas station receipts and college reading lists, always making me swear to only listen to the songs in the order he'd written them. He'd send me home with an armload of cassettes and make me promise to return them the next weekend. He claimed the playlists were important because he needed to set the mood for me, so I had the right context for the song we were about to discuss. (Although I was starting to wonder if the lessons Will taught were more his own interpretations of the lyrics rather than what Mick and Keith intended when they had written them.) But that didn't bother me much because, as my mom always said, "Every person is allowed to interpret art in their own unique way. That's what makes it so special."

Will assigned the tracks based on whatever theme he wanted to talk about that night. What a person would risk for love. What fate had to do with life's outcome. If fame and riches truly made you a success.

Of course, those themes couldn't be superficial or easy, the way I'd hoped when I first signed up for this. It was Will after all. I should have known nothing with him was ever going to be easy.

Tonight's pick was "Gimme Shelter", the song he said had started him on his Rolling Stones obsession.

"You got it yet?" He tapped his thumb on the steering wheel, watching me dig through his cassettes.

"I got it, I got it." I held up the plastic case. "Patience is a virtue, you know."

"Yeah, well, not one of mine," he said flatly.

Of course, I knew that already. If I was being polite, I would've called Will's energy "a bit excessive." But if I was being really truthful, I would've described it as "extremely intense most of the time."

Over the weeks, I'd begun to notice he was rarely ever completely still. He was always jiggling his leg, tapping his class ring on the steering wheel, breaking out in wild air drum solos, or compulsively searching his cassettes for the next song.

His nerves seemed the most frayed when he first picked me up at Pizza King each night. But as the hours wore on, and we listened to the music and talked, he relaxed and became a softer, more peaceful version of himself. I liked to believe I had that calming effect on him, but I knew that was probably only me getting my hopes up again.

Now, I slipped the cassette he'd asked for in the tape deck. A few seconds later, a set of eerie voices floated through the speakers, making the car feel like it had suddenly become haunted.

"Man, this part scared me at first," I told Will, peering out at the blackness flying past the car window. We were so far out of town there wasn't a streetlamp or porch light in sight. "I had to get up and shut the curtains in my bedroom when it started playing I was so creeped out!"

Will liked me to begin our lessons by telling him my first impression of a song. He said it gave him a starting point to work off, so he could judge how much I'd learned after he'd finished.

I tried not to laugh at how seriously he took my education. I knew it would hurt him if I made fun of how diligently he planned our nights together. Besides, I kind of liked how much effort he put into me.

He seemed pleased with my interpretation. "Yeah,

that's why I love it so much. It gets you in a certain mood right away. Just grabs you by the throat and drops you in. There's no getting away from it."

I nodded, agreeing with him like always.

After the ghoulish introduction, the song changed abruptly, an upbeat guitar chiming in, Mick singing about a storm threatening his life tonight.

Will and I sang together, the guitar plucking cheerfully now, a maraca shaking jauntily behind the beat, calming my fears the same way it had when I'd listened to the track in my bedroom. As the song progressed, a woman with a booming gospel vibrato joined Mick, the two of them singing together with such raging conviction it felt like their voices alone could've incited the lowliest servant to stand up and lead a revolution. They screamed about an upcoming war over and over, building the song to a fervent battle cry. As the notes faded away, it was like I'd been converted to something, although I wasn't quite sure what it was.

Will rewound the song, pushed *Play* again, but lowered the volume this time so he could talk over the sound. This was the part of the night when his teaching began in earnest.

"So, everything started with this song," he said, as if he were stepping to a podium in a college classroom. "When I was a freshman we had a student teacher from IU. He wanted to be a coach, so he helped my dad with the team. One of his ideas was to play this for us at the end of practice. It might have been a joke at first, you know? With the whole 'just a shot away' part? Get it? *Shot.* Like shooting a basketball?"

I nodded to show I understood but said nothing more. Discussion wasn't allowed until the end of the lecture.

He stared out the windshield wistfully. "Man, I loved that guy. It was great to have someone there to buffer my dad. He can be a bit intense at times. I mean, he's like that with everyone. But he's even harder on me..." He trailed off, even though it seemed like he wanted to say more.

It was well known around town that Coach was a hard ass with his team. He screamed and yelled and got so red in the face that you were sure he was going to have a heart attack over something as stupid as a referee calling his guard for a traveling foul. His practices were closed to outsiders, so no one really knew what went on in there, but there were lots of rumors about it. Supposedly, he hurled balls at the heads of kids who missed shots. And sometimes he assigned so many laps that new recruits collapsed and had to be dragged off the court until they either got up or quit. And if he was that rough on other people's kids, I could only imagine what he inflicted on his own son.

"So anyway," Will went on, "the student teacher guy would blast this song as we practiced our free throws. He was trying to distract us, make us learn how to concentrate around the noise and confusion and stuff. My dad liked his tactics, so he brought in these huge speakers to make it even more intense. Over time, I got used to hearing this song when I shot free throws. Eventually, when I was in a game, with the crowd screaming and trying to distract me, I could make myself hear the words in my head." He sang a few lines of the song as an example. "It would calm me down. Help everything else fade into the background. You get it?" He looked over at me, eyebrows raised, as if I knew exactly what it felt like to be at a free throw line with a crowd screaming at me.

I nodded, more to make him keep talking than in agreement. "Everything would get still inside me, and I would sink the shots." He let go of the steering wheel and shot an imaginary ball through the air, as the car plummeted down the straightaway like an arrow in flight. "*Swish... swish... swish*. I'd never miss. I was that good, Red. Which you might know if you'd ever come to any of my games."

I rolled my eyes. "I told you I was at some of them. I just didn't know it was you out there." I didn't mention that when he was a senior, I was only in seventh grade. And that, at the time, the candy they sold at the concession stand was more interesting to me than what was happening on the court.

"Yeah, well. Excuses, excuses." He winked to let me know he was only teasing. My stomach fluttered like a million butterflies were swarming inside. He always looked so sexy when he did little flirtatious things like that. I wanted so badly to reach out and casually lace my fingers through his, pull his hand over the console and press it right between my....

"I was a 75% free throw shooter," he went on, jarring me out of my fantasy. "And a guard too, so it was perfect. They'd inbound the ball to me, and I'd bring it up the floor. All those games when it was close at the end and the other team needed to get the possession back, I'd hold the ball, and they'd have to foul me. Which they didn't want to do because they knew how good I was. And there I'd be... *swish, swish, swish.* Racking up the score again." His eyes went soft like he was a million miles away, his toes lined up along the white stripe on a shiny gym floor.

He glanced over and tapped his temple, a wave of black hair spilling over his forehead. "That's the power of your mind. The power of focusing on what you want, to the exclusion of everything else."

I looked away, hoping he couldn't see that the only thing I wanted without exclusion was him.

He kept the volume down and said nothing more. That meant the floor was now open for remarks. Not knowing Will's story, I'd prepared my notes to address how the song became an anthem to protest the Vietnam war. (A fact I'd discreetly weaseled out of Karen under the guise of having to write a paper about the turmoil of the seventies for school.) As we discussed the lyrics' finer points, I pushed against some of Will's ideas. Not because I felt strongly one way or another, but because I knew Will liked the thrill of a good argument.

"So that's why you have to stand up for what's right," he told me after he'd explained the backlash the band faced after they'd released the apocalyptic song. "Always speak up. Always fight for what you think is right."

"Fighting's not really my forte."

"You don't have to have to fight with your fists.

You could do what the Stones did back then. Protest, or write something that tells everyone your beliefs."

"Yeah, I guess writing might be more my speed," I mumbled to my lap.

"Yeah. It probably would be for a brainiac like you." I fought back a smile. I loved when Will made comments about me being smart. He got a mischievous look on his face. "But I gotta say, fighting can be awfully satisfying too."

Scott had alluded to Will's notorious temper before. He claimed Will settled his disputes in high school with his fists more often than not, but so far, I'd never seen that side of him. I was beginning to wonder if Scott was just being dramatic again, inflating Will's vices to drive a wedge between us.

"Well, whatever you chose," Will said, "if you see something you don't like, you've got to stand up and say something. At least that's what I do."

I immediately thought about how I'd gone along with Jimmy when he'd asked me to help him bully Tommy. I shuddered, imagining what Will would say if I told him how weak I'd been that day. What I'd done in band class definitely hadn't been right. If Will knew what a coward I really was, would he change his mind about me? Would he even want me on The Ride anymore?

He was watching me. I tried to look transfixed by a road sign streaking by outside the window so he couldn't read my mind like usual. Still, something nagged at me about the story he'd just told. Something that made me think about what my mom said to me in my bedroom a few weeks ago.

"So that part you were talking about before," I said. "When you said you could make 'Gimme Shelter' play in your head whenever you shot free throws."

"Yeah, what about it?"

"Are you saying you used the song to change the way you felt when you stood on the free throw line?" I thought of the exercise my mom used to show me how to get in touch with my feelings. How she'd asked me to conjure something that felt good to ease my nerves. She'd said athletes used the same technique to heighten their performance, purposely getting out of their heads and into their bodies by not thinking so much and instead feeling more.

Will considered my question. "Yeah, I guess so."

"How did you figure out that trick?"

"It's just something I came up with to get me in the right head space. In the thick of the game, you're all amped up from playing so hard. There's a lot of nerves and adrenaline pumping. Especially when the score is close. But when you're shooting free throws, you have to become really calm and centered. It's a rough transition sometimes."

"So that's when you'd use the memory of the song?"

It was just like when my mom had told me to think about petting puppies or walking in nature or John Belushi. But instead of those examples Will thought of "Gimme Shelter", the song he could conjure with such clarity, it always calmed him down.

"Yeah, I figured out a way to connect with how I felt

in practice by singing the song in my head. And once I did that, it would drown everything else out and I'd always hit the shots."

"Hmmm. That's really cool."

It was exactly what my mom had shown me I could do. Nothing around Will had to change for him to achieve on the basketball court. The crowd could still yell, the score could still be the same, the stakes could still be just as high. None of that mattered because he'd learned to focus deliberately on something that relaxed him, something he knew would make him feel good.

"Yeah. I could control my mind out there," he said, "and in basketball, controlling your mind is just as important as controlling your body."

I wanted to laugh, since I already knew that lesson all too well. "Yeah, in gymnastics too."

"Pretty much with everything if you think about it," he said. "That's why I keep getting so mad when you only focus on all the things that can go wrong in your life."

I didn't even try to defend myself. I was too preoccupied by how strange it felt to be talking about such big concepts as thoughts and feelings with Will. He wasn't like the other boys at my school. All they ever talked about were sports and TV shows and whose truck had the biggest tires and wouldn't get stuck when they went mudding out on the flats on the weekend. Will was so different from every other boy I'd ever known.

"Speaking of that, how'd it go with your cheer captain?" Will asked.

My heart dropped. Last week I'd told him about

my ideas to improve the dance to our school song. And how I'd been too afraid to bring them up with our team captain Linda because she never listened to me.

"Uh, yeah, that," I stalled, knowing he wouldn't like my answer. "I didn't get around to saying anything to her."

"Red!" He threw up his hands in exasperation.

"It's pointless!" I wailed, hating the look of disappointment on his face. "You don't understand. I know what she'll do if I try to suggestion anything. She'll get all huffy and defensive and go to Miss Lancaster and say I'm giving her attitude like she did when Michelle wanted to try out a new tower formation. It's not worth it. She'll never listen to me!"

"There you go again with all your worst-case scenarios!"

"I've tried before and the same thing always happens," I argued. "My worst-case scenarios always come true. So technically, doesn't that make them *real*-case scenarios?"

"But *you're* the one that makes them come true," he said. "That's what I keep saying. You gotta get to a place where all you think about is what can go right instead of everything that could go wrong."

"As if it's just that easy," I huffed.

"It *is* that easy."

"Yeah, well, not for everyone. You don't know what it's like to be mortal like the rest of us."

He made a face. "So you're getting mad at me now?"

"I'm not mad. It's just frustrating coming from you. Of course it's easy for you to only think about things going right. Everything you do is perfect."

His expression clouded over instantly. "Well, obviously not *everything*," he spat bitterly. "But then again, you already know that."

I scoffed. "Right. What mistake have you ever made?"

The car sped up. "Like you don't know?" he said, refusing to look at me. The air between us suddenly felt eerily charged, as if lightning was snapping off Will's body, arcing over to mine.

I tipped my head at him. "Know what?"

He studied me hard for a few seconds. His leg began bouncing up and down furiously. It scared me how upset he seemed.

"Are you serious?" he asked. "You really don't know what I did?"

"I have no idea what you're talking about."

I thought back to the drive-in when I'd asked him what he'd wanted, but couldn't have, and he'd turned into such an asshole. Was this so-called mistake of his related to that?

"What is it, Will? What kind of big mistake did you make?" I'd shared so much personal stuff with him. Wasn't it time he shared some of his secrets with me too?

He gripped the steering wheel tighter. "Let's just say I learned the hard way the consequences of focusing on worst-case scenarios. Now I'm just trying to make sure you don't make the same mistake I did."

I opened my mouth to ask him more, but he cut me off. "Let's just leave it at that. I don't want to talk about."

I looked out the window, hurt by his steely tone. It was like I was back at the drive-in when he'd reprimanded me so harshly. What had I done to set him off?

After a few minutes of silence, he touched my shoulder to get my attention. When I looked over, his expression was sincere. "Sorry, Red. I promise. We'll talk about it someday. Just not right now, okay?"

I shrugged. "Whatever. I don't care."

"It's just," he hesitated, struggling for the right words. "It's so nice to be out here with you listening to the music, not thinking about the real world, you know? This is the one part of my week I really look forward to. Let's not ruin it by talking about the past."

I nodded, knowing exactly how he felt. Just like Will, I thrived on how isolated, how cut off from reality we were on these back roads. It sometimes felt like the Monte Carlo was a submarine plunging through the dark ocean of night, sealed airtight against the real world, Will and I the only two people alive on Earth. The simplicity of our self-containment always felt like such a relief. I didn't want to ruin that peace either.

"Of course," I said, again fighting back the urge to reach out and touch his hand. It was right there, resting so close on the console. "Believe me, I don't want to talk about the past either."

He grinned at me, relieved I understood. His sweet smile reminded me I'd lost focus on why I was here in the first place. I had to remember my job was to make Will happy. To hand him tapes and make him laugh; to talk about the things he loved and to love them right back with him. I shouldn't have been pushing him to think about things that were so obviously upsetting.

"Hey," I said, falling easily back into my assigned role, "have I told you the story of when I tried to do a round-off with my pom-poms in my hands and fell right on my head in front of the whole gym? No? Oh man, settle in. You're going to love this story…"

CHAPTER NINETEEN

SPIES

STACIE AND I were on a mission. (Okay, maybe we were just playing a game, but it sounded way cooler if we called it a mission.)

The game was named Spies, and we usually played it by hiding in the bushes outside a cute guy's house in the vain hope of glimpsing him taking out the trash or playing basketball in his driveway or, if we were lucky, standing in his bedroom window taking off his shirt.

We pretended to be as sly as two James Bond femmes fatales, me as Pussy Galore, Stacie as Agent XXX. But in reality, we were hopelessly inept. We'd always end up getting yelled at by a neighbor or else giggle so hard we fell out of our hiding spot in the bushes and have to race away looking as guilty as two kids trying to catch Santa coming down the chimney.

Today, the goal of the game was to find Will and Mark. It had all come together perfectly, even though we hadn't planned it ahead of time. We'd spent last night with Holly, and when she and her family headed to church in the morning, Stacie and I faked like we were asleep until they were gone. Then we'd shot out of the house, still in our sweatpants and messy ponytails, in search of our intended targets.

We were lucky because both Will and Mark went to the same church. That meant we could easily hide outside and spy on them as they walked to their cars after the service was over.

By the time we made it up to the red brick First Baptist Church standing just a block off the square, the faithful parishioners were already safely sequestered inside. All of them most likely praying for a winning basketball season and God's great mercy, in that exact order.

We set up our surveillance across the street, behind the hedgerow of the senior citizens' center. It was a beautiful late September morning. The air still warm but laced with just enough coolness to remind you fall was waiting in the wings. Stacie and I sat cross-legged behind the bushes, plucking blades of grass and drawing our initials in the dirt to pass the time.

"Do you think we're going to hell because we're not in there with them?" I asked, trying as always to make something I worried about a lot seem like it didn't matter at all.

It seemed like Stacie and I were the only two people in our entire school that didn't go to church. Now with the town so hushed and lifeless -no cars on the road, no one out on the streets- it felt like we were the last two people on Earth; as if the supposed Rapture had happened while we slept, Jesus plucking the cream of the crop from their beds and leaving heathens like Stacie and I behind.

"No, we're not going to hell," Stacie huffed. "You know organized religion was only developed as a way to control people, right? It was a fairy tale made up by the rich and powerful to scare the lowly into doing what they wanted. It's very sad when you really think about it. Believing blindly in something just because someone else tells you it's true? Such a case of misplaced trust."

"Yeah right. So misplaced," I mumbled. Stacie always had a way of making everything into a battle between smart people like her and everyone else. I went along with it because I knew she considered me a member of her elite tribe. But sometimes I wondered if it was fair to divide people up that way. Especially since I'd learned when I lived on the farm that there were more ways to be smart than just from things you learned in a book.

"Besides," Stacie went on, "they're all a bunch of hypocrites, those people in there." She lifted her chin to the church, glowing like a red ember in the sunlight. "They sin as much as everyone else. But they go in and ask for forgiveness, then walk out all holier-than-thou, thinking they're better than everyone else. It doesn't seem very Christian to me. In fact, I think old Jesus would be rolling in his grave, or wherever the heck he ended up, if he knew what they're all doing in his name."

I agreed with Stacie about the hypocrite part. It was the one thing I never understood about what happened to my mom. How could people who claimed to be so righteous and caring treat another person so cruelly, just for loving someone? I'd always thought that loving all people as equals was what Jesus walked around proclaiming from the mountaintops. But it seemed like most people in Cold Springs had forgotten that part of his message.

We didn't talk much as we waited. It was so quiet, the air so still, it felt like any word we said would shoot straight down the church belfry for everyone inside to hear. After a while I had to stand up and do a few jumping jacks to stretch my cramping legs. Just as I finished, I heard the squeak of hinges. Then organ music swelled through the air, the gigantic bubble of gospel bursting straight out the church door.

"They're coming out!" I hissed at Stacie, who was lying on her back in the grass watching a bunch of crows circling the sky above us.

We scrambled to our positions, trying not to laugh as we peered over the hedgerow like two of the characters from the *Hogan's Heroes* TV show spying on the Nazis.

My stomach churned, thinking of what I was about to see next. Scott had told me that Penny went to the same church as Will. It was going to kill me, but I'd come here because I wanted to see the two of them together. It was sick, I knew, but I needed to see the reality of what I was up against.

You would've thought Will having a girlfriend would've squelched my crush on him, but it had just the opposite effect. It made it easier to be with him. Will was now in the same category as my celebrity crushes: safe, off limits, fun to obsess over in a completely nonthreatening way. I reasoned the only difference between

Will and John Travolta was I could actually talk to Will in person, maybe even touch him by accident every once in a while. Unfortunately, that ease I had with him was only making my obsession grow stronger. Maybe if I saw Will and Penny together as a couple, I could finally come to my senses and let go of this stupid crush once and for all.

Scott came out of the church first. He was looming over Holly like a car salesman, gesturing wildly, obviously trying way too hard to make her laugh. Stacie and I looked at each other and rolled our eyes.

"That boy has got to dial it back," Stacie whispered. "He's going to scare her off."

"Yeah, we should talk to him about it," I said. But then I noticed Holly laughing. They were walking really close to each other, like they were in their own little world. Maybe Scott was doing okay on his own after all.

Mark came out next, clustered together with his family. He shoved his younger brother roughly on the shoulder, then his brother shoved him back, and the cycle repeated until his mom had to stop shaking hands with the pastor just to separate the two of them.

I made a face at Stacie. "Really?" I still didn't understand what she saw in Mark. He seemed like such a dunce, which in theory should've meant he wasn't her type.

"Hey, he's hot," Stacie defended herself. "I just like making out with him. I don't need him for long intellectual conversations."

I wanted to say, "No, because you already have Rob for that," but I didn't.

"Uh oh," Stacie said. From the tone in her voice, I already knew who she'd seen before I turned back around.

Will and Penny walked down the church sidewalk arm in arm. Will had on a pair of nice, pressed khakis and another one of his striped dress shirts. His hair, usually so ruffled and unruly by the time I saw him at the end of the night, was combed neatly, falling in sleek, black waves to just above the collar of his shirt. Penny was latched tightly to his side, wearing a ruffly white blouse and a floral peasant skirt. That skirt pissed me off because I'd been wanting to buy one exactly like it for months now but hadn't gotten the nerve up yet. I didn't think someone as short as me could pull it off. But Penny had no problem making it look good.

"Oh my God, oh my God, oh my God!" I squeezed Stacie's arm tightly as I stared at the two of them. A lightning bolt was probably going to strike me dead for taking the Lord's name in vain so many times in a row. The explosion would surely blow our cover.

Will and Penny stopped at a group of older people, which included Coach and a few others, who I assumed were Will's mom and Penny's parents. Scott told me that Will and Penny's parents had been best friends for years and they had fixed their kids up. Will stepped back a little, which made it easy for me to see Penny clearly. She looked almost the same as she had in the magazine, wings of brown hair feathered away from her face and makeup so bright I could see it all the way across the street.

"Geez. Where'd she just come from? A church or a brothel?" Stacie must have read my mind. I knew she was just saying that for my benefit, because there was no denying Penny was pretty. She had a round-cheeked, button-nosed cuteness that stood out even under the three pounds of Maybelline products plastered on her face. I stared at her, taking notes, thinking: *That's what Will likes. That's what Will thinks is pretty.*

I touched my hair. It was nothing like Penny's. Miss Lancaster made us keep ours long and one length so we could all have matching ponytails for cheerleading competitions. My hair was boring and stupid, just like my plain stupid face. In fact, all of me was stupid and childish and ugly compared to Penny.

Stacie nudged me on the shoulder. "You're way prettier than she is."

I was going to protest, but I was suddenly so exhausted I didn't even think I could make a joke. I should've never come. I thought seeing Will and Penny together would make me wake up and realize how futile being with him was. Then I could give up and let my feelings for him just shrivel up and die like they were supposed to. But instead of making me want to forget about Will, seeing him there with Penny standing on the sidewalk in front of the entire town only made me want him more.

The longer I watched though, the more something started to seem strange between the two of them. It took me a few seconds to realize it was because Will wasn't talking at all. Coach talked and Will's mom talked and Penny talked, but Will just stood there staring off into the distance.

He was shifting on his feet like he always did. Putting his one free hand in his pocket, then taking it out. Running his fingers through his hair, then tugging at his shirt. I noticed his foot tapping a little. I knew him well enough to know what was going on. He was hearing a Stones song in his head.

Just then, Penny turned and looked right at where Stacie and I were hiding. We let go of our branches and threw ourselves flat on the ground, but not before Penny's eyes landed directly on me. *Oh my God. Did she see me? Does she know who I am?*

Stacie and I clutched our hands over our mouths to keep from laughing. We stared at each other, eyes bulging, listening to car after car pull out of the parking lot. Finally, Stacie got the nerve to peek out again.

"All clear. They're gone," Stacie said.

I let out an enormous sigh. "She didn't see us, right?" I asked, struggling to my feet.

"No, we were too far away," Stacie assured me, although I wasn't entirely sure that was true.

"Good," I said, brushing the dirt off my sweatpants. *See? You didn't make a complete fool out of yourself after all*, I told myself. But I wasn't entirely sure that was true either.

◈

It was a bad idea right from the start. But then again, you have to remember I was a naïve fifteen-year-old girl trying to transform myself from boyish sidekick into full-blown love interest in a single night, so it made sense to me at the time.

The Wednesday after I saw Will and Penny together

at church, I drug Stacie up the five blocks from school to the town square and straight into Parker Drug Store's makeup aisle.

"This is crazy!" Stacie repeated the plea she'd chanted the entire walk there. "No guy in their right mind could actually like a girl that wears that much makeup!"

"Will's been with Penny for five years, so he must like it, right? It only makes sense," I reasoned.

"I don't know. It just doesn't seem right for you. You shouldn't have to cover up who you are for some guy."

"This coming from the girl who wore a Band-Aid over the zit on her chin so Mark wouldn't see it? I'm not sure you're one to talk about not covering up who you really are for a guy."

She rolled her eyes. "Well, that was disgusting. I had no other choice."

"Just help me out, okay? I need to find these exact things." I opened up a picture of Brooke Shields I'd ripped from my *Seventeen* magazine. Her face took up the entire page, eyes rimmed in smudged brown eyeliner, long eyelashes coated in black mascara, and cheeks sculpted in a rosy pink.

"It says Bonne Bell blush in Cherub," I read the tiny print at the bottom of the page. "And Maybelline eyeliner in Sienna Smoke."

We sorted through the sealed plastic packages hanging off the wall, holding Brooke's face up to each shade to make sure we got the right one.

It was crazy to think I could come anywhere close to looking like Brooke just by using the same makeup she did. With her perfect features, porcelain skin, and trademark thick eyebrows, she was the most beautiful girl I'd ever seen. My mom told me once my eyebrows reminded her of Brooke's. But even if I believed her (which I didn't) I knew it would take way more than just two eyebrows to make me as stunning as she was.

Stacie eventually forgot all her complaints and threw herself into helping me. It was the way things always went between us. If one of us truly wanted something, the other became like Kennedy's Bay of Pigs advisors: full support, no questions asked. Although looking back now, a few well-placed questions might have saved both me and Kennedy a whole lot of humiliation in the end.

Stacie became so committed to my plan she even agreed to help me put on my makeup that Friday night. We wedged ourselves inside the bathroom at Pizza King, Stacie painting and smudging and smearing colors on my face, trying to get as close to the picture of Brooke as possible, even though she admitted to having no idea what she was doing. She applied one round of cosmetics, then I lurched up from the toilet seat, studied myself in the mirror and commanded her to put on more. After we repeated that cycle a few times, Stacie finally put her foot down, wailing, "If I put on anymore, he'll think you're auditioning for the lead role in *Hello Dolly!*"

"I know it's a lot. But it's going to be dark and I want him to notice." I studied my reflection one last time. I was sure I'd aged at least two years just by the mascara alone. And the eyeshadow definitely made me look way more alluring, just like the package had promised. In fact, someone might even mistake me for a nineteen-year-old if the light hit me just right. (And if they didn't look down at my undeveloped chest.)

"Oh, he's going to notice all right," Stacie muttered to my back as I bounded out of the bathroom to meet Will at the curb.

And boy, was she ever right. He did notice. In fact, I'd barely made it onto the console before he circled his hand in front of my face and asked, "What's with all this?"

"What do you mean 'all this'?" I sputtered. "This is my face!" My heart sunk, hearing the tone of his voice. It wasn't at all what I'd hoped for.

He furrowed his brows, studying me. "Yeah, but your face looks different."

"Can we just go, please? Cars are backing up behind us," I begged.

Rob settled in beside me. I noticed he was making a concerted effort not to glance in my direction. He was probably worried that if he and Will caught eyes, they'd both burst out laughing. And Rob was way too nice to do something like that.

Will wasn't so nice though because he did, in fact, burst out laughing. "Are you wearing makeup?!" he asked incredulously.

"I always wear makeup." It wasn't a lie. I sometimes put on a little eyeliner and a tiny swatch of blush in the morning. But by the time I saw Will at the end of the day, it had usually all worn off.

"Not like *that* you don't!" He still refused to drive. He just sat in his seat smirking at me, like he'd never seen anything as hilarious as my painted face before.

I could feel my blood pressure rising as Will gawked at me. "Seriously, can we just go?!"

Someone honked behind us. I wanted to climb out of the car and kiss the person who had the nerve to tell Will to move his entitled ass. I'd have done anything to get out of the glare of the streetlamps so I didn't have to look at his shit-eating grin anymore.

"Fine. We'll go." He finally put the car in gear. But we were only two blocks out of town when he started in on me again.

"It's just that makeup is way too girly for you, Red. It doesn't look right on you."

"Did I ask for your opinion?!"

He breezed on without missing a beat. "No, but seriously... it looks weird. Don't you think it looks weird on her, Rob?"

Rob stared stony-faced out the windshield. "I'd rather not get in the middle of this," he said diplomatically. He had his hand on the door handle like he wished it was an ejection lever that would shoot him straight out the sunroof.

Will shook his head. "You're just not like that," he informed me in his bossy way.

"I'm not like what?"

He thought for a second. "I don't know... like a girl."

"Oh my God! I am a girl, Will!"

I couldn't believe what I was hearing. This was way worse than I'd ever imagined. Will had just confirmed my worst fears. Not only was I going to have to convince him I was old enough for him to date, now I was also going to have to convince him I was actually a *girl*?

My dreams were becoming more and more hopeless by the second.

"What? Don't get mad. It's a good thing!" Will said. "I told you I liked how different you are. You fit in with all of us. You're just like one of the guys."

"Ugh. But I'm not a guy!"

"But you act like one."

"I do not!"

Will huffed. "Don't you remember that blow job joke you told us last weekend?"

Rob sucked in a sharp breath, clearly trying to hold back a laugh.

"You loved that joke!" I wailed.

"I did! That's what I'm saying," Will said. "And remember? After the joke you played like three verses of 'Yankee Doodle Dandy' in armpit farts."

"Yeah? So? Girls do armpit farts too!"

He tipped his head at me. "Do they though?"

"Ugghhhh!" Everything was backfiring. I hated how he was laughing at me. Mocking me for trying to be something I'd obviously never be: a person he could ever be attracted to.

"I most definitely am a girl, Will! In fact, I'll prove it to you."

I leaned back and unbuttoned my jeans, pretending like I was going to strip down just to make my point. I really sold it too. I unzipped the zipper all the way down and yanked the waist of my jeans open wide, then lifted my ass up off the console like I was about to shimmy out of my jeans and show them my privates. (Karen always said you had to really commit to a joke if you wanted it to land just right.)

"Whoa... whoa... whoa!" Will cried, eyes bulging in disbelief. "Stop! I believe you, Red!"

I was glad he'd jumped in. I hadn't really thought of what I'd do if he had let me go through with it.

Poor Rob was now turned away, staring intently out the passenger side window like he was trying to pick the perfect spot to land when he threw himself out of the car.

"Good," I said triumphantly, zipping my jeans up. I liked how I'd shocked Will. It made me feel really powerful. But my victory was short-lived.

"You *do* realize you've just made my point for me, though," Will said.

"What do you mean?"

"Just that most girls wouldn't pull a stunt like that." He glanced down at my jeans. "Of course, a guy might however."

His self-righteous laugh was so infuriating it took everything I had to not punch him right in his beautiful jaw.

"Just don't talk to me anymore, okay," I growled, snatching Rob's beer out of his hand and taking a huge swig. I wished I could go back and listen to Stacie. God, it had been so stupid to think a few dime store products would be enough to get Will to see me the way he saw Penny. It mortified me that I'd even tried. Now I had to sit next to him for the rest of the night, knowing he probably had already figured out it was all an attempt to get his attention.

We rode along, each of us staring straight ahead like

three stone statues strapped into our respective leather seats. No one dared to say a word. Not even Will.

When I finally got the nerve to glance at Will out of the corner of my eye, he still had the shit-eating grin on his face. Yes, he most definitely knew what I'd been trying to do. Now I wished the console had an ejection lever too, because he would never let me live this down without teasing the hell out of me first.

He surprised me though, because after a few more minutes of driving, he bumped his shoulder into mine.

"Hey, I'm sorry. I didn't mean to make you so mad." His voice was conciliatory, a rare tone for him. When I looked over, his smile had disappeared. In fact, he almost looked a little worried about whether or not I was going to forgive him.

"I wasn't mad," I grumbled.

"Of course you weren't."

We caught each other's eyes, and both started laughing. Rob exhaled loudly, joining in with us.

"It's just that —" he started.

"Can we just not talk about this anymore?" I said, cringing.

"Let me explain. Please."

"Fine. I'm obviously not going to stop you."

He took a deep breath, hesitating like he wanted to choose his words carefully. "It's just that, think about it. Why is it even called makeup in the first place? It's because girls are trying to *make up* for something they think they don't already have."

I rolled my eyes, acting like he was so incredibly

stupid. But I had to admit, there was something in what he'd said. I'd never thought about it that way before.

He went on, ignoring my theatrics. "To me, it always seemed like girls use all that glop," he gestured at my face, making my cheeks burn again. (Thank God, my Cherub blush was so thick he probably didn't even notice.) "Because they're trying to compensate for some perceived flaw they have... trying to fix something they're lacking."

His voice was pleading, like he really cared that I understood.

"Yeah, I guess you're right," I begrudgingly admitted.

He stopped the car at a stop sign, then turned in his seat to stare right into my eyes. "So now do you understand why I don't think you have to wear makeup, Red?"

"Why?" I asked, heart pounding at what he might say next.

"Because someone like you doesn't need it."

CHAPTER TWENTY

"UNDER MY THUMB"

"I STILL CAN'T believe those two are dating," Stacie said, throwing the *Us* magazine onto her bed. I snatched it up and settled back on one of her quilted pillows.

John Travolta smiled up at me in all his blue-eyed, black-haired, cleft-chinned glory. It looked like he was waiting patiently for me to lean down and plant a kiss right on top of his glossy paper lips. (Which is what I would've done if Stacie hadn't been there.)

In the bottom corner of the page, there was a smaller picture of John with his arm wrapped around Brooke Shields' waist, a cheesy title about how the *Urban Cowboy* had now found *Endless Love* printed underneath.

"Yeah, my two favorite people are dating each other," I said. "I'm still not sure how I feel about that."

"I know exactly how you feel," Stacie said. "You're jealous as hell!"

"Yeah, I guess. But I love them both so much. Shouldn't I just be happy for them?"

"You get to feel however you want to feel. Happy, jealous, mad as hell. Just pick one and OWN it, man!"

She sounded just like Will, with all his "Stand up for yourself!" and "Say what you want to say!" platitudes. God, I wished life was as simple for me as it was for the two of them.

"If I were you, I'd be happy they're dating." Stacie pointed to the cover. "Brooke going out with John gives you and her something in common."

"Yeah? What's that?"

"Well, in this article…" She took the magazine from me and flipped it open, running a finger down the page. "It says he's 27, and she's only 16. That means Brooke's lusting after an older man, just like you."

I ripped the magazine away from her. I'd read the article a hundred times when it came out in August, but I'd forgotten that one piece of information. It had meant nothing to me back then. But now it meant everything.

I scanned the paragraph. Stacie was right. Brooke and I were almost the same age and yet she was dating someone eleven years older than her. (A span way worse than the measly five years between Will and me.) That meant John was a man and Brooke was a girl. And no one even cared. Not only did they not care, Hollywood was celebrating the two of them like their budding romance was the greatest coupling since Farrah Fawcett married Lee Majors.

"Oh wow. You're right. He's way older than she is," I said, my heart lifting with hope. Could dating Will really be a possibility? I thought back on what he'd said about me wearing makeup the other night in the car. *Because someone like you doesn't need it.* My stomach flipped in the same delicious way it had that night. Had Will actually been saying he thought I was prettier than Penny?

"Of course, I'm right," Stacie said, flopping flat beside me. "Although I'm still not sure what you see in that whacknut, Will."

I tensed at her insult. "What do you mean? You said yourself you thought he was hot."

"Yeah, he's hot. I mean, no one's going to deny that." It surprised me how proud I felt of her admission. Like Will's good looks had anything to do with me.

"But he'd be way hotter if he kept his big mouth shut."

I couldn't help but laugh. "Yeah, I had that same thought the first time I met him too." For some reason, I suddenly felt guilty for admitting that out loud. "But now that I know him better, it doesn't bother me so much," I clarified quickly.

"It doesn't bother you that he's a pompous know-it-all?"

"He's not a pompous know-it-all!"

"He is too!"

"Well, he just acts that way sometimes. He's different when you get to know him."

Usually I told Stacie every detail of my life, but there was a lot about Will that I'd kept to myself. I hadn't told her how Will changed when we were alone together. How when the car door slammed after the last person left each night, his pompous bravado faded away, leaving a quieter, more thoughtful boy in its place. A boy, I was pretty sure no one else knew existed but me.

"You're just mad he played that song last night," I said.

"It's a terrible song!"

"A lot of people like 'Under My Thumb'!"

She shook her head at me. Stacie had already been in a bad mood on Saturday night when Will played that song for her. Mark had stood her up at Pizza King, so she'd had no other choice but to go on The Ride with us. Rob and I had both begged Will not to play that particular song, but he'd ignored us. It was almost like he was trying to antagonize her. And it had worked because she and Will had gotten into a big fight over all its misogynistic lyrics. All the controversial lines that talked about how Mick wanted to keep a girl as a pet and only let her talk when she was spoken to. Terrible, sexist suggestions that were incongruously sung to one of the most cheerful and upbeat melodies in rock 'n' roll history. It was The Rolling Stones' specialty: taking something so undeniably offensive and crafting it into something so lovely, you forgot what you were even singing about in the first place.

Luckily, Stacie and Will had ended up laughing about their disagreement. It was the first time Stacie had smiled the entire night, so I couldn't stay mad at Will like I'd wanted to. They'd even agreed to pick up the argument where they'd left off the next time they were together. Stacie would probably never admit it, but I was pretty sure she enjoyed fighting with Will sometimes.

"The song isn't meant to be serious," I explained.

"Obviously Mick has a great appreciation for women. He's helped out tons of female performers. The song is just meant to get people thinking, you know."

"Sounds like a line of propaganda fed to you by your cult leader." Stacie glared at me.

"Stop it. Will is not a cult leader." I looked away, feeling a bit uncomfortable that I had, in fact, repeated the exact words Will had used when he'd explained the song to me the first time.

She lurched up and grabbed me by the shoulders. "He hasn't asked you to drink any Kool-Aid yet, has he?" She shook me back and forth hard. "Whatever you do, *don't drink the Kool-Aid!*"

I laughed but pushed her hands off my shoulder a little harder than I meant to. I rolled off her bed and wandered over to the window, peering out like I was checking on the weather so she wouldn't see how upset I was. I knew Stacie was just joking around, but still. She shouldn't have been talking about Will like that. Especially when she didn't know him like I did.

"Sorry, sorry," she said. "I know how much you like him. And if I'm really being honest, I do kind of like arguing with him."

I smiled over my shoulder at her. "I thought you kind of enjoyed it."

"Yeah, it's fun sometimes," she said lightly. "And I do like Will. Even though he is pretty annoying."

I nodded since it was mostly true. Will was difficult sometimes. But not with me. He hardly ever teased me anymore. I guess I'd passed all his tests, which meant he and I were on the same team now. Will believed teammates should always be completely loyal to each other. I loved how dedicated he was to me. No one had ever blindly supported me the way Will did now. I mean, except for my mom. And Stacie, of course.

"I'm just worried you're wasting your time hanging out with him so much," she said.

I nestled in the window seat that looked out onto the woods, then wrapped my arms around my legs, bracing myself for what I knew was coming next.

Lately Stacie had started harping about how she thought I was passing up all these great opportunities to go out with boys I might have a chance of dating because I was always with Will. What she didn't understand was that being able to turn down other boys was one of the best parts about hanging out with Will. I never had to worry about going out on an actual date when I always had plans with him.

"I keep telling you that Chad is dying to go out with you," she said.

I made a face. Chad Rindquist was Mark's best friend and a starting guard on the basketball team. He was definitely handsome, with his curly brown hair, dimpled cheeks, and All-American boy smile. Not Will-level handsome, of course. He wouldn't command a full page spread in a magazine the way Will had. Still, with as many girls in our school that lusted after Chad, I found it hard to believe that he was dying to ask me out like Stacie said.

"Why would he want to go out with me?"

"Because you're pretty!" Stacie said. Then, catching

her feminist slip, added, "And smart, and funny. Chad's always talking about the stuff you say in French class."

"He never gets my jokes! I think I've had to explain every one of them to him so far." I thought back to Chad's blank stares. The way he always seemed confused whenever I finished a story. "I know the guy is cute, but I think the old saying is true about him. God doesn't give with both hands."

"Yeah, you might be right." Stacie looked up at the ceiling, thinking. "But what does it even matter? All guys are pretty much dicks. You might as well go out with one who's nice to look at."

"Is that a direct quote from Gloria Steinem?"

"I think it is, actually." We laughed together. Stacie rolled onto her side and stared idly out the window behind me as a heavy silence settled over the room.

For a long time, I'd never really understood why Stacie distrusted boys so much. I knew her dad left her mom when Stacie was only two years old and hadn't been in contact with either of them since. But she was so close with her stepdad Frank that it didn't seem like losing her real father was even an issue. One night almost a year ago when Stacie and I had gotten drunk for the first time off some cooking wine we'd snuck out of the kitchen, she'd admitted she still thought about her real dad a lot. She said she knew she'd been a pain-in-the-ass toddler, always throwing tantrums and breaking things and climbing into her mom and dad's bed every night. She said she wondered if she'd driven her dad away by being such a bad kid. If his leaving had all been her fault.

I'd tried to tell her there was no way that could be

true, but I didn't think she really listened to me. She'd brushed it off like she did whenever anything got too personal. Made me swear to never talk about it again or she'd tell everyone I had a pillow with John Travolta's face on it that I practiced kissing on at night, so I'd never brought it up again. But I knew, deep down, it still bothered her.

"Listen, I'm sorry," Stacie said, tucking both hands under her cheek in a way that made her look like a little girl all curled up for her nap. "Here we are talking about stupid boys again."

"Don't forget the pact!" I reminded her.

"I know, I know. I just worry about you sometimes. It sounds sappy, but I just want you to be happy."

I pretended to gag. "That is seriously sappy! Which we both hate." I tried to think of a way to distract her from the subject. "Are we going to have to make another pact now? A No-Sap Pact?" I said, laughing. I kept saying the tongue twister over and over again until it came out No Pap Sact and I finally got Stacie laughing too.

When I caught my breath, I tried to reassure her again. "Seriously, you don't have to worry about me. I'm happier than I've ever been before."

She gave me a funny look. "Are you sure?"

"Yes. I'm sure. Trust me, I'm very, very…" I looked up in the air, searching for the right word, "content."

"*Content*?!" She spat the word out like it was coated in shit.

I nodded, looking out the window so she couldn't see my face. I watched a single orange leaf drop off a branch, then float downward, dipping slowly from side to side as if it were being rocked by an unseen hand as it fell. When it finally touched down on the grass really softly, I smiled to myself. The ease of that lone little leaf's journey made me feel hopeful somehow, like I was being sent a message that I was being cared for in that same gentle way. Like I had an unseen hand holding me too. I just had to remember to stop every once in a while and notice the feel of its grip around me.

She sat up on her elbow, peered over me. "So, you're content to spend every weekend riding around lusting after a boy who already has a girlfriend? Wasting your life away while the rest of us are having fun?"

"I'm not wasting my life away!"

"But you're missing out on so much stuff!" Stacie protested. "We're sophomores now. That means we can go to the prom this year if we get invited by an upper-classman. And there'll be Homecoming and dates to the movies and all kinds of other stuff. Are you really going to give all that up to ride around, doing nothing every weekend?"

"It's not doing nothing."

"Really? It certainly seems like nothing to me."

"Believe me, it's something." I stopped there, not wanting to divulge any more of what Will and I talked about when we were alone. "I like my weekends now. They feel so, I don't know…. just so natural… so easy…"

"Oh my God! Natural and easy? Now you sound like a maxi pad commercial!" Stacie groaned.

"Stop!" I waved her off. "You just don't understand!"

"Fine. Then explain it to me."

I let out a heavy sigh. "I'm not sure I can."

"How about you try?"

I knew Stacie well enough to know she wasn't going to let me get out of this. "Okay. But you have to promise not to laugh at me."

"I promise," she said, sitting up and swinging her long legs around to perch on the edge of the bed.

I tried to think of a way to say it that would make Stacie understand. At first the words got all jumbled up in my brain, but then I let myself imagine being in the car with Will, let myself feel the emotions in my body the way my mom had taught me to, and when I did, my thoughts began to flow freely.

"I guess I'd say that being with Will is like the first part of every romantic movie," I started slowly, keeping my eyes closed so I could stay in the feelings. "When the couple are just getting to know each other, and there's this montage scene, where they're laughing and talking, and talking and laughing. That's how it is between Will and me. That fun, silly, doesn't-really-mean-anything-yet part. Over and over again."

I opened my eyes and peeked at Stacie to see if I was making any sense. She was screwing up her mouth up the way she always did when she thought hard about something.

"Well, I do agree," she said. "That part with boys is pretty fun. But that's just the beginning of the movie."

"So? Isn't that the best part? I'm fine with just hitting the pause button right there."

"You're saying you're happy staying in the 'montage scene'?" she air quoted, "never going any further?"

I shrugged. I'd never really thought about it before, but now that I'd said it out loud, it made perfect sense. Never going any further meant I'd never have to risk getting hurt by a boy. Never going any further meant I could always stay safe.

"Yeah. The next part of the story is when all the bad stuff happens, right? That's when the guy and the girl fight and break up and people cry and have nervous breakdowns. Sometimes they even die! Haven't you seen *Love Story*?! That shit's rough!"

Stacie considered my analogy.

I went on. "I mean, I'd think *you* of all people would understand. Aren't you're the queen of staying in the first part? Dating Lite. Isn't that what you call it? Love 'em and leave 'em before they get too attached."

"Yeah, that is my philosophy, but I don't know," Stacie said. "I still think you're stopping yourself a bit too soon. You skipped the good part that comes right after the montage scene in the movies. The hot make-out session. The steamy sex scene."

My face flushed. "Oh my God. I've never even kissed a boy. I can't even think about the steamy sex scene right now!" Of course, that wasn't true. Stacie would've been shocked by the myriad of ways Will and I had consummated our love in my fantasies: in front of the fire like Brooke and that guy in *Endless Love*. On the beach, like Brooke and the other guy in *The Blue Lagoon*. In the back seat of the car, like John Travolta and that girl in *Saturday Night Fever*.

"I guess I get it," Stacie said. "But are you sure you don't want to find another guy you can 'montage' with?" She wagged her eyebrows. "Someone you could go a little further into the next scene with?"

"No. I don't want to find another guy. And I definitely do not want to move on to the next scene."

"So, you want to just keep everything exactly the way it is with Will now?" Stacie asked.

I hesitated for a split second. "Yeah. Everything is perfect just the way it is."

She narrowed her eyes at me, clearly not buying it. Luckily, she decided not to cross-examine me. "Alright. I guess I'll accept that. As long as you're…. content."

"Oh, believe me, I am!" But my over-enthusiastic delivery rang hollow, even to my own ears. Who was I kidding? I wasn't content with the way things were with Will. But what other choice did I have? He was a twenty-year-old college student with a girlfriend, and I was… well, I was just me.

CHAPTER TWENTY-ONE

COACH'S OFFICE

THE NEXT DAY, I was racing back and forth across the gym floor, trying to avoid being killed in a nasty game of dodgeball, when Coach Calder bellowed my name.

"Miss McCaffrey! I need to see you!"

When I turned to look at him, a ball whacked me right on the side of my head.

"Shit, hell, damn," I muttered under my breath as I jogged to sideline to meet him. Along the way I passed by Stacie, standing still as a statue with her arms crossed in front of her, as if she was just praying someone would hit her so she could finally sit out.

"Have fun with your future father-in-law," she whispered as I got closer.

I was still rubbing the side of my head, cussing a blue streak, when I made it to Coach.

"Nice language for a girl," he said with a wry smile.

I wanted to say, "well according to your son, I'm

not actually a girl," but instead I said, "Oh, sorry about that. I guess my ninja-like reflexes need a little work."

I did a couple slow karate chops, then a wildly off-kilter spin kick to show him how bad I was a dodging things. He shook his head at me, with the same this-girl-is-crazy look that Will gave me a lot. But since he was laughing, I didn't mind.

I made prayer hands and bowed deeply to him. "Did you need me for something, Sensei?" I tried to keep the laughs coming, but a more important topic already pre-occupied Coach.

"About this week's column…" It was how he started every conversation with me lately. All because of the new partnership I'd brokered with him.

When basketball season had started a few weeks ago, I'd come up with an idea to write features on each team member as a way for the community to get to know the boys better. Since The Cold Springs Gazette could barely fill their four pages on a good day, I was sure they'd jump at the chance for more content to print. The only tripping point came when I thought of float-ing the idea to Coach. I knew how protective he was of the boys; that he didn't take kindly to people butting in and asking too many questions about his team. But Will had pushed me to talk to him. He'd assured me his dad would love the idea, and (in an un-shocking twist) Will had been right. In fact, Coach was so excited about me offering more good press for the team I could barely get past him in the hallway without him pulling me aside to give me suggestions for what to write next.

From what I could tell, Coach considered my column

a kind of propaganda machine for his team; a way to get inside his opponents' heads and psyche them out before they ever stepped on the court. The first day I'd sat down with him, he'd patiently explained that basketball was a game of minor advantages. And he wouldn't be southern Indiana's most winning basketball coach if he didn't exploit every one of them he got.

"I have some notes in my office I want to talk to you about," he said, motioning for me to fall in beside him.

I obediently trailed behind but hesitated as we neared the boys' locker room. Girls weren't usually allowed inside, but Coach seemed to have forgotten that rule because he brusquely ushered me down the hallway. As I walked further into the shadowy interior, the stench of sweat, mildewed tennis shoes, and backed-up toilets became so powerful I had to cover my nose. (Which was saying a lot, considering how much time I'd spent in cow barns in my lifetime.)

Coach turned into his office, but I hovered the doorway surveying the crowded interior. Framed team pictures and newspaper clippings decorated the walls. Behind his desk stood a line of grey filing cabinets, their tops covered in trophies. Each statue was adorned with a gilded boy suspended in a mid-air jump shot, a frayed piece of basketball net hanging from his tiny golden hand.

"Have a seat." Coach motioned to a wooden chair draped with a pile of red practice jerseys. He deftly hurdled a bag of basketballs to take a seat behind his desk. Luckily, it smelled a little better in there. More like leather and Ben-Gay than the toxic mushroom cloud of the hallway.

I scooped up the jerseys, fighting back a memory of being yelled out by my Girl Scout leader for letting the American flag brush the ground as I gingerly placed them on the floor. I hoped Coach was so busy shuffling the papers around on his messy desk that he didn't notice my irreverent handling of his teams' uniforms.

As I waited for my next assignment, I examined the man that one day (in a distant fantasy) just might be my father-in-law, like Stacie said. Coach wore his standard ensemble: a red polo shirt, khaki pants, and white tennis shoes. Looking at him, it was hard to believe he'd once been a basketball star at Cold Springs just like Will, since he now had a big belly, and his hair was salt and pepper grey. Despite his looks, he was still pretty fit though. I'd seen him leap off the bench to yell at a ref during a game. The guy was so quick you'd think he'd had half his parts rebuilt just like Steve Austin in *The Six Million Dollar Man*.

Coach hunched over a clipboard, so engrossed in what he was reading it was like he'd forgotten I was even there. I used the opportunity to subtly scan the cluster of framed family photos on a cabinet just behind his right shoulder, Maybe they could feed me a few more scraps of information about Will.

In between a bunch of vacation snapshots, was a wedding portrait of a young Coach with Mrs. Calder. It shocked me how much Will looked like the younger version of his dad. Next, my eye was drawn to a picture of Will and his siblings. The three of them were lined up in a row: Will's older sister, then Will, then his younger brother Mitch, grinning into the camera with identical white smiles. All three kids were attractive, but Will clearly dominated the center of the frame with his pristine, dark beauty.

"Here's what you're going to do," Coach clapped his hands, jolting me out of my revelry. "You're going to write about Rob this week, got it?" He pointed at me in an all too familiar way.

"Uh, okay."

"I want you to go at it from the angle of how smart he is. Include how he can read defenses, anticipate presses, adjust on the fly. You know, stuff like that. Really play up his brains. Make sure you put in there how he's ranked at the top of the class academically. That'll surprise them for sure."

"Right, right." I looked down at my gym shorts, wishing I had a pencil hidden in my pocket. How did he expect me to remember all this?

"Man, you wouldn't think he was so smart by looking at him, huh?" Coach shook his head. "The guy looks like should be standing out in a cornfield trying to keep the crows away, if you know what I mean."

"Yeah. A lot of people underestimate Rob," I said, thinking of Stacie.

Coach tipped back in his chair, a faraway look in his eyes. "It took that kid a while to get the motor skills to match the brains. He was a mess at first." I could tell he was revving up for a much longer story. After spending so much time with Coach these past weeks, I was starting to understand that he and Will communicated in much the same manner: Long blustery stories, punctuated by dramatic gestures, driving home lessons they believed to be the one true gospel of the Calder Way.

"Yeah, Rob definitely needed some guidance, that's for sure," Coach went on.

I thought of Will telling me how he'd worked with Rob in his own time. How he'd taken him from an uncoordinated bench warmer to the starting center after months of one-on-one practice.

"But now that I've got Rob where I want him, he's a great asset to the team," Coach said.

I want to correct him and say, "you mean now that *Will* has gotten Rob where you want him," but I knew I couldn't.

Coach laced his hands behind his head and launched into his version of Rob's story, a progression woven so dramatically you'd have thought poor Rob had gone from a newly minted Frankenstein to Wilt Chamberlain and Larry Bird's love child in only one season.

"And now that he has all those skills matched up with his smarts, he's a force to be reckoned with," Coach concluded.

I scanned the piles of binders and folders on the desk. I really needed to take notes if I was ever going to keep up with his ramblings. "Do you have a piece of paper I can write this all down on?"

He pulled open a desk drawer and handed me a little notepad with *Finnegan's Real Estate* printed along the bottom of each page. I scribbled notes on my fictional boyfriend's family stationery as Coach kept talking. "And I really want to play up his height. Put in there he's 6 foot 7."

"*Is* he 6 foot 7?"

"Naww. He's listed at 6'5, but we can just say it's a misprint. By then we'll already be in their heads."

"Um... well... I'm not sure I can..." I trailed off, wondering what Jane Pauley would do in a situation like this. Jane had been my hero ever since she started helming *The Today Show* next to Tom Brokaw a few years ago. Not only was she the most famous woman reporter in the entire country, she was also from Indiana and graduated from the IU School of Journalism, just like I planned to one day. Surely Jane wouldn't compromise her journalistic integrity just to impress the father of a boy she liked. I clearly would however, because I didn't have the nerve to challenge Coach. What was the harm in fudging a few inches? No one would ever know, would they?

"And another thing..." Coach charged on about psychological warfare and keeping the opponent off guard and how there were so many nuances to the game of basketball that the run-of-the-mill fan never understood. When he started listing off those nuances one by one, I couldn't help but drift back to Will's lovely face floating just above his shoulder. I let myself become so engrossed in his perfect smile I didn't notice until too late that Coach had stopped talking.

When I focused back on Coach, he was studying me with a confused look on his face. He whirled in his seat to see what I'd been staring at.

"Oh, you like that picture of my kids, huh?" He grabbed the photo and brought it closer.

"Let's see, you already know Mitch," he said, pointing at Will's round-faced younger brother. Although Mitch had Will's crystal blue eyes, his face wasn't blessed with the same stunning angles as his brother's.

"Did you know Mitch was All-State baseball player last year?" he said enthusiastically. "Very athletic. And nice too. A real gentleman to the girls."

He raised an eyebrow at me.

"Um, that's interesting," I said, not quite getting why he was telling me all that.

"I'm just saying he's a real nice boy. And he doesn't have a girlfriend right now either."

"Yeah, I know. We have Biology together. He is very, very nice."

Coach must have sensed my disinterest. "I mean, not that I really care one way or another who he dates." He waved a hand dismissively. "It's the wife that never gives it a rest. I'd just like him to find some girl so we can finally talk about something different at dinnertime."

A twinge of guilt ran through me thinking of Mitch. Like all the kids in my grade, I'd known him ever since I could remember, but it had always been in a peripheral way. He was cute enough and sweet enough, but he had never been the kind of guy to catch my attention before. Yet after I met Will, Mitch had suddenly become a lot more interesting to me. Now I struck up conversations with him, picked him as my partner in biology class, found any way to be close to him in the vain hope that if we became friends, I could glean some more intel on Will through him. I'd even fantasized about Mitch inviting me to Sunday dinner so I could see Will and his family up close and personal. The only problem was, I had a feeling that Mitch had mistaken my sudden interest in him as something more than just friendship.

"You probably don't know my other kids though," Coach said, and I perked up immediately.

"This is my oldest daughter, Carol. She lives out on Route 37. Works at the real estate office. And this is my middle boy, Will. He goes to ISU." He turned the picture back to himself and shook his head. "Now this guy here." He tapped Will's face a few times. "He's the one most like his dear old dad. Which is probably why the two of us butt heads so much."

He laughed, but there was something sad in the sound. I thought of Will telling me he'd only just started coming back to Cold Springs because of some kind of falling out he'd had with his dad. I wondered what had come between them.

I leaned across the desk so I could get a better look at this son I supposedly knew nothing about. "Oh yeah, I think I've seen him before," I said, trying to sound casual. "I heard he's helping you out with the team this year."

"Yeah. He is." Coach eyed me suspiciously, like he was wondering how I knew that. My heart dropped. Whoops. I'd better be more careful or else I might slip and tell him about how I was out until 2:00 in the morning last weekend drinking beer with his middle son.

Luckily, Coach went on without questioning me. "He was a great ballplayer, this one." He smiled as he looked down at Will's face. "I'd even go so far as to say he was the best player I've ever coached." It sounded more like he was talking to himself than to me now.

"Just a really amazing talent. God, I loved working with him." There was something about the way he said it that made me think I was the first person who had ever heard those words out loud.

"That good, huh?" I said in a voice so soothing it might as well have been my mom's. *Just keep talking, Coach. Tell me everything you know.*

"Oh yeah. Plus, he's really smart," he said. I held my breath, waiting. "Knows the game inside and out. Probably as well as I do, in fact."

"Wow? Smart you say?" I prompted.

"Yeah. He's been so helpful with the team too. Maybe because he's closer to their age. I don't know. They seem to listen to him..." he trailed off. I caught myself before I blurted out, "And how does that make you feel?"

An idea came to me then. A way for me to finally understand something I'd been wondering about ever since I first met Will.

"So, he's going to be a coach like you, then?" I asked innocently, hoping Coach would take the bait.

He startled a little, then looked up at me for the first time since he'd taken the picture off the cabinet. "Oh, no, no, no."

"No?" I asked. "Why not?" I'd been so surprised when Will told me he was getting a business degree at ISU. The idea of Will stuck behind a desk, taking phone calls, tapping at a calculator all day long? It just didn't seem possible. How could someone who could barely sit still long enough to finish a Coke at Pizza King survive being holed up inside an office all day long?

Coaching would be perfect for Will. When he showed up in the gym after school, kids always swarmed around him. I'd watched him giving them pointers on how to improve their game, lifting their arms and squaring their shoulders so they could feel the right angles for a shot. I'd heard him bark like an overbearing brother, then shower them in cheers and high-fives when their balls swished through the net.

Those kids adored him. They hung on his every word; came back to see him week after week to report on how they'd improved, raving about how his advice had been right. They were better ball handlers now that they spent at least thirty minutes a night dribbling with their less dominant hand, just like he'd told them to.

Will was a natural leader, a natural coach. I'd told him that before, but he'd just given me a sad smile and brushed it off, saying his family had other plans for him. Plans that had been handed down a long time ago and weren't up to him to change.

Coach was shaking his head. "Naw, Will can't be a coach. I told him he had to get a degree that would make him some money. Then he could come back and take over the family business. Be successful. Not get stuck in a teaching job that pays shit like I did."

I wanted to point out to Coach that it didn't look like he was struggling to get by on his salary. Not with the enormous house they owned, all their brand-new cars and nice clothes and beach vacations they took (according to the pictures behind him). But then I remembered the real estate business Will's grandfather owned. I looked down at the notepad in my lap. There were four different locations in southern Indiana printed underneath the main heading. Scott had told me before that most of the Calder's money came from the Finnegan side of the family, not from Coach's teaching salary.

When I opened my mouth, I sounded scarily like my mom. "Well, I think that if you get to do something you love, then money doesn't really matter." It came out sounding righteous, but I didn't care. Will's happiness was on the line. I might have a chance to save him from a life of budget summaries and year-end reports, if I could just get Coach to listen to me.

Coach looked down his nose at me and laughed the same smug laugh that had made me want to slap Will across the face more than once. "Oh, out of the mouths of babes," he said condescendingly. "Listen, you're young. You don't understand it all yet. It's up to us parents to make decisions for you kids, so y'all don't end up making the same mistakes we did. You get that?"

I nodded dumbly, shocked that he was blatantly admitting to forcing Will into a career he didn't want. It was the exact opposite of my mom's parenting philosophy. She was always harping about how she trusted me to make my own decisions, telling me it was the only way I'd learn to navigate life for myself. I'd always thought her hands-off approach was just an excuse to cover up the fact that she was too busy with her own life to get involved in mine. But now that I saw the flip side to my mom's laissez-faire attitude, it made me realize how much I appreciated the freedom her blind trust afforded me. A freedom that Will didn't seem to share.

Coach looked down at the picture again. "Still. I wish he'd just let it go," he mumbled cryptically.

"Let what go?" I asked, heart revving in my chest as I waited. Was Coach about to reveal the secret Will refused to tell me?

It was almost like he hadn't heard me. "I mean, I told him I was over it," he went on. "I told him I'd forgiven him... that everyone had forgiven him. He's gotta know everyone makes mistakes."

I could barely breathe now. "What mistake did he make?"

He looked up at me like he'd forgotten I was sitting right there. "You don't know?" It reminded me of Will in the car. *You really don't know?*

"Know what?"

Coach waved a hand at me. "Oh well, if you don't know, then all the better." He whirled around and put the picture back. It was all I could do not to leap over the desk and grab his collar and scream, *"Tell me what it is!"*

"I told him everyone had forgotten about it. But then again, if you knew my son, you'd know he's kind of dramatic. He tends to make a big deal out of everything."

"Yeah, he is quite a drama king," I mumbled under my breath.

Coach furrowed his brow. "What did you just say?"
Shit.

"Uh, I just mean guys *in general* are dramatic," I stumbled over my words. "Drama here, drama there. Drama, drama, everywhere!"

Coach tipped his head at me. "I guess," he said,

looking unconvinced. I must have confused him with my inane rambling though because he didn't press the subject. He just gave me a few more suggestions for what to include in the newspaper column, then sent me on my way before I put my foot in my mouth again.

After he'd dismissed me, I surfaced from the locker room gasping the relatively fresh air of the gym, still reeling from everything that had just happened.

My mind whirled back over all Coach had just disclosed. Will had made some kind of mistake. One that Coach had forgiven him for, but that Will still couldn't let go of. I saw Will standing in front of me at the drive-in, admitting there was something he'd wanted but couldn't have. And in the car saying he'd learned the hard way what lack of focus can do to someone.

I had so many questions. I could go to Scott and ask him to tell me what Will's big mistake was, but that just didn't seem right. Not when I knew how much it upset Will. I'd experienced first-hand what it felt like to be the target of town gossip. I knew how humiliating it was to find out that people knew things about you that you hadn't told them yourself. I didn't want to talk about Will behind his back like people talked about me behind mine. Besides, finding out the details of Will's mistake wasn't even the point. What I really wanted was for Will to finally trust me enough to tell me his secret himself.

CHAPTER TWENTY-TWO

"25 OR 6 TO 4"

TIMING WAS EVERYTHING in band class, and unfortunately, today mine was off.

Usually when we finished playing a piece, I'd lurch back to my seat, taking cover in the crowd of boys so Jimmy wouldn't notice me. But today I'd slipped up and lingered too long at my music stand looking over the last stanza of Chicago's "25 or 6 to 4". I hadn't noticed how the tempo slowed at the end, so I'd played it too fast. I'd been trying to figure out how to fix my mistake for next time. But in doing so, I'd made a much bigger mistake. Because when I turned to sit down I was alone and defenseless, and Jimmy was there waiting for me.

I tried to sneak past him. "Come here," he said, reaching up from his chair with the speed of a cobra strike. He hooked my belt loop with two fingers and pulled me down onto his lap before I even knew what had happened.

I landed on him with a thud. "What do you need, Jimmy?" I fought to keep my voice light. Any hint of distress would be like blood in the water to him.

"I just wanted you to feel what a huge boner you're giving me today, Red", he purred in my ear. His arm was like a band of steel strapped across my hips, driving my ass hard into his groin, making it clear that the claim about his boner wasn't figurative at all.

I wanted to fight him, to try to get away, but I knew that would only make things worse. Instead, I had to think.

"I did that to you?" I said sweetly. "I had no idea."

Steve was giggling inanely in the chair next to us, watching Jimmy's hand caress my knee with the same expression the creepy old man at the town pool had given me this summer as I'd rubbed baby oil into my legs.

Mr. Weinreight was busy screaming at the saxophonists, telling them if they didn't learn to come in on the right beat he was going to march down to the elementary school and get the sixth graders to play it since they at least knew how to read music.

But even if Mr. Weinreight had been staring straight at us, it wouldn't have mattered. The drum section was perched high at the top of the tiered room. From where he stood down below, his view of us was blocked when we sat in our chairs. That meant normal school rules didn't govern this space. That meant a lot could happen back here without anyone ever knowing about it.

"You do this to me on purpose. I know you do," Jimmy said.

"Oh really? And how do I do that?" I looked down

on his face. I hated that my first thought was of how cute he was; how the little smattering of freckles across his nose made him look like an adorable little boy. Surely there was some of that little boy's innocence still left inside Jimmy somewhere. If I could just reason with that part of him, then maybe I'd have a chance.

"You dress like this to turn me on," he said.

"What? You have a long-sleeved polo fetish? That's a bit weird, but hey, whatever floats your boat."

He laughed, but unfortunately, his grip didn't loosen. He still had his arm bolted across my waist like a seat belt after someone had just jammed on the brakes.

All I could think about was a filmstrip Mr. Jones showed us in science class last year. It was of a fly trapped in a spider's web. The more the fly struggled, the more tangled up it became, until eventually all it could do was surrender to its fate and let itself be eaten.

Trying to learn from the fly's mistake, I put my arm behind Jimmy's neck and rested my hand on his shoulder, doing my best to relax, despite the fact that my heart felt like it was about to pound a hole right through the middle of my chest.

"Well, your shirt makes these look nice," he said, running a hand along the side of my boob.

I jerked away. *That's enough!* My body said. *We're out of here!*

"Stop! That tickles!" I laughed, trying to cover for my body's mutiny. Then I forced myself to settle back into his chest, chanting, *I can't piss him off, I can't piss him off,* over and over inside my head.

"It's these tight jeans you wear every day that really

makes me hard." He caressed the washed-out denim. Steve giggled and stared as Jimmy traced the inside of my thigh with his fingers, slowly drawing his hand higher and higher up my leg until....

"Jimmy, don't!" I grabbed his hand and pulled it away just as he was about to graze the place that only I'd ever touched before.

Hearing my outburst, Monica Staub, one of the clarinetists that sat in front of us, whirled around in her chair to stare. I could only imagine what the scene must have looked like to her.

"Turn around, bitch!" Jimmy snapped at her. "This is none of your business!"

Monica shot me a disgusted look as she turned back in her chair. Of course, she would be mad at me and not Jimmy. That's just how things worked at this school. By the end of the day, there'd be a rumor going around that I was on my knees giving blow jobs to every guy in the drum section. Including Tommy, who I noticed was sitting back in his chair, looking pretty relaxed. It was probably the exact same look I got whenever the guys picked on him.

Jimmy wrenched his hand back from where I was holding it away from me. God, he was so strong. He put it back on my leg, but luckily, not as close to my crotch this time.

I prayed for the saxophones to get their damn entrance correct so Mr. Weinreight would order us to our drums again and I could escape. There was more at stake than just fending off Jimmy. Tina was across the room, only one tier lower than us. From her higher vantage point, all she had to do was look up to see me sitting on Jimmy's lap. Then a boob touch and crotch rub would be the least of my worries.

"Come on, Red, you know exactly what you're doing when you bend over with that sweet ass of yours right in front of us," he whispered into my hair. "Don't act like you don't."

"I have to set my drum up. I'm not sure how I'm supposed to do that without bending over." This time, when I glanced back at him, he wasn't even looking at me. Instead, his eyes were trained across the room at Tina. When he shifted me a little taller in his lap, I realized what he was doing. He was actually trying to make sure Tina noticed me there on top of him.

"You play innocent." His breath tickled my neck. "But I know deep down inside, you like it when I look at you."

My stomach flipped, sick with the knowing that a little bit of what Jimmy was saying was true. I did like the attention he gave me. I just wished I could have all his compliments without all the groping that came along with them.

Jimmy kept me prisoner on his lap for a while longer until the saxophonists finally figured out the elusive beat and we were all called back to our drums. After the piece was over, I made it to my seat so fast there was practically a cloud of dust coming off my heels.

I sat there, my head tipped back against the concrete wall, taking deep breaths, celebrating how lucky I was to dodge that bullet. Then Monica Staub called out to me.

"Tina wants you," she hissed, looking so happy with

herself I wanted to slap her. Everything inside me went cold. I'd forgotten about the clarinet, to trombone, to saxophone gossip network that ran with service more reliable than Ma Bell's. Maybe I hadn't dodged that bullet after all.

Jimmy and Steve snickered from their seats as I slowly stood and inched forward to see Tina. Jimmy tipped an imaginary hat at me like he was saying farewell to Marie Antoinette as she was being led to the guillotine.

Mr. Weinreight was writing on the chalkboard with his back to everyone, so when Tina saw me, she stood up in front of the entire class. Her face was an unnatural shade of scarlet which, (coupled with the unfortunate Bruce Jenner haircut she'd recently received), made her quite a disturbing sight.

"I... WILL... GET... YOU!" She mouthed furiously, stabbing the air with her finger like it was a dagger and I was its intended target.

Instinctively, I ducked for cover behind a music stand, sure a saxophone mouthpiece was about to be hurled through the air straight at my head. Every boy in the drum section was laughing his ass off now and Jimmy was the loudest. He was having a grand old time celebrating the predicament he'd created for me.

I scurried back to my seat, crouched over at the waist, like a soldier diving for a foxhole, then collapsed on the folding chair. "Stop laughing!" I whined at the boys. "She scares the shit out of me!"

"Yeah!" Jimmy called over the four boys sitting between us. "She scares the shit out of me too! Man, I'd hate to be you right now, Red."

The boys burst out in more fits of laughter. I couldn't believe Jimmy would so blatantly use me as a pawn in whatever sick game he was playing with Tina.

"I hate you," I growled at him. I didn't even care anymore if he got mad at me. What did it matter? In five minutes the bell would ring and Tasmanian Devil Tina was going to whirl across the room and beat the shit out of me. Jimmy suddenly seemed harmless in comparison.

After milking a few more laughs at my expense, Jimmy finally came to my rescue.

"Relax. She's not going to beat you up." He stood like he was about to walk down the row to me.

"No! Don't come over here!" I cried, turning away. "You're only going to make it worse!" I briefly caught eyes with Tommy, sitting two seats away. Was he laughing at me too?

"Alright, alright." Jimmy sat back down in his chair. He stared straight ahead and called instructions out of the side of his mouth like he was the head of some kind of covert operation. "I've got a plan, okay? Just listen and you'll be fine."

"Are you sure?"

"Of course, I'm sure. We're drummers. We stick together, right?"

"We do? Because if that were true, then none of this would've happened in the first place."

"Just relax," he said, ignoring my insolence. "You and me. We take care of each other. Don't we?"

I glanced at him. He stared back, eyebrows raised and waiting. I looked at the clock. In one minute, class would be over and Tina would unleash her fury upon me.

"Yes, we take care of each other," I relented. My heart sunk, wondering what kind of pact I'd just agreed to. I had a nagging feeling that I'd just made a deal with Jimmy that one day I was going to regret.

�'

This was Jimmy's plan: When the bell rang, a group of the biggest drummers would close ranks around me and escort me to my next class, with him stationed at the back to fend off Tina's attack.

When Jimmy said drummers stick together, he meant it. Like literally. In fact, the guys stuck together so tightly on the way to my English class I could barely see anything beyond their heads and backs and shoulders. All I could hear was Tina shouting behind me, some squeaking of tennis shoes on the linoleum floor, and the sound of skin on skin, which I assumed was Jimmy wrestling her away from me.

"*STAY AWAY FROM MY BOYFRIEND YOU FUCKING BITCH!!*" Tina shrieked, her hysterics dividing the throngs of startled kids in the hallway like Moses parting the Red Sea.

"Just keep walking," Steve commanded to my right. (*Like I was going to do anything else?*) I felt a rush of air along the back of my head, the prick of a few stray hairs being pulled from my scalp. Jimmy must have slipped for a second and let Tina get too close. When I heard him laughing, part of me wondered if he had released her on purpose just to give himself another thrill.

The boys stared straight ahead as they marched me down the hallway, each of them so serious about their assignment I felt like I was being flanked by the Secret Service. In fact, if Steve had talked into his sleeve, mumbling, "Air Force One, we've got Red Robin secured and are delivering her to the drop off point," it wouldn't have seemed out of place.

When we finally got to my classroom, the boys deposited me inside with a cascade of chivalrous bows, then some high-fives to their fearless leader, Jimmy, who was now squared off with Tina outside the door.

As I sat down at my desk, Stacie glanced up from her textbook. "What was that all about?"

After I told her the whole sordid story, she gave me a look like I'd forgotten something really important. "Okay, so they got you here.... but how are you going to get to your next class?"

"I have no idea," I said miserably.

My English teacher, Mr. Boucher, watched indifferently out the doorway as Jimmy and Tina fought in the hallway. Tina was now dissolved in tears, beating on Jimmy's chest, screaming "I hate you!" while he smirked down at her with a satisfied expression. It seemed his plan had gone exactly as he'd wanted it to.

Watching Tina break down, I was surprised that I felt more sorry for her than anything. Yes, she was the girl who wanted to knock my front teeth out, but seeing her there, groveling to Jimmy in front of the whole school made me want to run to her side, shake her, and tell her to wake up, Jimmy wasn't worth it. That she should open her eyes and see how he was manipulating her. That in a perfect world it should be she and I banding together to knock Jimmy's front teeth out, not each other's. But then I remembered that's not how girls at Cold Springs High operated. These Packs had decided long ago their resources were scarce. They truly believed they had to compete ferociously for everything they got. They'd never consider working together against a common enemy. Even if it was in their own best interest.

Stacie leaned across the aisle and hit my arm. "I still think we should write that story on Jimmy and his bullies," she whispered.

I made a face. "I thought we talked about this. We couldn't take on the basketball team." I pulled my homework from my backpack and pretended to be enthralled with checking my answers so Stacie would drop it.

"We could and we should. Now that we have this platform, we have to use it for good. I mean, if we don't do something to stop them, who will?" she pleaded.

"I can't talk now. I need to finish this before class." I faked like I was adding to one of my answers. I really didn't want to get into this again. Because even though I knew Stacie was right -that someone should do something to stop Jimmy's reign of terror- that didn't mean that person was going to be me.

She leaned across the aisle and pulled my pencil out of my hand. "Jane would do it," she said with a mischievous grin. Stacie knew all about my latest obsession.

"Yeah, well, I'm no Jane Pauley!" I yelled. When the surrounding kids looked over at me my face flamed.

"Look at that." Stacie pointed out the door where Jimmy and Tina were now kissing passionately, hands running up and down each other's bodies. God, it was so disgusting. How could she give in to him so easily? Didn't she see what he was doing to her?

"You're just going to let him get away with that kind of behavior? Jerking everyone around for his own entertainment?" she said.

"He's not that bad."

Stacie huffed. "There you go again. Sticking up for him."

"I'm not sticking up for him. You're just making too big a deal about everything."

"Too big a deal?" Stacie's cheeks were red. "Why are you criticizing me? You're supposed to be on my side, not his!"

I blinked at her, surprised by how angry she suddenly become. Why wouldn't she just let this issue go?

"Stacie I'm sorry," I said, leaning closer. But she wouldn't look at me.

"It's fine. Whatever." She flipped open her English book and pretended to be engrossed in *Beowulf*.

I sat there waiting for class to start, stomach churning, cursing myself for screwing everything up so badly. Not only had I pissed Stacie off, but I also had no idea how the hell I was going to get to my next class now that my bodyguards were gone. I wished I could go back and play the damn "25 or 6 to 4" song the right way the first time. Then none of this would've ever happened.

I cringed, watching Jimmy and Tina give each other one last slippery kiss before she headed to her next class. She didn't even glance in my direction when she left. I guess I was nobody to her now. Just a faceless pawn in their game of love, or whatever the hell you called what was going on between them. Jimmy kept his eyes on Tina until she disappeared around the corner, then walked over and casually leaned in the doorway to my class.

"Hey, Red!" he shouted, ignoring the rows of heads bent quietly over their books. Mr. Boucher gave him a withering look but said nothing. Basketball players could do whatever they wanted at school. No teacher was brave enough to reprimand the boys who brought such glory to our town.

"I've got it all taken care of," Jimmy said. "You've got nothing to worry about now."

He winked at me, and a couple of girls glanced over with the same lucky-you expression I got whenever Jimmy talked to me.

"Like I said before," he called out, chest puffed up big. "We drummers stick together."

Stacie narrowed her eyes at me. "Yeah. That's exactly what I thought."

CHAPTER TWENTY-THREE

THE OATH

"Take out your Bibles, class," Mr. Boucher said.

Stacie and I rolled our eyes at each other. "I can't believe this. And in a public school!" Stacie whispered loudly.

Mr. Boucher looked over his glasses and gave her a thin smile. "We've been over this, ladies. Scholars have studied the Old Testament as a work of literature for years. And that's the only way we will be examining it in this class. As literature, not philosophy."

"Yeah, but still," Stacie said indignantly. "There are so many great books to read and you choose the *Bible*?"

I agreed with Stacie, but I'd never say it out loud to Mr. Boucher. Or even in front of our other classmates, most of who were now glaring at Stacie like a drop of water might melt her into a steaming puddle any minute. Stacie didn't give a shit, though. She said whatever popped into her head and never even cared what anyone thought about it. It was another of her many superpowers I wished I possessed.

Mr. Boucher read a passage out loud in a low drone. He went on and on, line by line, verse by verse, Lest Thou by Take Thee. I tried to concentrate, but my mind kept drifting back to the look on Tina's face as she was groveling with Jimmy in the hallway. There was something about the desperate expression that reminded me of an incident with my dad that happened when we still lived on the farm. It wasn't something I wanted to think about right in the middle of English class, but I couldn't stop. The images kept flooding back, no matter how hard I tried to keep them away.

It was around the time Karen and her friends had first started coming to our house, but before I understood the reason why. We were all in the living room, watching the movie, *The Rose* with Bette Midler. It was late, way past my bedtime, and it was an R-rated movie, so I really shouldn't have been there. But Karen had begged my mom to let me stay up.

Normally my mom wouldn't have allowed me to break the rules, since (being a military man) my dad was very strict about my schedule. But that night my dad wasn't home. Ever since the girls had started coming over, he spent more and more nights at the bar in town after work. Since he wasn't there, my mom had given in and let me stay up. It was an unusual act of defiance that, in hindsight, I should've seen as the first red flag that something big was changing in our household.

When my dad had come home later that night, Mom and Karen were squished together in an easy chair, I was sitting on the camel saddle that he'd brought home from one of his deployments, and the other girls were all piled next to each other on the couch.

The room was dark, lit only by the flicker of the TV light, so I barely noticed him in the doorway.

"Hi everyone," he said, waving awkwardly.

"Oh, hi," Mom said. The girls all joined in with stilted hellos.

He hesitated for a split second, like he was about to say something more, then thought better of it and headed up the stairs to their bedroom. When he disappeared, the girls all looked at each other and started laughing. My mom hit Karen on the leg and told her to stop, but for some reason Mom was laughing too.

I looked back at the TV to see what was so funny but all I saw was Bette Midler having some kind of horrible break down, screaming at the guy she was supposedly in love with, and collapsing on the floor of a hotel room sobbing her eyes out. I couldn't figure out what was so funny about that.

A second later, Mom whispered in my ear. "Go up and check on your dad for me."

I had no idea what she was asking me to do. "Check on him? Check on him for what?"

"Just see how he's doing," she said in a terse voice she hardly ever used with me.

I was furious at her for making me leave the movie. I climbed the stairs to their bedroom like a death knell was playing behind me, complaining the entire way to myself: *Why did she ask me of all people to check on Dad? What did checking on someone even mean? Wasn't*

that something grown-ups did to kids, not the other way
around? I'm not even a good choice for this job. Dad
doesn't even really like me that much in the first place.

When I appeared in his doorway, Dad looked as surprised to see me as I was to be there.

"Uh, hey there kiddo," he said. He emptied his pockets into the brass bowl on his dresser. It had the heads
of two Bedouin sheiks painted in enamel on the inside,
both staring off into the distance, with these strange, sad
smiles on their faces. It was another souvenir from his
time overseas in the Air Force.

"Hi," I said, surveying him up and down. I wasn't
sure, but I figured a good once-over was the first step of
checking on someone.

He looked tired, but that was normal for him. My
mom had explained last year that it was the pills that sat
next to the brass bowl that made him that way. The cancer
that had come from the chemicals he'd flown in Vietnam
was gone now, but he had to take all the pills to keep it
away for good. When she'd said that, I couldn't help but
think of the Keep Away game we played in gym class. The
one where you had to keeping running and darting and
zigging and zagging, doing whatever you could to stay
alive. I guess my dad was playing the same game, except
with the cancer. It was no wonder he was always so tired.

The room was painfully silent, and I was desperate
to think of something to say. Then I remembered the one
thing my dad and I had in common.

"It looks like Daisy's just about ready to have her
calf. Me and mom brought her into the barn today…
just in case."

"That's good." He smiled, then took a swig from a beer bottle I hadn't even noticed sitting next to the vials of pills. There were three more empty ones on his nightstand, a couple more on the counter in the bathroom. "I'd hate to be pulling a calf out next the pond like we had to do with Bertha last year."

"Yeah," I agreed, trying to think of what to say next. "And Poulet got all tangled up in that roll of fencing next to the barn. It took us almost half an hour to get her out. She was fighting us the whole time!"

"Stupid chicken!" He shook his head, exasperated. "That's what happens when your brain's the size of a pea." He unbuttoned the top button of the dress shirt he wore to his job at the bank. The job he hated but couldn't quit because it "funded this entire operation." At least that's what I'd heard him tell my mom when I'd eavesdropped outside their door on the way to the bathroom a few months ago.

My dad and I stood there smiling at each other for a few seconds, the silence seeping back to level off at where it had been before. Then he reached up and tugged at his ear and half of it came off in his hand.

It was a prosthetic. That was the new, big word I'd learned after the surgery my dad had the year before. The one to remove the lump on his earlobe that turned out to be melanoma, the kind of cancer he now took all the pills to keep away.

I remembered how shocking it was when I'd first seen my dad after the surgery. The top part of his ear was sitting there on his head like always and then, *bam*, halfway down, the rest was gone. The cut went straight across, its edge so sharp it was like the surgeons had laid a ruler against his ear and just whacked off the bad part in one precise slice.

It had only taken a couple of weeks for me to get used to the way he looked with the half ear sticking off the side of his balding head. Then one day, he and Mom came home from Bloomington with a plastic box about the size of my headgear case. Inside was the bottom half of an ear made out of rubber. The *prosthetic*. The fake ear fascinated my mom. She called it a work of art and made me hold it and look at it closely so I could admire all the details that made it look so real. The bumps and ridges and blue veins painted so subtly inside; the color of the "flesh" that almost perfectly matched the top half of my dad's ear on which it would be glued.

I didn't agree with my mom's assessment of that ear at all. Half a body part in a box was no work of art to me. I thought it was gross and creepy. Like something you'd find sitting on a table in a haunted house. When I said that out loud my mom had shushed me. She said my dad was really excited about the ear and I shouldn't ruin it for him. She told me he'd been self-conscious about the way he looked after the surgery and that's why he hadn't gone back to work until the new ear was ready, even though the doctors said he could. He'd been too embarrassed for anyone to see him with only half an ear on his head. Now this new, museum-worthy ear in a box was going to fix all that.

I'd made sure to never say anything about that gross ear again, but something always confused me about what she'd said. I couldn't understand why my dad, a retired

Air Force pilot with a drawer full of medals and accommodations, who had flown secret missions into North Vietnam to rescue downed pilots in the war, was worried about the way he looked. Why did he care about what other people thought about him? I thought only insecure kids like me were supposed to think about dumb stuff like that. Not a fully grown war hero like him.

That night, my dad had put his ear on the dresser next to the brass Bedouin plate. I took it as my cue to move toward the door, figuring my mission was complete. I had checked on my dad. Now I could go back to Mom, report that he was the same as always, and get back to the girls and the movie. Then maybe I could find out if Bette got her happy ending the way I hoped she would.

"Well... good night then," I said.

"Good night, honey."

I remember how close I'd been to being out of the room. If I'd only moved faster, I would've been in the hallway, and I could have just pretended I hadn't heard when he called out my name. But unfortunately, I was just a few seconds too slow.

"Just one more thing," he said when I turned around.

My heart sank hearing the hollow tone of his voice. I'm not sure how I'd known that what he was about to say next would be bad, but somehow I did.

"Uh huh?" I said, swallowing hard.

He looked down at the beer in his hands, scraping the label with his thumbnail as the seconds ticked by like hours in the quiet room. He didn't speak for so long I thought maybe I was going to escape after all. But then he'd asked the question that, still to this day, I wished he hadn't.

"When I walked by earlier... you know, when you all were in the living room," he started haltingly.

"Yeah."

He took a deep breath. Raised his hand to rub the sharp edge of his half ear. "Were those girls laughing at me?"

The hurt in his eyes made me look away before I even knew why. There was something in them I shouldn't have seen, I knew that much. He was a grown-up. I was just a kid. He was my dad. He wasn't supposed to look like that. I shouldn't have seen what I just had.

I remembered the girls laughing for no good reason. The way my mom had hit Karen on the leg and told them all to stop. Immediately, I knew Dad was right. They were laughing at him. And at the very same instant, I also knew I couldn't tell him that.

"No," I lied, "they weren't laughing at you. It was just a funny part of the movie." My face burned like I was standing on the surface of the sun, not the green shag carpet of his bedroom.

My dad nodded. But the sad look was still there. I thought I'd said the right thing. But somehow, he'd still known I was lying.

When I'd made it back downstairs, I was so mad at my mom I didn't even file my report on my dad's demeanor the way she'd wanted me to. I couldn't explain why I was so angry. I just knew she had done something to make him look that hurt. It took a few more months before I finally figured out what exactly it was.

That's why the desperate look on Tina's face when she was pleading with Jimmy in the hallway seemed so familiar. Why I couldn't help but think back to that night. It was the same humiliated look that my Dad had when my mom and the girls had laughed at him.

Now, sitting there, listening to Mr. Boucher drone on and on, all I could think about was the pain I'd seen in both my dad and Tina's eyes. About how stupid they'd both looked. What fools they'd been. My dad had been ridiculed at the bottom of his own staircase. Tina had been turned into a raving lunatic in the middle of the school hallway. And for what reason? Because of the whim of some stupid *other person*?

Now the questions wouldn't stop coming, no matter how furiously I tried to stop them. Was that what happened when you let yourself really care about someone? You risked being laughed at? Made fun of? Losing all control? Of your happiness... your sanity... your dignity too? I sure as hell hoped not. Because if that was what love was like, then you could count me out. I'd lay my hand on that Bible Mr. Boucher was holding and take an oath in front of this entire classroom:

I will *never* let that happen to me.

CHAPTER TWENTY-FOUR

"TUMBLING DICE"

"I THINK YOUR Dad likes me," I told Will as he handed me back my beer.

We had an unspoken ritual now. When I wanted a beer I'd hand him the bottle, he'd twist the cap off, then hand it back to me. For Will, it was a way to keep track of how many beers I drank. He still only allowed me to have two bottles a night, saying he didn't want anyone to think he was taking advantage of me. (He always laughed really hard when he said that part. Like the idea of the two of us ever being together in that way was so completely hysterical to him.)

For me though, our beer ritual was just one more little special thing that he and I shared; so rote and thoughtless now it was like we were an old married couple standing at the sink before bedtime, passing the toothpaste back and forth, taking turns to spit.

"He does like you," Will said, turning down the

stereo. It was another thing he did that made me feel special. Turning down Mick to listen to me. "He talks about you all the time."

"He does?"

"Well, he talks about the *column* all the time," Will corrected himself. "And about you too. At Sunday dinner last week he was going on and on about how smart you are. How great your writing is. He even called you his own little secret weapon." He lifted an eyebrow at me.

"Wow," I marveled. I couldn't believe Coach would bring me up at Sunday dinner of all places.

Scott and Will always talked about their family's weekly ritual of getting together for Sunday dinner at the Calder house. I'd fantasized for so long about one day being there, sitting next to Will, that I'd inflated it into something straight out of a TV show. I pictured the Calders like the Ewing family on *Dallas*. Coach the stoic patriarch J.R., Will's mom the classic beauty Sue Ellen, and Will the sexy Bobby. I couldn't imagine them ever sitting around their huge dining room table, inside their enormous house, talking about someone as unimportant as me.

"See? I'm not the only person who thinks you're pretty great," he said.

My face flushed. "Looks like I've got you both fooled."

"Red. We've talked about this," he warned.

"Oh yeah, sorry, I forgot. I'm supposed to say I'm the greatest of all time!" I pumped my fists in the air. "Just like Muhammad Ali. That's what you do, right?

Walk around telling everyone how great you are all the time?"

"Pretty much." He gave me a playful wink. "Although you might need to dial back your charm a little."

"What do you mean?"

"I think my dad might think you're a little *too* great. He's trying to fix you up with Mitch."

I tried my best to look surprised, although Coach hadn't been very subtle with his "he's a real gentleman to the girls" comment back in the office. I knew he'd been angling for something.

"Yeah, my mom's been on the warpath to find Mitch a new girlfriend after he got dumped last month. She's all worried he's going to end up with no one to take to Homecoming. I think the two of them have decided he should set his sights on you."

I swallowed hard, wishing it wasn't so dark in the car so I could read Will's expression. Was he bothered by that plan, or did he agree with his parents? Did Will think I should go out with Mitch too?

He glanced over at me. "Don't look so worried. I took care of it."

"What do you mean, you took care of it?"

"I just told them it wouldn't work. That you're way out of Mitch's league."

It took a second for what he'd said to sink in. And when it did, I was shocked. Not only had Will just admitted I was an actual *girl* capable of being dated, but he'd also placed me in some kind of league out of reach of his own brother. And yet, as thrilled as I was by the development, I still couldn't stand the superior look on Will's face.

"That's not very nice. I'm not out of Mitch's league."

His face clouded over. "Of course you are. You're way too good for him."

I was so confused I couldn't even think of a comeback.

He watched me for a second. "What? Why are you giving me that look? Do you actually *want* to go out with Mitch?" He took the corner so fast it threw me into the passenger side door.

For a second, I considered lying and saying yes just to see how he'd react. But I was too afraid of making him mad.

"No, I don't want to go out with him!"

"Well, good because.... because..." he stammered. "He's my *brother*, Red!"

"I know he's your brother. What's that got to do with anything?"

He stared out the windshield for a few seconds before he answered. "It just wouldn't be right."

I gave him a funny look, not understanding his vague rationale. "Fine. Whatever."

"Good." He seemed relieved that we'd reached an agreement.

I couldn't figure out what had just happened between us. Had Will been jealous at the idea of me going out with Mitch? It was too crazy to be true, and yet he'd seemed determined to squelch the possibility quickly. I stared out the window, thinking over the exchange. A fingernail moon hung above us, its glowing edges blurred, making it seep into the dark sky. I couldn't help but feel a bit of that same glow seeping inside me too.

We didn't talk for a little while. We both just drank our beer and listened to the Stones, letting the silence tamp down between us. I snuck glances at Will whenever he turned his head away. He was dressed casually tonight, in a worn St. Louis Cardinals jersey and faded jeans. He and Penny must have stayed home and watched TV together instead of going out like they usually did. The thought made me sick to my stomach because it meant they might've had sex. I tried to put the image out of my mind and instead focus on how handsome he looked. How the white of his shirt offset his tan skin. How the sleeves of his jersey fell just above his elbows, showing off the muscles of his forearms. *God, is it normal for me to get that turned on by looking at a boy's arm?* It didn't seem right, and yet my body- with all its random throbs and pulses- clearly wasn't interested in sorting out the rights and wrongs of the situation at the moment.

Will finally broke the silence. "You were great at the party."

"Great? What do you mean?"

"Your story. You did great. You had everyone laughing." He seemed proud of me for some reason.

I shook my head at him. "You shouldn't have made me do it."

I cringed, remembering how Will had called me over to the circle of older kids he was standing with and ordered me to tell my story.

I'd tried to get out of it. "Will, no... it's stupid," I'd argued. I was so nervous it felt like my heart was going to pound its way right out of my throat. I couldn't tell a story to all those people. What if they didn't think it was as funny as Will had?

"It's not stupid, Red," Will said patiently. "I loved it."

He'd been standing directly across from me, eyes locked on mine. It was like in the cartoons when one character hypnotizes the other by making those red and white circles whirl in their eyes.

Waiting until I was fully under his spell, he then commanded gently but firmly, "Tell them."

I'd started off slowly, looking only at Will, trying to tell the story like I'd told him in the safety of his dark car. It was about when I was showing my cow at the 4-H fair a few years ago. The huge red heifer had taken one step through the gate of the ring, looked at all the people in the stands and then frozen like a statue. No matter how I pulled and prodded, she'd made it clear that she was not budging. No way. No how.

The crowd at the fair had laughed, which made everything even that much worse. I'd ended up throwing my body into the cow to shift her off balance and get her to move. Luckily, it had worked. The only problem was, when she finally took a step, I was so close to her that her hoof came down right on the edge of my bell-bottomed jeans. That meant when I lunged triumphantly forward, my elastic-waist pants stayed bolted to the ground underneath the cow's hoof. Then simple physics took over (body in motion forward, pants at rest behind), and I ended up flashing my bare ass to a stadium full of spectators.

I'd gained momentum as I told the story at the party, bolstered by Will's eyes locked on mine. It was like all his overwrought confidence had somehow leapt right across the circle of kids and straight into my body. I'd added actions. Mimed the furious tugs. Described the out-of-fashion jeans in embarrassing detail. The surrounding group leaned forward, eyes wide as they listened to the mortifying story. Each of them nodding along like they were right there next to me in that ring until finally I capped it all off with my punchline:

"So, you could say the moon came out early over the 4-H fairgrounds that afternoon, if you know what I mean!" I slapped my ass for emphasis as everyone erupted in laughter.

The sound nearly levitated me right off the ground. Then suddenly everyone else fell away, and it was just Will smiling at me, his impossibly blue eyes shining with approval.

"But you were amazing back there!" Will gushed. "They loved it!"

"Yeah, but that kind of stuff makes me nervous. I don't like all that attention."

"Again, I don't understand you. Attention feels amazing. Like a shot of adrenaline right to the heart!" He pounded his chest hard. "You just gotta get used to it. Slowly but surely. All it takes is some practice."

"I don't like it when you boss me around like that," I grumbled. I knew I sounded like a baby, but I had to stand up to him a little. I'd been around Will long enough to figure out he didn't like things to be too easy.

If I gave in too much, he'd eventually get tired of me and decide to move on to his next fixer-upper project.

"I'm not bossing you around. I'm trying to make you better, remember? And how are you going to get better if you don't keep trying?"

When I didn't respond, he leaned toward me, flashed the same magazine smile that had launched busloads of his female disciples. "Remember baby, you have to do anything your heart desires," he sang, his voice low and breathy. I knew it was from a song, but I was too flustered to remember which one.

"You remember you're not Mick Jagger, right?" I snapped. I hated when he used his good looks to try to make me cave. Especially since it always worked.

He sat back, seeming to recalculate.

"You gotta keep putting yourself out there," he said. "Don't sell yourself short. You miss 100 percent of the shots you don't take."

I rolled my eyes. "Enough with the basketball references, Will. I thought I was here to learn about music."

"Music, basketball. Basketball, music. It's all intertwined for me."

Hearing him bring up basketball reminded me of the things his dad had said in his office about Will making some kind of mistake. I suddenly saw a way to finally bring up the topic.

"So tonight," I said, "I did what you asked me to. I told the story like you wanted."

"Yeah."

"I think it's time for you to tell me a story too."

He shrugged. "Sure. About what?"

"I want to know about this supposed mistake you made."

He squeezed the steering wheel, knuckles going white. "Oh, man.... not now.... I thought we were having a good time here."

"You said you'd tell me, eventually. I think it's time. I mean, it's only fair. Tit for tat, right?"

He laughed the way he always did when I used that phrase. *Do boys ever grow up?* Then he sucked in a great breath and blew it out heavily. "I guess you're right," he relented. "Fine then. If that's what you want. I'll do it. I'll tell you the whole damn awful story."

I couldn't help but think he was just being dramatic again. Especially remembering Coach's mumbled words "*I told him to just let it go...*"

"Are you sure it's that bad, Will?" I asked.

He shrugged. "Maybe it's not. Maybe I'm just being dramatic," he said, making me wonder for the hundredth time if he could truly read my mind. "Maybe I'm just a fucked-up has-been that can't move on. Do you think that's it, Red?"

"Well, I don't know. I guess I can't really say until hear the story first."

"Fine. Listen to the damn story," he grumbled. "But I hope you appreciate this."

"Appreciate what?"

"The fact that I wouldn't do this for anyone else but you."

Will found a tiny dirt path that cut between two over-grown cornfields and parked the car. I'd heard stories of couples parking on deserted roads like this to make out, but I knew better than to hope for something like that to happen between Will and me.

"Let me find just the right track first," he said, look-ing through his cassettes. A few seconds later, "Tumbling Dice" began pouring through the speakers. It was a song The Rolling Stones had written about a down-and-out gambler who'd run out of luck. In my head I fast for-warded over the depressing lyrics, hoping it was just another of Will's ploys to add drama where there wasn't any; that his story wasn't really as sad as he was making it out to be.

He fidgeted in his seat, brows furrowed, like he wasn't sure where to start.

I watched him. "All sixes and sevens and nines, huh?" I quoted the lyrics. When we first studied "Tum-bling Dice" Will told me the phrase meant someone who was mixed up and confused.

He blinked at me in the disbelieving way he often did. Gazing at me like I was someone he'd just met even though I was the same me that had been sitting next to him all along.

"You're good, Red," he said. "You know me so well."

He rubbed his hands up and down his jeans a few times and took some deep breaths, like he was prepar-ing himself to jump into a frozen lake. He looked so upset that for a split second I almost let him off the hook and told him to forget it, I didn't really need to know the truth after all. But the tantalizing prospect of what he was on the verge of saying kept me silent. I was about to find out just how much of himself he was willing to share with me. There was no way I was stopping him now.

Finally, he blurted out, "Well, it's obviously about what happened in the state basketball championship."

I stared at him blankly.

He rolled his eyes. "Oh, I forgot. You're the only person in this entire town that doesn't know what happened in the state championship."

"I told you. I was kind of busy back then."

"Oh, right. With your dad. Sorry."

I pushed on not wanting to get sidetracked. Now was not the time to talk about the years I'd spent watching my dad slowly succumb to cancer. "I know a little about the championship game. I know it was close and that we almost won. But then there was some sort of big heartbreak right at the end."

Will winced when I said the last part. "Yeah, well, that's just it," he said. "*I* was the big heartbreak."

I made a face. "What do you mean?"

"Okay, here goes. I'll try to set the scene for you." He swept one hand across the windshield in his theatrical way. "It was a David and Goliath story from the start. We were the underdogs. Tiny little hick school Cold Springs going up against giant Crispus Attucks from Indianapolis. They had all these huge black kids. It was practically the NBA, you know. And you gotta remember, we'd never even played against any black kids before. And those guys, man, they were all so —"

"Yeah, yeah. I know all of that. I read the article," I cut him off before he said something I'd have a hard time pretending not to hear. Not a single black family lived in Cold Springs, or in any of our neighboring school districts, for that matter. In fact, our area of southern Indiana was so segregated I'd even heard rumors that the KKK still held meetings at a pizza restaurant only 45 minutes away. I'd always believed that Will wasn't as racist as a lot of the other people in our town, even though I had no proof of that. I prayed my faith in him wasn't misplaced, but so far, I'd been too scared to press him any further on it. Too afraid to find out the truth about what he really believed.

"I got it," I prompted him, "David and Goliath. They were huge, you guys weren't. Go on."

"We'd been down the entire game, but somehow, we'd fought back. I mean, I was on fire. I was playing for my life. Hitting outside shots, inside shots, somehow pulling down rebounds over these guys that were like a foot taller than me."

His expression had softened like he'd slipped into a waking dream. "It was insane inside that field house. The crowd was so damn loud. I mean, we could hardly even talk to each other out on the court. Even if we shouted at the top of our lungs, we could barely hear each other."

He stared out the windshield, needing another deep breath before going on.

"It came down to five seconds left on the clock. We were down by one point with possession of the ball. So Dad called a timeout to set up our last play."

He studied me for a second, like he wanted to make sure I'd sorted out all the details before he went on.

"I got it," I assured him, conjuring the scene in my mind: Boys running to the sidelines, all sweaty and desperate and exhausted. Every one of them knowing all their hopes and dreams now rested on a few unforgiving ticks of a clock. My heart pounded as if I were standing right next to Will in that gym, desperately craning toward Coach in the huddle, trying to hear the directions that would ultimately change my life forever. For better or for worse.

"I asked for the ball," he went on. "I mean, it only made sense. I was a senior. The captain. I was the one hitting all the shots. It seemed like a no-brainer to me. I'd just let a couple seconds tick off, then take the outside jumper the same way I'd done to win regionals. Then it would all be over. We'd be the state champions."

I tensed, knowing that's not what happened. Seeing the look on Will's face made me want to hold my hand over his mouth so I didn't have to hear the rest of the story.

"But Dad told me no. He said they'd be expecting that, so he wanted me to fake the jumper but then dish it to Collins, one of our guards, who'd be standing under the basket ready to put in an easy layup." A bitter look hardened in his eyes. "He actually wanted me to give it away to fucking Collins, a guy who'd barely scored all night. He wanted me to let him take the shot."

"Uh huh," I said. Coach's logic seemed so clear to me sitting safely in that quiet car. But I had a feeling it wasn't so clear to Will that night in the hot, packed gymnasium.

"I begged Dad to let me have the shot, but he wouldn't back down." He threw his hands in the air, pleading to the nothingness of the night stretching before us. "He said I had to trust him. That he'd thought it all through. That he knew what was best."

"So, what did you do?" I asked, even though I was pretty sure I already knew the answer.

"Well, I acted like I was going along with it, but even as we broke the huddle, I knew I wasn't going to listen to him."

"Oh Will, no." I wanted to reach over and shake him hard. Yell at him to not be a hero. To listen to his dad for God-sakes.

"They inbounded the ball to me. One second ticked off. Then another." He cocked his head, mumbling like he was in a trance. "The weird thing was, they didn't even guard me that closely. It was almost like they were daring me to take the shot...."

I held my breath, waiting.

"And so I did." He dropped his chin to his chest. "And that's when it happened," he whispered to the floorboards. "He came of nowhere, this huge guy lunging at me. I saw him out of the corner of my eye and for a split second, I lost my focus. I took my eyes off the basket and looked at him instead. God, I can still see his face." He shuddered like a blast of cold air had just blown through the car. "His eyes were so big, just staring into mine like he could read every thought inside my head."

I felt like I was hanging there, suspended in the air right alongside Will.

He whirled in his seat, pleading with me as if I could somehow save him from what was about to come next. "I swear to God, it was only a split second, Red. But it was enough. The ball was just rolling off my fingertips and I felt something different inside. I don't know why, but instead of seeing myself making the shot like I usually did, I saw myself missing it." His eyes bored into mine. The pain I saw there made a chill run down my spine. "And that's exactly what happened. I missed the game-winning shot."

It took a second for me to catch my breath before I was able to speak. "Oh my God. That's awful."

"And the worst part was just as the ball was leaving my hands, I looked down and Collins was just standing there all alone under the basket. He would've had an easy layup, just like my dad said. But by that time, it was too late. The ball was gone. The buzzer was ringing. I couldn't take it back. It was all over."

He looked so miserable, slumped there, his face marbled red and yellow by the dashboard lights. I wanted to reach over and wrap my arms around him and give him the kind of hug my mom always gave me in moments like that, but I knew I couldn't.

Instead, I said, "But you did your best. The team wouldn't even have been in that position to win if it weren't for you."

"Yeah, yeah, that's what everyone tells me. But I still fucked up and everyone in this entire town knows it. If I'd just listened to my Dad, Cold Springs would have a state championship right now. My dad would have a state championship right now. And that's the worst part.

It's what he's dreamed of his entire career, getting that championship. And he had the chance to do just that, and I took it away from him." He narrowed his eyes at me. "Just by being fucking stupid."

The words hung there, snapping hot between us like a tangle of snipped electrical wires.

"Will, stop it. You're not stupid. It could have happened to anyone. Basketball's a game of chance."

His eyes went wide. "A game of chance?!" he said like I had no idea what I was talking about, which, of course, was true. I didn't know what it was like to put myself on the line like he had. I knew nothing of making a huge decision and then being forced to face the consequences of it like he'd had to in that gym.

"Well, if that's what you think," he said, "that it's all up to chance, then it looks like I rolled the dice and lost, huh?"

The song tapered to an end in the background, Mick ironically repeating, "*you've got to roll me.... you've got to roll me....*" over and over, almost like he was taunting Will.

Will scrubbed his face with his hands like he'd just woken up from a bad dream. "Wow. I don't think I've ever told that story to anyone before."

"Really?"

"I've never had to. Everyone around here just knows it already."

"Yeah. I guess that's true."

"I know it's the first thing every person in this town thinks of when they see me," he said. "They smile and pat me on the back and talk about everything I did for that team, but I see it in their faces. Underneath all the bullshit they're shoveling me, they're remembering that night. That shot. They're remembering how I robbed the entire town of a championship. They hate me for it."

I couldn't believe what I was hearing. "Will, that's crazy! No one hates you!"

I sat there, stunned. Will was so wrong about what people thought about him. I'd seen the way everyone looked at him. I knew how much everyone in the entire town still admired him. Shit, the old men at Hunter's Diner were still telling the story of his last second buzzer beater at the '79 regionals like it had happened only yesterday. People in Cold Springs didn't hate Will. They loved him.

Seeing how badly he'd misinterpreted the truth about himself made me think about my own situation. Every time a person in town passed by me, I conjured some sort of ghostly judgement in their faces. Was I doing the same thing Will was? Making up things that weren't actually true? Seeing condemnation in peoples' eyes that wasn't really there?

Will spun his class ring around and around on his finger. "I know for sure it's what my dad thinks about when he looks at me." His voice was so soft I could barely make it out. "Every time he sees my face, all he can think of is what a failure I am. That's why I stayed away for so long. So he wouldn't have to look at me and remember how I fucked everything up."

"But you're wrong!" I cried. "Your dad told me he loved coaching you. He said you were the best player he'd ever worked with. I could tell how proud he was of you."

His eyes shot to mine. "He said that?"

"Yeah. When I was in his office the other day."

"Why would he tell you that?"

I shrugged. "Probably because he thinks I don't know you, so it was safe to tell me how he really felt."

He considered that for a second. For the first time since he began the story, the edges of his mouth lifted the tiniest bit.

I plowed on quickly, trying to capitalize on the shift. "How could anyone blame you? I mean, think about it. You had the guts to be out there, to willingly put all that weight on your shoulders. Most people never take on anything as scary and hard as that, but you were asking for it! I sure as hell could never do that. I mean, what you did... all you accomplished... it's amazing." I hesitated, scared to say what I really wanted to. "*You're* amazing, Will."

He searched my face, like he was trying to figure out if I was being sincere or was another in the long line of people he could no longer trust to tell him the truth. I understood his scrutiny all too well.

"You're sweet," he said with a sad smile. Then he wagged a finger at me. "That's what's different about you, Red. You never look at me the way everyone else around here does."

"No, and I never will." I hated seeing him defeated like this. It was so out of character for him. I struggled to think of a way to make him feel better. "Seriously, you shouldn't be so hard on yourself. I think you're amazing." I'd said it twice now, which was double the amount of honesty I was used to, and yet I knew it was exactly what he needed to hear.

He scoffed. "Well, you also think Miller Lite is good beer," he pointed to the bottle in my hand, "so I'm not sure I can trust your opinion."

I knew he was trying to lighten things up and change the subject. And as the inventor of that game, I figured the least I could do was play along.

"Why do you keep buying Miller Lite then, if you hate it so much?"

He tipped his head like I'd asked a silly question. "Because *you* like it, Red."

The sincerity in his voice left me speechless. It was hard for me to imagine Will even thinking of me outside the walls of the car, much less taking the time to consider what I did or did not like.

I opened my mouth to thank him, but he cut me off. "So now that you know my whole awful story, can you see why I keep drilling into you all that stuff about believing in yourself? Why I keep telling you to stop doubting yourself all the time? Now do you get why I know about that so well?"

"Yeah, I get it now."

"When you see yourself losing, you lose. Just like I did."

"Will, stop..."

"I'm just trying to make sure you don't end up being as much of a disappointment as I am." His smile didn't reach his eyes.

"Okay, that's enough now. Self-loathing doesn't look good on you," I teased. "I want the old pompous, know-it-all Will back now."

"Oh, don't worry. He's still in here. Somewhere."

"That's good. Because I'd miss him if he left. Besides, you know you're contradicting yourself."

"How so?

"Weren't you just telling me how you miss 100% of the shots you don't take?" He nodded, and I went on. "So why don't you give yourself the same break? Give yourself credit for trying."

"Because I'm me. And I should've known better."

I burst out laughing. "Oh, because you're not a mere mortal like the rest of us?"

He shrugged, hesitating like he had to think it over. I was glad to see that smug part of him really hadn't completely disappeared after all. "Well, I'm just saying it had all worked so well up until then. Why would I have picked that moment to forget everything? I just don't get it. I knew better. And yet I still fucked up."

"You fucked up because you're human. Nothing more. Nothing less." I couldn't believe how much I sounded like my mom.

He sighed heavily. "Yeah, I guess," he said like he still couldn't quite accept his own flaws.

"Besides, I think you're still right about going for it and taking the shots," I said. "Its just that you're confused about the next part."

"The next part?"

"Yeah, Mick keeps saying it," I pointed to the stereo. "The lyrics are *you've got to roll me*. Remember?"

"Yeah, of course I remember. It's the refrain of the entire song."

"See what he's saying? You've got to roll me... that's all. He doesn't say you've got to roll me and then arrange everything so the exact perfect numbers come up. Don't you see? The only thing we're in charge of is rolling the dice, Will. None of us can control where they land."

The words that had just come from my mouth surprised me. Usually I was exactly like Will, constantly beating myself up for something I'd done wrong and trying desperately to find a way to fix it. But now, from seemingly nowhere, I'd just admitted there was so much of my life that I had no control over. Hearing it out loud was strange. Where had that idea come from, anyway?

"Ugh!" he growled, running his hands through his hair roughly. Then he slammed both hands on the steering wheel so hard the sound made me jump. "We have no control?! I don't think I like that!"

I slammed my hands on the dashboard really hard, mocking him. "Yeah! Me neither!"

"Ugh!" he slammed.

"Ugh!" I slammed back.

We did it a few more times, slamming back and forth until we were both cracking up.

"Just think about it this way," I said when we finally stopped beating up the car. "Isn't the whole not-knowing part what makes life so fun?" Again, it was like I was saying the words as much to myself as to him. "That's what makes this all a game. And you love games, right?"

He nodded slowly, considering. "Well, that *is* true."

I searched for another example. "Like when you asked me to join The Ride. I didn't know what was going to happen here. All I could do was roll the dice and then wait and see what happened next. And I think this turned out pretty well. Don't you agree?"

He stared out the windshield, thinking. "Yeah, I'd say it's turned out really, really well." He turned to me, a slow smile spreading across his face. "*Amazing* even." He gave me a little wink.

I knew he was making fun of me for using that word so many times before, but his eyes were back to dancing mischievously like usual, so I didn't really care.

"Man, I think my dad is right about you, Red. You're awfully smart."

"Hey, I'm not a genius. I just play one on TV," I said, using the voice of the fake doctor in the cough syrup commercial.

He shook his head at me. "I thought I was the one that was supposed to be the teacher here, not you."

"Well, maybe I have a few things to offer you too." It wasn't until he cocked an eyebrow at me that I realized how provocative that sentence had sounded. My mom would've called it a Freudian slip. And she would've been right.

Will held my stare as a light rain began to fall, walling the windows in opaque rivulets; turning the small space into even more of an isolation chamber than it already was. The sudden encasement made me feel even more acutely how alone we were on that dark little path. So alone that anything could happen in that front seat and no one would ever know about it.

Will suddenly startled, breaking the lock between our eyes. "Um, we better get going, huh? It's getting late." He turned the ignition and dropped the gearshift into reverse so abruptly it made me think that he'd just felt the same sense of possibility that I had too. And from how fast he was revving the car out of the road, he clearly wanted to squelch it quickly.

"Fuck, why did I tell you all that?" he moaned, glancing back and forth between his side mirrors as he gunned backwards down the lane.

"Because I got you drunk and took advantage of you?" I said flatly.

He gave me a rough, big-brother push on the shoulder, then whirled the steering wheel under his palm, aiming the car down a road that now seemed as expansive as the Autobahn compared to the tunnel of cornstalks in which we'd just been enclosed.

But before he sped up, he leaned over the console. "So, did it surprise you to find out the truth about me?"

"What's that?"

"That I talk a good game, but I'm basically full of shit."

It was now my turn to give his shoulder a shove. "Oh, not at all," I said cheerfully. "I've known that for a long time!"

He tipped his head back and laughed loudly. A flood of satisfaction poured over me, watching his clear relief. I couldn't hug him like I wanted to, but I could make him laugh. And for now, that would have to be enough.

ᡐ

We kept cruising around aimlessly and I swear to God, I tried my best to act normal. I switched out the cassettes and handed Will beers and teased him when I caught him fixing his hair in the rearview mirror. But inside I felt like I was standing on top of the Empire State Building thumping my chest after all he'd just shared with me.

That's probably why I got so cocky. Why, when Will got out of the car to take a piss, I thought it would be a good idea to chug the rest of my last allotted beer, hide the bottle beneath my feet, and help myself to another one before he got back in the car and noticed I'd gone over my limit for the night.

I was so sneaky I could barely contain myself. It was all I could do not to burst out laughing at how clever I was. I'd tricked him and he had no idea what I'd done. But after I'd guzzled my extra beer in record time, I started to wonder if it was more than just my sneakiness that was making everything so hysterical. And that's when I realized that maybe there was a good reason Will didn't let me have more than two beers a night.

The headlights blurred into two funnels of white on the road in front of me. And when I turned my head and look around, it took a second for my eyes to catch up. Everything inside the car seemed fuzzy, like the dashboard and windows and Will himself were all coated in this weird hazy glow.

I shifted sideways in my seat to watch Will drive. It was like I was in a dark theater watching a movie instead of sitting right there beside him in real life. The moonlight flashed bright and sporadic over his face, like a strobe light at a disco dance. He mouthed the words to the song on the stereo, his fingers tapping idly on the steering wheel in time to the music, the muscles in his arm moving just slightly with every drumbeat. *God, there I go, lusting over his arm again.* I couldn't help it though; it was just so beautiful. His arm and his wrist too, with the thin skin that looked so soft and the little blue veins that ran under his watch. Had anyone in the world ever looked sexier wearing a Timex watch? I didn't think so. And his face. I didn't even want to get started on how perfect that was. I could've written for two whole days just on the bones of his cheeks, the plump symmetry of his lips, the mysterious shadow along his jawline that I was dying to just reach out and....

"Are you staring at me?" he glanced over and gave me an odd look.

I knew I should've looked away, but I couldn't. It was like my eyes were magnetized to his face and I didn't have the strength to break the connection.

I felt the words coming and yet couldn't stop them. "What does it feel like?"

He furrowed his brows. "What does *what* feel like?"

I raised my hand up and rubbed my own jaw. "Your face... like along here... what does it feel like?"

Oh God. Did I actually just say that out loud?

He grinned and ran his hand along his face the same way I'd done mine. It made a funny sound, like when I ran my thumb across the bristles of my toothbrush.

"Oh, you mean this? This is just a five o'clock shadow. It's nothing really."

I could have easily saved myself then. Just said okay and dropped the subject. But the beer wouldn't let me shut up.

"But what does it *feeeeel* like?" I leaned my elbow on the console to get a closer look.

Will seemed surprised. "Do you actually want to feel my face, Red?" he asked, laughing.

It was my last chance to salvage my dignity, and yet I let it pass by with barely thought.

"Yes."

Has someone hi-jacked my vocal cords? What the hell is happening to me?

Will shook his head, like he couldn't believe what I'd just asked of him. I knew how he felt because I couldn't quite believe I'd asked it either. I was sure he was about to piece together that I'd snuck a beer when he wasn't looking and yell at me for breaking his rules. But instead, when we came to an intersection he brought the car to a complete stop, put it in park, and turned to me, eyes dancing in delight.

"Well then, if this is what you want." He reached over and gently took my hand in his. My heart pounded so hard that no amount of beer could calm it now. I knew if I looked into his eyes, I wouldn't be able to go through with it, so instead I concentrated hard on the edge of his cheek like the fate of all of beard science rested on the data I was about to collect.

He laid my fingers on the curved part of his jaw, close to his neck, then guided my hand down toward his chin. It seemed so simple, and yet he did it in this very slow and deliberate way, which made it incredibly sexy.

"It's so prickly," I breathed when we got to his chin, fighting the urge to inch even closer to him than I already was.

"Uh, huh." He lifted my hand and put it higher on his cheek on a spot where his skin was smooth and flaw-less. "But it's not prickly everywhere," he explained. I felt him staring straight into my eyes, but I still couldn't meet his gaze.

That time, when he guided my hand along his face, it felt like there was velvet underneath my fingertips.

"It's so soft," I said dumbly, all my cleverness completely robbed by the feel of his skin on mine.

When he finished, he didn't let go of my hand right away. Instead, he laid my palm flat on his cheek, covered it with his own hand, and pressed down hard. It felt like my entire body had been reduced to a single humming ache with a heartbeat pounding inside of it. He was so close I could feel the tickle of his breath on my lips. I finally met his eyes and when I did, it felt like every molecule of air inside the car had suddenly been vacuumed away in one gigantic whoosh. His sky-blue eyes pierced into mine, and in them I thought I saw a question that was only mine to answer.

One part of me felt like all I had to do was lean one millimeter toward him and everything I'd ever wanted would instantly be mine. But a bigger part of me screamed that I was an idiotic drunk girl who was about to make a huge ass out of herself.

I pulled my hand away quickly. "Uh, well, thanks for that," I croaked, bracing against the passenger door to quell my light-headedness.

He sat back in his seat and scanned my face like he was trying to solve a maddening riddle he couldn't quite figure out. "Why are you so weird, Red?" he finally asked, a faint grin playing on his lips.

"I told you already, I got kicked in the head by a pony when I was little. That's why I'm the way I am."

He looked up at the car roof and smiled. "Oh yeah, I remember that story. The one where you fell face first into a pile of horseshit when it bucked you off?"

"That's the one!"

"I love that story." He put the car in gear and started driving. "Tell it to me again."

And so I did. He drove and I talked, and we went back to playing our previously scripted roles like always: Will, the flamboyant hero of the romantic movie and me, the wishful little girl admiring him from her seat in the audience.

And yet, even as we were going through the same motions, it felt like something had changed between us. Maybe it was because I was drunk, or delirious, or way too damn hopeful. But the question I thought I'd seen in his eyes... every time he glanced over at me, I swore it was still there.

CHAPTER TWENTY-FIVE

"SHE'S SO COLD"

THE NEXT WEEKEND I was still flying high by whatever unnamed thing had passed between Will and me when he'd pressed my hand to his cheek. Although it was hard not to notice that he seemed to be making a concerted effort to never let the car come to a complete stop now that we were alone. Like he was genuinely afraid I might ask to touch him again. And he *had* picked the song "She's So Cold" for us to study tonight, which made me wonder if he was sending me a message that I needed to cool myself off, since Will never just picked songs randomly. But I decided not to get discouraged so easily (a lesson Will had drilled into me these past weeks), and instead focus only on the look I thought I'd seen in his eyes that night. (Focus was the key to getting what you wanted. Another one of Will's lessons.) I guess that's what gave me the nerve to ask what I did next.

"So why isn't she ever here with you?" I blurted out

as I busied myself looking for the cassette we needed for the night's class.

"Who?" Will asked.

"Penny."

I couldn't believe I'd had the guts to say her name out loud. Over the past weeks, I'd concluded there was an unwritten rule about not talking about Penny on The Ride. Even Rob and Scott, who both obviously knew Penny well, seemed to make a point of not mentioning her. I wondered if it was because, like me, they'd noticed Will was always agitated when he first got back from seeing her and had decided it would be better not to bring her up. Or maybe it was because they knew how I really felt about Will and were trying to spare my feelings.

"Penny?" Will scrunched his brow like he was struggling to place a face with the name. I knew he said he liked to not think about the real world when he was on The Ride but forgetting the existence of the person he had been dating for five years was some serious denial.

"Yeah. Your girlfriend. Penny." I had no idea why I was even bringing her up. I liked pretending Penny didn't exist as much as the next guy. But I had so many questions about the two of them. Something about their relationship just didn't make sense to me. I wondered if maybe I could trick Will into shedding some light on how he truly felt about her.

He shrugged. "Oh, Penny wouldn't like all of this." He tried to make it sound casual, but I picked up on how he started tapping his thumb on the steering wheel even though there wasn't any music playing.

"She wouldn't like spending time with you? I guess I get that. You *are* pretty annoying."

He shook his head, exasperated. "It's not that. It's just that she doesn't like all this stuff." He circled his hand around the empty car as if that explained everything. When I looked confused, he went on. "She doesn't like drinking and listening to music and driving around. She says it's pointless. A waste of time. She thinks the only reason a person should drive is to get somewhere."

"Geez, that's weird. That sounds like the complete opposite of what you believe," I said innocently.

"Yeah, I guess." He shifted in his seat. "Did you find the song yet?"

I waved the cassette in his face. "Of course. I'm a master at this. Remember?" *Unlike Penny.* I fought back a smile as I slipped the tape into the player and began to fast forward to the right track.

He reached out like he was going to grab my hand away then, seeming wary of touching me, pulled back. "Just let it play. We have time."

He was right. We did have time. It was only 11:00 and Will rarely took me home before 1:00 in the morning. He never minded staying out that late, even though I knew he had to get up early for work on Saturdays, even earlier for church on Sundays.

"I guess Penny doesn't quite get The Ride, huh?" I said cheerfully. "How we actually *are* getting somewhere, even if it's more philosophically than physically. We're solving all the great mysteries of life out here! I mean, doesn't that count for something?"

He brightened. "Yeah, of course it does. But I'm

not sure she understands all that like you do, Red." He raised his beer to toast me.

I clinked my bottle against his, toasting me too. I loved the way he celebrated our partnership. A partnership that didn't include Penny.

"Wow, so she doesn't like drinking and listening to music? That seems like that's all you do." *Whack, whack.* I hammered the wedge even further between them.

He looked at me skeptically, and I wondered if I'd gone too far. "Well, she *does* like listening to music. It's just that she doesn't like —" He stopped himself. Glanced over at me with a sheepish expression, like he didn't want to go on.

"What? What doesn't she like?"

He took a deep breath. "She doesn't like The Rolling Stones," he said, morosely.

Thank God I was taking a big swig of beer at that moment. I wanted to do a full-on spit take like what Karen and I practiced in the bathroom (showering the mirror with a mouthful of water after one of us fed the other a fake punchline) but I was too afraid Will would get mad at me for messing up his windshield. So instead, I pretended to choke on my beer; fake coughing and sputtering and dribbling some out of my mouth to soak my shirt until Will was practically driving off the road from laughing so hard. Yeah, it wasn't very ladylike, but that was okay. Sometimes you had to give up your dignity for the sake of a good joke.

I mopped my mouth with the back of my hand. "She doesn't like The Rolling Stones?!!" I bellowed, coughing a few more times for effect.

"I know. Crazy, right?" I loved how happy he looked at that moment.

"I thought a person would have to sign a contract agreeing to exclusive Stones listening rights before you would allow them within five feet of you!"

Somehow he grinned and looked miserable all at the same time. "I wish I'd thought of that. But you know, it was a long time ago."

"Back before you were obsessed with the Stones?"

He gave me a pointed look. "Back before I knew what I *really* wanted." His eyes bored into mine, making my stomach drop out from under me like the car had just plummeted over a cliff.

I told myself I was getting carried away again. Seeing signs and reading meaning into things that weren't really there. There was no way Will was saying what I thought he was.

And yet, the tantalizing flicker of hope gave me the courage to push him more.

"Does Penny know about me?" I asked quietly. It was a bold question; one that implied Penny might have a reason to worry about whatever was happening between Will and me all these nights we were alone together. As soon as the words were out of my mouth, part of me wished I could take them back. Will was probably going to laugh at me. Ask me what the hell did it matter if Penny knew about me or not? But the other part of me thought his answer might reveal a lot about what this elusive, achy truth between us really meant.

Will didn't laugh. In fact, his face was deadly serious when he finally answered. "Um, she's never really said anything outright." He kept his eyes purposely trained out the windshield. "But yeah, I think she knows about you."

"So, does she —"

"We should probably listen to the song now," Will interrupted, turning the volume up like he wanted to drown out my words before they touched air and became real. So that's what we did. We listened to the song. I never got to finish the question I'd started:

"So, does she know about the phone calls too?"

CHAPTER TWENTY-SIX

"HONKY TONK WOMEN"

THE CALLS STARTED a few weeks ago. One night when I was doing my homework, my bedroom door had flown open. Karen was standing there with the phone in her hand, the cord stretched tight from the kitchen, through the dining room, into the hallway, to just outside my bedroom door.

"There's a boy on the phone asking for Red?" she said, looking confused. My mom and Karen didn't know about the nickname the boys at school had given me.

I turned down the volume on my boom box. It must have been Scott, wanting me to go over his Latin vocabulary words with him again. He was so bad at memorization. I kept telling him if he'd just make up a song for them, it would make it so much easier, but he never listened.

Music blasted through the receiver Karen was

holding. "Jesus Christ, where's this kid calling from, a rock concert?"

When I recognized the song, everything inside me went still. It was "Honky Tonk Women" by The Rolling Stones.

I sat bolt upright in my bed. *No way. It couldn't be.*

I clamored for the ornate gold phone next to my bed that looked like it had been ripped from Louis the Fourteenth's home office. "I'll take it in here," I gasped. *Breathe. You have to remember to breathe.*

The music, now coming from both phones, swelled even louder in my room.

"Fine," Karen huffed, disappearing back to the kitchen as I put the receiver to my ear. The song was definitely "Honky Tonk Women". There was no question about that now.

I covered the mouthpiece with my hand. "*Hang up!!!!!*" I shrieked so loudly I was pretty sure I dislodged a piece of plaster from my popcorn ceiling. Karen muttered "Jesus Christ" again and then her line clicked off.

In a state of complete panic, I chanted to myself: *It can't be him. I'm sure it's not him. Why the hell would it be him?*

And then: *Is this really happening? This can't be happening! What the hell am I going to say?*

"Hello," I choked out. That seemed like a good start.

"Red!!" Will shouted through the phone.

Oh my God, oh my God, oh my God. It's him!

"Will, what's going on?" I stammered. "Why are you calling me? Are you okay?" Nothing made sense right then.

"Of course, I'm okay. Why are you asking if I'm okay?"

"It's just... just... it's pretty late and you've never called me before, so..."

"What's the big deal? I just had a free minute, so I thought I'd call and check up on you."

My heart pounded at the sound of his voice inside the walls of my bedroom. It felt like he was standing right next to the bed looking down on me lying there in my threadbare Holly Hobby night shirt.

"Yeah, me and the guys just got back from some parties," he said, "and I said Hey, I'm going to see what my friend, Red, is up to."

My friend, Red. Great. So this was a friendly phone call, that's all. Why would I have thought it was anything different?

"You're partying on a Tuesday night?"

"Every night's a party when you're in college. You better be prepared for that. It's all parties, and sex and drugs and rock 'n' roll."

I smiled at his familiar refrain. "So that's all there is to college, then? Sex, drugs, and rock 'n' roll?"

"Yesh, and *parrrrtiessss*... there's lots of parties too!" He was slurring his words really badly. I'd never heard him like that before.

"Aren't you forgetting something?" I asked.

"Like what?"

"Like classes maybe?"

"Oh, yeah. *Claaassses*. Uh huh, there's definitely those too. But those are *waaaay* not so fun."

The state he was in shocked me. Will always drank

when we were together, but I'd never actually seen him drunk. In fact, it was one of his rules on The Ride: Sloppy drunks were not tolerated. It was the reason he was so careful to keep track of how many beers I drank each night.

"Are you *drunk*, Will?"

"Naw. I'm just feeling *goooood*." He giggled a little at the end.

He was definitely drunk. I tried to think of a way to trip him up. "You're wasted."

"I'm not *wayshted*, Red!" he lisped.

I laughed. "You're shit-faced."

"I'm not *schiff-faced*!"

This was getting funnier by the second. "Yeah, and my hair isn't red."

"It isn't red. You told me yourself. It's... it's... cherry blonde... or something like that."

"It's strawberry blonde," I corrected him. "Get your facts straight, loser." I couldn't believe he remembered me telling him that.

I heard him sigh. There was the shuffle of footsteps, the click of a door, and everything got quiet on his end of the line.

"Fine, so maybe I'm just a little *teeeeeny* tiny bit drunk," he admitted softly. His voice had the faintest echo in it now. I pictured him locked inside a dark closet, the cord of the phone threaded through a crack in the door. "But you can't make fun of me 'cause it's all your fault."

"My fault? Why?"

He was silent for so long I almost thought he hadn't

heard me. Just as I started to repeat myself, he blurted out, "Because I just can't seem to drink you off my mind."

Everything inside me froze when I heard the line from "Honky Tonk Women". I took a deep breath and told myself to calm down. It meant nothing. He was only singing along to the words of the song. I waited for him to turn up the stereo and sing the chorus loud like he always did in the car, making his voice all twangy to match Mick's. But then I realized the music wasn't playing anymore.

The silence swelled, jammed packed with so much left unsaid. The pause became awkward, until I finally blurted out, "So, tell me more about these parties..." We talked for a while longer, both of us falling into the easy banter we had in the car. I could have stayed on the line with him forever, but after a while, Will abruptly said he had to go. I pretended like it was a tremendous relief to say goodbye since I had so much homework to finish.

When the line clicked dead, I felt like I was going to explode straight through my ceiling. I was so excited I couldn't contain myself in my tiny bedroom anymore. I had to get up and ping from room to room in the dark house with a smile on my face so big it felt like it was spring loaded there.

All I could think about was Will's voice. Of Will picking up the phone and calling me. Of Will saying he couldn't drink me off his mind. Had he really meant it? Or was it just a line in a song to him? It was hard to discount it as nothing, since Will was always so intentional about the words he hi-jacked from Mick and Keith to use as his own.

I was wandering around aimlessly, trying to figure out what had just happened, when I bumped into Karen outside the laundry room.

"What was that all about?" she asked, looking mad. I guess it had been kind of late when the phone rang. I hoped it hadn't woken my mom.

"Oh that? That was nothing. Just a friend calling." It took everything I had to wrench the smile off my face.

"At 11:00 on a Tuesday night? What kind of friend is that?"

"Oh, it's Scott's cousin. He's in college, so he stays up late."

"He's in college?" She scrunched up her face. "Why the hell is he calling you?"

"Oh, it's nothing. I think he was just bored."

"Just bored? Seems like more than that to me."

"Oh, pshaw! You're nuttier than a pee-can pie on Derby Day!" I said in the southern accent Karen thought was so funny. She didn't laugh like she normally did, though.

"Don't worry. It's nothing like what you're thinking, Karen," I assured her. "This guy has a girlfriend."

"Right. He has a girlfriend."

"Uh, huh. They've been together forever."

"He has a girlfriend, but he's calling you in the middle of the night?"

"Yeah. But, like I said before, it doesn't mean anything."

She turned sideways, squeezing past me to get to the kitchen. "You may *think* it doesn't mean anything. But I wouldn't be so sure about that."

CHAPTER TWENTY-SEVEN

THE AMENDMENT

"UGH. I HATE that monstrosity!" Stacie glared at the retreating school bus that had just dropped us off in her driveway.

We'd complained the entire 30-minute ride home about being reduced to lowly bus riders again. Scott normally drove us everywhere, but now that he and Holly were officially dating he was spending more and more time at her house after school. Which was great for him but sucked for Stacie and me as it only further exposed us as little baby sophomores, too young to even have our driver's licenses.

When we got inside the cabin, we threw our backpacks by the kitchen table and Stacie got us some snacks; our normal routine on Monday afternoons when we had to get our column churned out for the next day's submission. Usually, Stacie's mom was there to serve us since she didn't work, but today she'd left a note for us saying she was volunteering at the library. Luckily, she'd left a loaf of her homemade bread cooling on the counter. I salivated just thinking of the butter melting so salty and rich into the fluffy insides of the bread. Once again, I wished the Cunninghams would just adopt me. I pretty much lived at their house, anyway. If I moved out, my mom and Karen probably wouldn't even notice I was gone. In fact, they'd probably be relieved to not have to stop their busy lives just to drive down to Cold Springs and pick me up all the time.

Stacie put some slices of bread and butter in front of me, then went to the corner of the living room and threw some logs into the wood stove. The downstairs of the cabin was basically just one huge room, so the heat of the flames began warming my skin before Stacie even got our milk poured.

We devoured the bread as we read through our notes. I tried to concentrate on the work, but the fullness of the bread in my belly and the warmth of the wood stove on my back made me want to slip over to the denim couch and curl up for a nap next to Stacie's cat. My foggy brain defaulted back to what it always did whenever it got a free moment: thinking only about Will. As I watched Stacie read, I got the idea that if I revealed a little of what was going on with me, maybe she could help me untangle all the knotted-up thoughts inside my head.

I took a deep breath and dove in.

"He calls me sometimes," I said, my voice sounding way too loud in the still room.

She looked up. "Who calls you?"

"Will."

She dropped her pencil. "Will calls you? On the phone?"

"No. He leans out his window and yells like Tarzan." I snapped. I always got extra sarcastic when I was nervous. "Yes, he calls me on the phone."

"Really?"

"Yeah, it all started a few weeks ago. On a random Tuesday. Just out of the blue."

Her eyes went wide. "He called you on a random Tuesday? Just out of the blue?"

"Uh, huh." I told her about how Will was drunk when he called. And how he'd said he couldn't drink me off his mind.

"He said that?!" She snatched my hand across the table and squeezed it hard.

"Ow!" I cried. "Yes! He said that."

She looked past me, out the living room window. "Wow. I might have to rethink this whole thing then."

Stacie was still adamant I was wasting my time with Will. She'd even recruited Scott to talk some sense into me. He'd pulled me aside the other day to remind me that my obsession with Will was pointless. I'd lied and told him I totally agreed. That I thought it was time I stopped hanging out with Will so much too. I said I wanted to get back to being more of a normal high school girl like I used to be. But I'd only said that to make Scott leave me alone. I knew he and Stacie only wanted the best for me, but it had kind of pissed me off that they'd talked about me behind my back like I was some kind of freak. The rest of the school already whispered about me enough. I didn't need my best friends gossiping about me too.

"Do you think it means anything?" I asked, my heart lifting. "Because at first, I did. And then I didn't. And then I did again. And now... Oh, I don't know. I'm just so confused!"

"I can imagine. The guy is pretty confusing." Stacie rolled her eyes. "So, how long has it been going on?"

"For a few weeks now. Why do you think he calls?"

"Well, it could be because he likes you and wants to talk to you."

"You think?" I said, fighting back a goofy smile.

"Yeah. You know how the saying goes: 'What is said when drunk has been thought out beforehand.'"

"You mean, Will thought about the fact that he couldn't drink me off his mind *before* he actually tried to drink me off his mind?"

Stacie giggled. "Well, I think we may have just been sucked into a Rolling Stones black hole with that statement. But yes, I think that's what I'm saying."

"Oh man. That would be awesome!"

"Or," Stacie went on ominously.

"No!" I groaned. "I don't want there to be an 'or'. Can you just stop before you get to the 'or'?"

"I'm just thinking that we have to account for Will's egotistical nature. He could just be calling you because he gets a kick from how much you obviously like him and talking to you gives him a shot to his self-esteem."

I slumped in the chair, not liking how rational her argument sounded. I felt like I should say something about how Will didn't have an egotistical nature, but I couldn't think of one shred of evidence to refute the claim.

"He's always sober when he calls me now," I added, hoping it would bolster my case somehow. "It's not like it's a mistake. He knows what he's doing."

"Oh, I think he knows exactly what he's doing," Stacie said in a tone I chose to ignore. "He's called you more than once, then?"

"Yeah. He kind of has a schedule. He usually calls every Tuesday and Thursday. And sometimes Sundays too."

Her eyes widened. "Wow! That's a lot."

Again, I tried not to smile, but it was hard to hold it back. I liked how Stacie was saying aloud all the things I'd already thought to myself. "What should I do?"

She shook her head, thinking hard. "Honestly, I'm not sure I really know. Has he given you any other clues about how he feels about you?"

I thought about that electric feeling that had passed between us when I'd touched his face. But that was too hard to describe in words, so I went for something easier. "He calls me Marianne sometimes."

Stacie scrunched up her face. "Why would he call you that?"

"It's after Marianne Faithful. She was a groupie for the Stones in the sixties."

"He calls you a *groupie*?!"

"Not outright. He knows that makes me mad."

"Oh, well, how kind of him not to insult you to your face," Stacie snapped.

"It's not insulting to be called Marianne. In fact, I kind of like it."

Stacie looked unconvinced, but I still didn't explain

the reason the nickname didn't bother me. I didn't tell her I'd spent hours at the IU library pouring over tiny microfiche articles about The Rolling Stones trying to learn more about Marianne Faithful's relationship with Mick Jagger; and how what I'd found there had made me want Will to call me Marianne every minute of every day, for the rest of my life.

"I think that's strange, but you can get your kicks however you want I guess," Stacie said.

"How open-minded of you, Stacie. Thank you very much," I deadpanned.

"I just think you should talk to him about what the hell is going on. It's weird how he wants you with him all the time. You know, considering his situation."

Again, something inside me swelled. So, Stacie had noticed it too. I wasn't just making up how Will acted like I was important to him. I thought of Karen saying his phone call might have meant more than he let on. Was there a chance the signs I thought I was seeing were real?

"You have to be honest with each other," Stacie went on. "And, by the way, I'd appreciate if you were honest with me too."

"What do you mean by that?"

"Why didn't you tell me about him calling you until just now? Usually you'd be on the phone with me the second after you hung up if something that exciting happened to you."

I swallowed hard, realizing she was right. Why hadn't I confided in Stacie like I usually did?

"I guess I figured you wouldn't like it," I confessed. "That you'd say he was just leading me on, and then I'd feel like shit. And I wanted to feel good for a little while, before I had to face the truth. I wanted to believe it was possible I could truly mean something to him."

Stacie searched my face, her eyes softening. "Of course you mean something to him. How could you not? No one could know you and not think you were the funniest, most hysterical girl in the world."

"Lucky me... a regular Bozo the Clown," I grumbled, picking at the corner of my notebook.

"I'm sorry. You know what I mean." She sat back in her chair and groaned. "Ugh! Seriously. I don't know what to tell you about all this shit! I have no idea what's going on with Will. Or with you. I don't even know what's going on with *me* most of the time!"

Stacie's admission took me aback. I wasn't used to her admitting to not knowing something. She always seemed so confident, so sure about everything in her life.

She went on. "Listen, I know you think I've got everything all figured out, but honestly, this whole boy thing is so confusing sometimes."

"I know. What's happening to us?" I said. "Everything seems so complicated all of a sudden."

Stacie scribbled some loopy circles on her paper for a few seconds. "Yeah and I think things are only are going to get even *more* complicated in the future." She gave me a mischievous grin. "Especially since I've decided to go through with it."

"Go through with what?"

She slapped both palms flat on the table, making me jump. "I'm going to lose my virginity," she declared loudly.

"What?!"

"Yeah. I'm going to do it!" I couldn't believe how excited she looked. If I had made a decision like that, I'd be throwing up in the trash can right then.

"You're really serious about this?" I asked, dumbfounded. "You're actually choosing to become an old shoe?!"

We both burst out laughing. It was an inside joke that had come from the "sex education" talk we'd had in Health class last year. (The quotation marks are because our teacher did not once mention the word sex in the discussion. That gives you an idea of just how educational it was.)

For the talk, Mrs. Beasley, our seventy-year-old Born-Again Christian teacher, told a long story comparing girls to shoes. In a man's closet, she'd primly droned, there were new, fresh shoes that had never been worn. And there were also old, beat-up shoes that had been worn around the block over and over again. She asked us to imagine a man going into his closet and looking at his selection of shoes.

"Which shoes do you think a man is going to pick? The used shoes or the new shoes?" While the rest of the girls murmured "the new ones" in their monotone Sunday school voices, Stacie and I fought to keep our faces straight. But when Mrs. Beasley whirled around, pointed right at us and shouted, "*Don't be an old shoe!*" we'd completely lost all control. We'd ended up laughing so hard, for so long, she'd eventually sent us to the principal's office so we could "think about our childish behavior". Now we used the old shoe line every chance we got.

Stacie shrugged coolly, firmly back to her confident self again. "I figure what the hell, it's going to happen sometime." She swept a hand down her body. "I gotta break in this new loafer sometime. I might as well get it over with."

I blinked dumbly at her, still shocked by this plan of hers.

Stacie watched me, looking pleased with herself for having left me speechless.

"So you and Mark are really going to do it." She and Mark's on-again-off-again relationship had been on a lot lately, so she hadn't been joining us on The Ride much as she used to. A development I was sure must have bothered Rob, even though he acted like he was fine with it.

"Probably," she said brusquely. "We'll see what happens."

My heart pounded just thinking of what she was suggesting. I couldn't believe that Stacie, the girl I'd known since we were twelve years old, who still slept with the blanket her dad gave her for her first birthday, could actually lay down in a bed naked with a boy and let him put his penis inside her. Could that really happen?! And if so (since the two of us had always been so much alike), did that mean there was a possibility that I could do the same thing too?

"When did you decide all this?" I asked. Our development had always been perfectly synchronized, and yet there she was, on the brink of losing her virginity when

I hadn't even had my first kiss yet. I suddenly realized how far behind she'd left me.

"I've been thinking about it a lot lately," she said.

"I guess there are a few things you haven't shared with me, either."

She looked guilty. "Well, you've been busy with *other people*, haven't you?"

"I guess that's true. But let's not argue, okay?" I really didn't want to go back to talking about how much I needed to let go of Will.

"Maybe we need to add an amendment to our pact about never letting boys come between us," Stacie said with a little smile.

"Yeah? Like what?"

"How about we make a rule that says we have to tell each other everything from now on?"

"Of course," I said, trying not to think of all the other things about Will I hadn't told Stacie yet. Maybe this new amendment could have a grandfather clause?

"Another pinky swear?" Stacie asked.

I laughed, thinking of how many times we'd pinky sworn over one thing or another since I'd known her. (*You always have to sit next to me at the lunch table. We will never, ever say the word* ya'll *in a sentence. I'll only be your bridesmaid if you promise there will be no bows on the dress.*) I reached across the table and hooked my finger in hers. We squeezed them together tight.

"Hey, wait a minute," I said, tipping my head at her. "Doesn't this feel like a strange juxtaposition? I mean do you really think a girl who still pinky swears is mature enough to be having sex?"

"Of course!" she said, eyes shining. "My mom always says I'm a Churchill quote come to life. A riddle, wrapped in a mystery, inside an enigma."

"A puzzle without a key," I added the ending to her mom's favorite jab about her.

"That's right," Stacie said, looking proud. "It's my life's goal."

"What is?"

"To be so damn unpredictable no one will ever figure me out!"

CHAPTER TWENTY-EIGHT

"BEAST OF BURDEN"

WILL PULLED THE Monte Carlo down a lane dissecting an empty pasture, then parked in front of a little blob of water everyone in town called Peanut Butter Pond. We got out without speaking and climbed up on the hood, the Stones singing softly through the car's open windows as we stared out across the water.

"You've been here before?" Will asked, arching an eyebrow at me.

I kept my gaze trained on the surface of the water. With the light of the moon reflected off its still surface, it looked like a polished oval mirror nestled inside a frame of dried-up cattails.

"Yeah, I've swum here before. I know why it's called Peanut Butter Pond." It came out sounding defensive, but I couldn't help it. Sometimes Will acted like he knew everything, and I was just a naïve little girl he carted around explaining the world to. I was always trying to prove to him I knew more than he thought I did. Like now. I could've told him they named the pond that because when you waded in it the mud squished up through your toes and coated your feet just like peanut butter, because I had in fact experienced that sensation firsthand. But he just stared out into the night and didn't ask me anymore.

A beat passed. "So, you've skinny-dipped here too, then?" he asked, a challenge in his eyes.

"Well, um. No."

"Right." He gave me a satisfied smile. "I didn't think so."

I rolled my eyes, annoyed. *And the point goes to Will. Just another thing he's done that I haven't done yet.*

I wished it hadn't been early November, because maybe then I would've stripped off my clothes and dashed into the water just to rob him of the satisfaction of one-upping me. I imagined what it would feel like to do just that. God, he'd be so shocked. But then what would've happened next? Would he have laughed at my boyish body, my flat chest that couldn't compare to Penny's? Or would he have stripped down too, grabbed my hand, and run into the pond with me where we'd twine our bodies together in the silky slickness of the black water and kiss until we were both gasping for air?

My face burned at the thought. I shouldn't have been thinking such lurid thoughts with him sitting right there, only a few inches away from me. But then another forbidden thought came. The image I fell asleep to every night: Will climbing toward me from the foot of my bed, smiling his devilish smile as he settled his naked body into the open V of my legs.

God, I had to stop. I was just torturing myself. All these fantasies had been fun at first, but now the pain of not being able to have Will the way I really wanted him was becoming more than I could bear.

He tipped his head back and took a long drink of beer. I watched his Adam's apple slide under the smooth skin of his neck as he swallowed, then forced myself to look away.

"Could I maybe have just one more tonight?" I asked, pointing at the bottle in his hand. We'd spent the earlier part of our night celebrating Cold Springs' second basketball win of the season and I'd already blown through my normal allotment of beer. It had been a rowdy, fun night, all of us together in the car for the first time in a long while; Stacie, Rob, Scott and even Holly too.

"*Pleeease*," I begged, making my best puppy dog eyes. "I worked hard tonight. I think I deserve it."

It had been a long night of cheering in the sweltering gym. My legs and arms felt hollowed out and rubbery from tumbling on the wooden gym floor; my throat sore from screaming so loud.

Will sized me up, then broke into a broad grin. "You're right. You *do* deserve it." He hopped off the car hood. "You kicked some serious ass out there tonight, Red." He headed back to retrieve my reward.

My chest ached from his compliment. Basketball season had started last week, but this year was different because now Will was there. In the past, I'd always been jealous of the other cheerleaders whose parents came to watch them perform. I was so envious of the girls who had moms to hurry thermoses of hot tea to them on the sidelines to soothe their throats. Whose dads wrapped them in hugs after the game and told them how great they'd done as they ushered them out to their waiting car. I'd banished my mom from my games a long time ago, so I was always the one girl alone, quietly slipping away so it wouldn't be so glaringly obvious that no one was there for me.

But now I had Will. I mean, not that he actually talked to me during the games. He was too busy standing on the sidelines yelling directions at the team for that. But it still felt good knowing he was there. And he clearly kept track of me because he would always comment about how I'd done afterward, saying things like, "Man, the crowd went crazy when you did all those flippy things, Red," or "You were so high on that one pyramid. Do you ever get scared you're going to fall?" or "You know you're the best cheerleader out there, right?" It made me know he was watching. It was nice to feel like there was someone in the crowd who cared about how I did. It was nice to feel like anyone cared about me at all.

"Hey," Will called from where he was bent inside the car. "You look kind of cold. You need a sweatshirt?"

"Yeah. That'd be great. Thanks." The thought of wearing something of Will's thrilled me. Maybe when he dropped me off I'd pretend like I forgot I had it on and keep it. Then I could sleep in it the entire rest of the week.

When he walked back he shouted, "Think quick!" then hurled the balled upped sweatshirt straight at my stomach. I caught it, made an exaggerated *offff* sound and pretended to almost teeter off the hood of the car to make him laugh.

"You've got better hands than Chad, that's for sure," Will grumbled. Poor Chad had been so nervous about finally being a starter, he'd made all kinds of stupid mistakes in the first quarter. He'd let easy passes slip through his fingers, got called for traveling on his drives, forced simple layups to roll off the rim instead of dropping inside.

Will had pulled him aside as he came back to the court after a timeout. I could tell by Will's gestures- the smooth tamping motion of his hands, the furious pointing to his eyes- that Will was telling him to calm down and focus. After that Chad had settled into a better rhythm and ended up scoring in double digits to help cement Cold Springs' win.

I pulled on his ISU sweatshirt, soaking up the soapy smell of fresh laundry detergent, vaguely thinking how Will was probably the kind of boy whose mom still did his laundry for him.

"Here you go. For you, my sweet." Will handed the cold beer over, giving me a little wink when our hands touched along the bottle. A shock of electricity shot through me, making my stomach flip in such a pleasurable way. Ever since we'd started talking on the phone, we were much more flirtatious with each other. The anonymity of the phone line had made us looser, freer with each other. Now, it seemed that boldness was seeping into our real, in-person life too.

He hopped back up on the car hood again, sitting a little closer to me this time. So close I could almost feel the phantom brush of his thigh against mine. "I skipped 'Beast of Burden' when I was back there." He tipped his head toward the cab. "I know how you hate that song."

"I don't hate it," I protested, even though he was right. The suggestive lyrics always embarrassed me. Listening to Mick beg a girl to make love to him while I was sitting next to a boy I myself wanted to make love to did get a little awkward sometimes.

"You always act kind of weird when it comes on," he said.

"I don't act weird! It's just it's too mushy for me. Making love?" I shuddered. "Call it fucking, banging, getting laid... that's fine with me. But *making love?* Blech. That's just so... so.... sappy!"

Will fought back a smile. "Right. So sappy." He didn't believe me, I could tell. I hoped he never found out the truth about how obsessed I was with romantic movies. I'd never tell him I'd watched *Endless Love* countless times. (Which, side note: just so happened to involve Brooke Shields having sex with an older guy when she was only fifteen.) Although truthfully, not every part of *Endless Love* was romantic since the guy burned down Brooke's house at the end.

It annoyed me that Will had picked up on how uncomfortable I was listening to "Beast of Burden" with him. He probably thought I was such a little baby, getting all embarrassed at the mere mention of sex. I needed to prove to him I wasn't as squeamish about the idea as he thought I was, so I decided to throw the subject right in the middle of the ring. Just get it out in the open once and for all, so we could finally stop tiptoeing around it.

"Stacie decided she's going to lose her virginity," I declared boldly.

He choked on his beer, and I grinned to myself. I'd said it mostly just to shock him. I knew he considered Stacie and me too young to even think about something as grown up as having sex. But it was about time for Will to get a little eye opener and start seeing us in a different light. To learn boys weren't the only ones who thought about sex. It was about time he learned that fifteen-year-old girls got horny too.

He turned to me, his eyes big. "What do you mean she *decided*? Like she scheduled it on her calendar? Like a dentist appointment or something?"

I liked how flustered I'd made him. "Pretty much," I said flippantly, knowing it would annoy him even more. "She says it's going to happen eventually, so she might as well get it over with."

"Get it over with?!" He looked horrified. "That's how she looks at sex? As something you just have to get over?!"

"Yeah. What's wrong with that?" I shrugged. "I feel the same way. Why make such a big deal about it?" Of course, that wasn't necessarily how I felt about sex, but I was curious to see what his reaction would be.

His cheeks were stained pink, and he kept opening and closing his mouth like he didn't know what to say next. He searched my face like he was seeing me in a whole new light, which was exactly what I'd wanted.

"Sex isn't something to be taken lightly, Red," he finally declared in his holier-than-thou tone.

Something flared in me. "Oh really? I think what

you really mean is that sex isn't something *girls* should take lightly."

I sat up taller, waiting for him to spew the same double standard all guys believed: girls should wait to have sex or else they'd become whores, whereas guys could do it all the time because it was just a primal drive they couldn't control.

"Not just girls. Everyone should take it seriously. Boys and girls alike," he shot back.

"Right. Because boys and girls are so equal around here."

After our horrific sex education talk, Stacie and I had asked Scott what kind of lecture they'd received. Turns out there was nothing in their lesson about boys keeping themselves "brand new" for a girl's selection. In fact, their metaphor involved Oldsmobiles and Ferraris and something about just keeping the vehicle on the road at a safe speed without veering off into a ditch. (And always having a raincoat in the trunk, you know, just in case.)

"Of course, boys and girls aren't equal. We're clearly the superior sex," Will teased, giving me a playful bump on the shoulder. I could tell he wanted to the change the subject, but I wasn't going to let him off so easily.

"Oh, so you really think sex is so special, huh?" I pressed.

He looked out over the water, pondering for a moment. "Yeah, I think it should be reserved for when two people really care about each other. Not something you do to check off a list."

"What is this? You getting all religious on me?"

"I'm not getting religious. It's just what I believe."

His smugness rankled me again. There was no way he was telling the truth. All this bullshit about sex being so special was obviously just to cover his ass so I didn't find out what a hypocrite he really was. I'd seen firsthand how girls threw themselves at his feet. I knew all about his adoring female fan club. Hell, I was a card-carrying member of it myself. There was no way any boy who'd been offered as many opportunities as Will had could've turned them all down just to keep sex as sacred as he claimed it was.

I was so sure I was right about his double standard I blurted out the obvious question. "So, you're a virgin, then? You're saving yourself for marriage?"

"No. I'm not a virgin, Red!" he sputtered, like I'd just accused him of some heinous crime. *Ah ha. Just as I suspected.* I loved how my trap was working. Now all I had to do was give him a little more rope, then sit back, and let him hang himself.

"So how many girls have you done it with, then?" I lured him closer to my noose. "Five? Ten? Fifteen? Twenty?"

"I'm not telling you that!" His cheeks had deepened to red.

I was the smug one now. "Just like I thought. You can't answer the question or else you'll reveal what a hypocrite you really are."

He rolled his eyes at me. I could tell he was mad, but I didn't even care. "Just like a typical boy," I singsonged, "always with the double standards. I can screw whoever I want, but you girls have to keep yourselves holy and pure until we decide you're fit for us to marry you."

His face suddenly went steely. "Fine. You think you know me so well? You want to know how many girls I've had sex with, Red?"

From the triumphant look on his face, I instantly knew I'd miscalculated.

I swallowed hard. "Yes," I croaked, although now I wasn't so sure that was true.

He leaned closer, blue eyes piercing mine. "One. I've only ever had sex with one girl."

I sucked in a sharp breath. It felt like he'd just reached over and slugged me right in the stomach. I wished he'd admitted to screwing seventy-two girls, not just one. Because one girl meant he truly believed what he'd just told me about saving sex for some he truly cared about. One girl meant he loved Penny.

"Whatever," I snapped, trying to hide how upset I was. "You can think sex is *SOOO* special and I can think it's no big deal and we can just agree to disagree, okay?"

He shook his head at me. "Where is this even coming from? This doesn't sound like you. This is all Stacie talking, isn't it?"

"It's not just Stacie," I said, irritated. "I think about these things too. I'm not a little girl, Will!"

It came out sounding so childish. I cursed myself for letting him get to me again. But then his eyes flickered down my body, and I saw something fighting in his expression.

"Believe me, I'm well aware you're not a little girl," he said in a husky voice.

My skin prickled at the way he'd just looked at me.

As I sat there fighting to catch my breath, he slid off the car, took a few steps out into the pasture, looking out at the night with his back to me. After a few seconds, he whirled around.

"Just promise me you won't do anything crazy, okay?" he begged. "That you won't go out and get laid by some random boy just to keep up with Stacie."

His vehemence surprised me. "Right. Like you even care."

"I do care, Red. I care a lot!" He looked down at his feet, shaking his head like he regretted what he'd just let slip. "Listen, you can do what you want." He held his palms up, pleading as he walked closer. "Just promise you'll come talk to me before you make any rash decisions."

"You want me to tell you when I decide to lose my virginity?" I asked incredulously. Was what I was seeing true? Was Will actually upset about the idea of me being with another boy?

"Yeah." He'd come so close he was standing only inches away from me now.

I made a face. "Well, that's weird. But okay." Again, the satisfaction swelled over me, but I made sure not to let it show. "If I ever decide to have sex, you'll be the first to know."

He let out a breath, seeming relieved. "Good."

I had to look away so I wouldn't burst out laughing at what made my promise so hysterical. "Of course, you'll be the first to know Will," I whispered inside my head, "because when I do finally decide to have sex, it's going to be with *you*."

CHAPTER TWENTY-NINE

THREE OPTIONS

I TRUDGED THE quarter mile from school to Pizza King like someone had filled my tennis shoes with cement. I was exhausted, not only from staying up late talking to Will, but from the extra intense training my cheer coach had put us through after school. All I wanted was to go home and collapse in my bed, but I couldn't because Karen didn't get off work for three more hours. Now my only option was to hang out at Pizza King until she was able to drive down to Cold Springs and pick me up.

Even though it was a perfect fall day- the trees a tunnel of orange and red casting mottled shadows over the sidewalk- I was too preoccupied by trying to sort out my mixed-up life to notice the beauty all around me.

My head felt like a cement mixer full of rocks.

Will had called me.... but then said I was his friend.

Stacie had agreed he might like me... but then said he might not.

Will had held my hand on his face... then told me I was weird.

Every time I snatched one bit of truth, its complete opposite came along and whacked all hope out of my grip, sending me plummeting back into a whirling pit of confusion.

I still wished I could talk to my mom. She'd be able to help me figure this all out. But of course, she was too busy. Even if I could squeeze in a few moments of her time, I wasn't going to let her schedule me into her life like I was just another one of her clients. No. She didn't get to be my parent only when it was convenient for her. There was a price for her not being there when I needed her, and I was going to make her pay it. Even if it ended up costing me too.

The rumble of a car on the road next to me startled me out of my haze.

Rob smiled out of the window of the beat-up Ford truck now idling next to me. "Hey, you need a ride?" he called out. Sweat soaked the edges of his brown hair, and his cheeks were still flushed pink from the basketball practice that had just ended.

"That'd be great!" I said, relieved to be distracted from my own thoughts for a few minutes.

I climbed up into the passenger seat next to him.

"Weird to see me sitting on this side of you, huh?" he said, echoing the exact thought I'd had as I glanced over at him in the driver's seat.

"Yeah... really weird."

"Will always insists on driving on the weekends. But he's got a sweet ride, so I don't mind."

"Yeah, he says he doesn't get to drive when he's at college, so he tries to make up for it on the weekends," I said.

As Rob accelerated toward the town square, I told him how Will had been teaching me to drive the past few weeks.

"So as weird as it is to see you over there," I said, "think about what it's like to see Will in the passenger seat."

"That would be strange," Rob agreed. "Even at work, he doesn't let me drive. But the good thing for both of us is he's an awesome driver."

It was true. Despite driving too fast, Will was the best driver I'd ever ridden with. Even better than Karen. (Although I felt like a traitor admitting that, even if it was only to myself.)

Rob went on, "So you're lucky to be learning from the best. I mean, is there anything that guy can't do? He's just one of those people that's good at everything."

Admiration shone in Rob's eyes. I knew it was exactly what I looked like when I talked about Will too.

"Yeah, he's pretty much good at everything." I agreed. Although now that I knew Will better, I was beginning to realize his life wasn't as easy as he wanted everyone to believe it was.

Rob turned left by the courthouse. "Still, I can't believe he let you drive the Monte Carlo. That's his baby. He won't even let Mitch drive it."

"I didn't really want to," I admitted, thinking of how nervous I'd been the first time I'd begrudgingly slipped behind the wheel. "But he made me."

"Well, you must be special, then."

"So he tells me." The words came out before I could stop them.

Rob glanced over at me with a look I couldn't quite read. He opened his mouth to say something, but I cut him off quickly. "You can just drop me off up front." I motioned to the curb in front of Pizza King where we were just pulling up. I didn't need another lecture on how I was getting my hopes up by hanging around Will so much.

I sighed heavily, peering inside the empty restaurant. Kelly, the afternoon waitress, was polishing the napkin holders, what she always did when things were slow. My fatigue grew as I thought of sitting alone at a table in the back corner, doing homework for hours until Karen came and got me.

An idea came to me as I reached for the door handle. "Hey, where are you going now?"

Rob shrugged. "I just gotta run home and do a few chores, then I'm coming back for an FFA meeting at 7. Why?"

"Could I come with you, maybe? I could help you with those chores."

He seemed surprised, but in a good way. "Wow, Red. That'd be great." He smiled. "You sure you don't mind?"

"Mind? It would be my pleasure!"

Rob turned the truck around and started toward his house. My heart lifted like he'd just agreed to drive me straight to the gates of Disney World. Rob's farm might as well have been Disney World because I knew exactly who would be waiting for me when I got there: a pasture full of beautiful, black-eyed cows. Otherwise known as my long-lost best friends.

❧

As we drove up to Rob's house, his dad was coming towards us on a gargantuan green tractor that took up most of the driveway. I waved at Mr. Grinfield as Rob dropped one tire of his truck off the road to let his dad idle up beside him.

His dad was tall and skinny just like him, but with wrinkled skin that looked like the shrunken apple head dolls we made for our pioneer unit in fourth grade. He nodded at me as he briefed Rob on the chores still left to be done. There was no need for introductions since we used to be neighbors. And also because everyone in Cold Springs knew everything about each other whether they wanted to or not.

"You know your old place up there is sitting empty now?" Mr. Grinfield said to me, lifting his chin in the direction of my old house. He looked almost as sad as the day my dad had first told him we were selling the property. Mr. Grinfield was nice like that. Like all the other long-time farmers around here, he'd gotten a kick out of giving my mom and dad a hard time when they'd first moved to town; ribbing my dad about being a "gentleman farmer" with his measly 100 head of cattle and his tiny blue tractor that looked like the premature baby of the other farmers' huge John Deeres.

But after the joking died down, Mr. Grinfield was always there when my dad needed him. He'd drive over in his old truck to walk the fields at dusk, giving my dad advice on what strain of clover to plant for the best hay and how to treat a cow with milk fever without calling the vet. And when my dad got too sick to put up hay that last summer, it was Mr. Grinfield that organized all the other farmers to help get it done so our cows would have food for the winter. Thinking back on all of that now, it reminded me once again that there were parts of Cold Springs that I truly appreciated. That the entire town wasn't as bad as I always made it out to be.

He leaned down in his tractor seat so he could see me better through the car window. "It's a damn shame, I tell you. Your mom and dad got that place into good shape. Someone should be farming it instead of letting it just sit there and go to seed."

I wasn't sure what to say. It was strange to hear someone talking about my mom and dad in the same sentence again, like they were still the team they'd been when they bought the 75 acres on a whim and set out to live their dream of becoming farmers. Back before my mom traded in that dream for a new one, in what seemed like the blink of an eye.

"Yeah. It would be nice to see it back up and running again," I said, more because it seemed like what he wanted to hear, not because I truly believed it. I struggled to imagine our farm still up there, functioning the way it always had without me there to be a part of it. Half of me liked the idea of it sitting there all forlorn and dilapidated, frozen in time at the exact moment we locked the last barndoor and drove away. I kind of enjoyed thinking that the farm wasn't able to move past all it had been before. It seemed like a fitting end to its story. Maybe because it reminded me so much of my own.

Rob needed to feed the small herd of beef steers his

family kept in a lower pasture, so he parked us by the hay barn then commandeered his own matching green tractor with a long flatbed wagon attached. He lined it up next to a tower of hay bales, climbed up a few and started throwing them down for me to stack.

After a few minutes of watching me work, he called out, "You still got it, Red!"

"I guess it's like riding a bike," I agreed. It felt good to get back into the rhythm of stacking the heavy bales. When we'd first bought our farm, I was so small my dad had to teach me a method of first balancing the bale on my thigh, then using the thrust of my leg in combination with my arms to help me catapult the dead weight to where I wanted it to go. Although I must have grown, or gotten stronger or something, because the bales seemed a lot easier to lift now than the last time I'd done it two years ago.

Of course, Rob made it look easy. It was like he was tossing a piece of shredded wheat over his shoulder instead of a twenty-pound hay bale. He was way stronger than his skinny arms let on, although I took some solace in the fact that he was sweating almost as much as I was by the time the wagon was full.

I watched him, thinking of how he'd probably had to wake up early to do chores before school, then spend an entire day making straight A's, then run his ass off for two hours at basketball practice, then come home to do more chores before going back to school again to preside as the President of the FFA club. I'd come up with the Clark Kent/Superman analogy for him just because of his thick hair and glasses, but I was starting to see how it was way more fitting than I'd first thought.

I sat on the hay bales in the back as Rob drove us over the rutted pastures to our waiting customers. Whenever he glanced back to see if I was okay, I did something goofy. I bounced around dramatically, acting like I was about to fall over the side. Then I struck a bunch of iconic poses: George Washington crossing the Delaware, the Statue of Liberty in the harbor, Marilyn Monroe getting her skirt blown up on a New York city heating grate. He was laughing pretty hard by the time I hopped down to unhook the gate to the far lot. I hoped the amateur entertainment was enough to pay him back for letting me tag along.

The cows gathered along the fence stared at us hungrily. I barked "git cow!" at them and they politely yielded enough space to let Rob through. I leapt on the moving wagon, then fell easily back into the routine I knew so well: methodically wrenching open the baling twine, then flinging sections of hay like frisbees to the waiting herd as Rob drove slowly down the field.

On our farm, I used to play a game when I fed the cows. I'd pretend each flake was a gourmet entrée I was serving up on a silver platter. "Here's your Caesar salad, Bessie... dressing on the side, just like you asked," I'd call out as I tossed a chunk of hay into the grass. "Your order of breadsticks, Cookie. Still warm from the oven," or "Spaghetti with marinara sauce. It's my momma's recipe from the home country. I think you're gonna love it, Anabelle." (My mom and I named all the cows on our farm even though my dad said it wasn't necessary since they had ear tags to tell them apart.) I just had to remember to never serve the cows steak. I'd made that mistake once, and I'd felt terrible about it afterward.

When the wagon was empty, Rob parked the tractor, then walked back to where I was making hay angels in the leftover debris scattered across the boards. I stared up at a sky so expansive and blue it seemed to go on forever. Seeing that open sky made me realize how nothing in my life was that big anymore. It had shrunken so gradually I'd barely even noticed. Like the frog put in a pot of cold water on the stove with the heat turned up so slowly he didn't even notice he was being boiled. My carefree big sky life from the farm was now squished into a tiny ranch house life, packed mostly with worry about what people were whispering about me behind my back. In a flash of clarity, I saw how I'd now become that frog. But instead of being boiled by water, I was slowly being boiled by my own fearful thoughts.

"Here," Rob said, handing me a glistening glass bottle of Coke.

"Hey, where'd you get this?" I sat up and took the bottle from him, wondering where he'd hidden it this whole time.

"I can't tell you all my secrets," he said. I brushed the hay out of my hair and scooted down to sit next to him on the end of the wagon. Multiple rolling pastures surrounded us in all directions, their green edges seamed together with thin rows of trees, clusters of black and white dairy cows milling inside their patchwork borders.

I held out a handful of hay to a steer sidling closer, snorting at us with curiosity.

"I always tell people that cows are like big dogs," I said as the young steer tentatively reached out, gently curling his tongue around my offering. "But no one ever believes me."

"Yeah, you gotta know them, I guess," Rob agreed. He scratched the cow's topknot. In return the steer leaned into Rob's hand, adjusting his head up and down against it like he was saying "just a little higher... just a little to the left." I joined in scratching behind his ear and the steer gave a heavy sigh, like he'd never felt anything so heavenly before.

We laughed at his antics. "Do you miss it?" Rob asked, not looking at me.

I stiffened next to him. Immediately I started sifting through sarcastic comebacks: *Yeah, I miss it like a toothache!* Or *I miss it like Chinese water torture!* Or *I miss it like a hot poker in the eye!* But then something strange happened. The truth hurtled over all the lame jabs and shot straight out of my mouth.

"Yeah. I miss it so much."

Rob kicked at the grass. His legs reached the ground. Mine didn't. "I get that," he mumbled. "I know I would miss it too if I ever had to leave." There was something so kind in the way he made a point of not looking directly at me.

We both swigged our Cokes; the syrup somehow tasting sweeter enhanced by the surrounding beauty. It was a tradition at the end of each haying day for all the farmers to sit around drinking icy Cokes out of glass bottles, shooting the shit about how long they thought winter was going to last and what month the first plantings should go in and whether they thought the basketball team had a chance of making it past regionals this year.

When I was really little, I'd sit along the edge of the group and just listen quietly. I wasn't so interested in what the farmers had to say, I just liked the easygoing, can't-fight-the-flow-of-time way they had of saying it. To me, everything with the farmers seemed so relaxed, so trusting. Which was kind of surprising, considering their livelihoods relied on something as unpredictable as the weather. And yet it was like they knew that no matter what came their way, they'd always be able to handle it. Probably because they also knew if they wanted to keep doing what they loved, they had no other choice but to trust and believe, or else the worry would make them go mad.

Rob bumped my shoulder with his. "You can come here anytime you want, Red. You know that, right?"

"I know. But you might have to start selling tickets," I said, smiling up at him. "I mean, since you already have Stacie scheduled every Sunday."

Stacie had started visiting Rob on the farm about a month ago. She loved bottle feeding the calves and helping him with the chores like me.

He nodded. "Yeah. That has been nice. Although I know she's just coming for these guys." He pointed at the cows. "Not for me."

I shrugged, wishing I could tell him something he wanted to hear. "She *is* an animal lover."

"That's for sure."

"So, does she know what's going to happen to them?" I lifted a chin to the munching steers. Looking at their rippling hindquarters, I guessed they were only a few hundred pounds away from the slaughterhouse.

He laughed. "We *do* argue about that a lot."

"Oh, I can only imagine."

"Let's just say we've agreed to disagree."

I nodded, thinking of how I'd also come to a similar truce with Will. Except ours was about how sacred sex was supposed to be.

We sat there listening to the sound of the cows chewing, the far-off honk of geese passing over on their way south. I suddenly felt tired again. Like my muscles were all squishy and raw, but in the best kind of way. Almost like I'd shed a too tight skin and the new one underneath was just getting exposed to fresh air.

"Are you ever going to tell Stacie how you feel?" I blurted out, too exhausted to stop and map out where the rest of the conversation might eventually lead.

I expected him to be shocked. To sputter and deny and rationalize why I was way off base with my assumption of his feelings for her. But he didn't do any of that.

"No," he said simply. "I don't really feel the need to. Things are just fine the way they are between us."

I thought about Stacie saying she wanted to lose her virginity. How she and Mark were doing more and more together every weekend. I didn't think Rob had time to be so fine about what was between him and Stacie anymore.

"Well, you might want to say something to her soon," I warned. I didn't want to betray Stacie, but maybe I could at least give Rob a hint. Make him get a move on and whisk her out of that dummy Mark's hands before it was too late.

He shrugged. "You can't force things. If they're meant to be, they'll be."

I huffed, trying to think of a rebuttal, but it was a hard to come up with an argument. Just like his dad, Rob had this way of talking that made you feel like he had some kind of special insight that the rest of the world wasn't privy to yet.

"And are you going to tell *him* how you feel?" Rob asked. This time, he made a point of staring right at me.

I did all the things he was supposed to do before. I sputtered and denied and rationalized why the assumption he'd made about how I felt about Will was *way* off base. He let me go on and on for a while until I finally ran out of steam, then accidentally gagged on my last sip of Coke in a futile attempt to appear nonchalant.

Then he took a deep breath and said quietly, "I'm with you every weekend. I know how you feel about him."

It was clearly pointless to argue anymore. "Still," I said, shaking my head, "I could never, ever tell him the truth."

"Why not?"

"It would be too embarrassing. He might laugh at me!"

He gave a lazy shrug. "Maybe he would. Or maybe he wouldn't."

"Maybe he would or maybe he wouldn't?!" I yelled. "Good God, you say it like it doesn't even matter either way! Don't you get it? I'd be humiliated!"

"You mean all you're worried about is getting laughed at a little? That's your worse-case scenario?"

"Yes! Isn't it *everyone's* worst-case scenario?!"

"Red," he sighed heavily, like I was missing something really basic. "If I based all my decisions on whether or not someone laughed at me, I wouldn't have done half the things I have in my life."

"What do you mean?"

"Look at me." He swept a hand down his body. "You think I haven't had my fair share of people laughing at me? My God, I've been called every name in the book. Frankenstein, Stickbug, Scarecrow.... Lurch!"

I looked away, ashamed that I myself had called him Lurch last year. But that had been before I really knew him, although I knew that didn't let me off the hook.

I was glad when he went on. "People look at me, they hear the way I talk so slow, and they think I'm dumb. Do you know my third-grade teacher told my mom I didn't know how to read? Just because I wasn't good at reading aloud in class, she assumed I didn't know how to read. Whenever she'd make me stand up in front of the classroom to read, all the kids laughed at me. But that didn't stop me from trying. And look at me now."

"Yeah, you definitely know how to read. And talk too." Rob was one of the smartest people in our entire school. I thought of the long conversations Stacie and I had with him down in Mrs. A's classroom about Reagan's foreign policy and works of Steinbeck and what the United States needed to do to reduce their dependency on fossil fuels.

I remembered the speech Rob had given in front of the entire school when he was running for class president this year. Yeah, it was short and to the point. And he was pretty hard to hear, even with the microphone turned up to its highest setting. But despite that -in fact, maybe even *because* of that- he'd had the entire class body hanging on his every word.

"And basketball?" He looked off into the distance with a wry smile. "Talk about getting laughed at! Jesus Christ, I was terrible at first. In fact, I think I laughed at myself harder than everyone else."

"I'm sure you're exaggerating," I said, even though I'd heard enough of both Coach and Will's stories to know he wasn't.

"Oh, I was that bad! I mean, thank God Will took me under his wing and helped me out. I'm as surprised as anyone else by what I've accomplished now. But you know what?" He tipped his head, thinking. "I'm not sure that even matters because I still would've played. No matter if I'd gotten better or not. I loved it so much. I just loved how good it made me feel when I stopped thinking so much and just forgot everything else and just played, you know? People could've kept on laughing at me and it wouldn't have stopped me."

My eyes flew to his when I heard his choice of words. *How good it made me feel.* There it was again. The mantra from my "If It Feels Good Do It" pin. What Rob had just described made me think of my mom telling me how athletes got into that feeling, not thinking, place where all their talents flowed freely. It was from that place that magical things happened. How many examples was I going to get until I finally trusted my good feelings too, just like Rob had? When was I finally going to stop worrying, stop trying to control what was going to happen next, and just follow my instincts and let the next step unfold naturally?

"I'm just saying all this because you shouldn't let the fear of being laughed at stop you from doing the things you want. I know firsthand people can laugh at you and make fun of you, and you still get up the next morning and go on with your life. And you know what? It's never really as bad as you expected it to be. And the even better part is, a lot of times you actually get exactly what you wanted all along."

I blinked at him, shocked not only because I'd never heard him say so many words in a row before, but because it sounded so much like what Will had told me when I'd first confided in him that I wanted to write the column and change the school song dance and do features on the basketball team. Will said that unless I spoke up and put myself out there, I'd never get what I wanted. Was Will trying to teach me that the same advice held true when it came to him? Was he trying to get me to realize that all I had to do was ask and I could have him too?

Rob went on. "I'm just saying. I've seen how much fun you and Will have together. That's got to be a good thing, right?"

"It does seem like a really good thing," I said. "It feels really good. I know that much about it."

"So, what've you got to lose?"

I decided to tell him the other reason I had for not telling Will how I really felt about him. "Well, I have one big thing to lose." I twisted a strand of hay around my finger so tightly the skin on the tip went white. "I could lose him. If I told him how I felt and he didn't feel the same way, then The Ride would be over. It'd be too awkward after that. I'd never be able to face him. Then I'd never see him again."

Rob bobbed his head slowly, like he was considering that consequence for the first time. "Well, from the way I see it, you're either going to lose him now, lose him later, or never lose him at all."

I gawked at him, stunned by how clearly he'd summarized my situation.

"You're right," I said. "It's definitely going to be one of those three options."

Rob threw an arm around my shoulder and squeezed me into his bony frame. "So, I guess the real question is... have you got the guts to finally find out which one it's going to be?"

CHAPTER THIRTY

SURPRISE!

I FELT LIKE a superhero as I danced to the school song in front of the standing-room-only crowd. (I'm Super Pom Pom Girl! *Wham pow!* The Incredible Flying Cheerleader! *Swoosh, Bang!*)

My kicks were extraordinarily high, my back handsprings extra snappy, my twirls like the Tasmanian Devil all hopped up on speed. I was so light, so powerful, so completely sure of myself. All because I'd finally made a decision. After talking to Rob, I'd realized I was tired of wondering what the hell was going on between Will and I. Tonight after the game, I was finally going to find out how he really felt about me.

Of course, I hadn't quite figured out how I was going to do that yet. (Other than knowing it was probably going to involve chugging a bunch of beers to bolster my courage). But I'd work on the details later. Somehow, I just knew everything was going to be okay. Especially after Will had called last night and told me about some big surprise he had for me.

"What is it?" I asked, praying that the surprise was him admitting his love for me first, so I wouldn't have to risk making an ass out of myself after all.

"You'll have to wait and see," he teased in his sexiest voice. "But I promise you're going to love it."

So that confirmed it. Will was excited to see me and was going to give me something I would love tonight. Just like I thought. Everything was going to work out perfectly.

Out of the corner of my eye, I caught a flicker of Will's black hair by the entrance to the gym. My heart soared into the rafters as I watched him walk in. Then, the very next second, it plummeted straight to the floor because just behind him, holding onto his arm, was Penny.

I froze like a statue in the middle of the gym floor.

"What's wrong? Are you alright?" Holly mumbled through her plastered-on smile as she danced beside me.

I startled back to life and frantically struggled to get back into the beat of the dance. "Yeah, yeah, I'm fine." The pep band wailed behind me, the drummers playing so loudly it felt like their sticks were beating straight into my back. I twirled to the music, whipped around fast, then locked my eyes back on Will and Penny, feeling dizzy and off balance. The walls of the gym pulsed around me as if they were made of billowing fabric instead of concrete blocks.

Dancing maniacally, I watched them make their way along the sidelines, stopping every few feet to talk to someone in the crowd. My stomach burned as I took it all in. It was the same scene I'd imagined so many times before, except in my version it was *me*, not Penny, with Will. *Me* holding his hand in front of everyone in a crowded gym, *me* who all the girls envied, *me* the people of Cold Springs saw in a whole new light simply because I was on the arm of their golden boy.

I ran to the edge of the sideline to prepare for my final tumbling run. I had to calm down. This wasn't as bad as I was making it out to be. From what I could see, Will was barely even talking to Penny. And she was the one clutching onto him, not the other way around. They clearly weren't happy together. Anyone with two eyes could see that.

I pulled my focus back into myself and ran as fast as I could toward Holly, coming at me from the other side of the gym. We flipped through a series of synchronized back handsprings, then finished with our matching full layouts right in front of the squad's pyramid. The entire gym exploded into applause as we hit our final pose. I glanced at Will, now detached from Penny and standing alone on the sidelines. He looked right at me and nodded just slightly, looking proud. I could almost hear the words he would say to me later. *You were amazing tonight, Red.* The warmth of his approval flooded over me like the ceiling had just cracked open and showered me in a beam of noontime sun.

As we jumped and cheered our way off the floor, my eyes zeroed in on Penny, now in the bleachers, standing next to Will's mom. She was staring straight at me, clapping but not smiling like the rest of the crowd. I looked away quickly, my cheeks seared by the heat of her focus. I remembered Will's words. *Yeah, I think she knows about you.* All these months I'd been so sure that Penny never considered me a threat. But judging from the look on her face now, I was pretty sure that had all changed.

∽

For the first half I cowered in between Scott and Stacie in the student section, furiously sneaking glances at Penny across the aisle. She and Mrs. Calder were talking non-stop, clearly not watching the game. Didn't Penny know Will would want to talk about each play afterward? That he'd want to go through every detail of every quarter with a fine-toothed comb, analyzing where the team could improve, what strengths they could capitalize on, what weaknesses they'd have to address at the next practice? Will and I talked about nothing but basketball for hours after a game. I still didn't understand his relationship with her. If Penny didn't like basketball or The Rolling Stones, what the hell did she and Will even talk about?

It was discouraging to see how close Penny was with Mrs. Calder. Scott told me that Penny and Will's parents were best friends. I thought of all the history the two families had together, all the bonds Will and Penny had created in the five years they'd dated. I sat with Will in a dark car for a few hours every weekend and thought I was an expert on his every thought and feeling. But maybe that was just me being delusional again. I was starting to realize there was a whole side of Will's life that I knew nothing about.

At halftime I stayed in my seat and watched as Will held court on the sideline, graciously entertaining the people who lined up for their turn to talk to him like he was a groom in a wedding receiving line. I waited until the game was about to start again, when most people had taken their seats, to head to the bathroom. That way, there'd be a better chance of Will seeing me as I walked by.

I made my way down the bleacher stairs, thankful our squad had worn our sleeveless vests tonight instead of our bulky sweaters. I knew the uniform made my arms look good. And the V in the front dipped down just low enough to hint at a promise. (Which, in my case, was a pretty empty promise, but Will didn't know that... at least not yet). I'd had my skirt fitted, so it was tight across my ass and really short and flounced at the very top of my thighs when I walked. I'd already had enough second glances by boys (and a few fathers too) to know I looked good. Now if only I could get Will to notice me too.

I acted like I didn't see him leaning up against the wall looking sexy in his white Henley shirt with two buttons open at the top, the sleeves pushed up his fore-arms just a bit. When I got closer, I saw his gaze flicker off the man he was talking to and slide down my body, then back up again, taking all of me in. When our eyes met, the corners of his mouth raised into just the hint of a smile before he quickly glanced away.

That look, that tiny smile, propelled me down the hallway and into the bathroom where I threw myself in front of the mirror, beaming at my reflection like I'd just been crowned Miss America. All I could think about was being alone with him later. Sitting next to him. Talking to him. Laughing with him. Maybe even touching him. Just thinking about the possibilities made me realize that I'd never wanted any person in the entire world more than I wanted Will Calder at that moment.

When the buzzer rang to start the second half, I bounded out of the bathroom and ended up crashing straight into Will's chest.

I stumbled backward. "What are you doing here?" I sputtered, wondering if I'd somehow conjured his presence from sheer desire alone.

He reached out and put his hands on my shoulders to steady me. "I just... I just need to talk to you for a second." His voice was low. He glanced over his shoulder nervously, then maneuvered me a few steps down the hallway, back by the metal gate that closed off the rest of the school to the fans. *Wait a minute. Will never talks to me at games. What's going on?*

Once we were in the shadows, he let go of me. Then he took a deep breath, like he was trying to work up the courage to say something.

"What's wrong?" My stomach dropped looking at his face. The sexy grin from the gym was completely gone.

"How do you know something's wrong?"

"Will it's me. I know you."

He nodded. "Yeah. I guess you do, don't you?" From the tone of his voice, I couldn't tell if he thought that was a good thing or not.

I looked up at him, waiting with mounting dread for what was about to come next.

"Listen, I'm really sorry, but something's come up. I can't see you tonight," he said.

I suddenly felt like I was falling backward from some great height. "What do you mean you can't see me? Why not?"

Nothing made sense. I'd talked to him after school only a few hours ago. We'd made plans. He was going to pick me up at Pizza King after the game. We were going to listen to "Jumpin' Jack Flash". There was going to be a surprise.

He glanced over his shoulder again. "My parents want to take us to the new steakhouse in Lindale after the game, so I won't be able to make it after all."

Us. The word was like a knife to my heart. Of course. He and Penny were the *Us*, not he and I. Why did I keep forgetting that?

"I'm sorry," he said, looking miserable. "I don't even want to go."

"So don't go," I snapped.

"Red. You know I have to."

The injustice of it all burned in the pit of my stomach. "What about all that stuff you're always telling me about standing up for yourself and not being a pushover and letting your voice be heard? Was that all a bunch of bullshit?"

He looked pained. "But this is my family. It's different."

"Is it? Or are you just using it as an excuse to take the easy way out?"

It was one of the standard lines he'd used on me a million times; challenging me whenever I gave him a perfectly good reason I couldn't do something. *I know you, Red. You're just trying to take the easy way out.*

"Alright, you got me." He held up his palms, looking wounded. "I'll admit sometimes it's a lot easier to give the advice than to take it for yourself, okay? I told you before, I'm full of shit. I'm not sure why this comes as such a surprise to you."

He didn't sound like his usual blustery self at all. In fact, he sounded lost, confused even. Emotions I wouldn't even have thought were possible for him if I hadn't noticed them slipping into our phone conversations a lot lately. Doubt and worry that revealed the truth of what was hidden underneath his confident facade. For a split second I felt sorry for him, but then I remembered he'd just ditched me, and the anger flamed back again.

"Whatever, I don't care," I said, looking away, hoping he wouldn't see how upset I was.

Then I remembered something. "So, was this your big surprise, then? You were going to say we going to meet up and then *Surprise!* bail on me at the last minute?"

"No. Not at all. Listen…" He reached out for me, then forced his hands back to his sides. He seemed to do that a lot lately. Start to touch me, then stop. Start to say something, then stop. It was like he was fighting with himself all the time. Why couldn't he just tell me what was really going on inside of him?

He went on. "Believe me, this is as much a surprise to me as it is to you."

I rolled my eyes, not sure I wanted to believe anything he said anymore. He'd seemed so excited about tonight, but in the span of a few hours, everything had changed. I felt like a piece of trash being tossed around by the wind. Will wants to see me, I feel fabulous. Oh wait, now Will doesn't want to see me, now I feel like shit. This was all too confusing. Too exhausting. And infuriating too. Why did Will always get to decide everything? Why did he always get to be the wind, blowing in whatever direction he wanted depending on his mood? No, he didn't get to have it his way all the time. It was time for me to start blowing too.

"Whatever," I shrugged, coming up with a plan as I went along. "It's all probably all for the best anyway...."

He furrowed his brow. "What do you mean? For the best?"

"Well, because of Chad." I tried to make my best lovesick face. It wasn't easy, but luckily I'd become an excellent actress over the past few years.

Will scanned my expression like he didn't understand what he was seeing there. "What about Chad?"

"Oh, he keeps begging me to go to this party tonight, so now this frees me up to go out with him." Maybe *begging* was a bit of an exaggeration, since technically Chad hadn't asked me out to my face. But Will didn't need to know that.

"Go out with him?"

"Yeah... like on a date. Ever heard of it, Will? It's what high school kids do these days."

"I know what a date is," he said in a stony voice. I knew that jab would get to him. Will hated the idea of getting older, of being left behind. "It's just... just.... you want to go out with Chad?!" He hooked a thumb back to the gym looking mystified. "That loser? He doesn't even know how to box out for a rebound!"

I burst out laughing. Not just because it was such a Will thing to say, but because he'd set me up for a perfect comeback. "Well, that won't matter since I doubt we'll be playing much basketball together, if you know what I mean." I wagged my eyebrows at him.

It was so satisfying to watch the realization of what I'd just said slowly spread across his face. "Oh, right," he said. "But umm... ummm...."

"But umm what?"

He threw his hands in the air in frustration. "Well, just... you should be careful. I mean, I'm not going to be there to watch out for you, so —"

"What do I have to be careful about? I'm just one of the guys, remember?!" I tossed my head in defiance and the end of my ponytail landed along the bare skin of my chest. I hadn't meant for it to do that, but when his eyes dropped and lingered there for a second, I was glad it had.

"Red, you're not just one of the guys," he whispered.

"Oh, I'm not, huh?" I jutted out my chin at him. "What am I then, Will? Tell me." My heart pounded hard in my chest. What was I doing? I'd never pushed him like this before. It scared me to think of what he might say next.

He opened his mouth, then shut it quick. It felt like I had him against the ropes. There was no way he was getting away without revealing at least some of the truth now.

Just as he started to answer, the door to the gym

burst open, the cheers of the crowd swelling loudly into the hallway. When I looked over Will's shoulder, Penny was walking straight toward us.

"Oh, there you are!" she called down the empty hallway to Will. I could tell she was taking in the scene, trying to make sense of what was happening between Will and me. She narrowed her eyes at me as she got closer. It reminded me of a picture I'd seen in *National Geographic* of a lioness sizing up her prey. I had an image then of Penny in high school, stalking the halls alongside Will, scanning her perimeter, always on the lookout for threats. Seeing her, I was sure she'd been a member of The Pack back then, just like Tina was now.

Will didn't turn around, but he took a step away from me. It was only then that I realized how close the two of us had been standing.

I gulped, my heart rising into my throat as Penny made it to Will's elbow.

"Um, so can you let Mitch know about the party, then?" I said to Will, trying to cover for something I didn't quite understand. I expected him to make a face and say, "what the hell are you talking about, Red?" like I'd gone crazy, but he didn't.

"Sure. Where was it again? Chad's, you said?" His cheeks had gone pink. The way he played along with my ruse told me everything I needed to know.

"Yeah, Chad's. Tell him it starts right after the game." I took a step to leave, but before I could get away, Penny stepped in front of me.

"Wait a minute," she said. "Aren't you going to introduce us, Will?" She latched onto Will's arm and wrenched him tight to her side like she had when they'd walked in.

Will glanced around uncomfortably, like he wasn't sure where to let his eyes land. "Oh um, Penny, this is Red. Red, Penny."

"Oh, Red," Penny said, looking me up and down deliberately before turning to Will and stage whispering, "she's the one who's so messed up, right?"

My stomach lurched at her description.

Will swallowed hard, looking almost as sick as I felt. "She's not messed up —"

"No, I remember you telling me about her," she said, pointing at me like I was a piece of trash in the street. "You said you wanted to help the poor thing. You said she had her head so far up her ass she couldn't find her way out. Those were your exact words. I remember."

"Penny... stop," Will said.

"And that you felt sorry for her," she went on without skipping a beat. "That she was probably hopeless, but it didn't hurt to try. Wasn't that what you said, honey?" Her words were so sickly sweet they made my teeth ache.

My body froze into a block of ice. I couldn't believe what I was hearing. Will had talked about me to Penny? I pictured it, their two beautiful heads bowed together, both of them laughing about how sad and hopeless I was. It was my worse-case scenario come true.

"Penny, I didn't say it that way, I just said —" Will stammered.

"No. I clearly remember the part where you said you felt sorry for her," she repeated, eyes boring into mine as she watched for my reaction. I blinked back at her, trying my best to keep my face relaxed, to not break her stare. I knew if I looked at Will, Penny would see how badly I wanted to slap him across the face. Then she would know everything.

Penny gave me a big smile. "Although honestly, I don't think you're a total basket case like he said." Another insult straight to the gut. "I thought you were pretty good out there."

Her sudden warmth threw me off. "Uh... thanks," I said, stupidly. *Why the hell is she complimenting me?*

"I mean, you're good for being so *young*." She pulled out the last word extra-long. Now I understood where she was heading with this.

She tipped her head at me, eyebrows raised. "Like what are you? A freshman?"

"Actually, I'm a sophomore." Will shifted on his feet, looking over at the trophy case like he was suddenly enthralled by how many sectional titles the cross-country team had won.

"A *sophomore*?" The girl was certainly good at emphasizing certain incriminating words. "So, how old does that make you anyway?"

"I'm fifteen," I said. When she broke into a shit-eating grin, I blurted out, "And a half! No. More like three quarters really...." I trailed off weakly and she started to laugh. Will cringed beside her. *Oh. My. God.* I couldn't believe I'd fallen right into her trap.

"Fifteen? Oh, you're still such a little girl!" She glared pointedly at Will, her lips set in a hard line. He refused to look at her. He just stared straight ahead, quietly fuming. I waited for his eruption, but he just stood there, rigid as stone, like he'd turned into one of those big-headed statues on Easter Island.

Why wasn't he saying anything? Why wasn't he telling Penny to back off and leave me alone, like he always did whenever anyone dared bother me on the weekends? Will always stood up for me, no matter what. He and I were a team. But where was all his so-called loyalty now?

The sound of a ref's whistle and the muffled explosion of Coach's voice came through the closed door.

"Uh, I gotta get back in there," Will said, trying to pull his arm away from her.

But Penny didn't let him go. "Don't be rude, Will," she said sweetly, wrenching him back to her side. "You need to say *goodbye* to Red before you go."

Her ultimatum echoed with crystal clarity through the empty hallway. For the first time since Penny arrived, Will looked directly into my eyes. There was a stabbing sensation in my chest as I held his stare; a pain that didn't feel like it was mine alone.

"Right," he said, hesitating.

I held my breath, hoping this would be the moment Will finally spoke up and came to my defense. Praying he would wrench himself out of her grip and tell her the truth: that he wanted to be with me and not her. The muscle in his jaw flexed as he thought, and for a split second, I truly believed that was exactly what was going to happen. But then he looked down at his feet.

"Goodbye, Red," he mumbled through clenched teeth.

And that's when I knew it was over.

CHAPTER THIRTY-ONE

STUPID

I LOCKED MYSELF in a bathroom stall and collapsed on the toilet.

The only thing I knew for sure was I would not let myself cry.

I would keep control. I would bottle up my pain because I knew it would hurt worse if I kept it trapped inside. And since I deserved to hurt as badly as possible right then, I would not give myself the satisfaction of letting one teardrop seep out of my disgusting body.

I sat like a statue on the toilet and chanted one word over and over again, letting it silently slash me apart from the inside out:

Stupid. Stupid. Stupid.

How could I have been so stupid?

Why had I let myself even hope? I knew better than this. I knew not to let Will in. I knew I could never get what I wanted. I knew all those things he kept telling me couldn't be true. I was not special. I was not a star. I was not pretty and smart and fucking funny as hell.

I was me.

And I was stupid. *Stupid. Stupid. Stupid.*

People came in and out of the bathroom. Voices droned. Faucets splashed. Toilets flushed. But I still didn't move. It was like I wasn't even there anymore. On the outside I was a quiet shell of a body, but inside there was a tornado whirling. I was spinning, flailing, trying to grab hold of anything that made sense, so I could turn myself right side up again.

My stomach burned as I imagined Will and Penny talking about me behind my back. Laughing at me. Worse yet, pitying me. I remembered the night I'd first climbed onto Will's console alone. When Will had called me a groupie and I'd been so sure he and Rob were laughing at me, that they only wanted me there as a joke. And now I knew that all this time, it had been true. I'd only ever been a joke to Will, after all.

But Will had been so convincing when he'd said all that stuff about wanting me on The Ride. And over the weeks, he'd confided so much to me. He'd been so sincere. At least I'd thought he'd been sincere. But again, that must have just been me being stupid. *Stupid. Stupid. Stupid.*

Why hadn't I listened when everyone told me I didn't have a chance with him? Instead, I'd clutched at the idea that Penny didn't like The Rolling Stones or basketball as much as I did, so there was no way they could be happy together. I'd gotten all pompous and overconfident and barely even asked Will anything else about their relationship. I hadn't asked because I hadn't wanted to know. I wanted to put my head in the sand and pretend Penny didn't exist, that *THEY* didn't exist. All I wanted was my romantic movie fantasy. I didn't have the guts to see the truth staring me right in the face the whole time.

Stupid. Stupid. Stupid.

I clutched my sides and rocked back and forth in the toilet seat.

Why would Will care about me, anyway? I was just some insignificant little girl he kept around to make himself feel important. Someone he dragged along to hand him beers and put cassettes in the player and stare at him adoringly when she was too drunk to know better. What had Stacie said about him? That I had to account for his egotistical nature. It wasn't like I didn't know that was true. The fact that he behaved like a pompous ass was at the basis of almost every joke I told about him. So why had it taken me so long to see what he'd never even tried to hide in the first place?

The words Stacie and Scott had said more than once echoed in my head:

We don't want you getting your hopes up. You can never be with him.

I sat up, eyes flailing around the metal walls surrounding me. Why hadn't I listened to them? They were my friends. They were trying to help me, not be mean like I thought. And yet I still chose to believe what I wanted about Will instead of the God's honest truth.

I curled into a ball, rocking harder now, hating myself even more. My shame built tighter and tighter under my skin, making me ache with a pain I'd never known before. I wished I had a knife so I could slice open my arm and somehow release the pressure of the hurt. Let my humiliation ooze out all over the bathroom floor until I floated away into nothingness. Desperately, I clawed at the soft part of my wrist with my fingernails, slashing at my skin over and over so I could feel even more of the pain I craved. The pain I deserved for being SO. FUCKING. STUPID.

CHAPTER THIRTY-TWO

THE FALL

"WE'RE GOING TO have so much fun tonight you're going to forget all about that asshole..." Stacie hesitated as we got out of the car at the bottom of Chad's driveway. "I refuse to even say his name because he doesn't deserve my breath!"

Ever since Stacie found me barricaded in the bathroom (there was no way I could've ever gone back into that gym. Not with *them* out there), she'd done everything she could to distract me from what had happened in that hallway. She'd convinced Scott to give us a ride to Chad's party, sweet-talked a boy in the parking lot into giving her a fifth of peach schnapps (which we'd chugged back and forth the entire ride there), and kept up an ongoing diatribe about the wonders of being a woman free in a world, unencumbered by the agenda of dickhead boys.

Now as we stood staring up at the house perched

high on the hill above, I was just drunk enough, just swayed by Stacie's reasoning enough, that I thought I might actually be able to go to the party and forget about Will. At least for one night.

"Are you sure you're going to be okay?" Scott asked from the driver's seat. He wasn't coming in with us because he had a hot Trivial Pursuit tournament at Holly's house to get to. I'd begged him to blow her off, but he'd refused. Ever since he straightened up and stopped drinking, Scott wasn't much fun anymore.

I started to make a crack about him having a botched personality transplant ever since he met Holly, but then reconsidered. Scott had been good to me tonight. When he'd heard what had happened, he'd wrapped me up in a tight hug, told me how sorry he was and (in the most shocking turn of events), hadn't even said "I told you so" which I knew was probably killing him. I guess his newfound sobriety wasn't all bad.

"Just be careful," Scott said, looking up at the house. You could hear the thumping bass of the music blasting all the way down to where we stood. It was common for the basketball players to host a party after the games, their parents clearing out to "let the boys have their fun." Chad's older brothers must have started the party early, as there were already so many cars parked along the snaking driveway that Scott had to drop us off along the main road.

"Just don't do anything crazy, okay?" Scott warned, this time looking only at me. It sounded exactly like what Will had said to me at Peanut Butter Pond last weekend and in the hallway tonight. It almost made me wonder if Will had found Scott after the game and asked him to relay that message to me. I dug my fingernails into my palms again, letting the sting of pain remind me I had to stop thinking like that. I had to remember that things weren't like I once believed they were. That Will had never cared about me the way I'd thought he had. That the whole time we'd been together, I'd been wrong about who he really was.

Stacie and I started trudging up the driveway but only a few steps in, our friend Michelle stumbled out from between two parked cars.

"Whoops," she said, clumsily zipping up her jeans. Her wild brown curls were disheveled, and she was swaying on her feet almost as badly as Stacie and I were. "Just hanging a hose there. Hope I didn't flash you."

"Michelle!" Stacie and I gushed in unison, drunkenly holding our arms out to her.

"You guys!" She ran to us, acting like she hadn't seen us in ages, when she'd sat only two rows over at the basketball game. We latched elbows together and, for some inane reason, began skipping up the dark driveway. I burst out, singing "Lions and tigers and bears, oh my!" at the top of my lungs and the other two joined in, all of us laughing like we'd never heard anything as funny in our entire lives.

We hadn't made it far when a car roared up beside us.

"Hey beautiful!" Chad called to me from the driver's seat. His hand was draped casually across the wood steering wheel of his red Mustang convertible, his body cocked back at a cool angle as he sized me up. He had on his red letter jacket and his white smile gleamed in the moonlight. I hated to admit it, but he looked kind of hot. Not Will-level hot, of course. But I figured it was time for me to start readjusting my expectations. Time for me to come to terms with the fact that every boy I would ever meet from that day forward would pale in comparison to Will Calder.

"Chad! Just the person we wanted to see!" Stacie drug Michelle and me to his side. I noticed how she'd made a point of not acknowledging Mark, sitting next to Chad in the passenger seat. A gaggle of girls packed the backseat. They chugged their beers and shot us dirty looks when Chad and Mark were turned away, clearly telling us to back off their property.

"Oh really? Did you want to see me too, Red?" Chad asked, slurring his words a bit. He grabbed my hand and pulled me closer to his door. From the number of empty beer cans littering the floorboards, it was obvious he'd gotten a jump on the celebration on his drive home.

"Yeah, of course. I've been looking forward to this all week," I lied.

"Really?" Chad looked genuinely excited. Maybe he really *did* like me as much as Stacie claimed. "Well then, climb in. I'll give you guys a ride up. Then we can really have some fun." He wagged his eyebrows at me.

Stacie surveyed the packed car. "Where are we supposed to sit?"

Chad patted the console in between the seats. "You can sit here, Red."

I snatched my hand away from him. *I would never sit on anyone's console but Will's!*

Chad made a face. "What? What's wrong?"

Stacie elbowed me hard. "Get your shit together," she hissed under her breath.

"Oh uh, we should probably just walk. We all won't fit." I laughed nervously. "I mean, where are we going to sit? On the hood?"

I only said it as a joke. Everyone knew Chad was nuts about his precious, classic car; that he treated it like a baby. Our jeans had rivets that could scratch its custom paint. Our asses could dent the antique metal. There was no way he was going to let us on that shiny red hood.

"Great idea!" he exclaimed cheerfully. "Hop on!" I was so shocked he'd agreed I made him repeat himself twice. Each time he was just as insistent, so the three of us walked around the front and climbed up on the hood: Michelle near the center, me next to her, and Stacie along the edge, her back directly in front of Mark in the passenger seat (which I didn't think was a coincidence at all).

When the car began slowly inching forward, I waved like a parade queen to the audience of trees around us. Michelle and Stacie joined me, all of us laughing drunkenly together again. I was actually glad I'd suggested sitting up there. The way the woods were shuttering by, the cool night air lifting my hair and tickling my skin was all quite thrilling.

That feeling of invincibility I'd had at the beginning of the night flashed back for a moment. Maybe there was still a little of that superhero girl inside me. All I'd needed was a fifth of peach schnapps and the adoration of a slow-witted boy to bring her out again. Maybe I wasn't quite as stupid as I'd thought I was before.

But then Chad pushed his foot down hard on the gas and everything changed. The speed of the car turned the wind from gentle to menacing. The air lashed our hair across our faces and snatched our cries for Chad to slow down straight out of our mouths, flinging them uselessly into the night. A sick, helpless feeling grew in the pit of my stomach as the car gained more and more speed. How much had Chad had to drink, anyway? Why was he driving so fast? Didn't he realize there was nothing for us to hold on to up here?

Laughter and whoops came from behind us as Michelle, Stacie and I clutched onto each other in an attempt to stay on top of the car. Clearly, no one inside understood how precarious our situation was up there, or how close we were to falling off. When we hit the first turn, the three of us slid across the shiny hood, Stacie almost dangling off the edge. She clawed at me, desperately trying to stay upright.

"Chad, stop! We're falling!" she screamed into my ear in a last-ditch effort to save us. Chad finally noticed we were careening off the side and slammed on the brakes. It was the worst thing he could've done because it sent us rocketing off the hood like we'd been shot out of a cannon.

Time slowed to a crawl as I flew weightlessly through the air, the shadowy forms of Stacie and Michelle floating along beside me. Then the unforgiving black asphalt rushed up fast. My hands, trained by countless falls in the gym, instinctually snapped up to break my fall as I hit the ground hard. The momentum of the car sent me skidding across the pavement like a skipping stone, tearing layers of skin off my palms and knees along the way.

Headlights swelled bright and brakes squealed sickeningly close to my ears as my body came to a rest along the driveway. For a second, I was sure Chad was about to run over all three of us, but he somehow got the car stopped. Still, I leapt to my feet and dashed to the edge of the road, my survival instincts screaming for me to get out of his way. I bumped into Stacie struggling to stand along the side of the road. She was brushing dirt off of her clothes, pulling leaves out of her hair, cussing at Chad for being such an asshole. We huddled together to inventory our injuries as the rest of the kids piled out of the car.

It turned out Stacie was better off than I was. Since she'd been sitting on the side, she'd landed on the dirt edge of the driveway, so her hands had only been scraped up a bit. Mine, however, were so mangled it looked like I'd dipped my palms into a tray of red paint. I stared down at my bloody hands, thinking of how odd it was that they didn't hurt at all. Then I felt a brush of air along my knees, and when I looked down, I saw two frayed holes in my jeans, blood soaking through the edges in red ruffled streaks.

Michelle was still laying on the ground only a few feet in front of the parked car moaning for someone to help her. Chad and Mark and the girls from the backseat huddled around, trying to help her up. When she finally got to her feet, the group gasped at the sight of her. She looked like a zombie who'd just crawled out of an open grave. She must have taken most of the impact with her face. Ragged, seeping wounds covered one side of her cheek and forehead and blood dripped onto her cream sweater in macabre red splatters.

Things got fuzzy after that. Michelle was crying and Stacie was still swearing really loudly. People closed in tightly around me, telling me I should get into the house. That I needed to sit down. Get some Band-Aids. Wash the dirt out of my scrapes. Chad took me by the elbow and led me up the hill, blabbering something in my ear that I knew was an apology but sounded more like the grownups in the Charlie Brown TV shows... *wahhhh, wahhh, wahhhh.*

"I can't believe I ruined my jeans," I grumbled to Chad as I limped up the hill. He just stared at me wide-eyed, like he couldn't believe I was worried about my jeans at a time like that.

Things got even blurrier when I got to the house. It was like I was looking at a bunch of individual snap-shots cobbled together to make a jerky stop-motion movie: Mark swooping to Stacie's side, whisking her away through a dark doorway. A voice saying they were taking Michelle to the hospital. Kids parting in a too bright hallway to stare at me as I passed by to get to the bathroom. I yelled at Chad to get the hell away from me, telling him I was fine, I just needed to get washed up and put a few bandages on and I'd be good as new. Then I slipped into the bathroom and locked the door behind me.

I stared at my reflection in the mirror and laughed like a crazed person. There I was, alone and battered, nursing my wounds in a bathroom again. There seemed to be a common theme to tonight. My emotional wreck from the gym hallway had now turned into an actual wreck at Chad's.

When I looked down at my beat-up body, it felt like it wasn't even me I was seeing, but the shape of someone else wearing the clothes I'd changed into at Pizza King after the game. I sat on the toilet, thinking of the mess I'd made of everything. Wondering if maybe I could just stay locked up in the bathroom forever because I was too tired to face one more minute of this shit show I called my life.

I must have stayed in there for a long time because after four or five rounds of polite knocks, someone started pounding loudly, yelling "Who the hell's in there? I gotta take a piss!"

I finally forced myself up off the toilet seat and pushed past a couple of disgruntled girls and back out into the hall. Thank God I didn't see Chad anywhere. I didn't need him whining his fake apologies in my damn ear anymore. I hadn't found any Band-Aids in the bathroom, but I had washed the dirt out of my hands and dabbed at the hamburger skin of my knees with one of the white hand towels which I felt terrible about ruining with my blood.

I made my way through the crowd in the hallway, on a mission to get outside to the keg. It was the only thing I could think of that might make me feel better. I started to lean on the porch railing to help myself down the stairs, but my hands screamed in pain, so I ended up doing a weird stiff-legged-soldier walk to get down to the driveway. I was concentrating so hard on the effort that when I finally made it to the bottom and looked up, I nearly fell backward by what I saw there: Will walking up the driveway straight toward me.

He started running when he saw me. "Red, what the hell?! Are you okay?"

Every single second since the accident, all I could think about was how badly I wanted him there. And now there he was, in flesh and blood, reaching out to put his hand on my elbow to steady me as I teetered in the driveway. I'd never been so happy to see someone in my entire life.

My legs felt like jelly, muscles misfiring out of synch from the aftermath of the adrenaline from the accident. It was all I could do to not wrap my arms around his neck and ask him to hold me; to squeeze me as tightly as possible to help me get back to the normal shape of myself again. But I knew I couldn't do that.

"I'm fine, really." It came out as a whisper. I was so happy to see him I forgot everything that had happened between us only a few hours ago.

His eyes were wild, searching my face. "I just got here and someone said you'd been hit by a car and... my God, I was so worried!"

"Well, you know how people exaggerate around here." *Whose voice is that, anyway? Is that me?* "I wasn't hit by a car. I just kind of fell off of one." I didn't want to tell him what happened. How the whole stupid thing had been my idea. Just another instance of me having my head up my ass exactly the way he'd told Penny.

He grabbed my wrists and stared down into my bloody palms. "Who the fuck did this to you?!" he yelled, clearly enraged.

I was so transfixed by the sight of his hands on my body, the feel of his skin on mine, I couldn't answer him.

His fingers felt so strong wrapped around my wrists and the sensation suddenly made me feel a lot steadier on my feet. I wanted to stare at where we were joined together for a little longer, but then he shook me and yelled, "Tell me who it was. Because I swear to God, I'm going to kill them!"

I startled out of my stupor. "No one did this to me," I mumbled, understanding all at once where his anger might lead if I didn't squelch it quickly. "It was my fault. I did this to myself."

"That's bullshit. Who was driving? Tell me. Now!"

He narrowed his eyes at me, and when I didn't answer right away, he knew. "It was Chad, wasn't it? It was that asshole, Chad." He let go of me so suddenly that for a second I thought I might collapse in a heap on the driveway. He started pacing back and forth across the asphalt like a caged tiger, throwing his hands in the air, yelling to no one in particular, "Where is he? Where's the fucking asshole that did this to her?!"

A group of kids on the porch whispered to each other, then quietly tip-toed inside the house one by one, clearly not wanting to get in the crosshairs of Will's wrath. Will whirled and charged down the driveway toward a group of kids gathered around a fire pit in the yard.

"Will, stop!" I started to follow him, but when I moved, my knees screamed in pain. That's when all my anger from before came raging back. I was the one who was hurt and now Will was making me chase after him? Like everything else that had happened tonight, it just didn't seem fair.

"*WHAT THE HELL ARE YOU EVEN DOING*

HERE!" I shouted so loudly every person in at the entire party, both inside and out, must have heard me.

Will stopped in his tracks. The kids down at the fire all turned and stared up at the two of us silhouetted in the driveway. Will rushed back to my side quick.

"Shhhh…. just calm down now," he said in a low voice.

The fact he was trying to quiet me only made me angrier. "I don't have to calm down! You're not even supposed to be here!!"

Will seemed panicked by my volume. I'd never raised my voice to him like that before. "I got done earlier than I thought, okay?" he said. "Now, how about we go over here by ourselves and talk for a second?" He took my elbow and tried to lead me into the shadows so no one could see us. But the gesture just reminded me of being back in the gym when he'd led me into the shadows to tell me he was breaking all his promises to me.

I pulled my arm away roughly. "No. I don't have to do anything you say!" I knew I sounded like I baby but I didn't even care. What did it even matter anymore?

"Okay, okay… you're right. You don't have to do what I say," Will said in the soothing voice of a highly trained hostage negotiator. "But maybe I could just have a few words over here, in private?" He backed up and circled his arm around in the air the same way he'd done when he'd called me to his side the first time I'd seen him in the gym. I couldn't help myself. I took a few steps toward him. But when I got closer, I stopped and made sure I stayed on the lit driveway so he was the one forced to hide in the dark.

"I know you're pissed at me," he started.

"I'm not pissed! I don't even give a shit anymore!"

He threw a hand up. "Right... so this display of yours.... all this yelling is you not giving a shit?!"

How dare he yell at me *at a time like this?* I was so mad I lunged forward, raising one mangled hand in the air to slap him. He threw his arm up, blocking me before I made contact.

"Don't tell me I'm making a display! *You're* the one making a display. All your charging around, threatening people, saying you're going to kill them! When you're not even supposed to be here!"

He blinked at me for a second before he went on. "You have to let me explain."

We both stared at each other, an unspoken reality becoming harder to ignore with every line of our argument. As Will's friend, I had no right to be mad that he'd been with Penny. And as my friend, he had no obligation to defend himself about being with Penny. And yet there we were, both of us so obviously upset, and yet neither of us willing to admit why.

"I can't believe you said all those things about me to her." My tongue felt fat, each word tender and swollen as it tumbled out. "All this time you were telling me how special I was. How if I put my mind to it, I could have everything I wanted. Saying how smart and funny I was and then going to her and laughing about me! Saying I was a basket case, and hopeless and had my head up my ass?! I can't believe you've been lying to me all this time. I mean, what was this all to you? Was it all just one big joke?! Was *I* just one big joke to you?"

"No! Of course not. You gotta believe me," he pleaded. "I meant everything I said to you. I do think you're all those things I told you. It wasn't a joke. And it's not a joke now, I promise. I just said all those things so she wouldn't get jealous of you. So she'd leave us alone."

"Jealous? Of this basket case?" I pointed to myself, "Look at me!" I held up my butchered hands, waved an arm down to my shredded jeans. "What the hell does Penny have to be jealous about?"

He tipped his head, eyes softening in a way that made my stomach drop out from under me. "Oh, Red. Do you really not know?"

"Know what?" I asked, part of my blustery resolve crumbling.

"Penny has a lot to be jealous of when it comes to you."

I swallowed hard, still afraid I was too naïve and stupid to understand what he was trying to say. I'd gotten it all wrong before, hadn't I? I'd seen signs where there really were none. I'd stood in that hallway with Penny humiliating me, commanding Will to say good-bye to me with him never once standing up to her. Even if he was telling me the truth right now, even if he did think I was smart and funny like he'd said, that still didn't mean I was anything more than just a friend to him. That didn't mean that after tonight he'd ever want to see me again.

There was only one way to find out if everything between us was ending. I took a deep breath and asked the question that had been looming in my mind ever since Penny burst through the door in the gym.

"Is The Ride over, Will?"

Are we over, Will?

He hesitated, searching my face, seeming to struggle to find the right words. He opened his mouth, but just as he was about to answer, Chad appeared out of the shadows.

"There you are!" he called out to me, weaving drunkenly up the driveway. He must have left me bloodied in the bathroom and made a beeline straight to the keg because he looked even drunker than he was before. "I've been looking everywhere for you!" He was almost at my side, arms stretched wide like he was about to engulf me in an enormous bear hug.

But just as he got to me, Will stepped out of the shadows.

"Don't you fucking touch her," he growled, shoving Chad so hard that he stumbled all the way across the driveway and fell into the ditch on the other side.

"Will, stop!" I called weakly as he rushed to where Chad had fallen. I moved to follow him, but my knees screamed out in pain again, so I stopped short. That's when I realized I didn't give a shit if the two of them beat the hell out of each other because I kind of hated them both at that moment.

Chad struggled back up and looked around, dazed. "What the fuck, man?" he said, puffing himself up to face his shadowy attacker. But when he realized it was Will, his demeanor instantly changed. "Oh hey, man. It's you. What's going on?" he asked, looking nervous. Will's reputation for fighting was clearly hadn't been forgotten in town.

Will pressed his chest against Chad. "Did you see what you did to her, asshole?" he shouted into his face.

Out of nowhere, almost like he'd dropped from the sky (could that have been possible?), Rob materialized by Will's side. I nearly fainted from relief when I saw him.

Rob pulled Will away from Chad. "Hey, buddy... calm down now." Rob's voice was low in Will's ear. "The guy's fucked up. Just leave him alone." When Rob glanced at me, I had the distinct impression that this wasn't the first time he'd had to talk Will out of a fight.

"He could've killed her!" Will threw a hand at me. Luckily, his voice was a little softer now.

Chad weaved a little, brushing the dirt off his letter jacket. "I'm sorry, man. I feel terrible about that."

Will glanced over at me and rolled his eyes. He hooked his thumb at where Chad was now stumbling around in circles.

"You picked a good one there, Red," he grumbled. "What a catch."

I couldn't help but laugh at his hypocrisy. The guy was practically engaged and yet he still had the nerve to give me dating advice?

Rob had just started guiding Chad back to the fire pit when sirens began wailing in the distance.

"Great. Just what we need now. The cops," Will said.

Rob abandoned Chad and rushed up the driveway to Will. "We should probably get out of here."

Will looked back and forth between to the two of us. "Yeah. They probably heard about the accident and are coming to find out what happened. We should go before they get here."

Rob looked over my shoulder, pointing to the house. "Is she in there?"

I knew he was asking if we should find Stacie and take her with us too. He looked so hopeful. Like he was already imagining the two of them together in Will's backseat talking the rest of the night away. But I remembered a bedroom door. Mark leading Stacie inside and closing it behind them.

"I think she's... um... busy."

"Oh right, right." Rob nodded furiously. It broke my heart how he tried to act like it didn't bother him.

Will was already heading toward his car, which I noticed he'd parked right in the middle of the driveway, only twenty feet away. Of course, he hadn't parked at the bottom and walked up like everyone else. Will did what was best for Will. Rules were meant for other people, not for him.

It was obvious he just assumed I'd follow because he never even turned around to check. He was all the way to his car door before he realized I wasn't behind him.

"What are you doing? We have to get out of here!" he called up to where I was still standing, arms gingerly crossed, in the driveway.

"You go," I said. "I'll be fine here."

Will and Rob exchanged a glance, then Will walked back up to me.

"C'mon, Red. The cops are almost here."

"Yeah," Rob chimed in. "You should go with us. Once the police see you, they're going to ask questions and want all the details. Do you really want to deal with that?"

When I still didn't move, Will tried reasoning with me. "Listen, I'm sorry for everything," he pleaded, contrite for once in his life. "But we can talk about that later. You need to come with me now. *Please.*"

The sirens swelled louder through the trees. Will looked so concerned I was pretty sure that if I'd insisted on staying, he would've stayed too and faced the cops with me. But I didn't really want to spend the rest of the night listening to Will schmooze a bunch of troopers, while I answered questions about why I thought it was a good idea to ride on the outside of a car instead of the inside where there were perfectly good seats.

The moment suddenly seemed monumental. Like my decision of whether to stay or go might change the entire trajectory of my life. I took a deep breath and thought of my mom's words. How she'd said I needed to check in with how I felt in my body before I took action. My skin still danced with the relief I'd felt when I'd seen Will walking up that driveway. My heart still soared the way it always did whenever he was near me. Yes, I was angry, but boy, it had felt so good to see him there in front of me, eyes pleading in some unnamed and yet hopeful way. There was nowhere in the entire world I wanted to be at that moment than with him.

I reached out to him; the rightness of my choice confirmed by the way my body hummed as he gently grabbed my wrist. I let him guide me to his car, even though I didn't really need his help. But as we plunged down the steep driveway, slipping away just as the cop cars pulled up, I couldn't help but think it might be the last time Will whisked me away from anywhere ever again. He hadn't had time to respond when I'd asked if The Ride was over. But after everything that had happened tonight, I had a terrible feeling I already knew what his answer would be.

CHAPTER THIRTY-THREE

"AS TEARS GO BY"

MY HAND SHOOK as I reached for the beer Rob was holding out to me.

As we'd been driving, I kept flashing back to scenes from the accident. The terrifying sensation of sliding helplessly across the hood. Flying through the air and hitting the ground so hard. The horrible sounds of Michelle crying. I'd finally asked for the beer, hoping it would make all the scary memories go away.

I snatched the bottle quick, but both Rob and Will had already seen how badly I was shaking. I felt them exchange a glance above my head.

They both started talking at once.

Will: "Are you sure you're okay, Red?"

Rob: "I can hold that bottle for you if you want."

"Just leave me alone!" I snapped. They clammed up like scolded schoolboys.

I felt bad for yelling. "I'm fine, really. Look." I

pressed the cold bottle against my palm. "This actually feels good!"

Will had stopped a few miles back and ordered me to sit on the hood of the car under the neon lights of a closed Mobil station so he could put some Band-Aids on my scrapes. He'd straighten each of my legs in turn, bracing my ankle under his armpit as he expertly covered my mangled skin with bandages. He'd moved so carefully, touched me so gently, it was like one of my fantasies come to life. But in such a strange and surreal way.

As he'd tended to me, my throat had felt funny, like there was a wadded-up lump of cotton in the space right behind my tongue. Then the pinpricks had started behind my eyes. *Please, don't let this happen now*, I'd pleaded with myself, fighting back the urge to reach out and run my aching fingers through the waves of his black hair. It would've been easy with as close as he'd been, bowed like a servant in front of me. Luckily, I'd been able to get myself under control before I embarrassed myself by bursting into tears while he held my hands.

Now with my wounds covered, everything felt so much better. All that was left to do was try to forget what had just happened at Chad's house.

"Sorry if I'm being weird," I tried to explain, "it's just... I want to get back to normal now. Can we do that, please?" I didn't add that if this was the last night of The Ride, I didn't want to waste all my time talking about my stupid decision back at the party.

"Sure Red, whatever you say," Will acquiesced. "How about I play you a song then?"

I nodded, but then he added a caveat. "I'll play something that reminds me of you."

I groaned as he dug through his cassette box. What song would make Will think of me? I waited with mounting dread, expecting him to pick out "Can't Get No Satisfaction" or "She's So Cold" to tease me like he usually did.

But, as always, Will surprised me. When the first guitar strums of "As Tears Go By" wafted through the speakers, I instantly regretted giving him free rein with his choice. Because in only five seconds, the prickling behind my eyes had started up all over again.

"You like it?" he asked, dipping his head to catch my eye.

"Yeah, I like it," I choked out. But it wasn't the whole truth. Because I didn't just like "As Tears Go By", I thought it was the most beautiful song the Stones had ever written. It was so different from their usual stuff. Mick's voice was much more innocent than usual, delivering each word of the lyrics clipped and methodically, making it seem more like a spoken-word poem than a song.

Will bumped my shoulder. "It's your song, Marianne."

I smiled at him, barely able to breathe. Will always called "As Tears Go By" my song because it was first released by Marianne Faithful back in the sixties. It wasn't until a few years later that the Stones recorded their own version, the one he was playing now. The song that now had such a stranglehold on my throat, I wasn't even sure I could sing along.

Truthfully, I'd always thought of it as Will's song

too. The lyrics told a nostalgic story of Mick watching children playing on a playground, remembering when he was once their age, tears falling as he wished for the happiness he'd once had. The song (threaded with a series of violin swells so beautiful it made my chest ache), was about regret, about longing, about looking back on better times. It always reminded me of Will and how he wished he could go back to the way things used to be in high school. Sometimes Will seemed like such a Peter Pan to me; the boy that never wanted to grow up. The boy who kept coming back to his hometown trying to relive his glory days and yet never quite being able to recapture what he'd once had. I knew he said he was playing the song for me, but I wondered if maybe some part of him was playing it for himself too. I just hoped he hadn't picked it as some kind of foreshadowing; a message that our time together really was over, just like Mick's days on the playground were too.

Will and Rob started talking back and forth over my head about a house out on West Hill Road they were fixing up for Will's grandpa. I knew they were purposely ignoring me, trying to go back to normal just like I'd asked them to, and the sweetness of their gesture made me choke up all over again.

I should've just told Will to drop me off at Pizza King, or at least demanded some more answers about how he'd treated me in that hallway with Penny, but I was too tired to keep up my outrage anymore. The car was swaying so gently, the heat blasting warm from the vents, the song playing low as Will and Rob's voices droned melodically above my head. If this was going to be my last night on The Ride, I didn't want to fight any-more. I wanted to listen to music and talk and laugh and not think about all the ways I'd misinterpreted Will's signs. I was going to have the rest of my life to sort through all that. Tonight was all I had left with him.

Fence posts swished by in measured increments outside the windshield, and I let my eyes blur until the repetitious movement slowly began to hypnotize me. I took a deep breath and let it out slowly. It felt like the first full breath I'd taken since I'd woken up that morning. I smiled, thinking of how surprising it was that something so simple as a lungful of air could feel so good. In my relaxed state, I glanced around the car, making a point to soak up every detail so I could remem-ber it forever: the dashboard lights reflected on Will's face, his body pressed against mine, the music wrapped so snug around us, binding us together in our own little bubble of happiness.

I finished my beer and let the bottle drop with a *thunk* to the floor. After a while, everything around me started to fade into one fuzzy blur. Without even think-ing, I let my head drop onto Will's shoulder. Then I turned and curled into him, wrapping my arms around his arm, and pulling it tight to me like a security blanket. Then I closed my eyes.

It seemed like such a natural thing to do that it wasn't until I felt the pulse of his heartbeat on my fingertips and the heat of his neck so close to my cheek that I realized how intimate the gesture was.

I froze, expecting him to pull his arm away and say, "what the hell are you doing?" but he didn't. In fact, he and Rob didn't miss a beat in their conversation. They just kept talking back and forth like it was completely normal for me to be holding onto Will the way I was. Then, a second later, Will took his hand off the steering wheel and rested it on my leg, just above my throbbing knee.

It took everything I had to not sit bolt upright when I felt his hand on my leg. Will had never touched me like that before, and the sensation shocked me in the most literal sense possible. It felt like I'd just been electrocuted at the point where our bodies were now joined. I took a deep breath and told myself to calm down. If I didn't act casual, I might scare him off and make him pull away. I couldn't let him know that currents of electricity were now running from under his palm, circulating throughout my whole body, then pooling into a throb between my legs. I couldn't risk making a complete fool out of myself all over again.

I told myself I was making too big a deal out of his simple movement. Resting his hand on my thigh like that probably meant nothing to Will. In fact, he probably had no choice but to put his hand there with the way I had his arm wrenched to my side. But then his thumb started gently stroking my leg, back and forth, back and forth, and I decided that maybe none of this was a mistake after all.

I stayed that way, eyes shut tight holding onto Will, and pretended to be asleep. I focused only on the scintillating stroke of his thumb on my leg and the ticklish spot where the rest of his fingers draped along my inner thigh. It was everything I'd ever wanted. I wasn't going to ruin it by trying to figure out what was really going on inside his head. All I knew was his touch felt really good. And that was all that mattered to me.

I must have let myself become a little too relaxed because it seemed like only a few seconds had passed when an icy blast of air hit my cheek. I groggily opened my eyes and saw Rob standing in his driveway, leaning into the car, telling us goodbye. My God, how long had I been asleep?

"I hope everything works out okay, Red," Rob said. It sounded like he was talking about my injuries, but I had a feeling he was alluding to something more. He gave a purposeful glance at where I was hugging Will and added, "I have a feeling it will."

Rob slammed the door, and I was suddenly wide awake. I started to scramble into the empty passenger seat like I always did when Rob left, but Will didn't let go of me. In fact, his fingers only gripped around my thigh tighter.

Surprised, I glanced over at him. His expression was more serious than I'd ever seen it before.

"Stay," was all he said.

And so I did.

CHAPTER THIRTY-FOUR

"START ME UP" REPRISE

I WAS WIDE awake now. Wide awake and sober and chattering so incessantly you would've thought I'd just eaten a handful of Pixie Stixs then chased them with a gallon of Mountain Dew. I didn't feel too bad though because Will was blabbering on like an auctioneer at a livestock fair himself. Ever since we'd left Rob's house it was like we were trying to not let one moment of silence slip into the car, or else we might have to address why the hell we were driving around holding on to each other the way we were.

So far, we'd talked about a bunch of meaningless stuff. The basketball team's poor defense tonight. What Will was doing at work tomorrow. Which Stones songs would go on our top ten playlist. The funny thing was that Will, always so whirling and jittery, was finally still for once. In fact, he hadn't moved his hand off my leg once in the past hour. Not even to change the cassette.

He finally slowed the car to a stop, then looked over at me, eyes wide. "What do you want me to do?"

My heart galloped in my chest. *Oh my God. This is it. This is the moment I've been dreading for so long. Will is asking me point blank what I want from him. I'm finally going to have to tell him the truth about how I really feel.*

I tried to stall. "What do you mean? What do I want you to do?"

He motioned to the fork in the road in front of us. "Which way do you want me to go? Right or left?"

"Oh, my God!" I exploded in relief. "You mean the road! You mean, which way do I want you to *drive?*"

He gave me a funny look. "Yeah, what else would I have been asking?"

"Right, right," I said, kicking myself for reading too much into things once again. I looked up at the road signs, trying to figure out where we were. When Will started turning right, I realized what I'd just said. "Whoops, I didn't mean to go right... actually, can you turn left instead?" A plan began formulating in my mind.

As we drove, I could almost hear a phantom clock ticking in my ears. It was getting late, and time was running out. Not just on the night, but it felt like on Will and me too. Now that Penny knew about me, there was no way she was going to put up with him seeing me anymore. Especially if she was supposedly so jealous of me, like Will said. She was definitely going to put an end to The Ride. That was, if Will didn't do it first.

I had to do something to make Will remember all the fun we'd had, how much we'd shared, how good we were together before it was too late. His thumb grazed along my thigh again, sending shivers along my spine, and into the space between my hip bones that ached for so much more.

"Now turn right," I ordered at the next intersection, my plan taking further shape. I proceeded to direct him down so many twists and turns he finally said, "Wow. Listen to you, Red. Ordering *me* around for once."

It was a strange role for me since I usually just sat back and let Will take me wherever he wanted to go. But tonight was not the night for sitting back, for being a helpless passenger. If I was going to get what I truly wanted, it was time for me to stop letting life simply happen to me. It was time for me to finally grab the wheel and take back some control.

"Stop here," I said when we came to a long stretch of deserted road.

Will put the car in park and turned to me with a knowing smile.

"You recognize where we are, then?" I asked, my heart lifting at his expression.

"This is where I brought you the first night we met."

"I thought it might be nice to remember," I said, still not sure what I was going to do next. I hoped the memories of us dancing in the headlights and all the other lovely moments we'd shared, would flood over Will and he'd be so overcome with emotion he'd admit his love for me and I wouldn't have to risk telling him how I felt first.

"I've got a question for you, Red," he said, pointing at me. "Do you remember what song was playing when we got here that night?"

"Of course. 'Start Me Up'."

We both stared out the windshield, nodding to ourselves. The greatest hits tape was playing "Brown Sugar" now. "Start Me Up" was on a completely different cassette. One that neither of us made a move to find.

Our mutual paralysis eventually became so awkward we both finally blurted, "let's get out," at exactly the same time. We cracked up, which made everything instantly lighter. I reached for the door handle, hating I had to let go of him, yet at the same time knowing there was no way I'd ever be able to sort out my muddled thoughts if he kept touching me like that.

"I just have to do one thing first," Will said, reaching for the stereo. "Hey, roll down your window before you go." A few seconds after I was out of the car, "Start Me Up" began blasting from the speakers.

I walked slowly down the road in front of the car, still trying to figure out what I was going to do next. Gravel crunched from behind as Will followed where I led. When I turned around, he was facing me, bathed in the soft glow of one headlight. I scanned his face, his body, thinking how almost everything about him was exactly the same as the first night I'd met him. The night he'd stood so handsome and defiant in front of me, bathed in that same headlight. But now he seemed so different.

Now I knew the way he always tapped the edge of his ring on the steering wheel in rhythm with the song on the stereo. And how many times he rolled up his shirt sleeves. (Three, by the way). And how his lips parted a little bit when he listened intently to one of my stories.

How he ran his fingers through his hair when he was frustrated and how he always played a slow ballad at the end of the night, just before he let me out in my driveway and said goodbye.

Now, I'd seen him angry and sad and happy and every emotion in between. And what's more, now I knew exactly what *made* him angry and sad and happy and every emotion in between. Now he was standing in front of me, the same boy as before, but somehow completely changed. Now he was so much more.

I stood in the headlight across from him, heart pounding, thinking of how we looked like two actors on a dark stage, each illuminated in our own spotlight, waiting to launch into the dramatic finale of our story. Or maybe, just maybe, I prayed, it wouldn't be the end of our story. Maybe it would be the beginning of our next act.

Thankfully, Will spoke first. "You scared me tonight," he said, kicking at a rock by his foot. "If anything had happened to you... if I had lost you, I don't know what I would've done."

"Well, you don't have to worry anymore." I waved a hand down my body. "I'm perfectly fine. See? I'm right here in front of you. You haven't lost me."

"Yeah, but for how long?" As he met my eyes, it felt like he was asking the question as much to himself as he was to me. "How long will you be with me?"

Seeing the pain in his expression hurt, yet it also gave me hope. "I guess that depends. I mean, you never answered my question from before." I hesitated, afraid to face the answer that might follow. "Is The Ride over, Will?"

He lifted his chin at me. "Do you want it to be over?"

I still wasn't sure I was ready to say all I had to, so I started off slowly. "Well, we haven't solved all of life's great mysteries yet, have we?" I laughed nervously.

He looked so sad. "Yeah, well, I'd be glad if I could solve just one of them."

A cool breeze washed over us, lifting a curl of his hair, making it flutter along his neck. He shoved his hands in the pockets of his jeans and pulled his elbows in tight, shielding himself from the cold.

"What do you mean by that? What mystery do you need to solve?" I asked.

"I don't know." He tipped his head up, searching the night sky as if the answer was hidden in the stars above. "I guess I just don't get it, Red. You do what people tell you to. You go to school, you work hard. You try and try and try and they tell you that one day you'll be happy. And then after a while, after you keep doing all the so-called *right* things," he air-quoted, "you stop and say, 'now when was it again that I was supposed to be happy?' And they say, 'Oh, you have to put in your time, son. You just have to be patient, just keep trudging along. Keep your nose to the grindstone. It takes a while, but one day," he waved a hand through the air, "one day far, far, down the road... you'll finally get there. One day, *way* off in the future, you'll be happy'."

He shook his head, clearly fighting some inner turmoil. Then his eyes locked on mine. "But I don't want to wait that long. I'm just tired, you know? I've done what they've told me to and it hasn't worked." His voice was pleading now. "I haven't been happy. And now I finally am... now I think I know what I've wanted all this time. In fact, I think I actually *have* what I've wanted all this time, but now everyone says it's wrong. They say *I'm* wrong. So what am I supposed to do? I don't even know what's right anymore. Maybe you can help me. What's more important, Red? That *I'm* happy or that I do what makes *everyone else* happy? That's the great mystery I can't solve."

My heart hammered so violently against my chest it felt like it might crack open my ribcage. Was he talking about what I thought he was?

"You have to tell me more. What exactly is it that makes you happy, Will?" I croaked; my mouth so dry I could barely get the words out.

He threw his hands in the air. "That's just it! I can't even say what I want to say, because it's supposedly not right!"

We blinked at each other. I felt like I was standing on a razor's edge and the world was slowly tipping sideways and I had to decide which side to jump off on. And yet I was still so scared of making the wrong choice I could barely speak.

"My mom says you can't base your decisions on what other people think," I blurted out.

He seemed surprised at the mention of my mom. Will had asked me about her more than once, but every time he'd brought her up, I'd skirted around the issue with a joke or distraction. After a while, he'd finally gotten the message and stopped asking about her.

"Oh, does she?" he said lightly, like he was afraid he might scare me off the subject again.

"Yeah, she says you need to figure out what you feel deep down inside. Then follow only that."

He nodded, considering what I'd said. I wondered if he was having the same trouble I'd had at first of not being able to find where the deep down inside part of myself even was.

"She says you have to stop and check in with your emotions," I went on. "Take a deep breath and really hone in on how different thoughts feel in your body when you think them."

"Really? That's it?" he said, looking skeptical. "I don't know. This thing I can't figure out... it feels way more complicated than something that could be fixed by just closing my eyes and seeing how I feel inside."

"But that's just it! It doesn't have to be any more complicated than that." I pulled my pin out of my pocket, thanking whatever intuition had nudged me to grab it when I was leaving my room this morning. "Here, look at this."

I handed it to him. He tipped it into the headlights to read the words. When he finished, he broke into a slow smile. The same beautiful smile I'd seen the first night we met. The one that had swept me, kicking and screaming, to a place I'd never known before.

"If it feels good do it," he read, not looking entirely convinced. I wondered if he thought it was just another one of my jokes.

"Seriously, it works!" I said, "I've tried it. It's my new motto."

"I don't know," he said, looking miserable again. He handed the pin back to me. "Can it really be that easy?"

"Believe me, I thought the same thing at first. But I'm here to tell you, it can be."

I didn't add the reason I knew it could be that easy was because following that motto had led me to spending these past months with him, and nothing in my entire life had ever felt as good as that.

"Feeling good, leads to feeling good, leads to feeling good." I hoped so much he could see the perfect logic of it all. "Like magnets clicking together. Building blocks stacking up on top of each other. You just have to start with one tiny, good feeling and then the rest will follow. I promise." *Follow your good feelings about me, Will.*

He gazed into the wide expanse of fields surrounding us, seeming to slip into some kind of inner argument with himself. His expression contorted back and forth from what looked like relief to confusion, then back to relief again, until he finally threw his hands up again in exasperation. "I wish I could believe it was that simple, but there's so much more I have to think about!"

"I know… but…" I stopped, still not sure how to explain it.

"But what, Red? Tell me," he pushed.

I frantically tried to come up with a way to make him understand I was worth whatever risk he thought he had to take, but I just couldn't put the words together.

He went on. "You don't understand. My life is complicated."

"I know… but still…"

"Still what?" Another shove. He wanted me to take the lead. He wanted me to admit the truth first, I knew it. But maybe I could make him slip up. Maybe I could make him show me his hand before I ever had to place my bet.

"I know Marianne Faithful wasn't just Mick's groupie!" I shouted. I had no idea why I'd said it, but once it was out, it felt like the perfect way to lead him where I wanted to go.

He laughed, then wagged a finger at me. "Looks like someone's been doing her homework, huh?"

"Yeah. Just a little." On one of my afternoons at the IU Library, I'd found the truth that had fueled my dreams of Will and me one day becoming more than just friends: Marianne Faithful had never been *just* a groupie for the Stones. She and Mick had been lovers for a long time. Marianne had even been pregnant with Mick's baby until she'd miscarried after an overdose.

Will gave me a rueful grin. "You're right. Marianne was *way* more than just Mick's groupie."

"So, why do you call me her name?" I asked.

His eyes sparkled. "Why do you think?"

I should have known he wasn't going to make this easy for me. "Ugh! Don't tell me. This is another one of your tests, right? You ask the questions and I answer them. That's just the way this works?"

He shrugged. "I'm sorry. But that's the way it has to be."

From the car window, Mick's voice trailed off as the song ended. *You make a grown man cry. You make a grown man cry....*

I thought back to last night when I'd decided I was finally going to find out how Will felt about me. It seemed like a lifetime ago. So much had changed since then. Did I really have the guts to go through with it now that he was standing there in flesh and blood, right in front of me?

"Just tell me what you want. Say it out loud." He took a step closer, narrowing his eyes at me like he was trying to lure me forward with just his thoughts alone. I remembered the quote in the magazine article. How the kid said Will had 'willed them to the championship by his sheer determination alone'. I knew exactly what he was talking about because I felt like Will was doing the same thing to me right now. And yet, I still wasn't sure I was strong enough to do what he was asking me to.

"I can't just *say* it!" I sputtered.

"But don't you get it? You have to. It has to be you."

Dammit. I thought I could do this, but now that the moment was real, I felt like I needed more time.

"Just say it. Roll the dice," he pleaded, taking another step closer. "Tell me exactly what you want."

I smiled, realizing how he was using my own words against me now: *We're only in charge of rolling the dice, Will. None of us can control where they land.*

"But I'm afraid it would be pointless. You're with Penny. That's just how it is..."

He sighed loudly, blue eyes desperate now. "But that's just it, Red. I'm not asking you to tell me how things *are*. I'm asking you to tell me how you *want them to be*."

The measured tone of his voice made everything clear. This wasn't just a simple request; it was an ultimatum. So, this was it. I had no other choice. Either I told Will the truth about how I felt about him, or I cracked a stupid joke and avoided the subject like usual. I knew what would happen if I did that. We'd both get in the car, he'd drop me off at home and drive away and I'd never see him again. The decision was simple, just like I'd said. Simple and yet still the hardest thing I'd ever had to do in my life.

"Fine…. fine!" I yelled. "You really want to know what I want?!"

"Isn't that what I just asked?!"

I swayed in front of him. I felt like I was standing at the top of the two-story high dive at the town pool. "Okay. I'll tell you then. I mean, it's pretty simple, really." I took a deep breath and lept into my swan dive. "What I really want, Will, is *you*."

When the sentence tumbled out, it felt like an anchor that had been sitting in my stomach for three months had been pulled out along with it. The relief was instantaneous. *Wow! Who knew that finally speaking the truth would feel so good?*

I hurried on, afraid that if I didn't keep going, I'd never be able to start again. "I want you and I to be together. Not just as friends. Not just drinking beer and telling jokes and slapping each other on the backs. No, I want more than that. Like *WAY* more than that…"

The truth poured forth like a fountain now. "I want to hold your hand and sit right next to you in the car even when no one else is there with us, just like we did tonight. And I want to touch you whenever I want. Yeah, that's it! That's a big one. I want to touch you. Like a lot! And I want you to touch me too." I felt like I was on a runaway train barrelling downhill fast.

"And I want to run my fingers through your hair," I added, barely even thinking straight now. "I want to touch your hair because it looks really soft and I have a feeling it smells really good because I'm sure your mom buys you, like, the best shampoo..." he gave me a funny look, which was enough to stop me from telling him I wanted to run my tongue down the middle of his chest and taste the sweat on his skin.

But then one extremely important thing I'd been thinking about for a long, long time popped into my head and I figured, what the hell, if I'd already told him all that, I might as well swing for the fences.

"And you know what else I really want, Will?"

He raised his eyebrows, urging me to go on. What I was about to say next terrified me but had to finish what I'd started.

"I want my first kiss to be with someone special. Someone so extra special that I'll never, ever, forget it for the rest of my life. And I want it to be with you."

I was breathing so fast by the time I finally shut up, I felt kind of faint; even dizzier than after I'd fallen off the stupid car. *Oh, my God. What have I done?*

"There. I said it!" I shouted, "Are you happy now?!"

His face was maddeningly unreadable. His eyes were wide, lips parted a little, like he couldn't believe all he'd just heard. He wasn't smiling, but he wasn't frowning either. I wanted to grab him by the shoulders and shake him hard and scream: *I did what you asked me to, Will! Now tell me what the hell you're thinking!*

"Am I happy now?!" he asked, eyebrows raised in exasperation.

I could barely hear him over the pounding in my ears. *Please, please be happy now, Will,* I prayed.

The edges of his mouth tipped up just the slightest bit. "Hell yeah, I'm happy!"

Then, as if in slow motion, he reached out to me. I watched his hand cross the space between us, unable to fathom what he was doing. Then he grabbed my waist and pulled me tight to his body and I finally understood.

"Because guess what, Red?" He was so close his breath tickled my lips. "All of that stuff you just said. That's exactly what I want too."

Then, before I could even process what was happening, he dipped his head down and did what I'd dreamt about every single minute, of every single day, since the moment I first met him:

He kissed me.

CHAPTER THIRTY-FIVE

MILESTONE

A MILLION THOUGHTS poured through my head all at once:

Close your eyes! Now do something with your lips. Should my mouth be open or closed? And my hands... what do I do with those? Whatever you do, just keep your damn eyes closed. We'll worry about the hands later! I don't think I'm doing this right. I most definitely am not doing this right. Please, someone tell me how to do this right!

The spiraling voices built to a crescendo in my ears, then solidified into a wall of black that, surprisingly, seemed a lot like outer space. Then, either a split second or full minute later (I wasn't quite sure which), something moved in front of me. I realized it was Will pulling away.

Wait a minute. It's over already?

"What just happened?" I stammered, feeling as if I'd just woken up from a dream.

Will gave me a lopsided smile. His face was still so close to mine. "What do you mean, what just happened? I just kissed you."

I shook my head hard, still trying to figure out what was going on. "I know.... but I.... I think I might have missed it."

He pulled back and gave me an odd look. "What do you mean you missed it? I'm pretty sure you were right here."

"I know, but I was just so surprised and so... I don't know... just so *freaked out,* I think I may have blacked out a little."

"Red, is this another one of your jokes?"

"No! I'm serious!" I wailed. "God, this is terrible! That was my first kiss, and it was supposed to be everything I've ever dreamed of, and I went and ruined it! And now... now I'm never going to remember it, and it's supposed to be something you remember forever, Will! Forever you know. Like a memory you tell your children and your grandchildren about!"

"You plan to tell your grandchildren about kissing me?"

"Of course!"

He tipped his head, considering. "That seems a little weird."

"It's not weird, it's a milestone! A big milestone in a person's life! Don't you understand? Oh God. How could I have messed this up?!"

I could tell he was fighting hard not to laugh. "Calm

down. It's alright. You didn't mess anything up. I mean, as far as I'm concerned, it was fantastic."

"It was?"

"Yeah." His voice was low and sexy. "Like really, really, good."

He still had me pulled tightly to him and, for the first time, I stopped to savor the feel of his body on mine. *His body was on mine.* I couldn't believe I'd just said that. *Will's body was on mine!* I wanted to scream it so loudly they could hear me all the way back to the town square. But I knew I had to calm down and stop acting like a little girl or else Will might change his mind about me.

"I've got an idea," he said. "How about we have a do-over?"

"What do you mean?"

"A second chance at your first kiss."

"We could do that?" My heart was pounding so hard he could probably feel it right through my denim jacket.

"Of course we can. But first you gotta take a deep breath. It's going to be fine, really. Just relax."

I did what he told me to, trying out the method I'd learned at meditation workshop my mom and I had taken at the Buddhist temple last year. *Breathe in for five seconds. Hold for five seconds. Breathe out for five seconds. Hold for five seconds.* And it worked because after a few rounds, I didn't feel like I was strapped into a Tilt-A-Whirl anymore.

"Okay. I think I'm a better now," I told him.

He looked down at where my arms were hanging limply at my sides. "You know you can touch me, right?"

I thrilled at what he was suggesting. "Oh, yeah... I

guess I can, huh? Well, what do ya know about that?" I hesitated, surveying his beautiful body. "But there are so many good choices. I'm not sure where to start!"

He laughed. "How about you start with putting your arms around my neck?" God, he was probably wondering what he'd gotten himself into with me. I didn't even know where to put my arms when I kissed someone? What a rookie.

"Now just stay calm, alright." He reached up and gently cupped my cheek in his hand, exactly like a leading man in a romantic movie. How did he know I'd always dreamed of someone doing that to me? His thumb brushed lightly back and forth across my skin. "Are you ready?" he asked softly.

"I'm ready," I lied.

"Alright, here we go. Red's first kiss. Take two."

This time when he leaned into me, I let the blackness come again, but just enough so I could focus on every little sensation of what it felt like to finally kiss him.

After fantasizing about him for so long, I'd worried that if we ever did have a first kiss, it would pale in comparison to my dreams. But Will's kiss was not at all pale. It was bright and vivid. And warm and welcoming. And focused and all-consuming in the best way possible. Like falling headfirst into a chasm of pleasure, with no fear of ever hitting the ground. His lips were softer than I'd ever imagined possible. And man, he tasted so good. Like beer and peppermint, which sounded like a strange combination, but coming from Will's mouth was the most heavenly concoction ever.

He pulled away after only a few seconds. "Are you

okay? Did you miss that one too?" he asked with a sly grin.

"No, I got it this time. Just keep going," I mumbled, reaching up for him again.

He kissed me harder then. One hand in my hair, another pulling my hips tighter into his. A tiny part of me wanted to break away and find a piece of paper in his glove compartment, a receipt, the car registration, anything so I could scribble down my new feelings so I could remember them forever. But the bigger part of me wanted to not think anymore. To just disengage my brain. Pull a lever here, open a valve there, and do nothing but feel the satisfaction of finally getting everything I'd ever wanted.

I thought I was doing a pretty good job of letting myself sink into all the delicious feelings, but then Will's tongue slipped inside my mouth and I was so surprised, I jerked away.

"Oh, sorry, sorry," he said. "Was that too much?"

The answer that sprung into my head surprised me. "No. Actually, I liked it."

And I wasn't even lying at all when I said it. I did like it. *A lot.*

I'd always thought having a boy's tongue in my mouth would be gross. But Will's was the exact opposite of gross. The sensation of having a part of him inside me made me slide my hand behind his head and pull him down hard into my lips. The impulse was more instinctual than anything I'd ever felt in my life before. Like my body was telling my brain that no matter much I had of Will right then, it was going to need a whole lot more.

We kissed for so long when he pulled away, I was

light-headed. "Wow!" I knew I should've been playing it cool, but the feel of his lips on mine had erased any chance of pulling that off.

"You liked that, huh?" he asked, smiling his devilish smile.

"Yeah, I liked it. In fact, let's never talk again. Let's only do this."

He laughed. "Sounds good to me!" We kissed again. Even longer this time. I was really getting the hang of it now. Will was right about the relaxing part. It made everything just sort of, *blend* so much better when I wasn't so tense. But when we finally broke apart again, I still had one problem.

"So, when are you supposed to breathe when you kiss?" I gasped. When I scanned the surrounding blackness, it looked like little pieces of glitter were falling from the sky.

"You're so fucking funny, Red."

I stared at him wide-eyed.

"Oh. You're serious!" he said. "Well, I don't know. You just do, somehow. Like through your nose. You're not underwater."

"I kind of feel like I'm underwater, though."

All around me, everything seemed to pulse with a new, unseen energy. I couldn't believe I was now a girl who had touched Will Calder's skin and tasted his tongue. Who had run her hands through his hair. Everything I'd dreamt about for so long. And in a split second, all those dreams had come true. It was almost too much to comprehend at one time.

"What are you thinking?" he asked.

"I'm just wondering if this is all real."

He bent down so his lips were so close to mine, his breath tickled me when he spoke. "Oh, it's real alright."

"But why are you —" My words got garbled in his lips as he kissed me.

"I thought we weren't talking anymore. Only doing this," he reminded me in between kisses.

I pushed him away. "Now that was a joke, Will." I couldn't believe after all this time of trying to pull him to me, I was now pushing him away. And yet I had to, because I needed to figure a few things out.

His shoulders slumped like a kid who'd been told they can't have any more cookies until after dinner. "What? What do you need to talk about right this very second?" His eyes were half-closed as he stared at my lips with a glazed expression.

"What does this mean?" I asked.

"It means I want to be with you. And you want to be with me. I thought we cleared all that up just now." He bent and started kissing my neck, up high by my jawbone first and then lower and lower and lower.

The lightness of his kisses felt so good. Each one tickly and damp and hot all at the same time. It made my body pulse. And not just in the place where he was kissing me, either.

"I've wanted to do this for so long," he breathed into my skin of my collarbone.

"Wait a minute... wait a minute..." I pushed him away again. "What did you just say?"

"I said I've wanted to do this for so long," he mumbled, staring hungrily down at my neck.

"Like how long?"

He strained against my hands. "Just a long time, okay?"

He tried to kiss me again, but I wouldn't let him. "Tell me exactly. Since when?"

He sighed loudly, pulling away to gaze over my shoulder, eyes searching the field behind me as if the answer lay there. A slow smile spread across his face. It was the expression of someone reliving a fond memory. "Since the night at the drive-in when you told me I was a fucking asshole."

I was so surprised I actually took a step backward. "You mean the *second* time we were ever together?!"

"Yeah, then. You were so mad and so... so pretty. I wanted to grab you and kiss you right then and there."

I couldn't believe what I was hearing. "Oh my God! That was so long ago!"

He shrugged sheepishly. "Yeah, I guess."

"So why didn't you do something before now?"

"Well, c'mon. What did you want me to do? I mean, this is all pretty complicated, don't you think?"

"I guess," I said, hating his gloomy tone. And also how he'd used the current tense in that sentence. We'd just told each other exactly how we felt. Everything was out in the open. Why did anything have to be complicated anymore?

He took my hand and gently kissed my bandaged palm. "I'm so sorry about this. If I'd gotten my shit together sooner, none of this would've happened to you."

"It's not your fault. You came to the party when you got done with dinner."

"Yeah, well, that not the whole truth. I didn't even go to dinner."

I looked up at him, confused. He went on. "I broke up with Penny. Right there in the parking lot. I didn't even stick around long enough to explain it. I just told her I couldn't do it anymore and left."

"You broke up with Penny?!"

"Red, I just had my tongue in your mouth. Are you really that surprised?"

I blinked at him, heart swelling by what he'd just admitted. "I can't believe you really did it."

"Yeah, I decided at the game. In the hallway. When I heard her talking to you like that, something kind of snapped inside of me. All these little incidents over the past few years. All the nagging and jealousy and checking up on me and the... the *coldness*." He shook his head like he was trying to rid himself of the memories. "It came rushing up on me all at once and then it just became so clear. I didn't want to be with her anymore. I *couldn't* be with her anymore."

I remembered how he'd stood like a statue in the hallway. How he'd seemed so angry and yet had done nothing to defend himself. Now it made more sense. He hadn't argued because there was no point anymore. Because in his mind, he'd already decided it was over.

"My mom and dad were super pissed. They saw me leaving and asked what happened. I told them I broke up with Penny and had to go. Man, you should've seen their faces. I'm going to catch hell when I get home tonight."

"I'm sorry."

"No, don't be sorry for me," he said, grinning big.

"I'm finally happy now. I know I did the right thing. Besides, I'm the one who should be apologizing to you. If I'd just stuck to my original plan, you wouldn't have ruined these super-hot jeans." He squeezed my ass for emphasis.

It was weird to hear him say something so flattering to me out loud. Will thought I looked hot in my jeans? It sounded like something a boyfriend would say to their girlfriend. Was that what I was to him now? Was I now Will Calder's girlfriend?

As tantalizing as that idea sounded, I forced myself to concentrate on what he'd just revealed. "What do you mean, your original plan?" I asked.

"I'd decided to finally tell you how I really felt about you tonight."

"Really? Tonight?" I couldn't believe Will and I had devised the exact same plan for this night. We really were meant to be together.

"So what happened? Why did you cancel on me instead?"

"Because I saw Scott right before the game. I told him about the surprise I had for you. What I had planned for us —"

"The surprise!" I interrupted. "I forgot about that. What was it anyway?"

"The surprise…" he said, looking off in the distance like he'd forgotten about it too. He waved a hand dismissively. "I'll tell you about that later. Let me try to explain all this first." He took a deep breath. "When I saw Scott, he told me I had to leave you alone."

"Leave me alone?!"

Wait. What? Why would Scott have said something like that? He knew how much I wanted to be with Will. Why would he have sabotaged my chance of being with him? Especially after all I'd done to help him get together with Holly.

"He was worried about you," Will said. "I guess Penny had asked him about you. She was angry and trying to pump him for details. He was convinced I was just using you as a pawn. Trying to get some cheap thrills because I was bored with Penny."

"But that's not true, right?" I needed him to say it out loud.

"Of course not! But Scott doesn't understand what you and I have together. He doesn't understand the bond we share. He told me I was ruining your life. Keeping you from having a normal high school experience, whatever the hell that means. He said I was making you miss out on a bunch of stuff just to be with me."

"But I was never missing out. I told him that! I like being with you!"

"Well, he was awfully convincing. He said you'd finally decided you wanted to move on and I needed to step aside and let you do that."

Now I understood. I had told Scott and Stacie I was going to stop hanging out with Will so much. I'd even promised to go on some dates with other guys. But I'd only said that to make them stop hassling me. I'd never intended to go through with it. But Scott hadn't known that. He must have truly believed I wanted to move on.

"Scott said I had to stop holding you back," Will said. "Then he said it wasn't right how I felt about you.

That I was too old to be hanging around with you and that I was... I was..." he hesitated, looking pained.

"What?"

"He said I was taking advantage of you. Of your innocence." He cringed as he said the words out loud. "But I wasn't! Really, I wasn't. I didn't mean to feel this way about you. It just happened. I tried to stop it, but I couldn't."

"Will, you're not taking advantage of my innocence!" I gave him a little shake, forced him to meet my eyes. "For one thing, I'm not that innocent!"

He laughed. "Well, that is true. No one tells dirtier jokes than you, Red."

We laughed some more, but a few moments later, Will became serious again. "So can you see now why I cancelled on you?" he asked. "I started to believe Scott was right. I started to believe the voices in my head telling me how bad I was. I didn't want to do anything to hurt you. And I really didn't want to ruin your life."

"Believe me. This," I motioned to where our bodies were pressed together, "is the exact opposite of ruining my life."

We kissed some more. I wanted to just get lost in the fact that I was finally living the fantasy I'd held for so long, but a million questions were still pinging back and forth inside my head.

I pushed him away again. "So, what made you change your mind?" I remembered how he'd looked in the driveway, so frantic to find me. How he'd put his hand on my leg. He didn't have to do any of those things, and yet he still had.

"After I broke up with Penny, I told myself I was only going to the party to apologize for what happened in the hallway. I couldn't let you think I'd said all those bad things about you. It would've killed me if you'd believed what she'd said."

I swallowed hard, remembering how hurt I'd been when I thought Will had betrayed me. Thank God I'd forgotten that pain long enough to admit I was happy to see him when he'd shown up at the party, instead of forcing myself to stay mad like my rational brain wanted me to. I'd stopped, checked in with myself, and then been honest about my true feelings. That's why I'd decided to leave with him. Now that decision had changed everything between us.

Will went on. "I told myself as I drove to the party that if I saw you and you were happy with Chad like Scott said, I was going to say my piece and then leave you alone. Let you have your normal high school experience." He rolled his eyes, clearly not convinced by Scott's argument.

"But then I got there and you were hurt and I was so upset. I realized how awful it would be if you weren't around. And then when you fell asleep on my shoulder in the car. It seemed like you really wanted to be close to me, that it wasn't just me wanting you. That you wanted me too. It all just felt so right, you know? You by my side like that. I knew at that moment that's what I wanted. I knew I wanted to be with you."

I rolled his words around in my head, trying to make sense of it all. Tonight, after the accident, I'd leaned on him in the car without even thinking. It had seemed so natural, so right, just like he'd said. I couldn't believe it.

Again, one simple, unplanned impulse had led me to the exact place I'd always wanted to be.

Will went on. "I guess I rationalized it would all be okay if you said you wanted to be with me first. Then I wouldn't be so bad. Because then it would be *your* decision. It wouldn't be me doing anything to hurt you."

"Oh Will, you had to know how I felt about you. Did you really have to make me say it first?"

He cocked his head at me. "Well, I kinda suspected how you felt. But you know me. I had to give you one last test."

I punched him on the shoulder, which, since he deserved it, was worth the pain of making a fist.

"Hey! This isn't going to be easy, Red. I had to know you wanted it as much as I did."

I looked up into the sky, wishing he didn't sound so ominous about what was coming next for us. I knew Will's family loved Penny, and it was going to be a while before they got used to the fact that he was with me now. But they'd have to accept me eventually, right?

Will's face brightened. "Hey, I almost forgot the surprise!"

"Geez, can this night get any better?" It felt so strange to gush aloud like that after all these months of trying to hide my feelings around Will.

"You know what this means now?" Will asked excitedly.

"What?" I volleyed back, even though I already had my answer: *It means that we can walk into Pizza King holding hands and announce to everyone in town that we are now officially a couple.*

He let go of me and started talking fast. "I mean, I didn't think it was going to happen because of what Scott said. And then you and Chad and all that bullshit... I was just going to throw them out and say it wasn't meant to be...."

"What wasn't meant to be?" Hearing those words, I couldn't help but think of Rob. Wait until I told him which of his three options had come true.

Will ignored my question. "But now everything's changed!"

"Yes, everything's changed. So what's that got to do with the surprise?"

"Wait here," he said, racing back to the car. "Everything's changed so we can do it! We can go after all!" he called out to me.

"What are you talking about? Where are we going?"

He bent in the passenger window and rummaged around in the glove compartment, then jogged back, waving something triumphantly above his head.

"Here. Look!" He handed me two long rectangles of cardstock, which I quickly realized were tickets. I held them down in the headlights to read them. Just as I made out the three bold words printed at the top, Will grabbed my shoulders, and gave me a little shake.

"Tomorrow, Red," he said, eyes dancing in delight. "You and I are going to see The Rolling Stones!"

CHAPTER THIRTY-SIX

"YOU CAN'T ALWAYS GET WHAT YOU WANT" REPRISE

WILL GRABBED ME by the waist, dipped me over, and kissed me so hard you would've thought we were in Times Square celebrating the end of World War II instead of an arena packed with 40,000 Rolling Stones fans.

"I can't believe this is happening!" I shouted when we broke apart.

I wasn't even sure what part I was talking about. I couldn't believe he'd kissed me like that? Or I couldn't believe we were about to see the Stones live and in person? Or I couldn't believe we had floor seats only a few hundred feet away from the stage? (Although I *could* believe that last part. I was here with Will, after all. The guy definitely had connections.)

I guess what I really couldn't believe was how much Will seemed to like me now. It was as if the invisible wall between us had crumbled and now he couldn't get enough of me. It felt like an actual miracle had been performed in my life; one so big it needed to be submitted to the Vatican and broadcast worldwide on the six o'clock news, like when that lady from South Bend saw the image of Jesus in her toast last year.

Ever since we'd left my house for Louisville that afternoon, things had been getting better and better and better. Will had given me one of his Rolling Stones shirts to wear and we'd kissed at all the stop lights once we'd gotten to the city and now here we were, holding hands and making out in front of a crowd of thousands after all these months of just being friends.

On the drive down, there had been this one crystal clear moment that I already knew I would remember forever. The car was skimming over the dips in the road like a boat on the water and Will had turned and smiled at me, his pale blue eyes mirroring all the thrill, all the adoration I felt inside too. For a split second, he seemed like a mirage shimmering next to me in the driver's seat; something so beautiful, so hoped for, I was scared to blink and risk him being gone when I opened my eyes again. We'd just stared at each other, and the intensity of our connection had made my chest ache, but in such a pleasant way, like when you accidentally rub your hand against an almost-healed bruise. That's when I'd had the most amazing thought.

I did this. I followed my good feelings and now here I am. Everything that is happening right now is all because of me. I'd never felt so powerful, so sure of myself, in my entire life.

Now, inside the arena, I twirled around, staring up at the thousands of faces surrounding us, feeling that same invincibility again. Just as I turned back to Will, the lights of the arena snapped off, plunging us into darkness. A gigantic roar of voices thundered through the air. But after bellowing into the dark for what seemed like five whole minutes, there was still no sign of movement on the vast stage in front of us.

Just as our cheering waned, six notes of the marimba plinked playfully through the air. The crowd went insane. Every good Stones fan knew those notes by heart. And the legendary song they belonged to.

"LADIES AND GENTLEMEN," a man's voice boomed from the loudspeakers, "PLEASE WEL-COME.... *THE ROLLING STONES!!*"

The curtains parted. An explosion of lights and music erupted from the stage, blinding my eyes, slapping my face with a tidal wave of noise. And then there they were: The Rolling Stones. Real and in person and right in front of me. Mick skipping down the center of the stage waving his microphone over his head, Charlie tapping merrily on the drums, Keith, Ron and Bill casually spilling from the wings to flank the sides of the stage.

"Under my thumb...." Mick sang, his voice nearly drown out by the frenzied crowd.

A flood of sensations coursed through my body. It felt like someone had thrown a lever and sent a surge of electricity up through my toes, illuminating me from the inside out, like a human light bulb. Then, the weirdest thing happened: I started to cry. It happened so fast I couldn't even fight the tears back before they squeezed out of my eyes. It must've been the shock of seeing all the guys in person. Or the assault of sound piercing my ears. Or just the raw energy of the crowd undulating around me. But the tears came, completely disconnected from any kind of rational thought. Just a simple bodily response, as involuntary as a breath, or a sneeze, or a heartbeat.

Thank God, it was so dark and Will was too preoccupied by *completely freaking out* to notice what had happened to me. I would've been so embarrassed if he'd seen me like that, especially after I'd been so adamant about never crying over anything. I wiped the tears away quickly, then concentrated on the details of the spectacle unfolding in front of me to keep them from coming back.

Charlie smiled like a Cheshire cat on the drums in the back. Bill, in his blue track suit, played his bass guitar, looking as bored as if he were entertaining at some kid's Bar Mitzvah. Ron ran back and forth across the stage, his white fringed cowboy shirt shaking as he wailed on his electric guitar. And then there was Keith, standing stock still on the stage, looking the epitome of cool. His hair was all crazy like he'd just rolled out of bed five minutes before walking onstage, and he was wearing a black leather jacket and white shirt with a thin tie, a cigarette dangling precariously from his lips as his fingers flew over his electric guitar. *God, I wish Karen were here. She'd be losing her shit, seeing him play like this in person.*

I was almost scared to look directly at Mick in case the tears came flooding back again. But the force of him was so strong, coming closer and closer as he pranced down the catwalk in the middle of the crowd. There was nothing I could do but stare.

He had on tight white football pants with black knee pads and a bright turquoise jacket over his bare chest. His hair was long and shaggy, and he held the microphone so close to his curling lips as he sang it looked like he might accidentally swallow it whole. He gyrated and kicked and convulsed like he was possessed by the song he was singing. That he wasn't as much dancing, as physically channeling the notes into some kind of bodily incantation.

I screamed louder, jumping up and down in time with the music as Mick came closer, thankful the rush of adrenaline had numbed my tender knees and palms. I felt like I was at the zoo, seeing an exotic animal I'd only ever read about in books before, standing right in front of me. Will and I waved our arms over our heads with the rest of the crowd as Mick turned our way. I knew I was probably delusional from lack of oxygen from screaming so much, but I could've sworn he pointed right at me when he sang the line about the Siamese cat girl. Like I said, the day just kept getting better and better and better. It's little magnets of goodness snapping together, one after another, to become more and more and more.

⥈

The Stones played hit after hit with barely a moment's pause in between. We danced and screamed and jumped up and down for a solid two hours. My sides ached from exhaustion, but the excitement distracted me from the pain. I was only fifteen years old and I thought I might be on the verge of a heart attack. But, although Mick was sweaty, none of the band showed any signs of slowing down at all. You had to give it to the old guys. They really had some stamina.

Will was still as amped up as when the concert started, but he looked as worn out as I felt. The edges of his hair were wet and his face was red and his shirt was soaked with sweat. It was so hot down there with everyone smashed together that I'd pulled the bottom of my shirt up and tucked it into my bra, making a bikini top like we used to on really sweltering days at camp. I was glad I'd done it, because Will kept touching the bare skin of my back as we danced; letting his hand glance over the flat part of my belly every once in a while, making my legs turn even weaker than they already were.

So far, Mick had convulsed through "Let's Spend the Night Together", charged up and down the side wings during "Brown Sugar", rolled around on the stage with Ron during "Shattered", and mimed some pretty risqué hip thrusts during "Beast of Burden".

But the best part had been when he let the crowd take over the vocals to the chorus of "You Can't Always Get What You Want." I thought I might've burst a vocal cord from singing so loudly, but it had been worth it. I'd never felt so aligned with so many other people ever in my life.

Now Mick disappeared from the stage, leaving Keith to sing lead vocals on "Little T & A" which sent the crowd into a frenzy, since he rarely took the center mic.

When Keith finished his song, the stage went completely dark for the first time all night. After a minute passed, Will and I gave each other a funny look, wondering if we needed to get our lighters out for the encore. But before we could grab our Bics, a spotlight flamed to life in the rafters above the stage. There, in the metal basket of a huge mechanical crane, stood Mick, shirtless and waving a long purple scarf. Then another spotlight lit on the stage. Inside it's yellow funnel stood Keith, strumming a tinny guitar riff.

Will and I screamed "JUMPIN' JACK FLASH!!" into each other's faces before Mick even had time to reveal he was born in a crossfire hurricane. I started laughing hysterically, not just because of how stupid we must've looked, but because there wasn't much else you could do when your bloodstream was made up of 99.9% pure joy.

We sang with Mick at the top of our lungs as the arm of the crane extended over the crowd. Mick punched the air like a boxer as he sang, the fans underneath his metal basket reaching frantically up as he passed by, arms waving and bodies swooning like a bunch of Born-Again Christians at a Sunday morning tent revival.

As the contraption headed our way, I grabbed Will and shrieked into his ear, "Let me on your shoulders!!! Let me on your shoulders!!"

He looked confused, but I was so frantic I barely waited until he crouched down before catapulting myself up on his back and scrambling to his shoulders.

"Get me closer!" I screamed down to him, thrusting my hips like I was riding my horse, not my boyfriend. I knew I was acting crazy, but I didn't even care because

I was sure I could get Mick to see me up there above everyone else.

Mick sang and sang, but the basket moved slowly, and he hadn't made it to our side of the stadium yet. I was starting to lose hope because I could tell from where he was in the lyrics he might not make it to us by the time the song was over.

When he got to the last verse, Mick reached down, grabbed a handful of something by his feet and flung the pieces out over the crowd. It took me a second to make out that it was flowers he was throwing; red and white carnations, showering over the pulsing heads of the crowd like hundreds of colorful raindrops.

"Oh my God! Oh my God! I have to get one!" I yelled down to Will, even though there was no way he could hear me over the screams. Underneath me, he was clutching my thighs hard, doing all he could to get me closer; elbowing and pushing people like the great defensive player he was. But it didn't matter because the song was almost over.

Finally, Mick handed his microphone to the guy working the controls of the crane. Then he reached down and flung the last of the flowers out, dousing the devout heads underneath him like he was performing a mass baptism by carnations.

When he finished, he stood up and stretched his arms out wide to his sides. He threw his head back and the spotlight bathed his entire body in white, exposing each rib of his skinny torso. His football pants hung low on his hips and brown hair fell in tangles to his shoulders. Even though I was a dunce when it came to religion, I still saw an uncanny resemblance to a certain other deity who had once hung almost the same way above a cheering crowd. Although I was pretty sure Mick's night was going to end a helluva lot better than that other guys did.

I was so transfixed by the image of Mick up there, it took me a second to realize the song was over. Since I was above the heads of the crowd, I could see all the people celebrating their once-in-a-lifetime moment, clutching their flowers to their chest like they'd just experienced the rapture. I couldn't believe I wouldn't get one after all. I was so close. And yet, just the tiniest bit too far away.

Mick peered down on the crowd from his perch, holding the railing and panting hard, trying to catch his breath. I frantically waved my arms at him like I was stranded on a deserted island sending out an SOS to a passing airplane. But he still didn't look my way.

Then I saw it: One red carnation balanced on the edge of the basket right by his foot.

I waved even more frantically now. Mick was only a few hundred feet away. Maybe I could somehow get him to see my distress signal. "THERE!!" I pointed to the flower, screaming. "Mick! There's still one more!!"

But Mick was looking the other way. The band onstage was retreating. Switching guitars. Taking drinks. Shedding jackets. The crane arm rocked to life and started moving away. That was it. It was over. There would be no once-in-a-lifetime moment for me.

"NO MICK!!" I screamed with every ounce of cheerleading voice I could muster. "THERE'S ONE MORE!!" I was flailing so crazily it was a wonder I didn't take

flight right off Will's shoulders. I wanted that damn carnation. And just like Will had taught me, I wasn't going
to give up until I got it.

I wasn't sure if he heard me, saw me out of the
corner of his eye, or simply felt the laser focus of my
desire beaming at him from my perch atop Will, but
something crazy happened next. Mick turned around
and looked directly at me.

"THERE'S ONE MORE!!" I shrieked again, pointing at the flower by his foot, even though I knew there
was no way he could hear me.

He looked down, then turned back to the crane
driver. A few seconds passed, and I thought for sure I'd
only imagined his attention, that he hadn't really seen
me after all. But then the crane stopped.

Mick lifted the mic to his lips. "Wait a minute…
wait a minute. Hey Donnie, get me over there," he said
to the driver, pointing straight at me. "Get me over to
that pretty little thing… she seems to have something to
say to me."

Oh my God! He's talking about me!

Suddenly, everything became like a dream. Mick
started floating toward me, illuminated in his spotlight, all
flowing scarves and big lips and naked chest and messed
up hair. When he got right over me, I was blinded for a few
seconds. I panicked, thinking that maybe I was just about
to pass out, but then I realize the white in my eyes was
from the edge of Mick's spotlight that was now encom-
passing both Will and me, teetering there below him.

The crowd had caught on that something unusual

was happening, so they hushed to hear what was going on.

"THERE'S ONE MORE!" I stabbed my finger at the dangling flower, my voice seeming much louder now in the quieted arena.

My eyes had adjusted to the light so I could see Mick clearly hovering above me. His skin glistened with sweat and his chest heaved hard. He was so close I could almost see his heart beating in his emaciated chest. Thick black eyeliner circled his eyes, making their vivid green stand out among the wrinkles on his face. But what I noticed most about him was his smile. It was huge and genuine and seemed like it was just for me.

He bent down and picked up the flower by his foot, then raised the microphone to his lips. "Is this what you're wanting, my dear?" He asked in his British accent, arching one eyebrow at me.

"YES!" I screamed just in case he was still too high up to hear me. I barely even remembered that Will was underneath me anymore. I thought he might have been saying something, but I couldn't make it out.

"Well then," Mick said, dangling the flower over the edge of the basket like it was a piece of bait above my head. I reached for it, but it was way too high up and he still hadn't let it go.

He waited, letting the drama build before he finally opened his fingers. "Catch!" he called to me. The flower floated down through the dust-pocked air, twirling, and dipping erratically. My heart lurched, thinking of the possibility that I might not catch it. But by the grace of God, it somehow landed straight in my out-stretched hands.

The crowd roared as I pumped the carnation into the air in victory. Then, I put the stalk between my teeth like a flamenco dancer and shimmy my shoulders just to milk the moment a bit more. Mick burst out laughing. *Oh my God. I can't believe it. I just made Mick Jagger laugh!*

"There you go... are you happy now?" he asked me.

"YES!!" I screamed back, then added another shimmy for effect.

He laughed at me again. *That's two times now. I just made Mick Jagger laugh twice!* I felt like I might self-combust from sheer happiness alone.

Mick said something to the guy behind him and the basket started moving back toward the stage.

I struggled to catch my breath as the words from before flashed back in my head. *I did that. All of that happened because of me.*

As he floated across the crowd, Mick called out on the microphone, "Hey, Keith!"

Keith leaned into the microphone on stage where he'd been waiting. "Yeah, Mick?" he called back, arms crossed leisurely over his guitar. That's when I realized Keith had been standing there watching the entire scene unfold. That meant for the past 30 seconds, both Mick Jagger and Keith Richards had actually known I existed in the world. How unbelievable was that?

"I think we're going to have to change the lyrics to one of our songs," Mick said, silencing the crowd again.

"Oh yeah? Why's that, Mick?" Keith volleyed with perfect Vaudeville timing.

"Because," Mick paused dramatically, pointing back to where I was still waving my red carnation. "It looks like sometimes you *CAN* always get what you want."

The force of the crowd's roar almost knocked me right off Will's shoulders.

CHAPTER THIRTY-SEVEN

WORTH IT

IT WAS REALLY late when we drove home. In fact, once we got out of Louisville, the roads were so empty it felt like Will and I were the only two people alive in the world, which was just fine by me.

I was a hollowed-out shell of myself; my skin still buzzing from the relentless pounding of the speakers, my ears ringing in tinny monotone, my throat so hoarse from screaming I sounded like a five-pack-a-day chain smoker whenever I talked.

Will hadn't even turned on the stereo when we got in the car. Probably because, like me, the songs from the concert were still screaming in his head.

I sat on the console next to him, my arm entwined in his, reliving every amazing moment over and over again.

"Oh man, that was the best night of my life." I dropped my head over on his shoulder, exhausted.

"Yeah, mine too," Will said. "People are saying this

might be the last time the Stones ever tour. And we'll be able to say we were there, that we saw them live. Think about it. We may have just been a part of history!"

I tried to take it all in, but once again, everything seemed too big, too perfect for it to be real. "I can't wait to tell Stacie about it. She's going to freak out when she hears I actually talked to Mick Jagger!"

Will's arm tensed against my side. "Um, Red," he said softly, "I thought I told you. You can't tell anyone about this."

"Well, yeah," I said, remembering the instructions he given me when he'd dropped me off last night.

When we'd parked in my driveway, he'd gotten this serious look on his face, which I'd just assumed was him being all dramatic again.

"We can't tell anyone about us yet, okay?" he'd said. I'd agreed without asking more. I figured he wanted to keep us quiet for a little while, to be considerate of Penny's feelings. In fact, I thought it was kind of sweet that he didn't want to rub our relationship in her face so soon after their breakup. It was nice how he wanted to treat her with that kind of respect.

Still, Will respecting Penny had nothing to do with me telling Stacie about us.

"You said not to tell anyone *yet*." I reminded him of his exact words from last night. "But you just meant for a little while, right? Just till the shock blows over. I can at least tell Stacie, can't I? She won't tell anyone."

I'd felt so bad when Stacie called earlier and asked where I'd gone after the accident at Chad's party. I'd fibbed and said I'd gotten a ride back to Pizza King and called Karen to come get me. Because of Will's instructions, I hadn't told her the truth about how he'd admitted his feelings for me and about finally getting my first kiss.

It had killed me not to share my big milestone with her. Killed me even worse when I'd outright lied when she asked me to hang out and I'd told her I couldn't because I was going to Karen's gig tonight. I rationalized that what I'd done wasn't so bad because I was only going to have to withhold the truth from her for a little while. Stacie would understand why I had to wait to tell her everything. Yeah, she might be mad for a day or two, but she'd get over it. Stacie and I never stayed mad at each other for very long.

Will gently extracted his arm from mine and reached to turn the stereo down, which was weird because it wasn't even on. Realizing his mistake, he ran his hand roughly through his hair. I sat up, wide awake now, a foreboding gathering in the pit of my stomach.

"What's going on?"

"I thought you understood," he said, looking pained. "I told you this was going to be complicated."

"I *do* understand. I mean, at least I thought I did...."

I ran back over what I thought I knew. Will wanted to give it a little time before people started seeing us together to be sensitive to Penny. He was worried about his mom and dad being mad at him, which truthfully, I didn't quite understand. Will was 20 years old. In college, for Christ's sakes. Why did his mom and dad care so much about who he dated? I was only in high school, and my mom never even asked me who I was with on the weekends. She didn't give a shit who I went out with. Why were the Calders so involved in Will's life?

"It's going to take way more than just a little while to figure this out." He motioned back and forth between us like we were a complicated knot to be untangled, instead of just two people who liked being together. "We have to keep our relationship a secret for a lot longer than just a couple of weeks."

A secret? What was he talking about?

"But what about earlier?" I hooked a thumb back toward Louisville. Will had spent all night holding my hand, pressing me close, kissing me in front of a stadium full of people. He hadn't seemed like he was hiding anything about us at the concert.

"We were two hours away from Cold Springs," he explained. "No one at the concert knew who we were."

My heart sunk as I thought back over the night. How Will hadn't wanted me to sit on the console next to him until we were two towns away. How when we'd met up with the security guard friend of his that had gotten him tickets, he'd let go of my hand, and introduced me as simply Red, not as his girlfriend.

"Oh, right," I mumbled, suddenly seeing everything in a whole new light. I felt so stupid. How could I have overlooked so many signs? A heaviness settled over me as I began to understand where this conversation was headed. "So how long exactly do you think we're going to have to wait to tell people about us?"

"Well, not forever. But like I said, this isn't going to be easy. I just pissed off a lot of people. Not only Penny, but my mom and dad. Her mom and dad. The rest of my family. Penny and I were together for a long time. This is kind of a big deal."

He looked at me with the you-just-don't-understand expression he always got when he explained some great nuance of the world that I was too young to comprehend. I forced myself to smile; to ignore the burning in my stomach.

"I get it." I said, trying to let it all sink in. Why hadn't I thought about all Will would have to go through to be with me?

He sat up taller in his seat, eyes darting back and forth between me and the road before us. He seemed desperate to make me understand. "It'll be alright. I just need some time. Like I said, we'll tell people about us. Eventually."

I swallowed hard, somehow already knowing that Will's idea of *eventually* and my idea of *eventually* were two different things. All the images of Will and me walking into Pizza King hand in hand, of him guiding me through a crowd at a basketball game, of me sitting beside him at his family's Sunday dinner, slowly crumbled before my eyes.

"So, it's going to be more than just a few weeks?" I said, trying to hide my disappointment. I knew there was something more to him wanting to keep us a secret. A reality I kept refusing to look at because it threatened to shoot a hole right through the walls of my fairy tale castle.

"Yeah, it is going to have to be more than a few weeks, Red. Because it's not only about breaking up with Penny. It's more than that. It's well…. we can't tell people just yet because you're so —"

"Young," I finished his sentence, voice hitching on the dreaded word. There it was again. The age difference thing I kept pretending was nothing, but in truth was everything and more. God, I hated myself for being 15 right then. Especially since there was nothing I could do about it, which made it even that much more infuriating. It was all so unfair. Why did it even matter how old Will and I were? We enjoyed being together. We made each other happy. What was so wrong about that? It was the same thing that had confused me when everyone shunned my mom for loving Karen. Why did other people get to decide what was best for the two of them? Why couldn't everyone just mind their own business? Just live and let live? It was such a simple concept, and yet no one in Cold Springs seemed willing to even give it a try.

Suddenly, I thought of something that might make Will see us in a different light.

"But John Travolta is dating Brooke Shields, and she's 16 and he's 27, which is a way bigger age difference than you and me!"

He made a face. "Are we really talking about John Travolta right now?"

"There's never a wrong time to talk about John Travolta, Will." I teased, hoping to lighten the mood.

He laughed. "I hate to break it to you, but that's Hollywood, and this is Cold Springs. The rules are a bit different around here."

I deflated a bit. "Yeah, I guess you're right."

Then something else popped into my head. "But I'm going to be 16 in only a few months."

To me, 16 sounded so old, but from the way Will winced when I said the number, it obviously sounded very differently to him.

"I'm sorry. Really, I am," he said. "I don't want it to be like this either. And I promise, it won't be forever. You just gotta trust me."

"I trust you. I do." But the pact from Stacie's bedroom whispered in my mind.

We have to promise to tell each other everything from now on.

"Can I at least tell Stacie, though? Just her. No one else."

"No, you can't. We can't risk it. You know how gossip spreads in this town."

"But I swear, I know her. She won't tell anyone. *Pleeeeasse*, Will." I cringed at the sound of my own voice.

"I said no." His sharp tone reminded me of when my dad used to tell me I couldn't stay up late to watch TV when I was little. I was glad I was inside the car because otherwise I might have stomped my foot at Will like I did at my dad back then.

Will pulled the car over in the empty parking lot of a furniture store. My heart pounded as he slipped the gearshift into park and turned to me, looking grave. Man, the vibe on this night certainly had changed quickly.

"Look, I know you think this is all unfair," he started. The neon *Closed* sign in the window cast the angles of his beautiful face in an eerie, red glow. "But it's just the way it has to be."

"I know. I get it."

He furrowed his brows. "So, why do you still look so upset?"

I shrugged. "I guess I just wanted people to know about us."

His face dropped. Immediately, I knew I'd said something wrong.

"Why do you care so much if people know you're with me?" he asked.

"Um... I uh..." I realized I was ashamed to say the real reason out loud. Embarrassed to reveal how many of my fantasies revolved around the reactions of people in town. That set off a warning bell in my head. Why *was* I so desperate for everyone in Cold Springs to know about us, anyway?

"Sorry, sorry, that came out wrong," I sputtered, trying to repair the damage. "I just meant that I want to be a part of your life. Out in the open, you know. I want to know more about you. Like all of you."

He relaxed a little. "But you do already know all about me, Red. More than anyone else in the entire world, I think. And all the rest of that stuff will come, in time. I promise. I'm looking at the big picture. I want to be with you for a long time. So long that one day we'll look back on this and it will seem a blip on a screen."

I sat back, surprised by how much he'd thought about our future together.

He narrowed his eyes at me. "But if you're not happy with this arrangement," he said, his voice suddenly hard, "then maybe you should rethink this. If being with me isn't enough for you, then maybe we should end this right now, before it goes any further."

The steely look on his face froze me in place. *What's happening? Why is he so upset that I want people to know about us being together?* I couldn't believe I was on the verge of messing up our entire relationship before it even got started.

"Of course you're enough for me," I reassured him. "I could never want anything more."

I held my breath, waiting for his reaction, silently cursing myself for being so stupid again. I shouldn't have complained about being kept a secret. I was lucky to even be with Will in the first place. I had no right to make any demands of him.

He tipped his head, searching my face. "You sure? You sure I'm worth it?" Luckily, his voice was lighter now. He raised his eyebrows as he waited for my answer, like he was praying I was going to say yes. He seemed so sweet, so innocent in that moment. Not like someone so much older than me, but more like a little boy with his fingers crossed behind his back, hoping Santa had brought him everything he ever wanted.

I grinned at him. "Yes, of course you're worth it, dummy." I shoved him roughly on the shoulder.

He broke into a huge smile. Seeing it, I let out a sigh of relief.

"Oh, really?" he teased, his voice low and sexy. "Why don't you tell me all the ways I'm worth it, then? I've got some paper in the glove compartment. We can start a list."

I shook my head at him. God, I loved when he was smug like that. "No way! I'm not going to tell you how amazing you are every other second. And I hope to hell you don't expect me to be all gushy over you now. Because *yuck*!" I made a face like the thought of complimenting him turned my stomach. "I'm not that kind of girl, Will."

He laughed as he leaned over and kissed me tenderly.

When he was done, he whispered in my ear, "All I know is, you're the perfect kind of girl for me." My stomach twirled violently feeling his breath on my skin.

He kissed me again and everything I'd just been so worried about disappeared; erased completely by the pillowy softness of his lips. After a few minutes, I pulled back so I could look him in the eyes.

"Alright. Prepare yourself. I'm going to say one teeny, tiny, little sappy thing, but then that's it. Don't expect me to gush anymore after that, okay?"

He gave me a sleepy grin. "Alright, Little Miss Hard Ass. Lay it on me."

I paused, clearing my throat, trying to make a big deal of delivering my speech. "All I've ever wanted is you, Will. And now that we're together, nothing else matters but that." I went on, trying to sound as confident as he always did. "You're worth everything to me. And you don't have to worry. I promise I can handle the fact that our relationship isn't going to be easy."

He wrapped me in a huge hug. I felt the relief softening his body as he held me. I hugged him back as hard as I could, sucking in his warmth, his stability, the strength of his arms around me. All the while praying the promise I'd just made him was one that I could keep.

GIRL TO GIRL

Karen and I walked down the wide hallway of the Bloomington mall, eyes adjusting to the overhead lights that seemed so harsh compared to the dark movie theater we'd just left. We'd seen *Stripes* with Bill Murray and now were volleying the funniest lines from the movie back and forth, trying to get our timing just right. By the time we got home and reenacted the scenes for my mom (who had been too busy with work to come with us), we'd have our act down pat.

It was the same routine Karen and I went through every time we went to the movies together (which was a lot); adding the latest catchphrases and slapstick pratfalls to our repertoire, then repeating them so often my mom would get sick of us and beg us to stop. Which, of course, only made us do them more.

I tried to imagine what it would it be like to go to the movies with Will, to go on any kind of real date, instead of just riding around in the car together every weekend like we always did. We'd been secretly dating for almost a month now and I'd thought about asking if we could go to the mall in Bloomington together sometime. But I'd decided not to bring it up because I already knew what his answer would be. *"Bloomington is too close to Cold Springs, Red. There's still too much of a chance that we might bump into someone we know from back home."*

I knew it wasn't right to be disappointed about something as trivial as going to the movies. I needed to trust what Will always told me. That the truth about us would come out soon enough and I just had to learn how to be more patient.

As Karen and I passed by the B. Dalton bookstore, three women turned the corner and headed straight toward us. Normally, I wouldn't have given them a second glance, but my eye caught on the Cold Springs Warriors sweatshirt one lady was wearing. When I looked up, I realized it was Will's mom. That alone almost froze me in place but then something even more shocking came into focus: the girl in the middle of the two women was Penny.

It felt like every drop of blood in my circulatory system drained straight into my toes. I had the sudden urge to duck behind Karen so Penny wouldn't see me, but we were so close I didn't have time. Instead, I kept my eyes trained forward and pretended not to see her. But at the last second, just a few feet before they were about to walk by, my resolve cracked, and I glanced over. At that exact moment Penny looked right at me.

She took me in. Then she noticed Karen beside me which set off an almost comedic chain of events: Penny whispered to the dark-haired lady beside her, who must have been her mom. Then Penny's mom turned to stare at Karen and reached over to get Mrs. Calder's attention. Once alerted, all three stared openly at Karen, heads bent together whispering so furiously you would've thought they'd just come up with a plan to end the Cold War with Russia right there in front of the Orange Julius. From their reaction, it was clear they knew Karen was one half of the infamous lesbian duo that had rocked Cold Springs' world a few years ago.

Karen was still repeating Bill Murray quotes, oblivious to the women staring at her, but my cheeks burned like someone had pointed a thousand-watt spotlight straight at my face. I didn't breathe until the group had passed. Then, so flustered by what I'd just witnessed, I stumbled right past the McDonald's entrance and was almost to the RadioShack when Karen yelled, "Hey, where are you going?! I thought we were going to eat?"

I cringed at how loudly she'd yelled. Now she was just making it even more obvious that the two of us were together. "I've just got to run to the bathroom," I hissed, trying to distance myself further from her. "Go ahead and order for me."

I rushed to the bathroom on shaky legs then sequestered myself inside a stall to play back every horrible moment of what had just happened. The whispers, the stares, Penny's expression as she'd looked at me. Why was she even here with Will's mom anyway? Penny and

Will had been broken up for so long. Shouldn't she be out of the Calders' lives by now?

Someone came in and started washing their hands, so I finally got up off the toilet lid. I couldn't stay in there forever. If I didn't get back soon Karen would probably ask me if I fell in or had a bad case of the shits or something gross like that.

When I swung open the door, I almost fainted dead away. Penny was standing at the sink washing her hands, staring at me in the mirror's reflection.

I froze in the stall doorway. For a split second I considered ducking back inside, slamming the door, and hiding until she left.

Good grief, Universe. I know I said I'd wanted my life to be like a movie, but not a movie like this!

"Don't worry, I'm not going to hurt you!" Penny said with a big smile. "I come in peace." She held up her dripping palms as if in surrender.

I tried to laugh but it came out sounding like a goose honk. "Right. Of course," I said, joining her at the sink. I had to keep my cool and act like everything was normal. No one knew about Will and me, so logically there was no reason for me to be completely terrified by the sight of Penny.

I furiously washed my hands but the whole time I could feel her staring at me. "Nice shirt," she said.

I glanced down at The Rolling Stones shirt I was wearing. Will had given it to me a couple of weeks ago. He'd kissed me sweetly on the nose as he'd handed it over, insisting I'd look much better in it than he ever had.

"Thanks," I said to Penny. *Does she recognize it as one of his?*

"I have one just like it," she said brightly, turning off the sink and walking over to get some paper towels.

"Oh, really?" I swallowed hard. "That's cool."

I watched her in the mirror as the water burned hotter and hotter on my skin. She was still smiling and surprisingly, it looked quite genuine. Maybe I'd over-reacted when I'd first seen her. Maybe she wasn't mad at me after all. What if she'd been relieved to break up with Will? Maybe she was as tired of him as he was of her. Now she was just here to thank me for setting her free. Yes. That was possible. That was the kind of movie I wanted this to be. One where everyone turned out to be friends in the end.

"Listen, I just wanted to talk to you for a sec," she said, walking over to prop her tiny butt on the counter next to me. "You know, girl to girl. I thought I might be able to help you out."

"Really?" I said, hope swelling even bigger in my chest. See, I'd just been too dramatic before. Penny was here as a friend, not as an enemy. "Help me out with what?"

I thought I saw her smile drop just a millimeter; a hardness take hold in her eyes. "You don't have to play dumb with me. I know what's going on."

My heart seized in my chest. *What was it that Will always told me? Trust your first impression. It's almost always right.*

"I don't know what you're talking about." I turned the faucet off, then shook the water off my hands as casually as I could and retreated to the other side of the room to get some paper towels. I was relieved she couldn't see my face.

"Don't get all nervous," she said, following behind me. I wanted to tell her I'd be a lot less nervous if she wasn't standing so close to me. And if she wasn't blocking the path to the door.

"I want you to know I'm not upset," she said to my back. "You see, this has happened before. It's not a big deal now. Will gets antsy and decides he wants to be single again, so he breaks up with me for a few weeks," she sing-songed way too cheerfully. "Then he eventually gets tired of whatever distracted him and comes back to me. Simple as that. It happens the same way every time. I'm used to it by now."

She sounded as bored as if she'd just finished explaining the stages of the water cycle to me.

"Oh. Well, I'm glad you two have a system down," I said to the wall. Funny, Will never mentioned that he and Penny have broken up before.

"You know how Will is. How he gets all obsessive about stuff." It was weird how she was acting like we were two friends casually chatting when, in fact, we were quite the opposite.

There was only so long I could dry my hands without looking like a freak, so I finally threw my paper towel away and turned to face her.

She went on. "He always gets obsessed about some stupid thing. The Rolling Stones, basketball, his car. You know, dumb stuff like that."

"Yeah, I guess." I felt like a traitor to Will by agreeing. But I needed to shut her up so I could end this bizarre encounter as fast as possible.

She blinked sweetly at me, the ends of her long eyelashes clumped with so much mascara they looked like tarantula legs. "And now it just so happens that his current obsession is you." She didn't look away, so I didn't either.

She shrugged nonchalantly not waiting for a reply. "But, like I said, none of it ever lasts. He always grows out of whatever it is. Eventually he moves on."

I tipped my head, confused. Will hadn't grown out of his love for The Rolling Stones or basketball or even his car for that matter. He'd loved them forever and still did to this day. Was she even talking about the same person I knew?

"Don't you see?" she said matter-of-factly. "Will has a bit of a problem with growing up. Now he's just using you as an excuse so he doesn't have to."

"I don't even know what that means," I said. I hated the way she talked about Will so condescendingly. She acted like he had all these terrible flaws that needed to be fixed. Couldn't she see he was perfect exactly the way he was?

"What it means is he's being ridiculous," she scoffed. "Coming home from college every weekend? Cruising around the back roads like he used to, trying to relive his old glory days like he's still in high school? It's so, so... immature!" she spat. "Does he think he can just spend his entire life having fun?"

"What's so wrong with having fun?"

She huffed loudly. "Having fun might be okay when

you're young. But when you grow up you have to think about more important things. Like getting a job and making money." She leaned closer, narrowing her brown eyes at me. "Getting married."

I almost laughed right in her face. The thought of Will getting married was ludicrous. Yeah, other kids in Cold Springs got married when they were really young. In fact, there were some kids in the senior class now who were not only married but had babies together. But that wasn't Will. Did Penny even know him at all? Hadn't she listened to Will going on about how sex, drugs and rock 'n' roll were all that mattered to him? Will wasn't ready to get a real job, to buy a house, to chain himself to a desk to provide for a wife like her, who wasn't even smart enough to share his good taste in music. She was kidding herself if she thought he was.

She turned back to the mirror to check her makeup. As much as I hated to admit it, spider lashes aside, she was awfully pretty with her adorable round cheeks and perfect little nose. For the millionth time I wondered why Will had chosen me over her.

"Everyone told me he'd get cold feet." She tilted her head to the side, seeming to talk more to herself now than to me.

I winced at the term *cold feet*. She was serious about this marriage stuff, wasn't she? No wonder Will wanted to get away from her.

I startled, hearing my own words. *Wait a minute. Is Penny right? Is Will just using me as an excuse so he doesn't have to grow up and get married like everyone expects him to?* I shook my head hard, trying to rid my mind of the awful thought.

She turned back to me. "Although I will say he's taken his fantasy a bit too far this time. Running around with a cheerleader five years younger than him? C'mon. You've got to admit it's all a little crazy."

It didn't seem like the right time to bring up the fact that at fifteen and three-quarters-years-old I wasn't actually a full five years younger than Will. So instead, I just stared dumbly at the door behind her, praying that someone would walk in and interrupt us. "Listen Penny," I said, plastering on the most innocent expression I could muster. "I don't know what impression you have, but Will and I are just friends."

"Just friends. Right." She glanced back at the mirror, fluffing her brown hair. "I seriously doubt that. Although you may wish you were 'just friends'" -she furiously air-quoted- "soon enough."

"What do you mean by that?"

"Just that I don't know if you really understand what you've gotten yourself into," she said, arching an eyebrow at me. "You know Will is a man, right? A man that has certain needs." She pulled her sweater taunt over her ample chest. "Do you really think you're equipped to keep him happy?" She stared pointedly at my microscopic boobs in the mirror.

This was becoming utterly ridiculous now. Was she really insinuating what I thought she was? I mean, yeah, I was a virgin who didn't know her ass from her elbow about sex. But if Will asked, I would have sex with him tomorrow. So far it had been him, not me, who'd stopped us from doing more when we made out in the car. Penny clearly knew nothing about what Will did or did not want in his life.

"Like I said, I think you have the wrong impression of what's going on." I started for the door, eager to end the absurd conversation.

"Hey now, don't get all flustered." She whirled around and grabbed my elbow as I tried to pass by her. "I told you I just came in here to help you." Her big smile was back. "Maybe save you some time. And a whole lot of heartache too."

"Why do I find it hard to believe you have my best interest at heart, Penny?" I pulled my arm out of her grip. "I'm going to go now."

I'd almost made it to the door when she called out to me. "Oh right. I forgot. You have to get back to your *lesbian* mom." The word echoed so loud against the tiled walls it froze me in place. I was afraid to open the door in case it might slip out into the crowded mall and expose me even more than it already had.

Penny went on. "You know what the Calders think about that?" Her voice was syrupy sweet.

I turned to her, wishing so much I could just tell her I didn't give a shit and have the words be true.

Penny barreled on, knowing she had me right where she wanted. "The Calders are good Christians. You know that, right? They have strong morals, not only for themselves but for their kids too." I hated how much she was clearly enjoying herself. "You actually think they're going to want their son hanging out with a girl with a *lezbo* mom?" She made a face like she was trying not to throw up. "You think Will is going to ever bring you home to dinner knowing how they'd feel about you? No way. You're never going to fit in there. So why even try? Like I said, I'm just trying to save you some heartache. Because this thing between the two of you. It's never going to work. The Calders will never accept someone like you."

I stood there with my mouth hanging open, wanting to tell her she knew nothing about what the Calders thought about me. I wanted to tell her that Coach liked me a lot. That he even called me his right-hand man, his secret weapon. Hell, Coach and Mrs. Calder had even tried to set me up with Mitch a few months ago, that's how much they liked me. But then I wondered if that was only because they hadn't pieced together who I really was yet. And now that Mrs. Calder had seen me here with Karen and knew the whole truth about me, maybe her entire opinion of me would change exactly the way Penny claimed it would.

A wave of anger pulsed through me, the heat of it slicing deep, hurting all the worse because everything Penny had just said made so much fucking sense.

"Talk about pointless!" I yelled, tired of being on the defense. "You following me around and threatening me, that's what's pointless! Is this what I have to look forward to now? You popping out of toilet stalls and lurking behind potted plants, jumping out from behind trees to scare me away from him?" Whoops. Did I just give too much away? "Which is really pointless since Will and I are just friends!" I added quickly.

Penny gave a smug laugh. If I thought Will's smug

laugh was annoying, hers was a million times worse. "Oh, you won't have to worry about seeing me again," she said, holding up her palms once more. "You see, that's the great thing about all of this. I don't have to do anything. I just sit back and let nature take its course. Just let the inevitable happen and be there waiting for him when everything between the two of you falls apart."

I clutched the door handle, struggling to catch my breath. "Like I said, I have no idea what you're even talking about," I croaked. "But thanks for all your help, Penny. It was real thoughtful of you."

I clamored out the door, thankful to finally get away from her. But Penny got in one last jab as I escaped down the hallway.

"I'm just saying enjoy it now!" she shouted from the bathroom entrance. "Because whatever fantasy world you two are living in... it's never going to last!"

A QUICK NOTE FROM ME TO YOU....

Every author knows the lifeblood of a book is reader reviews. But since I'm too shy to ask someone to review my book face to face, I'm going to take the coward's way out and do it here.

Dear Reader,

If you happen to have a spare moment, would you please consider reviewing this book on Amazon and/ or Goodreads? It doesn't have to be fancy, just a few sentences. It can even be anonymous. (You could make up a fun Username like "MimiHotPants" the moniker my friend's 70-year-old mother used for her email address, which I still find completely hilarious!)

I would appreciate your effort immensely.

Much love,

Kiersten

ACKNOWLEDGEMENTS

This book began in the smallest of ways. I heard a song. A memory popped up. I got the slightest urge to find my old high school scrapbook. More memories came. I felt compelled to write them down. I decided to embellish them with my imagination. I wrote more. And more. And more.

From a broad view, a book seems like a really big thing. Just like life does. But it's really just a bunch of little things put together. Tiny impulses, small decisions. Nudges to go right. Urges to go left. So, I'd like to start my acknowledgements by encouraging you to acknowledge your own feelings, just like Red's mom encouraged her to. I can attest firsthand that good things come from listening to that voice inside you. Who knows what will happen if you really start listening to yourself? Maybe you'll end up writing a book!

There are so many people I'd like to thank for helping me along this journey:

To my writing group, who took a timid first-time writer who could barely read a page of her work out loud and helped her become someone who could put her story out into the world. Your thoughtful critiques, suggestions, and warm camaraderie were exactly what I needed to begin seeing myself as a writer and not just some crazy lady who spent way too much time living inside her own imagination!

To Jack, your championing of my work from the early, rough stages meant more to me than you'll ever know, especially coming from such an accomplished writer as yourself. (I still have some of your critiques in the drawer of my desk to bolster me when I get discouraged!) Thank you for your generosity, and for your meticulous copy-editing of my subsequent books.

To my Schiffer and Hafner family, who always asked how my project was going and took an interest in my work. You listened to my idea when I was still so tender and timid about sharing and didn't laugh at me or make me feel silly. Instead, you got excited and made me feel supported and told me I could do it. You will never know how much one small word of encouragement can mean to a person. Kindness matters. A lot. And you all have shown me a boatload of it!

To my Indiana girlfriends, Cheri, Terri, Julie, Amy, and Rhonda, who were always so eager to hear more of my story and had unwavering faith in me from the beginning (even though digging up some of our glory days might have seemed a bit scary at first I know!) Thank you for being a real-time reminder of those wonderful (and sometimes tumultuous) years growing up together when our friendships were the sun around which everything else in our lives revolved. Slumber parties and games of Light As A Feather and summer camp and proms and trips to the tanning bed wouldn't have been the same without you! Here's to all the fun left to come. *Friends 4 Ever!*

And an extra shout out to Rhonda, whose hours of editing this story honed it into something even better than I could've imagined. I'll never be able to repay you for all the care and wisdom and thoughtfulness you put into this project. You are a very, very Bon Ron!

To my sister Kendall, whose daily doses of encouragement kept me balanced and focused on the things that really matter: the love of the process, expressing my own voice, seeing the big picture of the magnificent life I'm living. The way you live your own life, always learning and loving and pushing yourself to do more, is such a great example of how I want to be in the world. I know the best is yet to come for both of us, and boy, is it going to be fun!

To my mom, who may not be alive to physically read this book, but whose words and essence are instilled throughout every word. Thank you for your gentle hand raising this wild child, and for trusting me so much in my teenage years. I would've had nothing to write about if you hadn't given me the freedom to figure out things on my own! You were the purest example of unconditional love anyone on Earth could've ever known and I thank God every day that I was lucky enough to have you as my mommy.

To my children, Lauren, Andy, Ben, Sam (Alli & Scott too), thank you for pushing me to challenge my self-imposed limitations and not accept the boundaries my generation sometimes too readily accepts. When I told you I was writing a book, you weren't embarrassed like I thought you might be, instead you all got excited and encouraged me and even acted like I was cool! What more could a mom want? The way you live your lives with such kindness and love, the way you pursue your own dreams, inspires me every day. I am constantly in awe of the wonderful people you've become and are still becoming! (Now, if I could just get one of you to go on Jeopardy....)

To my adorable grandson Finn, whose never-ending awe, wonder and joyous belly laughs (as well as his determination to get what he wants!) remind me of what this life is really all about.

And last, but certainly not least, to my husband, Andrew. Thank you for being my f1 fan for all these long years we've been together. You've graciously shared me with this story both physically (when I sequestered myself in my office for hours) and mentally (when I zoned out on many car rides home from the cabin.) Hubby: "You're in your story right now, aren't you?" Me: "Huh? What? Where am I? Who are you?" I would've never been able to pursue this dream without the support and freedom you've so lovingly provided me. We truly are the Wonder Twins! Any love story I could ever write would pale in comparison to the real-life version I'm living with you.

ABOUT THE AUTHOR

Kiersten Schiffer grew up in the farmlands of Indiana and now lives in Connecticut with her husband and boxer dog, Sable. After years of working at summer camp, Kiersten earned a degree in Outdoor Recreation from Indiana University and later put all her song-singing, game-playing, nature-hiking skills toward raising her four, now-grown children. She is addicted to stories in every form: books, TV, movies, and enjoys blogging about creativity and spirituality and the sweet spot where the two intersect. If she's not at her writing desk, you can usually find her burrowing down the rabbit hole that has currently snatched her attention. (Usually involving the latest reality show competition.) You can read her musings and get more information about her upcoming projects at kierstenschiffer.com

Made in United States
North Haven, CT
24 August 2022

23213532R00296